THE
TRINITY
GENE

by
Tim Newcomb

Published By Lagumo Corp.
Cheyenne, Wyoming

TM

ISBN 1-878117-07-6

Cover Design by
Paulette Livers Lambert

DEDICATION

Dedicated to John Levy of San Diego, for twenty years of long-distance laughter and friendship.

ACKNOWLEDGEMENTS

In memory of Goldie Fisher, Kenneth Newcomb, Virgil Tsuluca, and Floyd Hall—you did not live to see this but I never forgot you, nor the genius of your gentle natures.

Thanks to Lucia Van Bebber, Jane Eakin, Shelly Ackerson, Cassandra Messersmith, Steve Ruzicka, Mark Bazzone, and Kent Spence.

Special thanks to Dave Gosar, Maynard Grant, Bob Nicholas, Ward Newcomb, Andrea Richard, Mike Golden, Deidre Bainbridge, Bill Simpson, and Tom Young, all of whom helped guide this work to the world of form.

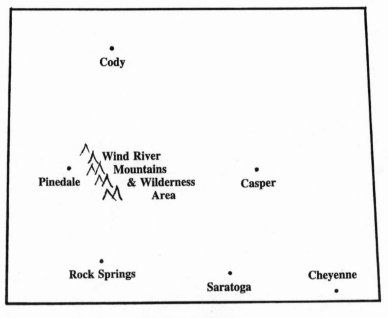

WYOMING

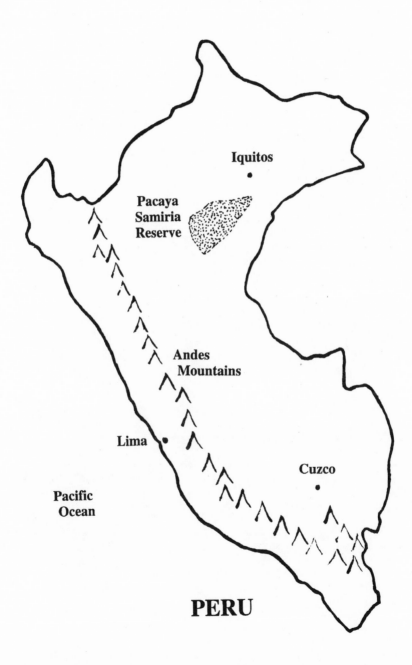

Iquitos

Pacaya
Samiria
Reserve

Andes
Mountains

Lima

Cuzco

Pacific
Ocean

PERU

THE PRIVATE JET vanished into the clouds shrouding Wyoming's Snowy Range Mountains to make the final descent into Saratoga. Thirty seconds later, the clouds vanished and two young priests gazed below to the green valley coming into view.

A telephone rang deep within a private compound several miles beyond Saratoga. "Mr. Mullen, we are on final approach."

"Thank you."

"You're welcome, sir."

With old hands spotted by age, John Mullen quietly replaced the phone and turned to gaze out the window toward Saratoga and the valley below. He watched the plane descend from the clouds.

Father Antonio de Montesinos glanced toward Father Manuel de las Casas. Manuel was gazing down to the pristine alpine valley. The cabin began tilting as the jet angled to align with the landing strip.

Antonio tightened his belt. "Do you know Mr. Mullen, Father Manuel?" his voice was deep.

Manuel stirred from his thoughts and turned to Antonio, shaking his head. "Do you?"

"No." Antonio shook his head and returned his gaze out the small oval window as a tiny cloud streaked by at 200 miles an hour.

Antonio had been on board when the jet climbed out of Brazil and headed for Peru. Although each knew the other by reputation, they had met at sunrise. Manuel boarded the plane in Iquitos, at the head waters of the Amazon, where they had cleared U.S. Customs. Except for occasional remarks during the flight, each remained silent, lost to private thoughts, to the magnitude of Mullen's plan.

The glistening white Gulfstream landed as smoothly as glass then rolled slowly to a stop near a dark blue Range Rover with heavily tinted windows.

Antonio emerged first from the plane, blue eyes squinting in the high altitude sun. Strong fingers raked a lock of black hair from his forehead. He stood as a giant at the top of the steps and looked across the valley. Manuel emerged beside him, wearing thick glasses.

The two young priests descended the steps to the concrete landing strip, drinking in the high mountain air.

Michelle Cumberland extended long legs as she stepped from the Range Rover. A strong head wind swept back her blond hair. Long strands followed the wind, trailing behind her. She locked eyes with the young priests.

Michelle's ancestors had been Vikings. She was a commanding athlete who stood six foot two, with silky blond hair that reached her waist. Her grandmother had been John Mullen's only sister.

Michelle approached the plane, extending her hand. "Thank you for coming. I'm Michelle Cumberland, an associate of Mr. Mullen. I will take you to him."

Fifteen minutes later, the Range Rover turned onto the highway leading to Medicine Bow Peak. After crossing three bridges, they turned onto a gravel road bordered by rugged mountain pastures.

Michelle wrestled the Range Rover as they bounced up the slope toward Mullen's compound. One hand gripped the steering wheel, the other worked the gear shift as they mounted the final incline. She explained the compound was built on the site of a large mining operation abandoned early in the century. The tunnels were extensive. Some extended thousands of feet into the granite mountain.

Buckled into the back seat, Antonio could not take his eyes from Michelle. Her poise and beauty, streaked with raw determination, riveted his attention to her.

When the Range Rover came to a stop, Antonio finally looked around. The late afternoon shadows along the mountain had begun to stretch in anticipation of evening's darkness.

Above them, the mountain continued to climb into the sky like a giant fortress.

The compound lay midway up the western slope of the great mountain and blended into the delicate patchwork of timber, wild flowers and glacial debris.

The three departed the Range Rover and walked along the gravel driveway toward the entry, an expanse of black glass built flush with the face of the mountain. The glass darkly reflected their images and the sweep of valley behind them.

Michelle ushered them inside, through a long hall to the library, where enormous windows overlooked the valley.

A lone figure sat facing them, silhouetted in the setting sun. An ancient hand invited them to the chairs in front of the desk.

Michelle quietly left the room as they sat.

"Thank you for coming." Mullen's voice rasped.

He touched a desk switch near the telephone and heavy metal plates began descending silently over the spread of windows that separated them from the valley below. The interior lighting increased to match the loss of sunlight as metal shutters sealed the room. With the plates secured, he came slowly around the desk and extended his right hand.

Both priests rose.

"I am John Mullen." Deeply set gray eyes stared from the weathered face.

He turned to Antonio and looked up, "You are Father Antonio de Montesinos." They shook hands and John turned to Manuel, "You are Father Manuel de las Casas."

He smiled, "Please be seated." John pulled up a chair to sit between them. His old hands lowered slowly into his lap. "Father De Montesinos, I understand you have spoken recently with Father Bernadine."

"Yes, I have," Antonio answered quickly.

"And you Father De las Casas?" John asked.

"Yes." Manuel adjusted his glasses.

"You reviewed the technical specs provided during your flight?"

They nodded.

"You are both convinced the blood within the relic Father Bernadine provided was Christ's and the child within Carlota was cloned from that blood?" John asked, studying their faces.

"Yes." Manuel answered firmly.

Antonio nodded.

John touched a button on his watch. Seconds later, Michelle returned to the room.

"Would you like to meet Carlota now?" John asked.

The two priests looked apprehensively to one another.

"Yes, Mr. Mullen," Antonio responded for both and breathed deeply.

"Her journey will not be easy, gentlemen." John's tired gray eyes roamed their faces until their discomfort became visible. "You will help her with her journey?"

"Yes," Antonio nodded and crossed himself.

"With our lives," Manuel said solemnly.

John rose from his chair and stood beside Michelle. "Let us introduce you."

The two priests followed John and Michelle down a hallway to an elevator.

"Good evening," the resident computer greeted. Bronze elevator doors opened silently.

"Carlota Cabral," Michelle instructed the machine as they entered.

"Thank you," the machine answered, closing the bronze doors and initiating their descent.

Antonio and Manuel gripped the recessed chrome railing as the elevator plummeted. Their stomachs jumped as the fall caught their breath.

Both knew they were plunging deep into the mountain. Both were aware they were dropping down a mine shaft, with millions of tons of granite overhead.

Michelle touched a green button on the panel near the elevator's door. "Carlota, we are on the way."

The elevator eventually slowed and stopped. The four stepped into a new corridor. A large metal doorway glistened at the distant end of the well-lit corridor. Their footsteps echoed down the granite tunnel.

When they reached the end of the corridor, the computer confirmed John's presence. Heavy doors parted slowly, revealing a receiving room of enormous proportion. A young woman stood squarely at its center.

Huge granite walls sloped outward to the ceiling a hundred feet overhead. An array of brilliant lights sunlit the cavernous room. A thin slice of water cascaded down the entire far wall, disappearing into mist at the edge of a shallow reflecting pond. The flooring was polished granite.

Carlota stood erect, facing them, her hands clasped gently together in front of her waist. She beamed as they entered.

Carlota was of average height, but average ended there. Hers was a young angel's face, with child-like brown eyes. Black hair was gathered to the crown of her head. Her skin was golden brown. And she was eight months pregnant.

She walked slowly to John and Michelle, extending a hand to each. "John . . . Michelle."

John touched her hand before turning to introduce his guests. "Carlota, this is Father Antonio de Montesinos and Father Manuel de las Casas."

She smiled delicately, offering a warm hand to each in turn. "Father De Montesinos . . . Father De las Casas. I am honored."

"As are we," Antonio replied as Manuel stared.

"I understand you are from Brazil, Father De Montesinos," Carlota said in Portuguese, looking up to Antonio who stood a head above her.

He nodded.

"Boa Vista, I am told," she prodded.

"Yes." He smiled gently.

She turned to Manuel, a fellow countryman. "I understand you, like me, are from Peru?"

"Yes," he said, nodding nervously.

"Father De Montesinos and Father De las Casas will dine with us tonight," John said.

Carlota smiled gently. "Delightful," she said, still looking at Manuel.

"You will join us at eight?" John asked.

"Of course," Carlota answered.

"We'll see you then." Michelle softly squeezed Carlota's hand.

John and Michelle turned to leave. The priests quickly followed.

Manuel looked back as they re-entered the corridor. Carlota remained motionless where they had left her. Mesmerized, he could not help but stare. When she smiled in response, he turned and hurried to catch the others.

• • •

ACROSS THE ATLANTIC and earlier that day, in a second floor Vatican office, Cardinal Hans Rajunt eased thin reading glasses from his brow and breathed deeply before placing them upon his desk. He closed his dark eyes for an instant, then looked up to the bishop trembling before him. "And when was this?" he hissed softly, his eyes squinting.

"We do not know, your Eminence." The bishop cleared his throat.

"What do we know?" The cardinal asked icily, glaring through the man's soul.

"We know one of the three fragments of the Holy Cross, upon which our most perfect Savior was crucified, is missing."

"Which of the three fragments is gone?"

"Fragment I, your Eminence."

"When was it last inventoried?" The cardinal asked, with long, thin fingers tracing the gold wire rim of his glasses.

"Two years ago," the bishop answered nervously.

"Bring me its inventory file." The cardinal slowly swiveled his high-back chair to face his window overlooking the distant gardens. "Go," he commanded.

The red chair squeaked softly as he turned and the bishop departed the room.

The cardinal sat motionless and stared into space, dark eyes unblinking.

• • •

A YOUNG ROMAN soldier kneels to clutch the rabbi's muscular forearm with both hands, slamming it across the rough wooden cross-beam.

The rabbi's eyes open wearily and peer through dark clots of blood covering his eyes. He hears the weeping of his family and friends over the voices of the Roman soldiers gathered around him. He watches the young soldier. A white aura radiates about the soldier's head, which had eclipsed the blazing Mediterranean sun.

The soldier sets his jaw with determination, gripping the rabbi's forearm and carefully positioning the long, thick iron nail. Another soldier kneels beside them, raising a large mallet high into the air as a cloud of dust rolls across the rabbi's face.

The young soldier watches the rabbi. The mallet descends. The young man recoils as blood squirts across his face, the thick nail embedding warm flesh and blood deeply into the freshly timbered cross-beam.

The rabbi grimaces. The soldier stares. Their eyes meet. The rabbi ignores his pain and tries to speak. The soldier bends down and eases a warm ear onto cracked and dusty lips.

"Bless you," the rabbi whispers.

The young soldier stands to help his fellows hoist the beam into position. Finishing, they look up at their work and nod to one another with definite approval, deaf to the screams of anguish around them.

The young soldier picks up a spear to guard the criminal's slow execution. He watches the other soldiers play dice for the man's garments amid the wailing of the onlookers. His thoughts drift to his beautiful young wife and their child. He will be glad to return to his family. He tries to wipe the blood from his dusty face with the back of his sweaty forearm, wishing the criminal would hurry and die. He wants to bathe with his wife. He glances up to the darkening sky. Perhaps it will rain.

• • •

THE BISHOP RETURNED with Fragment I's inventory file. A sinewy hand snaked from behind the red, high-backed chair. A bone thin finger uncurled and pointed to the desk. The bishop quietly laid the file on the cardinal's desk and vanished.

When the click of the door announced the bishop's exit, the cardinal turned back to his desk. He positioned the gold frame reading glasses near the end of his long, thin nose and opened the manila envelope.

The first document was a glossy black-and-white photograph of the fragment. The second document was a color photograph. Both glistened under the glare of the desk lamp.

The third document listed the fragment's history and lineage of possession from the time of Joseph of Arimathea. The wooden fragment had been carbon-dated twice at Oxford University's Archeological Research Center.

A thick iron nail, surrounded by a dark stain, was deeply embedded in the center of the fragment. The fragment was near perfectly preserved.

The discoloration, the document explained, was the stain of human blood which had long ago soaked deep into the resinous timber of the cross beam. A battery of tests had convinced church scholars the fragment was genuine and the blood was Christ's.

On the front of the manila file were the signatures of museum curators accounting for its inventory over the last eighty years. The signatures of Father Bernadine accounted for the last sixty.

The cardinal did not look up from the file as he reached over and touched his intercom button. "Summon Father Bernadine." Father Bernadine, he cursed to himself.

• • •

THE FAR WALL was a floor-to-ceiling glass pane, sealing the small dining room from the night air. Flames glowed softly and crackled within a granite fireplace along the interior wall. Mozart serenaded the room.

A full moon bathed the valley below in ashen gray, its reflection frolicking atop the North Platte River. The silver river wound its way through the twinkling lights of Saratoga. Small white steam plumes shimmered into the night air from the hot springs sprinkled along the valley.

Sounds of the annual summer festival radiated from Saratoga. Music and laughter danced up along the mountain's slope to the compound but remained outside as Carlota entered the room and everyone stood to greet her.

• • •

THE INTERCOM SQUEALED its shrill announcement. "Father Bernadine said he is too busy to come up. He invited you down."

Cardinal Rajunt's eyes narrowed but did not look up from the inventory file. Bernadine, he cursed again.

The cardinal shoved away the high-backed red chair as he rose. The chair rolled to a stop as he vanished from the room.

Father Ross Bernadine's right hand trembled with age as he poured himself a second cup of steaming coffee. He attacked his bagel and cream cheese before returning to his book. His old dentures were loose and clicked when he chewed.

The wait for Hans Rajunt, high priest for the Society, would not take long. He'll come, no doubt, cloaked in his favorite scarlet robe, Bernadine thought to himself, chuckling aloud.

• • •

MANUEL GESTURED ABOUT the room. "John, may I ask about your compound?"

John leaned forward slightly. "Of course."

"On the way up from the airport, Michelle said your compound is situated atop an old mining operation."

"Yes. Over a hundred years ago mining enterprises were engaged from Saratoga," he gestured to his right, "to Encampment and south into Colorado. When the boom ended, the mines were abandoned."

"How long have you owned it?"

"I acquired this particular property twenty years ago from the federal government," John lifted his wine glass to his lips. "Our renovations were more recent, however."

"How deep are the tunnels?"

"The deepest tunnel descends beyond 4,000 feet," John took a sip of wine. "Combined, the tunnels cover over 50,000 linear feet."

"You have to move a lot of air to keep such tunnels breathable. What's your power?"

"Geothermal."

Manuel's eyes twinkled. "Ingenious." He turned his head and looked out onto the tiny white steam clouds escaping the valley floor.

"The heat radiates from three central pockets, one lies 4,200 feet beneath us."

"Is there a danger?" Antonio wondered aloud.

"No," Michelle reassured him.

"Where are you from, John?" Antonio asked.

"I was raised in western Nebraska, in a small Sandhills town that was flooded over by a dam built during the Depression."

John silently remembered his boyhood days in the tiny dust bowl town. He recalled howls of high-pitched laughter as he and his friends hurled themselves from the town bridge to plunge into the frigid waters of the North Platte.

After the new dam had been sealed, the Platte swelled from its banks, slowly maturing into a lake. As it swelled, he and his father would drive to the grassy hills overlooking the valley and the abandoned town. When the lake eventually swallowed their home, they never returned.

Manuel's voice returned John's attention to the room. "Michelle said the compound has three surface buildings but I saw only one."

"They are difficult to detect and were designed to blend with the landscape," John said. "Michelle is an architect. She designed the compound."

"I'm impressed." Antonio turned to Michelle.

"Thank you," Michelle replied, eyeing him warmly.

John continued, "We minimize our interference with the mountain's wildlife. Two buildings are simply small reinforced concrete bunkers that require no maintenance. One houses a back-up computer system and one houses an emergency power source. The geodesic dome is the heliport."

"What computer system do you run?" Manuel asked Michelle.

"It is not a commercial system," John said matter-of-factly. "The system is a prototype, designed by a company developing machine intelligence, and is continually upgraded."

"One of your companies?" Antonio broke in, then wished he had not.

"Yes," Michelle answered for John.

"Voice responsive?" Manuel continued to probe.

John nodded.

"Have you named it?" Manuel recalled an M.I.T. professor who named her personal computers.

"Yes . . . Socrates."

"Socrates is aware of every significant human expression, from cave drawings to Hawking's cosmology," Michelle said. "He speaks all known languages."

"His logic gates are chromophore proteins," John explained quietly. "He monitors all media broadcasts around the world, as well as the Internet. Three hundred people are employed simply to feed him new information twenty-four hours a day."

"Will he respond to me?"

"If I wish," John answered and, without raising his voice, continued, "Socrates?"

"Yes, John," the deeply masculine voice resounded from the walls.

"Please meet Father Antonio de Montesinos and Father Manuel de las Casas." John shifted in his seat. "As you know, they are our guests." While he spoke to Socrates, he stared at Manuel.

"How do you do, Father De Montesinos?" Socrates asked in Portuguese.

"Fine. Thank you for asking," Antonio answered hesitantly in English.

"And how are you, Father De las Casas?" Socrates asked in Spanish.

"I am fine, Socrates," Manuel answered calmly in Spanish. He inclined his head toward John, "My compliments." Manuel had begun a deep admiration for the old man sitting before him.

"You know this machine?" Antonio asked Carlota quietly.

Carlota nodded her head gently. "Oh, yes. We have become good friends over the last several months," she answered softly. She raised her voice slightly, "Good evening, Socrates."

"Good evening, Carlota."

• • •

THE SCARLET ROBE billowed as Rajunt strode down the stretch of hallway along the Belvedere Courtyard. As he descended the giant winding staircase leading to Father Bernadine's sanctum in the basement of the Sacred Museum, the red hem of the robe slithered in pursuit several stairs behind.

Rajunt did not bother to knock. He pushed open the door with one hand, "Father Bernadine."

Ross Bernadine looked up, "Hello, Hans."

Rajunt despised such informality from anyone, but especially Bernadine. "I would speak to you."

Bernadine put down his book and motioned for Rajunt to take a seat. The cardinal ignored the invitation and remained standing.

"I understand Fragment I, which had been under your care," Rajunt stressed, "is now missing."

"It's not in the museum, but it's not really missing," Bernadine corrected the cardinal, his voice crackling with age.

Cardinal Rajunt hated replies that delayed an accurate understanding. "Do you know where it is?"

"Yes."

"Where is it?"

"I'm not ready to tell you." Bernadine returned to the last bite of his bagel.

"Oh, you will and now."

"No, I don't think so," he said, chewing the bagel.

"You will not leave the Vatican until Fragment I has been secured," Rajunt announced. His eyes had become black ice.

"I'll let you know if I need your permission." Bernadine blinked. Deep crevices etched his aged face.

"Where is it?"

"It is safe."

"Where is it, Father Bernadine?"

Bernadine's attention returned to the book in his lap and he dismissed Rajunt with a flick of his hand.

The cardinal's eyes fell to the pages held between Bernadine's gnarled fingers. They were written in a language that escaped him. The words escaped him but the author's name at the top of the page did not. FATHER MANUEL DE LAS CASAS. Rajunt's eyes widened.

Rajunt's silence caught Bernadine's attention. He looked up to see the cardinal surveying his desk.

The cardinal sidled up to the desk, lifting the top article to his face. He reviewed the title, an obscure archeological writing. Nothing. He dropped the article. His long fingers brushed aside papers of no consequence. The few shards of clay pottery scattered along the edge of the mangled old desk held no fascination. He was searching authors in the piles of papers littering the desk. He sought particular names.

Bernadine struggled from his chair and tried to wedge between the cardinal and the desk. He looked up to the cardinal, "May I help you?"

"You already have." The cardinal turned and strode from the room.

Bernadine's eyes followed him until the red cape disappeared around the corner. He walked to the door, closed it, and returned to stand over his desk.

He looked at the thin book Rajunt had pulled to the top of the pile. TOMORROW'S MESSIAH by Father Manuel de las Casas.

"*You old fool*," Bernadine thought to himself. His hands trembled as he swept all the papers from his desk and into a dog-eared cardboard box beside the desk.

● ● ●

"AFTER FATHER BERNADINE gave us the crucifixion relic our genetic engineering lab, SYNGENTEC, extracted enough blood for cloning. Several weeks later, we implanted the embryo into Carlota. That was eight months ago." John said, finishing the explanation to Antonio and Manuel.

John had faced the fireplace so his guests could enjoy the spectacular view of the valley at night. The dining room table was thick glass and circular, with several small candles set in the middle. The fireplace glowed softly.

"Aren't you frightened?" Manuel asked Carlota. Reflections from the tiny candle flames danced along the surface of his thick glass lenses.

Michelle sipped wine as she watched Carlota.

"Of what?" Carlota asked. Her face hardened but the soft brown eyes never strayed from Manuel's face.

"Think what you're doing," Manuel insisted, lifting his hands palms up. "The implications . . . ."

"Have ever you visited the *pueblos jóvenes*, the shanty towns of Lima?" Carlota asked.

Manuel nodded sadly, "Of course."

"Then you have seen how the poor are treated." Carlota paused, "I grew up in the slums of Lima, Father De las Casas." She glanced at John then back to the priests. "I more fear doing nothing to help my people than to bear the Christ child. So I agreed to give birth to him if John would permit him to be born among my people, the poor of Lima."

"But why?" Manuel asked.

"My son will free my people."

The table was silent for several moments. Antonio turned to John, asking, "Why have you done this?"

John's eyes softened and stared into space as he travelled down a tunnel of old memories. "Father Antonio, I began my pharmaceutical company fifty years ago, searching for medicines from the rainforests around the world, decades before it became vogue. Since that time I have witnessed some of the most brutal poverty in the world and have given to causes and relief organizations that try to help such people."

"Billions." Michelle interrupted softly.

"But despite the efforts of such groups, millions of people across the world remain consigned to economic slavery as their station in life, confined to poverty, disease, and death. Nothing has changed but the numbers. Now there are more poor than when I began," John's raspy voice softened to a whisper.

He rubbed his eyes and continued, "Five years ago, I was diagnosed with chronic lymphocytic leukemia. You are a physician, Father Antonio, so you know how valuable my time is. I decided to try something that might finally make a difference. If I can return the world their Jesus, things will change forever, for better or not." His eyes probed the priests. "But the world *will* change."

"Why did you pick us to help?" Manuel asked.

"We looked at several hundred people, but none came with the recommendation Father Bernadine gave you two," John said then focused on Manuel. "He considers you a kind of prophet, Father Manuel. And Archbishop De Gonzales regards you both as highly as Father Bernadine. In short, your reputations preceded you."

"How did you meet Father Bernadine?" Antonio asked.

"I've never met him," John answered quickly, "but I came to know of him through Archbishop De Gonzales. De Gonzales arranged everything through Bernadine."

"How did you meet Archbishop De Gonzales?" Manuel broke in.

"He contacted me in 1968, after the push of Vatican II. Your church needed some medicines in bulk for its South American relief organizations but couldn't pay," John answered. "We've become friends over the years."

Manuel nodded, shifting in his seat.

"What was Vatican II?" Carlota asked, "I wasn't born in 1968."

"I forget how old I have become." John smiled to himself and leaned back, running gnarled fingers through his thick mane of white hair.

Manuel answered Carlota, "In 1965, His Holiness Pope John convened a world conference of bishops and cardinals and directed the church to open its temples to the sunlight and its coffers to the poor. That was Vatican II.

"Clergy from Central and South America soon gathered to discuss the Church and the poor. When the conference ended, some suggested the Vatican examine its contribution to such neglect. More than a few argued that church officials should live no better than others," Manuel said, staring at Carlota.

"We are proud of that conference," Antonio said to Michelle. "Christ asked that we serve those who suffer as we would serve him if he so suffered."

"He comforted the poor, the diseased, and the despised," Manuel joined in quickly. "Those who invoke his name should do no less than live his example."

"We have chosen these two priests well," John thought to himself as Michelle smiled at him. They were well aware of the war raging within the Church of Rome between the privileged clerics of the Vatican and the liberation priests of South and Central America. If the Vatican learned of John's plan and tried to intervene, only liberation priests would remain fearless, even the Americans would retreat.

"We understand you know Father Bernadine well." Michelle turned to Antonio.

"Yes, I do. We met when I did research at the Vatican Library," Antonio answered. "Father Bernadine has been the curator for the Sacred Museum for the last sixty years. He was transferred there from Ireland early in his calling because of advanced degrees in archeology and his command of ancient languages."

"Were you surprised he released the crucifixion relic to your people?" Manuel asked John.

"Not entirely, although we were cautious when we approached him," John responded softly. "Archbishop De Gonzales assured me he merited our trust," white eyebrows arched, "and we had no choice."

"Did he fully understand what you intended to do?" Manuel asked carefully.

"Absolutely, as did Archbishop De Gonzales," Michelle answered for John. "They were delighted with the idea."

"I'm not surprised Father Bernadine helped," Antonio said. "He has never suffered fools silently. He was appalled by the papal silence that nourished the Nazi's campaign of hate. He urged the papacy to speak out against Hitler, that no matter the cost, Christ would never remain silent in the face of such slaughter. But to no avail . . . ." Antonio's words trailed into silence. He stared deep into the glass of dark red wine in his hand. "Father Bernadine was imprisoned and badly treated by the Germans until the war ended."

The table remained silent.

Antonio looked about the table. "He remained demoralized until the liberation pope came to power. But after Pope John died, the Society began securing the Vatican and settled into privileged comfort," Antonio paused. "Quite a blood feud developed between Father Bernadine and the Society."

"What is the Society?" Carlota asked suspiciously. The child within her kicked suddenly. She quieted him by placing her soft hand atop her stomach.

"The Vatican's heretic hunters," Manuel answered slowly. "They control the Opus Dei."

"What is the Opus Dei?" Carlota probed deeper.

"In 1931, Spanish elections proclaimed a republic and stripped the church of its power to rule over the people. Father Jose Escriba y Albas de Balaguer was outraged with the Spanish people. He founded Opus, his personal crusade to install theocratic governments around the world by guiding the careers of powerful people. He began by recruiting and training young lay professionals," Antonio answered.

"He even founded special universities to train them," Manuel interrupted then added, "which are well funded."

Antonio sat back in his chair. "When the Spanish militia began killing priests in 1936, Escriba scurried to a psychiatric hospital, pretending to be mentally ill. Can you imagine Christ pretending to be mentally ill when the Roman soldiers arrived?"

Michelle laughed aloud.

"Escriba then founded the Sacerdotal Society for clergy control of the Opus. The Society lives in luxury while many who follow the church starve." Antonio finished.

"Hence the feud between Father Bernadine and the Opus?" Carlota asked.

"Exactly," Manuel nodded. "Neither their numbers or their power frighten him."

"How large are they?" Carlota asked quietly.

"They have over seventy thousand members around the world, two thousand of which are bishops. They are wealthy, well organized, and well established throughout South America," Manuel answered.

"When Vatican II directed the church to open its coffers to the poor," Antonio paused with a smile, "Bernadine could barely contain his delight."

"But after the liberation pope died, the Society began trying to intimidate the new generation of clergy spawned by Vatican II," Antonio explained.

"Spawned from hell according to the Society." Manuel smiled delinquently.

"That's when Father Bernadine declared war on the Society," Antonio said.

"When Karol Wojtyla became His Holiness Pope John Paul II, he raised the Opus to the status of personal prelature, answering only to him," Manuel explained. "With such papal backing, Cardinal Hans Rajunt began driving liberation priests from the church and its universities. Anyone who questions the Society's authority or doctrine is instantly cut from the church—especially Americans."

"Why has Father Bernadine been allowed to stay?" Carlota questioned.

"A mystery." Antonio shrugged.

"What happens when they discover you've cloned Christ?" Manuel asked John.

"I have no idea how they'll react. Obviously, we hope they don't discover it until after the child is born," John said.

Michelle leaned back in her chair, staring at Antonio. "How do you think they'll react?"

Antonio turned to Manuel, smiling. "Would Cardinal Rajunt welcome that news?"

"He would become dangerous," Manuel answered solemnly. "He would fear the child."

"Many people would," Michelle said.

"Whole governments would fear Him," Antonio added, "His existence would necessarily threaten their power."

• • •

THE BILLOWING SCARLET cape swept so quickly into the reception room that the cardinal's secretary had not registered his return. Bellowed commands peppered the air.

"Summon the head of the *Gendarmerie* and then ask Cardinal Klodiński to join me in the Vatican Gardens." Rajunt hissed.

The secretary immediately picked up his phone as the cardinal turned and headed for the gardens.

Rajunt met Cardinal Klodiński at the outskirts of the Academy of Science grounds. They greeted one other warmly and walked toward the gardens.

"Cardinal Klodiński, thank you for joining me."

They walked without a word and followed the familiar path that wound through shadowing trees. Łukasz Klodiński knew the signs of trouble in his old friend. Rajunt walked slowly, studying the ground, his hands clasped behind his back. Klodiński knew Rajunt would not speak until he had scripted in his mind what he would say. There would be no spontaneity.

As Klodiński waited for Rajunt to speak, they followed the pathway, finally coming out of the shadows, past vast rose beds. They stopped under the giant sequoia planted by Pope Pius XI between the world wars. Rajunt looked to his old friend. "Father Bernadine has departed grievously from his holy duties."

"What did he do?"

"You are aware of Fragment I?"

"Of course, the most sacred of our relics. It holds the precious blood of Christ."

Rajunt locked his eyes on Klodiński's and inhaled deeply, "It is gone."

"Gone? How long?"

"Perhaps two years," he answered woodenly. "Bernadine knows where it is but will not say."

"He must. He cannot disobey you."

"For now, he will not say. I ordered him to remain within the Vatican until the fragment is secured."

"Will he obey?"

"The *Gendarmerie* will ensure he does."

"What are we going to do?"

"I have some thoughts." Cardinal Rajunt fingered one of the ropes that braced the giant tree. His eyes followed the rope to the tree and the tree to the heavens. His head bent back. He eyed the Mediterranean sky and, after several minutes, looked back to Klodiński. "You are familiar with TOMORROW'S MESSIAH and the other writings of that Peruvian priest, Father Manuel de las Casas?"

"Heretic," Klodiński replied coldly.

"I suspect a relation between him and Bernadine. Contact the Society in Lima. I want De las Casas brought before me."

"Done."

Cardinal Rajunt left his old friend and returned to his office.

Victor Semani, the head of the Vatican police, the *Gendarmerie*, was sitting in his reception room. Semani rose as Rajunt entered.

"Father Bernadine is not to leave the Vatican grounds. If he attempts to do so, imprison him."

Semani's eyes widened. He had never heard such an order but was not about to debate Rajunt. "Your will be done, Eminence."

"Go."

Both men turned, Semani heading from the reception room and Rajunt to his private office. Rajunt turned back when he reached his door, "Semani, make no mistake. Bernadine must not leave the Vatican unless I tell you otherwise." The cardinal's secretary looked up and stared at Semani.

Semani turned back and nodded.

• • •

AS MICHELLE STARED across the table to Antonio, her mind began to wander. For the past three years, she and John had considered many clergy, searching for spiritual guides for the new Madonna. Their search had narrowed to these two liberation priests sitting at their table.

Father Antonio de Montesinos had been born on a small farm outside Boa Vista, Brazil, near the Venezuelan border. Even as a child, he had insisted on becoming educated, despite his family's poverty. His parents turned him over at an early age to Iam Ignatious, the local Jesuit priest. Antonio learned all he could and became a Jesuit, leaving Brazil for medical training in the U.S.

When he became a physician, he returned to his people and to Ignatious, now old and frail.

Antonio had lived with the 9,000 Yanomamö Indians of Brazil before the military expelled all doctors, nurses, missionaries, and anthropologists from the region, and left the Yanomamö to the mercy of 50,000 invading gold prospectors.

After the gold prospectors seized control, Antonio began to chronicle the stark contrast between the suffering of the Yanomamö and the privileged lives and pampered comfort of the Vatican's Society.

Antonio also chronicled the speed with which the Vatican began replacing rebellious Brazilian liberation bishops with those selected by the Society, those less offended by the suffering of others.

Antonio's excommunication was imminent.

Manuel, however, was a Franciscan priest and engineer, who lived with some of the poorest people in Peru, near the headwaters of the Amazon.

Like Antonio, Manuel penned what he preached and his writings are passed hand-to-hand across South America, echoing the call for compassion, the liberation epoch.

Manuel had been tutored intensely from infancy, the only child of a wealthy banker and an advanced mathematics professor. By the time he entered college at sixteen, he spoke eleven languages. After becoming a Franciscan priest, he earned two advanced engineering degrees from M.I.T. in record time, with a wizardry that could not conceal itself.

He returned to Peru to live with the Indians along the Peruvian headwaters of the Amazon.

Manuel was considered an oddity by his relatives, whose great wealth and contributions to the church prevented his excommunication. As they did Antonio, the Vatican's Society decried Manuel a religious leper . . . a liberation priest.

But Manuel was hated even more by the *Sendero Luminoso*, Peru's Maoist guerrillas because he helped the tribes remain independent. Michelle and John were amazed Manuel still lived.

Michelle had studied the file photo of Manuel, kneeling before several village farmers and tracing his finger through dusty red earth, outlining an irrigation system. He wore thick glasses over large brown eyes and sported a thick and unruly head of sandy hair. She was fascinated by his eyes, they were the eyes of a visionary.

Michelle had also scrutinized the file photo of Antonio, taken while he had lived with the Yanomamö. She gazed across the table at Antonio, hoping not to stare. But he was profoundly handsome. The powerful image from his black-and-white photo refused to budge from her mind's eye as he sat on the other side of the dancing candle flames, smiling back at her with penetrating eyes.

The photo showed him wading through black swamp water as he carried an injured child. Only khaki shorts covered him. Streams of sweat matted his black hair and coursed down the bronze face as he held the child protectively in his arms. Large black leeches clung to his thighs.

Thick biceps bulged under the child's weight. Prominent veins webbed his broad chest. He grimaced under a dense cloud of large insects swarming about his head.

Standing six foot four, Antonio's muscular body looked chiseled from marble. The khaki shorts clung wetly to narrow hips and glued to the dense mound of his crotch. The intelligence behind the eyes stared through the camera's lens, as if he could then see her now.

". . . those addicted to power will fear Him." Manuel continued.

Michelle's attention returned to the conversation.

Carlota gazed out the floor-to-ceiling glass wall, to the twinkling lights of Saratoga in the dark valley below. A full moon challenged an army of blazing stars for control of the night sky.

John and Michelle looked to one another.

Carlota refocused her attention, looking to Antonio and Manuel. "Soon, I return to Peru to give birth to my son," she paused, "and we must come to understand one another."

She smiled gently at the intensity of Manuel's stare and continued. "I would appreciate some time to come to know you. Michelle has offered to take us to the Wind Rivers, for a day or so."

"The Wind River Mountains cut diagonally across Wyoming's northwest corner." Michelle said quietly, not wanting to interrupt. "They are quite beautiful and we have a home on the shores of Fremont Lake."

"Would you consent?" Carlota asked.

The priests nodded quickly.

John's eyes drifted to the moonlit valley and the dark peaks of the Sierra Madre Mountains to the west, crowned with bright stars. He preferred her to stay within the protective cocoon of the compound until she had to leave. "Aren't you comfortable here, Carlota?" He asked, hoping she would change her mind.

"You are worried about me, aren't you?" Carlota smiled delicately, her face transformed into a mother speaking to a concerned child.

"Yes," John nodded, "and the child."

"You must not, my dear friend. If we are meant to finish this journey, nothing will stop us." As if peering out from an ancient universe, Carlota's child-like eyes moved to each person at the table, deliberately and slowly. "I have placed myself in God's hands all my life. I cannot stop now."

The two priests crossed themselves.

"I have somewhat less trust than you in those matters, Carlota. But if that is your wish, we will make it so," John said.

"We'll be back soon, John." Michelle assured him.

John nodded in silent accord. He reached for Carlota's hand and gently squeezed it. "You've been here within the mountain for eight months. I worry needlessly. You go enjoy yourself, and when you're ready to return, let me know." He smiled with old and steady eyes.

Carlota brightened, looking eagerly to the priests.

• • •

FATHER BERNADINE FED the lapping blue flames of the incinerator with every paper that had been on his desk, as well as any writings by Father De las Casas or Father De Montesinos. He knew Rajunt would soon confiscate his papers and relieve him of his duties at the museum.

By the time he returned to his office, it had already been sealed. A young and kind-faced *Gendarme* stood in front of his office door.

Bernadine looked up and smiled to the young man, "May I enter, please?"

"No, Father, you may not." The young *Gendarme* set his jaw with determination.

"I see."

"Cardinal Rajunt has asked that you go to your quarters and remain there, Father."

Bernadine shuffled to his small room on the other side of the Vatican. After closing the door, he sat on the edge of his bed for a moment, caught his breath and sighed. He reached for the phone by his bed stand. The first call was to Brian O'Riley.

• • •

AN HOUR AFTER they had finished the meal, Manuel tried to stifle a yawn.

John turned to Michelle, "Would you see our guests to their suites? This has been a long day for Father Antonio and Father Manuel."

Carlota remained seated as John bid the priests good night.

Michelle led them down the hallway to the elevator and eventually back to the great room where they had met Carlota. Walking past the waterfall, they entered another room with a long curving wall and a series of large bronze doors.

With a priest on each side, Michelle walked to the third bronze door until it caught their reflection. "Socrates, this is Father Manuel's suite." The door slid back into the granite wall.

Michelle and Antonio each bid Manuel good night.

As the door slid shut, Manuel turned to look about the room. Recessed lights at the edges of the ceiling softly lit the room. Like the great entry room, the walls had been carved from the granite mountain, but were polished to a mirror finish. The granite floor was covered with a cream colored Persian rug. He recognized the design and estimated it to be three hundred years old.

Tiny running lights glowed along the edges of the floor, lighting pathways to other rooms.

He walked to the bedroom and gazed in. The room was smaller than the entry room and had a lower ceiling. A large bed lay at floor level and abutted the far wall. Cut into the granite wall above the head of the bed was a small and dimly lit alcove for personal affects.

Manuel's day had begun long before sunrise and the bed was inviting. But he wanted to shower before he slept.

The bedroom lights dimmed as he left. He followed the path between the running lights that led to the bathroom. The bathroom lights brightened at his approach. Shiny green exotic plants with fragrant blossoms adorned the warm room. The walls to his left and right were solidly mirrored. The opposing mirrors stretched the bright jungle of exotic plants infinitely in both directions.

An enormous sunken tub abutted the far wall. Four brass shower heads glistened high above the tub, suspended from the ceiling.

Manuel removed his clothes and walked to the steps that led to the bottom of the tub, hanging his toes over the edge. He stood at the top of the steps, looking for faucets to turn on the water.

"Father De las Casas."

"Socrates?" Manuel's great mind reeled with surprise. He caught himself and smiled.

"Yes. May I fill the tub for you?" Socrates asked in Spanish.

"May I shower instead?"

Streams of warm mist began spraying from the ceiling, shrouding the bottom of the tub with a steamy mist. Manuel stepped into the tub, reaching out with fingertips to test the water. Satisfied, he joined the waters, threw back his head, and faced the hot spray. For several long minutes, he stood lost in his reveries. His mind burned. So much to understand. "Christ," he whispered to himself, "help me."

"Would you like to soap?" Socrates asked.

"Please."

Within seconds, Manuel began lathering his torso under a warm, soapy spray. Ten minutes later, Socrates ended the shower at Manuel's command.

Manuel settled into bed, pulling flannel covers to his chin.

"Sleep well, Father De las Casas," Socrates bid him good night.

"Good night, Socrates," Manuel mumbled back and drifted away.

Socrates dimmed the room and stood vigil.

Six hundred feet above, Carlota and John gazed from the dining table upon the valley below. The stars of the western sky silhouetted the crest of the Sierra Madre range. Saratoga sparkled as an oasis of light in the blackness below.

"John." Carlota rose and walked to the massive window. She placed a finger gently upon the cold glass and gazed out. "What have we done?"

• • •

ABANCAY, PERU IS a ten hour journey by land cruiser from Cuzco, the former capital of the Incas. A frontier town high in the

Andes Mountains, soldiers guard its gates from the *Sendero Luminoso*, the Shining Path.

Within Abancay, the Society's seminary instantly separates itself from the town's grime and muddy streets with high, imposing walls. Within the walls, two fountains splash and dance in the sun amid elegant flower beds. Goldfish swim lazily in their basins.

Bishop Jesus Gómez had knelt in prayer before the altar in one of the garden's two chapels. Beyond the altar was a painting of the holy family, ornately framed with gold. The footsteps of one of his charges quietly entering the chapel broke his concentration. He ended his prayers and rose, turning. "What is it, Brother?"

"This was delivered by courier moments ago."

Bishop Gómez accepted the manila envelope and walked into the gardens. The young charge followed several paces behind. Gómez opened the envelope to find a communiqué faxed from Cardinal Klodiński in Rome to the Lima office. Gómez must locate Father Manuel de las Casas immediately. The instructions were unyielding. He turned to his young charge, "Has the courier left yet?"

"No."

"Instruct him to wait for me, I must return to Lima."

The sun had begun to set.

• • •

"GOOD MORNING, JOHN," Socrates broke the dark silence four hundred feet within the mountain.

John stirred slowly in the darkness, rolling onto his back. "Good morning, Socrates."

"Jacob Brigham is on the line, he asked that I wake you." Only Jacob and Michelle had instant access to Mullen.

Jacob Brigham had been John's closest friend and business associate for forty years. While Mullen had proved unsurpassed in creating wealth, Brigham was without equal in safeguarding it. When John's wife, Sarah, had been killed thirty years earlier, Jacob had been John's source of comfort through many difficult years. John's trust in Jacob was absolute. Jacob was second in command of the vast Mullen empire.

"Patch him in." John's eyes remained closed.

Socrates activated the scrambler and transferred Jacob's call. "John?"

"Jacob, good morning. Where are you?"

"Seattle."

"What's up?"

"Brian O'Riley called me during the night. Father Bernadine had called him earlier. Cardinal Rajunt has discovered the crucifixion fragment is missing and has ordered him confined to the Vatican, he's under virtual house arrest. Bernadine is convinced Rajunt has made the connection to Father De las Casas." Brigham waited for a response. When there was none, he continued, "O'Riley indicated a fax was transmitted between the Vatican and a hot number in Lima, Peru two hours after Father Bernadine's call."

John opened his eyes, staring deep into the quiet darkness for several seconds. "Did you contact Lima and Iquitos?"

"Yes, immediately. I related O'Riley's communiqué."

"Did you make any recommendations?"

"No, not at this point."

"Did they?"

"No. Ray Stauffen will remain in Iquitos to see if inquiries are made about Father De las Casas there. Janice McClain said Bishop Gómez is in Abancay. She will let us know if he returns to Lima."

"Have you contacted Brian in Rome?"

"Yes, moments ago. His people in the Vatican will try to learn more about Father Bernadine's situation. Anything else, John?"

"No, just keep me abreast."

"Done." Jacob Brigham hung up the phone.

"What time is it, Socrates?" John asked quietly.

"Nine-fifty a.m."

Several minutes of silence passed as John grouped his thoughts for the day. "How are our guests?"

"Fine. They joined Michelle outside for breakfast earlier and are with her now. Would you like to speak with them?" Socrates asked.

"No. Let 'em be." John's legs hurt and he tried massaging some age from his thighs as he spoke. "Is it nice out?"

"Yes, a pleasant day."

John swung his feet to the floor and the lighting around his bed brightened. He showered, dressed, and headed outside to join the others.

As he walked from the mountain entrance, he spotted Carlota and Manuel twenty yards beyond. He crossed the gravel driveway to join them.

Carlota clutched the binoculars. "I see it!" she exclaimed excitedly and handed the glasses to Manuel. "There," pointing to a dark spot in the blue sky, circling lazily above the valley river. When she saw John, her eyes brightened even more. "It's an eagle," she explained.

"Can you see the Canada geese?" John pointed to a narrow peninsula formed by an abrupt bend in the river below. "They usually cluster on that sandy bank along the middle bend in the river."

"I don't see them," Carlota shook her head.

"I do," Manuel responded. He quickly handed the binoculars back to Carlota and pointed toward the river.

"Where's Father De Montesinos and Michelle?" John looked around.

"They went for a run down the mountain about forty minutes ago," Manuel answered.

"Can you spot 'em, Carlota?" John asked.

She trained her binoculars on the roads below for a minute. "I think I can," she paused and pointed, "There they are, coming back."

After a few moments, John spotted them and estimated they were a half mile away. One followed the other by a hundred yards. John knew a steep climb lay ahead of them so he settled onto the nearest comfortable rock.

The three visited until Michelle crested the slope. When she reached John, she took one deep breath and bounced to a stop. She was sweating but still vigorous, with cheeks flushed red and long hair dangling in a pony-tail.

"Good morning, John," she said, catching her breath.

"Did you have a good run?" Carlota asked.

Michelle smiled her answer and they waited quietly for Father De Montesinos.

Moments later, Antonio crested the slope. His face was pale and his breathing rapid and shallow. Baggy gray jogging togs were dark with sweat. Several sweaty locks of hair stuck to his forehead. He looked dizzy.

"Are you all right, Father?" John stared at him with pity.

Hunched over at the waist, elbows locked, and hands gripping his knees, Antonio nodded breathlessly, staring blankly to the ground in front of his face.

"Michelle?" John's tone reproached her before turning to Antonio. "The air is somewhat thin here, Father," he said comfortingly to Antonio, who had caught John's disapproving look to Michelle.

Antonio quickly straightened, took several deep breaths, and swallowed hard. "Don't blame Michelle. I asked if I could run with her, insisted she go at her regular pace, and was foolish enough to try to keep up." He wanted to collapse to the ground. He just smiled at Michelle.

"We better get you into dry clothes," Michelle responded.

Carlota turned to John as they all approached the expanse of black glass at the entrance, "Could we go out today?"

"Of course," John answered.

"How about lunch in town?" Michelle suggested. John nodded.

As Carlota and Manuel smiled, Michelle tugged at Antonio's sweatshirt sleeve, "Let's clean up."

Antonio followed her wearily as the others stood talking.

An hour later, the Range Rover made its way back down the mountain. As they pulled north onto the highway leading to Saratoga, Socrates interrupted their conversation.

"John, Jacob Brigham is on the line."

"Patch him in," John said and Socrates engaged the scrambler. "John?"

"I'm here, Jacob."

"I just got a call from Janice McClain. Bishop Gómez returned to Lima and boarded a flight to Iquitos. He's in the air now. Obviously, the Society is looking for Father De las Casas. I called Stauffen and let him know."

"Thank you."

The line cleared.

Manuel looked to John.

"Cardinal Rajunt has discovered the crucifixion fragment is missing and has confined Father Bernadine to the Vatican. Rajunt seems to have gleaned some connection between you and Father Bernadine," John explained. "The Society has begun to search for you."

Carlota's face tightened and her hands moved protectively over her stomach. Soft warm hands pressed lightly against the kicking in her womb. *"Peace my child,"* she thought to herself. The kicking subsided.

"What do we do?" Manuel asked, adjusting thick glasses to the bridge of his nose.

"Carlota, do you still want to spend some time in the Wind River Mountains before you return to Lima?" John looked back to her, asking softly.

"Yes," she said firmly. "It is important that I have some time with the Fathers, so that we might be friends before returning to Peru."

"It might be best then to leave tomorrow," John suggested reluctantly.

She acknowledged with a nod and turned to watch a small herd of antelope off to her right, barrelling up the mountain's lower slope.

• • •

THE PLANE'S TWIN propellers roared as the wheels squealed against the concrete. Bishop Gómez sucked in his stomach and gave his seat belt a final tug as the plane bounced onto the runway at Iquitos, Peru.

Ray Stauffen was the sole unmoving figure in the crowd as he watched the plane taxi to the terminal. When Bishop Gómez emerged from the plane, Stauffen turned and left the building.

Stauffen was watching the next morning when Bishop Gómez headed for the mission church five miles from Iquitos.

The tiny church, made of unpainted concrete blocks and roofed with aluminum sheeting, was tied to civilization by two overhead lines hung through the trees from Iquitos. Two overhead fans spun lazily through the humid air.

Bishop Gómez went inside and placed a call across the Atlantic to Cardinal Rajunt. He was suffocating under the equatorial heat. His sweat-soaked shirt clung like molasses to his back. He ignored his discomfort. After several seconds and a series of electronic clicks, the phone began to ring.

"Yes."

"This is Bishop Gómez calling for Cardinal Rajunt."

"Hold."

Gómez pulled up a chair with his right foot and sat, pressing the phone to his ear.

"Hello."

"Cardinal Rajunt?"

"Yes."

"Your Eminence, this is Bishop Gómez." Gómez paused.

"Yes."

"Cardinal Klodiński asked that I locate Father De las Casas and then call you."

"You have located him." The statement betrayed hope.

"No."

"Then why are you calling?" The voice developed the cold edge of impatience.

"I flew into Iquitos yesterday and have been trying to locate him, but," Gómez leaned forward, placing his elbows on his knees, staring at the floor, "something strange is happening here."

"What?" Rajunt snapped.

"The local priests are telling people the Messiah is returning as one of them. And soon."

"I doubt that. They would not dare."

"It is true."

"How do you know?"

"That is what they are preaching," Gómez answered.

"The priests told you that?"

"Yes. They are confident it is true."

"Archbishop De Gonzales' priests?"

"I suspect they are."

"Do the people believe them?"

"Absolutely. That is all they are talking about."

"Find De las Casas," Rajunt followed each word with a pause.

"But he is nowhere to be found." Gómez looked up suddenly as a moving shadow caught his eye. He followed the angled shadow to a silhouetted figure in the doorway.

"May I help you?" Gómez asked.

"What?" Rajunt asked.

The silhouette approached until it became a barefoot old Indian woman, with combed black hair and a tattered and soiled white cotton dress. "Are you the devil?" she asked Gómez in Spanish.

Rajunt hung on each word of the distant dialogue.

Gómez' forehead curdled. He put his hand over the end of the receiver. "I am busy on the phone, please go away." Gómez snapped.

"Take your hand from the phone," Rajunt ordered instantly.

Gómez' hand dropped away.

"They say you are the devil, that you fear the child." Her jeweled black eyes stared defiantly.

"I am a bishop," Gómez replied. "I can assure you I am not the devil. Now go!"

She turned and left the church.

"Find De las Casas, Bishop Gómez," Rajunt repeated.

"I don't know how," Gómez whined nervously.

Several seconds of silence suspended the conversation between continents. "Determine where he was last seen." Rajunt's voice was ice.

"I don't think anyone here will confide in me." Gómez reached out with his foot and squashed a spider as it crawled along the floor.

"When you have tried, call me back."

The line went dead.

Rajunt hung up the phone, shook his head in irritation, and lifted his copy of TOMORROW'S MESSIAH from his desk. Easing back into his enormous red leather chair, he brought the thin book to his lap and examined the cover. TOMORROW'S MESSIAH by Father Manuel de las Casas.

Rajunt positioned his reading glasses and began to read. Dark eyes tried to follow the words swiftly but soon slowed to a snail's pace. For the first time, Rajunt's pale lips began to move as he read.

An hour later, Rajunt slowly lowered the thin book into his lap. His face was pale.

• • •

MICHELLE ENTERED JOHN's suite.

"John?" She called out and waited.

The room remained silent.

"Socrates, where is John?"

"In his Zen rock garden room."

Michelle walked through the sitting room into John's bedroom. She hesitated beside his bed, at the stairway tunnel leading up to his meditation chamber. John's Zen rock garden was the only room in the mountain she had not designed. It was his sanctuary, his place of peace.

"When did he go in?" She asked.

"About an hour ago."

Michelle headed up the tunnel until she reached the massive hardwood doors. She pried them open quietly. She was reluctant to disturb John and instead stood motionless, surveying the dim room.

The low ceiling arched gently to the center of the circular room. From the ceiling's high point, a thin beam of light led directly below to a single slab of stone, sitting atop a spread of white gravel that covered the entire floor. The tiny chips of white gravel had been raked into wave patterns radiating from the stone. In the darkness, the encircling granite walls simply blended unseen into nothingness.

The spot-lighted stone looked like a distant fortress island rising in miniature from a serene sea. A gnarled and twisted bonsai clung to its side.

John sat atop a thick leather cushion at the edge of a small deck. The deck, fashioned from weathered planks, protruded but a few feet into the silent room.

Michelle stood looking down to the back of John's head. She knew he was aware of her. He remained motionless, facing the stone island. His mane of silky white hair shimmered in the dim shadows.

"John," she had to interrupt him.

He turned back, looking up to her.

"We're ready to leave."

"Yes, I know." He signaled for her to join him.

She sat next to him. "Are you frightened?" she asked softly.

"Yes. What we have begun will soon be independent of us."

"It already is," Michelle said, squeezing his hand and resting her head on his shoulder. For several minutes, they gazed at the distant solitary island.

John turned to her, "You must go now." He kissed the top of her blond head.

She sat up, looking over at him. "What do you think will happen?"

"The child will be born. The rest . . . ," he inhaled deeply, ". . . will unfold by its nature."

"Why does she want to return to Lima? The child would be safer here."

"She is deeply religious, Michelle. She does not seek your sense of safety."

"But why return to Peru?"

"She and Angelica grew up together on the streets of Lima. The child is her best hope for her people, the poor of South America. He will be born as one of them. That is her wish, which we shall honor."

Michelle rose to her feet, "We'll be back soon." She brushed her fingers over his white hair then left the chamber.

John breathed in slowly then released his breath. "Socrates."

"Yes, John," the deep voice resonated through the chamber.

"Alert me when they have left." John sat passively for ten minutes, staring across a dimly lit sea to the fortress island.

Unheard from several hundred feet above the chamber, the heliport began to open as the Jet Ranger's blades blurred. Michelle looked back to Antonio, Manuel, and Carlota, checking that their safety belts were buckled.

She maneuvered the machine off the ground.

"John."

"Yes, Socrates."

"Michelle has cleared the compound."

The Jet Ranger tilted forward and headed down the mountain's slope for a hundred yards before leaping into the sky. Michelle radioed the tower at Saratoga's airport for clearance. The flight would only last a few minutes.

John cleared his throat, "Security."

Within seconds, a phone in Mullen's hangar at the Saratoga airport began to ring.

"Pete Riner," Riner answered by speaker phone.

Riner had begun a meteoric rise through the ranks of the F.B.I. soon after he graduated from Notre Dame law school. His career with the F.B.I. ended ten years later when John Mullen asked him to head Mullen's corporate security and offered to quadruple his salary and establish substantial college trust funds for his five children. Before Riner had agreed, he brought his family to Saratoga that summer. After their first visit, they refused to live anywhere else. Saratoga was home.

"Pete, John Mullen here."

"Yes, Mr. Mullen."

"Michelle and her guests are en route. She will be taking the Mercedes."

"Yes, sir. Everything is ready."

"Keep 'em safe, Pete."

"Yes, sir."

"I have asked Dr. Groussman to travel with your team in case Ms. Cabral needs attention. You can pick him up in Saratoga."

"He's already at the hangar, sir. Michelle called me earlier and gave us their departure time."

"You're ready to follow?"

"Yes, sir."

The whine of the Ranger's powerful engine began invading the hangar. Riner looked out his office window to the eastern sky. "They're in view, sir."

"Keep me posted."

"Yes, sir," Riner ended the conversation and headed out into the hangar, signalling to others. The hangar doors began sliding apart.

John breathed several deep breaths and returned his attention to the twisted bonsai clinging to the brightly lit stone.

Riner hurried to the Ranger as soon as Michelle cut the engine, bending low as he made his way beneath the blurring blades. He opened Carlota's door and extended a hand, "Ms. Cabral."

She smiled gently and took his hand, easing out of her seat. Riner accompanied her away from the twirling blades to the hangar. Antonio and Manuel followed close behind.

When Michelle joined them, a dark blue Mercedes sedan emerged from behind one of the jets. The black tires squeaked against the slick concrete of the hangar floor as the car pulled alongside.

A young woman stepped out, leaving the driver's door open and the engine running.

"Thank you, Denise," Riner said.

Denise nodded and headed to the back of the hangar.

"Ms. Cumberland, I hope your journey is pleasant."

"Thank you, Pete." Michelle walked to the driver's door and signalled Carlota to sit up front with her. Riner opened the door for Carlota. Antonio and Manuel climbed in back.

The Mercedes rolled from the hangar and, as the hangar doors closed, passed through the airport's side gate. They headed north on Highway 130 toward Pinedale, nestled along the western slope of the Wind River Mountains.

Moments later, a silver Lincoln Continental left the hangar, following the Mercedes. A red and white Suburban Wagon soon followed the Lincoln.

John rolled back his head, stretching his neck. He inhaled deeply and uncrossed his legs, hanging them over the edge of the deck. The tips of his toes just reached the white gravel floor. "Socrates."

"Yes."

"Jacob Brigham, please."

Socrates instantly dialed three numbers. All the lines answered within two rings. Capable of simultaneous conversations, Socrates located Brigham and terminated the other conversations.

"Jacob Brigham."

"Mr. Brigham, this is Socrates, please hold for Mr. Mullen." Socrates alerted John that Brigham was on line.

"Patch him in."

Socrates engaged the scrambler.

"Jacob?" John asked.

"Yes."

"Where are you?"

"Over the Pacific, between Seattle and Anchorage."

"Anything from O'Riley?"

"He has confirmed that Father Bernadine is definitely confined by the *Gendarmerie*."

"The Vatican police?"

"Yes. We're preparing to get him out tomorrow. If we wait longer, they will discover he's been making overseas calls from his room." Jacob warned.

"Who has he been calling?"

"He told O'Riley that he called seven different bishops throughout South America."

"Did he say who he called?" John questioned.

"No. O'Riley asked but Bernadine said he'd tell him later."

"What is he doing?"

"I'm not sure, but Stauffen called from Iquitos. It seems the local priests have begun telling their congregations the Messiah is returning soon to deliver them," Jacob paused. "Are there parts of your plan that I'm not aware of John?"

"Absolutely not, Jacob. Why?"

"We're picking up reports from six of our South American operations that local priests are telling people they don't have long to wait for the Messiah's return."

"They don't have long to wait, but how could the priests know? Where are your reports coming from?"

"Iquitos, Ayacucho, and Lima in Peru and Manaus, Brazilia, and São Paulo in Brazil. This isn't something that will pass quietly, John. Some villages are starting to celebrate." When John made no response, Jacob continued, "We've asked Bernadine to discontinue his overseas calls."

"What did he say?"

"He agreed. What do you think he's up to, John?"

"I have no idea Jacob, but it appears there may be some linkage between his overseas calls and the prophecies of the South American priests, wouldn't you say?"

"Definitely."

"Father Bernadine seems to have a plan hitched to ours."

"It appears so. In any case, O'Riley wants to get him out of the Vatican quickly, before Rajunt catches the scent."

"Let me know when he's out. I would like to talk to him. Jacob, find out what you can about these priests who are telling people about a new Messiah."

"I'll call you as soon as I can give you a good picture of what's happening. But I can tell you, John, the *Sendero* guerrillas in Peru are going to overreact if any ray of hope hits their people. They'll be in a killing mood."

"Tell Ray Stauffen and Janice McClain to be on guard."

"I already have, we discussed that."

"Can we track the numbers Bernadine called in South America?" John asked.

"Not without Socrates."

"Socrates," John called out.

"Yes."

"Assist Jacob."

"Standing by, Mr. Brigham."

"Jacob, keep me posted," John added.

"Will do."

"The line has terminated," Socrates informed John.

The chamber remained still for several minutes as John gathered his thoughts. "Can you help Jacob?"

"Yes," Socrates responded, "I have accessed G. T. & T.'s computer in Omaha. It is currently searching codes in its European cable for Vatican billing access."

"Will it take long to get Jacob his information?"

"No, the encryption systems are primitive."

"Can you be traced?"

"No."

John rose from the deck, his joints aching, and made his way to the tunnel that led from the chamber.

• • •

THE NEXT MORNING Rajunt returned to the Vatican Gardens to again meet Klodiński and waited near the great rose beds. It was unusual for Klodiński to be late.

Movement caught Rajunt's eye and he turned to see Klodiński hurrying along the path.

"Pardon my tardiness, but I received two calls from South America after I called you."

"Pay it no mind, my friend," Rajunt eyed him with disapproval.

"Bishop Gómez called me. He has been unable to find De las Casas."

"I know. He also called me."

"What did you tell him?"

"To keep looking," Rajunt snapped.

A distant siren broke the peace of the garden.

"Has Bishop Cardoso called you?" Klodiński asked.

"No. Why?"

"He and Bishop Sánchez called me soon after I had called you to meet me here."

"Sánchez, from São Paulo?"

"Yes. They said Archbishop De Gonzales' priests have begun preaching the Messiah will soon return. Bishop Sánchez said he and Cardoso have begun alerting the Society throughout South America to stop this heresy."

The siren's distant scream was increasing. Rajunt and Klodiński briefly looked toward its direction.

"An ambulance," Klodiński noted by the undulating wail.

Rajunt immediately redirected their conversation. His eyes had become glass and did not waver as he stared at Klodiński. "You must tell me exactly what they said."

"Bishop Cardoso . . . ."

"Is he still in Lima?" Rajunt interrupted sharply.

"Yes. Bishop Cardoso attended mass at the Lady of Our Light in Lima yesterday and said the priest was promising people that the Messiah was soon at hand. He immediately removed the priest from his duties but said many other priests are repeating it all across Peru. It spreads like wildfire, he said." Klodiński drew his brows together. "The people trust De Gonzales' priests." "What did Sánchez say?" Rajunt felt his chest tighten.

The crying ambulance swerved toward St. Peter's Square and slowed as it entered an ocean of tourists milling about with cameras trained on the Basilica. The siren's sharp wail parted the sea of people. "Keep going," O'Riley commanded from the back of the van.

Across the Vatican, Klodiński shrugged in holy confusion. "The same thing is happening in Brazil. The slums of São Paulo and Rio de Janeiro–that's all the people will talk about–the Messiah is returning as one of them."

The ambulance picked its way through the crowd and again gathered speed, heading down a side street to the Vatican's apartments for resident foreigners.

"They are almost here, Father. I can hear the siren." Fear gripped the face of the young *Gendarme* who had denied Father Bernadine re-entry to his office. He had found Bernadine sprawled on the floor of his meager apartment, nearly unconscious and clutching a phone after calling the ambulance.

"Bless you, my child." Bernadine looked up stoicly from his bed and breathed irregularly. He grasped the young man's hand.

"I'm going to carry you down the stairs, Father." The young man nodded reassuringly. "The stairwell is too narrow for a stretcher," he explained.

"You are too kind." Bernadine looked up at the kind-faced young man and smiled bravely.

Across the Basilica in the Vatican Gardens, Rajunt snapped a rose head from its stem. "I can already tell you, this is Bernadine's doing," he hissed.

"It makes no sense," Klodiński retorted and noted the standing veins at Rajunt's temples.

"Trust me, my friend, it makes perfect sense. We simply don't understand how it does, yet." Rajunt's cold lips pinched into a narrow furrow.

At that instant, the siren stopped wailing and Rajunt glanced back toward the Basilica.

"They're here, Father!" The young *Gendarme* broke Bernadine's weak grip, hurried to the tiny window and looked down at the small courtyard. The back of the ambulance doors swung open and scrambling medics pulled out a stretcher. The medics were locking its metal legs into place when the young man left the window, set his jaw with determination, and scooped Bernadine from the bed with powerful arms.

Bernadine weakly laid his head upon the young man's uniformed chest. "Am I too heavy for you, my son?" He looked up with hound dog eyes.

"Not at all," the *Gendarme* answered and rushed down the hallway with the frail old man tucked against his chest. He kicked open the stairwell door and bounded down the stairs two at a time.

Across the Vatican, Klodiński followed Rajunt from the rose garden. Rajunt walked slowly, studying the ground, his hands clasped behind his back. Klodiński waited for Rajunt to speak. When they reached the trees, Rajunt stopped and looked up, pausing.

"I shall go to Peru to visit Bishop Cardoso," Rajunt announced softly.

"You must be very careful, my friend. The *Sendero Luminoso* is ensconced all around Lima."

"God's will be done," Rajunt dismissed Klodiński's fears.

"He's having a heart attack!" The young *Gendarme* exclaimed to a white frocked doctor and, as gently as he could, laid Bernadine onto the stretcher.

"We'll take care of him, son," O'Riley responded and signalled the other medics to get Bernadine into the ambulance quickly.

O'Riley could see the young *Gendarme* was determined to accompany Bernadine.

"Is he on any medications?" O'Riley barked.

"I don't know," the *Gendarme* replied in frustration.

"I can't believe you people aren't better prepared! Go find out and call this number." O'Riley handed him a card from Rome's largest hospital. As they shoved Bernadine's stretcher into the ambulance, O'Riley scowled at the young man. "Now!" he snapped.

As he climbed into the back of the ambulance he glanced back. The young man was running through a crowd of nuns hurrying out of the foreign visitor's residence in curiosity. One nun was excitedly taking pictures.

O'Riley slammed the ambulance doors shut behind him. "Go."

"Do you want me to go with you?" Klodiński asked Rajunt hesitantly.

"No. I want you to stay here and keep an eye on Bernadine. He's part of this, I can tell," Rajunt's tongue flicked the air.

From the rear of the van, O'Riley watched the crowd of nuns and excited on-lookers become smaller and smaller as the ambulance rocketed away. He looked down at the old man and smiled. "Father Bernadine, you can sit up. We're clear."

• • •

MICHELLE STRETCHED SLOWLY, opening green eyes to a dawn breaking behind the Wind River Mountains. Lake breezes followed the morning sun through open patio doors to her bedroom. Perched on a pine branch overhanging the patio deck, a yellow-winged black bird chirped.

Michelle slipped into a flannel robe and wandered onto the wooden deck, which ran the full rear of the house. She stood at deck's edge, sixty feet above the rocky shore, and looked out across the lake. The breeze caressed her face and lifted wispy blond strands from her shoulders.

Fed from glacial melt high in the Wind River Mountains, Fremont Lake spread for a mile to the opposite shore. The sound of a slowly churning outboard carried across acres of mirrored water.

Michelle yawned and headed for the kitchen. A mug of coffee steamed from her hand when she returned. She pulled a chair to the deck's edge and eased back to watch the lake come alive.

An hour later, other bedroom doors opened to the patio. Manuel emerged and waved, buttoning the top of his shirt. He left the doors open and hurried to Michelle.

"Good morning," he said softly and sat beside her.

"Good morning. Did you sleep well?" She smiled.

"Yes."

"I'm sorry you and Father Antonio have to share a room. But John and I built it for our own retreat."

"It is palatial by my standards." Manuel responded matter-of-factly.

"Is Father Antonio still sleeping?" she asked.

"Dead to the world. Is Carlota awake?"

"You and I are the first awake. But I thought I heard her stirring earlier. Would you like coffee?"

"Please." Manuel rose from his chair. "Let me get it. In the kitchen?"

"A full pot." Michelle lifted her mug in explanation and Manuel disappeared into the house.

Michelle rose and headed for the patio doors to Carlota's bedroom. She walked past the open patio doors of Manuel's and Antonio's room and glanced in. Antonio lay sleeping, sprawled across the nearest bed.

His large frame overran the length of his bed. He lay on his back, his right arm covering his face. He had kicked away most of his cover. His upper torso was bare but a single white sheet had twisted about his hips. A long leg hung limply over the edge of the bed.

Michelle continued toward Carlota's room. When she reached the door, she knocked gently. "Carlota?"

Carlota turned off the water. "One moment, Michelle," she replied loudly, pulling back on her robe. She left the bathroom and opened the patio doors.

"I thought I heard you moving about earlier and wondered if you might want to join Father Manuel and me for morning coffee."

"How sweet. I need to shower first. I'll be out soon."

"Take your time," Michelle answered.

Manuel had not returned as Michelle made her way back. She paused at Antonio's room, glancing in.

Her eyes surveyed his sleeping body. The muscular chest rose and fell in slow breaths. Her green eyes eagerly followed the fine line of dark hair that trailed down the center of his ridged stomach and disappeared beneath the white sheet tangled around his hips. Antonio sighed deeply, rolling onto his stomach, losing his cover.

Michelle studied his rear appreciatively for several seconds. She sighed and returned to the deck chairs.

Manuel emerged from the house. "I helped myself to breakfast," With a cup of coffee in one hand, he held up a dark brown cinnamon roll in the other. "I hope that was all right."

Michelle smiled, "Father Manuel, you make yourself at home."
Manuel walked to the open patio doors and called for Antonio
to wake. He closed the doors and returned to sit beside her.

Fifteen minutes later, Carlota joined them and soon all four
sat near the edge of the deck, watching the morning lake and
talking.

Antonio was barefooted and wrapped in a heavy cotton robe.
Blue eyes sparkled relentlessly in the bright morning sun.
Contentment coated his face as he listened to Carlota and
Manuel.

"I appreciate that you have come to help me," Carlota said to
Antonio and Manuel.

The priests stared reverently at her, lulling the conversation.

"What would you like to do today, Carlota?" Michelle asked.

"I'm still a little tired, do you mind if I rest this morning?"

"No." Antonio and Manuel replied sympathetically.

"Would you like Dr. Groussman to come up to the house?"
Michelle asked.

"No, no." Carlota said softly. "I'm just tired. You three go enjoy
yourself, please," she insisted gently. "By the time you're back, I'll
be rested."

The priests looked to Michelle.

"We could water ski for a little while," she suggested.

"We've never skied," Antonio warned.

"Wanna try?"

Carlota smiled at the fire in Michelle's eyes.

"Is it hard?" Antonio quizzed.

"If you can stay up the rest is easy," Michelle laughed
throatily.

"I'll try," Antonio said.

"Manuel?" Michelle dared with the arch of a brow.

He smiled, shaking his head in declination.

"I have to try this alone?" Antonio smiled at Manuel. Manuel
nodded playfully.

• • •

BISHOP GÓMEZ STEPPED over fresh piles of burro dung as he
scurried along the footpath leading deep into the jungle from the
little church outside Iquitos.

His young native guide hurried along the trail and Gómez was
trying his best to keep up. Sweat poured down his face, burning

his eyes. The equatorial heat made the air thick and difficult to breath.

Overhead, the canopy of trees blocked out chunks of sky. Sharp shadows and bright patches of sunlight striped the footpath. Shrill calls of exotic birds occasionally pierced the heavy air and joined the constant drone of insects.

"Hold up, my man!" Gómez exclaimed in Spanish to the young guide disappearing ahead along the path. Gómez stopped to catch his breath. By the time he felt rested, he knew he had been abandoned.

"Heathen," Gómez grumbled aloud and pressed on, pushing leafy green branches away from his face. Fifty yards on, he rounded a bend in the path and stumbled into a clearing. Several *Sendero Luminoso* stood waiting, machine guns pointing at his face. Machetes hung from their waists.

"Priest," the leader hissed in Spanish. Her nostrils flared and brown eyes boiled with hatred, the corners of her mouth twisting into a cruel smile. Her tattered rain cape, gathered at her neck by a metal clasp, hung loosely across the forearm that held the machine gun. She motioned him to the ground, next to his young Indian guide.

He stared in terror a moment too long. Barking orders in Spanish, she pulled her machete from the sheath coupled to her belt. Two men grabbed his arms and kicked the back of his knees, knocking him to the ground. They held him kneeling before her. She lowered the razored edge of the machete to the tuft of skin between his right ear and his skull.

"Blood sucking leech," she snarled and pulled the blade along his ear. Gómez screamed. He struggled to grab the side of his head but the two wiry men held his arms in place.

As Gómez cried out, she shoved a machine gun muzzle between his teeth. He froze and rolled his eyes upward, his screams silenced. She stared down at him. "Suck on this, priest," she ordered.

Gómez was petrified. Not a muscle moved or twitched as blood poured down his neck.

She rattled the barrel against his teeth. "Suck or die, you decide," she growled, her unblinking eyes glowing fiercely.

Trembling, Gómez complied. He hesitantly wrapped his lips around the barrel. His quaking clattered his teeth against the metal. She slid more of the barrel into his mouth. Gómez' eyes bulged and he threatened to gag as she teased the barrel down his throat.

"Mmmmm, you're good priest. Get ready to swallow," she said with a throaty growl, her trigger hand tightening appreciably. The men holding Gómez pivoted quickly to the side.

"María!" Anita, the youngest of the *Sendero*, called out.

María's blazing eyes snapped from Gómez to Anita. "*¿Qué?*"

"We should take the priest back alive."

María looked back to Gómez, who had wet himself, and slowly withdrew the barrel from his quivering lips. A thin strand of saliva followed the glistening muzzle as it pulled away. "You're lucky today, priest," she snarled and inclined her head toward the guide.

The young guide cried out in fear as the rest of the *Sendero* descended on him. They tore off his piecemeal shirt and trousers in quick moves. Within moments, he lay naked on his back, staked spread eagle to the ground.

María walked over to him and lightly kicked his head with the muddy tip of her boot. "You're no priest."

He rolled his head toward her, his eyes frozen in fear. Gómez whimpered loudly in the background.

"You are a collaborator." She hurled the words at the young Indian guide in Spanish and spit down onto his face. Her dark eyes were filled with fury.

He responded with a phrase in his own language.

María stepped over his tight body and kneeled between his wide-spread legs. "Speak Spanish, collaborator," she ordered in Spanish.

The young man raised his head from the ground and looked down the length of his body to her. With powerful lungs, he blew a saliva glob onto her face and defiantly repeated his previous phrase.

"Brave little man." She reached between his legs, smiling broadly as her long fingers encircled their prey. She stretched him with one hand. With the other, she laid the strap edge of her machete against his lower belly.

He mumbled a prayer in Spanish.

"Spanish at last," she noted and continued pulling until he winced, the tendons of his neck flaring. "I want the priest to watch!" she commanded.

One of the men holding Gómez kneeled beside him, wrenching him into a headlock that faced María and threatened to snap his neck.

Gómez stared in horror as María gently slid the razored edge slowly back and forth, amid wild screams of anguish. The animals in the canopy above shrieked with excitement, piercing the jungle's peace with shrill calls of alarm.

María's lip curled back to show a glint of teeth when she had triumphed. She raised her severed trophy high above her head, looking to the others. The women of the group cheered wildly. The men winced.

"Mother of God!" Gómez whispered to himself.

Leaving the convulsing young man in a growing pool of blood between his legs, María walked over and yanked Gómez to his feet. "Move priest!"

The young man began to scream uncontrollably.

Moments later, the *Sendero* guerrillas herded Gómez with them as they tunneled into the green foliage of wet undergrowth. The last of them, one of the men who had held Gómez, glanced back to make sure no one followed.

• • •

JOHN STOOD BESIDE the wall of glass that framed the valley below. From the mountain fortress, he stared down to the tiny town of Saratoga with hands clasped behind his back.

"Jacob Brigham is calling," Socrates interrupted the silence.

"Patch him in."

"John, Brian O'Riley got Bernadine out a few hours ago. He talked Bernadine into faking a heart attack and took him out by ambulance."

"Where is he?"

"O'Riley took him out of Italy on a corporate plane. They just landed in Amsterdam about twenty minutes ago to refuel."

"Is Bernadine still on board?"

"Yep."

"Jacob, hold on a minute." John's hands dropped to his sides. "Socrates, Father Bernadine please, conference link."

Within seconds, a new voice entered the room. "Mr. Mullen?" The voice sounded distant until Socrates boosted the signal.

"Brian?" John asked.

"Mr. Mullen? Brian O'Riley here."

John walked back to his desk. "Is Father Bernadine there?"

Several seconds passed. "Hallo?" The voice was old and sounded hollow on the speaker phone.

"Father Bernadine?" John sat at his desk as he spoke.

"Yes."

"This is John Mullen."

"Mr. Mullen. We meet at last!" Bernadine declared with Leprechaun-like inflections.

"We do. How are you, Father?"

"I'm fine, quite fine."

"Ms. Cabral hopes to meet you before she returns to Lima," John said.

Jacob Brigham listened quietly in Anchorage.

"I look forward to meeting our new Madonna." Bernadine responded swiftly.

"Fathers Antonio and Manuel are here, too. I know they will want to see you," John added.

"You are too kind." Bernadine said sincerely.

"Brian?" John asked.

"I'm here," O'Riley shouted from the far side of the jet cabin.

"How soon can you get him here?" John's voice rasped.

"We'll clear customs after I transfer him to a corporate G-4 Gulfstream being flown in from Edinburgh."

"Mr. Mullen asked how soon can you get him there?" Brigham repeated the question to his subordinate.

"Sixteen hours, give or take a little for refueling," O'Riley added swiftly.

"Good job getting him out, Brian." John paused, "We'll see you soon, Father Bernadine."

"Yes, quite so, quite so," Bernadine chirped.

"Have a pleasant flight, Father," John bid him farewell, which Socrates interpreted as a command to terminate the Atlantic link.

"Are they off the line, Socrates?" John asked.

"Yes."

"Anything on those South American priests yet, Jacob?"

"Nothing of substance. Socrates identified the numbers Bernadine called overseas. We're checking out the addresses. I don't have anything solid yet, but we're working on it."

"I know."

"Is Michelle there with you?"

"She's at the Fremont Lake house with our guests."

Several seconds of silence ticked by. "John, do you think it's wise for them to be away from the compound now?"

"No, I don't. But Carlota insisted on visiting this area before we return her to Lima. She wants to spend some time getting to know the priests before she returns home, which I can understand."

"Can you persuade her to cut her time there short, given the developments in Rome?" Jacob asked somberly.

"I can only try to motivate her to do so, which is why I invited Father Bernadine to Saratoga."

"There is no danger yet from the Society but let me know if anything develops. I'll get back to you when we can confirm who Bernadine talked with in South America."

"Thanks, Jacob. I'll be talking with you."

"The connection to Brigham is terminated."

"Thank you, Socrates." John leaned back in his chair and rubbed his eyes.

• • •

MICHELLE WAVED AT Carlota then looked back and thrust forward the throttle. The front of the speed boat lifted from the icy waters and the ski rope snapped tight. Antonio began rising awkwardly from the lake.

From the deck above, Carlota watched Antonio plunge face first into the lake amid wild spray.

The boat lurched forward.

Manuel yelled instantly, "He's down!"

Michelle quickly circled the boat then cut the throttle, letting the floating handle of the ski rope drag within range of Antonio's long arms.

He signaled with a nod of his head and the front of the boat again lifted from the waters. Seconds later, he fell and the boat lunged forward.

"He's down!" Manuel yelled again and laughed.

The same false starts repeated several times.

Michelle went to the back of the boat. "Do you want me to show you how?" she yelled at Antonio's head as it bobbed in the icy water.

Antonio began pulling himself along the ski rope, back to the boat.

"You can run this, can't you?" Michelle asked Manuel as she tossed a ski into the lake with a splash.

"I'm an engineer as well as a priest, Michelle," Manuel replied. "I can drive a boat."

Michelle positioned a ladder over the side for Antonio and stepped up onto the edge of the boat, ready to dive.

Antonio looked up through water running into his eyes. Michelle towered overhead. Her silver swim suit glistened in the sun, glued to her perfect torso.

She smiled at him then dove when he lifted himself out of the water. The spray from her dive filled the air as Manuel held the ladder.

"She'll show you how it's done," Manuel predicted with a smile, positioning behind the throttle.

Antonio settled in at the back of the boat to watch Michelle, his pale blue eyes never leaving her. She was too beautiful not to appreciate.

Manuel looked back to Michelle, who was signaling go. He swiftly shoved the throttle.

The engine roared to life and the boat bore down into the water, shooting ahead. Michelle rose from the water.

Carlota smiled and returned to her room as the boat headed north to the cliffs.

Michelle cut to and fro over the wake, leaping waves with only one hand gripping the handle. The other hung limply to her side. Antonio knew this was child's play for her.

Manuel knew it, too. He raised his head high above the windshield and looked around. The wind laid back his unruly brown hair and teared his eyes.

"Hold on, Antonio," he shouted, spinning the steering wheel. The speedboat banked sharply to the right. After fifty yards, he spun the wheel to the left.

Michelle grabbed the ski rope handle with both hands. She had an eagle eye on Manuel's hands at the steering wheel, anticipating the boat before it could respond to his commands.

With a throaty laugh, she prepared to ride out his challenge. As the centrifugal force of the turn started into play, she edged her ski into the water. Strong legs held her body parallel to the water as a plume of icy water sprayed into the mountain air. She blasted past the boat with a rooster-tail spray following her for a hundred yards.

Manuel straightened the craft and headed for the distant rocky cliffs. In the distance, another boat followed.

Michelle zig-zagged effortlessly across the speed boat's swollen wake, her shoulders skimming the water at each change of direction. A spray of liquid diamonds followed behind her.

Admiration stretched into a smile across Antonio's face as he watched Michelle ride the wind.

● ● ●

RAJUNT'S FACE TELEGRAPHED silent fury as he listened quietly to Victor Semani, head of the Vatican police, explain Bernadine's newly discovered escape. By the time Semani finished explaining how the young *Gendarme* had even carried Bernadine down to the deceptive ambulance, Rajunt exploded.

Rajunt slammed down his hands and rose from behind the desk like a demon from the sea. His words were spoken in a near hush, but dripped with venom. "I told you Bernadine must not leave the Vatican."

Determined to endure the verbal whipping as a man, Semani stood silently.

Rajunt leaned forward, resting his weight on his palms. "Do you recall that order?"

"Yes," Semani answered without hesitation.

"Good." Rajunt leaned forward, "You realize you failed?"

"Yes."

"You realize you failed pathetically?"

"Yes." The veins along Semani's temples rose to the surface.

"You are not paid to fail. You realize that also?"

"Yes."

"You would not want to be unfair to the Society."

"No." Semani's fingers curled into tight fists hanging beneath the edge of the desk. Semani could see it coming, he knew Rajunt.

"You will insist that your salary be suspended until you at least locate Father Bernadine, won't you?" Rajunt leaned even closer.

"Yes, your Eminence."

Rajunt pulled back. "Come to me when you have located Bernadine and I will insist your salary be reinstated."

"Yes, your Eminence."

Rajunt returned to his seat, easing into the high-backed red chair. "If you do not return to me soon with that information, I know there is nothing I could say to dissuade you from resigning your commission." Rajunt cradled his chin between his thumb and index finger, his elbow on the desk. "Go."

Semani bowed his head, "Your Eminence." He hurried from the room.

When Rajunt heard the door to his outer office close, he depressed the button of his intercom. "Get me on the first flight to Lima," he ordered his secretary, "then call Bishop Cardoso in Lima and inform him of my arrival."

"Yes, your Eminence."

The secretary soon returned to the intercom. First-class booking was possible on a flight that would take him to Mexico City, with a three hour layover there, then on to Lima.

Rajunt ordered the ticket purchased and instructed his secretary to pack and deliver his luggage to the airport ahead of him. He returned to his residence overlooking the Courtyard of St. Damasus, positioned directly below that of the Holy See. Rajunt's apartment exceeded the Pope's in plushness and elegance.

Rajunt ordered a light meal brought to his apartment. As he waited, he soaked in his marble tub and sipped red wine from a thin crystal goblet, listening to Bach. After the meal, he napped while his secretary packed for him and transported his luggage to the Leonardo da Vinci airport.

When Rajunt awoke, he was ready for the flight.

He was seated in the first row of the Alitalia 747 when it rose from Rome, banked sharply over the green Mediterranean, and headed west for Mexico City.

Hours later, he slid open the telephone console beside his seat as the pilot announced in Italian that they had entered Mexican airspace. Thin fingers quickly keyed in his card number and Semani's private number. Several rings then an answer.

"Semani," the voice harshly announced.

"Cardinal Rajunt."

The tone shifted submissively. "Your Eminence, I am glad you called."

"Then you found Bernadine?"

"No, but we've made progress."

"What do you call progress, Semani?" Rajunt smiled politely at the stewardess handing him another glass of red wine.

"A Sister happened to take pictures when Bernadine was loaded into the ambulance. We enlarged the photo and discovered who got Bernadine out."

"Who?"

"Brian O'Riley." Semani sounded triumphant.

Rajunt's eyes narrowed. "Who is Brian O'Riley?"

"He directs John Mullen's Italian operations."

"Who is John Mullen?" Rajunt's impatience telegraphed itself across the Atlantic.

Semani hesitated, "You are unaware of John Mullen, your Eminence?"

"Who is he, Semani?"

"One of the richest men in the world, perhaps the richest."

Rajunt put down his wine glass and slowly wiped the corners of his lips with a white linen. "What do you know of him?"

"A good deal."

"American?"

"Yes, he lives in Wyoming."

"Wyoming . . . the state?"

"Yes."

"How rich is he?" Rajunt asked hesitantly.

"It's hard to say because he buries so much through cross-ownership but our bankers say conservatively he's worth over $29 billion. They also say his wealth is accumulating faster than that of anyone else."

Rajunt shifted in the soft leather seat. "Did he inherit his wealth?"

"No, he began a little pharmaceutical company fifty years ago with his own patents." Semani detected Rajunt's discomfort and smiled from the safety of his office on the other side of the Atlantic. "What he touches turns to gold," he added gratuitously for Rajunt's displeasure.

Rajunt closed his eyes to focus his mind. "What does he own?"

"It is easier to explain what he does not own, your Eminence."

"Get to the point, Semani. What is the source of his money?"

"A pharmaceutical conglomerate, bank holding companies, tracts of land around the world, a construction company, a computer company, a genetic engineering laboratory. . . ."

Rajunt's dark eyes snapped opened. He did not move or blink. His mind's eye spotted purpose against a backdrop of chaos—Bernadine, the missing relic, the blood of Christ, a genetic engineering laboratory. Semani's voice began again to register.

". . . and an investment firm. There is much more, as I said, he disguises his wealth."

"A genetic engineering laboratory?" Rajunt asked slowly.

"Yes, a secretive genetics research company called SYNGENTEC."

"I want the dossier on Mullen immediately."

"Yes, sir."

"Does he have family?" Rajunt pressed the phone to his ear as the pilot made another announcement.

"His sister's granddaughter is the only family he has left. His wife was killed in a plane crash years ago."

"Are they close?"

"Yes. They work together."

"Who is she?"

"Michelle Cumberland."

"How old is she?"

"Early thirties. She's an architect. Her parents were killed in the same crash as his wife. One of his corporate jets crashed in the Atlantic when she was an infant. It was a freak accident. Mullen has looked after her ever since."

"How old is Mullen?"

"Around eighty."

"How is his health?"

"He is rumored ill."

"With what?"

"We don't know."

"If Brian O'Riley is still in Rome, have him arrested."

"He left Rome for Amsterdam by corporate jet the day Bernadine was kidnapped."

"He wasn't kidnapped Semani, he escaped and you are responsible."

Semani remained silent, the unseen smile dropping from his face.

"Is Mullen in Wyoming now?"

"We believe so."

"Then that is where you will find Bernadine. Call me when you confirm." Rajunt terminated the call and instantly called his secretary, giving his commands without greeting. "Find Gómez and tell him to return to Lima to meet me there. I know where Father De las Casas is." He slowly replaced the phone into the console, lost in thought.

Rajunt's bony fingers trembled slightly as they reached into his attaché to retrieve his copy of De las Casas' TOMORROW'S MESSIAH. He began to read with a new eye.

• • •

GÓMEZ STUMBLED FROM a shadowy tangle of undergrowth, his face whipped from vines and branches. A glob of blood covered his ear stump. His hands were tied behind him and a long leather leash connected him to María. Tears of fear blurred his eyes.

María and the others followed him into the *Sendero* camp.

María held Gómez' leash high as armed men and women wearing ponchos gathered to inspect him. "Another priest!" she cried victoriously in Spanish.

Bishop Gómez knew better than to correct her. He looked to the ground, frightened of eye contact with any *Sendero* as they inspected him.

They cheered when María reached into her leather pouch, lifting Gómez' ear and her bloody trophy from the young guide high above her head. Then she turned to Gómez. "The priests in Iquitos are telling the peasants that Jesus is returning to save them. I want to know why."

He looked at her dazed. "I don't know why," he said nervously.

"Liar!" she screamed and back-handed him so hard he dropped to one knee. She turned to the *Sendero*. "I'll deal with him later."

One of María's comrades swaggered to Gómez, yanked him onto his feet, and sliced the leather band from his wrists. "Strip off your clothes," he ordered.

Gómez' fingers so trembled he could not unbutton his shirt.

"Help the good priest," María ordered.

Gómez soon stood naked and encircled by laughing and pointing *Senderos*. He stared at his clothes and boots, piled at his feet.

"We'll give these to some deserving *cocalero*," María bellowed as she swept up his clothes from the ground and pushed Gómez toward a small, windowless tin hut baking in the equatorial sun. The hut sat at the far edge of the compound.

Another *Sendero* hurried ahead to open the flimsy tin door and María pushed Gómez to the threshold. A sharp angle of sunlight cut along the hut's dirt floor. An acrid smell rolled out of the darkness.

"Bind his hands again," María ordered.

Gómez peered into the murky shadows of the hut as they tied his hands behind his back. Several older men and women were huddled inside, all as naked as he. "I hope you can keep the flies from laying their larvae in your head." María jabbed her gun barrel where his ear had once been and reopened the wound, bloodying the tip of the barrel. Lifting her muddy boot to his back, she pushed him face first into the dirt.

The door slammed behind him, returning the room to darkness.

Gómez could hear movement in the dark. The air was unbreathable. The humid heat boiled with bitter scent of human excrement.

"Are you a priest?" someone asked from the darkness.

"No, I am a bishop, Bishop Jesus Gómez," he spoke with pride.

"They have hurt you." A soft hand reached through the darkness, gently touching the side of Gómez' head. "I am Sister Agnus McDermott."

Gómez pulled his head away. The unseen hand retreated. "Who else is here?" Gómez demanded.

"Sister Teresa Pryor is here with me. We were captured together two days ago," Agnus explained quietly.

"Where?" Gómez refused to lower his voice.

"Near Concordia, inside the Pacaya Samiria Reserve," Teresa answered quietly for Agnus from an unseen corner, her legs pulled up to cover her naked chest.

"Why were you there?" Gómez demanded.

"We had come from Lima—the Drink of Milk program, for the children," Agnus whispered.

"Who else is here?" Gómez asked impatiently.

"Speak quietly, Bishop Gómez." someone ordered in hushed tones from a darkened corner. "They punish us when they hear us talking."

"Who are you?" Gómez demanded of the intruder without lowering his voice.

"Bishop Samuel Hyndman, from Canada," the man answered softly but with equal authority. "There is a priest here, but he is very old and weak. He's sleeping now."

"Who is he?"

"Father Iam Ignatious, from Boa Vista, Brazil."

"How did you get here?" Gómez had adopted Rajunt's inquisitorial tone.

"Father Ignatious and I are with Universal Relief. We were taking antibiotics to Puca Urco, along the Putumayo River, when the *Sendero* descended on our group. They slaughtered everyone but us," Hyndman explained.

"They seem to be collecting clerics," Teresa whispered.

"If they are, they've got a reason," Agnus predicted cautiously.

The tin door swung open. María stood in the sunlight, her legs spread wide and arms crossed at her chest. Two burly men stood beside her.

"You learn slowly," she said matter-of-factly as the men entered the dark confines for Agnus, dragging her by the hair into the sunlight.

Agnus suddenly became visible to Gómez. She looked to be about fifty and overweight. Her pale white skin was badly bruised by previous beatings.

The door slammed shut, returning them to darkness.

They listened from the darkness and could hear Agnus lifted to her feet.

"Stand up!" María barked. "We heard you talking to the new priest."

They heard her slap Agnus hard several times.

"Who else was speaking to him?" María asked.

The group within the hut listened in terrified silence.

"No one. Only me," Agnus choked out her answer as blood dripped from her mouth.

"That is a lie," María responded. "Hold out your hand."

They heard struggling. Agnus was fighting back. Another series of slaps ended the fracas and Agnus screamed what Gómez thought a death cry.

María wiped her bloody machete across Agnus' forearm. An index finger lay on the ground, pointing nowhere. "Bandage her so she doesn't bleed to death."

Agnus fought not to collapse. Her legs trembled. Someone tied a bandanna around her bleeding hand.

"Who else was speaking to him?" María asked again.

"Only me," Agnus chewed her words through clenched teeth, glaring defiantly.

María laughed unexpectedly. "Throw her back," she ordered.

The *Senderos* swung open the hut's tin door and tossed her in. When the door closed, Teresa crawled through the darkness. "I'm here, Agnus," she whispered. Agnus groaned softly.

Gómez settled back into the dark.

After an hour of dark silence, someone stirred when Agnus moaned.

"Samuel?" the voice was weak with age.

"I'm here, Iam."

"Who's crying?" the voice asked.

"They hurt Agnus," Samuel whispered.

Father Iam Ignatious crawled slowly in the dark toward the muted cries and gathered Agnus' head into his naked lap. "Their time is almost gone. The time for the Messiah is at hand, Agnus. Trust in God," he whispered assuredly.

Gómez opened his eyes to the darkness.

Iam could feel Agnus nod in agreement as he gently rocked her head in his withered lap.

"Why do you say the Messiah is at hand?" Gómez demanded with a sharp whisper edged in disbelief.

"Who is this?" Iam asked Samuel in the blackness.

"I am Bishop Jesus Gómez," Gómez answered for himself.

Iam's voice turned to ice and stabbed the dark. "I know who you are, Gómez. You're one of the Lima Society."

Gómez sat up proudly in the dark and repeated his question. "Why do you say the Messiah is at hand?"

"Because he is," Iam responded swiftly. "I suggest you repent."

"Hold down your voices!" Teresa hissed furiously.

"I have nothing to repent!" Gómez declared.

Ignatious said nothing.

Everyone settled back into silence as the light of day dimmed and night swept the jungle.

Hours later, Gómez awoke suddenly in the heat and darkness to a small snake slithering over his leg. He froze. As it moved on, he became aware of tiny feet marching across his scalp, heading for the bloody stump of his ear. He cursed the darkness and pressed the side of his head against the tin siding, trying to crush the insects and guard the wound.

Thirty yards from the hut, the *Senderos* sat around their campfire. A match flared as María lit her cigarette. "They know more than they let on." White smoke hung in the still air.

"There is nothing to know. They are all lies. There can be no new Messiah. The peasants don't know what they are talking about," Anita, the youngest *Sendero*, replied impatiently.

"Of course not, but the people can easily believe such lies. If they do, they will not fear us." María looked directly at Anita through the campfire flames. "If they do not fear us, they will destroy us.

"I intend to find their new Madonna, open her belly," María brandished her machete into the air, "and butcher her first born in front of the world!" The blade reflected the flames licking the night air.

"What should we do?" asked another.

"We gather more priests and nuns. We shall skin them one by one if necessary until someone tells me what I need to know."

"We should kill them now," Anita responded impatiently.

María's cigarette glowed as she inhaled slowly. "No one is to harm them until I order. Do you understand?" White smoke billowed from her mouth with each word.

Anita nodded her understanding. "If you want to learn about this Madonna, you should allow them to talk inside the hut and have someone listening outside."

María thought for a moment. "Tell them they may speak with one another," she told Anita before turning to the others. "I want someone to listen outside the hut at all times." She turned back to Anita, "Beginning with you."

• • •

SEVERAL HUNDRED FEET beneath the mountain, the bonsai suckled from the overhead spot light, gnarled roots fused to the cold stone.

John sat on the thick leather cushion atop the small deck, his long legs overhanging the edge. Barefoot, his toes touched chips of white gravel. Weary eyes never strayed from the tiny tree. "Socrates?"

"Yes," Socrates' deep voice resonated along the invisible granite walls of the dim circular room.

"Where is the plane carrying Father Bernadine?"

"Over the Atlantic, it is scheduled to enter U.S. airspace in five hours."

John eased from the deck. Tiny chips of white gravel crunched softly beneath his feet as he walked toward the bonsai. "Let me know when they do."

"Acknowledged."

John entered the sharp circle of light around the miniature stone island. Deep gray eyes studied the brightly lit bonsai while

the beam overhead cut deep shadows into John's weathered face.
"I want to better understand the *Sendero Luminoso*."
"How would you like to proceed?"
"You begin. I'll interrupt as I need."
"*Sendero Luminoso* translates as Shining Path. The *Sendero*
is a political movement that seeks absolute power in Peru. They
couch their need for such acquisition in Maoist terms, coupled
with teachings from Jose Carlos Mariátegui, who founded the
Peruvian Communist Party in the 1920's. To that end, they
openly intend to wrench apart Peru's social fabric with violence
and terror. Their goal is to rise to power amid chaos.
"*Sendero* strategy argues that violence is the only means to
liberate the poor.
"*Sendero* followers are taught their revolution will triumph
only when the Peruvian people cross over the river of blood.
"The *Sendero* attempts to intimidate or destroy anyone who
resists their authority."
"Begin with its history." John's face drew closer to the tiny
tree, studying its detail.
"The *Sendero* was formed in 1970 at the National University
at San Cristobal de Huamanga in Ayacucho, high in the Andes
Mountains 230 miles southeast of Lima. It evolved, in part,
through a series of struggles within the PCP, the Peruvian
Communist Party. In 1964, the PCP had divided into pro-Soviet
and pro-Maoist factions. Professor Abimael Guzmán Reynoso, who
later founded the *Sendero*, aligned with the Maoists.
"The *Sendero*, like all Andean political organizations at that
time, competed for popular favor by supporting the mass movement of Andean Indians who sought to have their government
provide public education.
"The Peruvian government strongly opposed the public
education movement and employed force to repress it. Eventually,
Guzmán was arrested. While he was imprisoned, a conflict for
control occurred within the Maoist faction and Guzmán was
expelled from the PCP. He then founded the *Sendero*. His
followers have come to know him as 'President Gonzalo.'"
"Explain Guzmán." John bent even closer to the tiny tree. Its
tiniest intricacies came to life.
"He was born to . . . ."
"Begin at San Cristobal University time frame," John said.
"Professor Guzmán taught at the National University in
Ayacucho, where he led the Communist party.

"Fellow professors considered him polite but reserved. He would dine only with the daughter of the head of the Communist party.

"His students, children of Andean Indians, found him charismatic and an excellent teacher. He taught education and ran the teacher training school for several years. The education program, which was the university's largest, gave him access to more students than any other professor.

"His teachings provided his students an historical context to the circumstances of Andean people as a consequence of European conquest. That context promised the means for a rebirth of pre-Columbian culture and provided psychological comfort to its adherents.

"Guzmán gained power within the university and his teachings crystallized to underpin the *Sendero*."

"What were his initial actions as he acquired power there?"

"He began by driving the American Peace Corps from the university.

"But primarily, Guzmán used his energies to shape the organization that became the *Sendero*. Today, the *Sendero*'s internal structure, use of local satellite cells, the rationale for violence, and its goals reflect his initial efforts."

"Guzmán was captured after Fujimori's *autogolpe*, when he declared martial law?" John slowly circled the slab of stone, gravel crunching softly beneath his feet. His eyes never left the bonsai. He was considering it from every angle.

"Yes. President Alberto Fujimori assumed dictatorial power on the evening of 5 April 1992 and ordered an assault on the Canto Grande Prison in Lima, which he called a *Sendero* indoctrination camp.

"The Canto Grande raid ignited a *Sendero* bombing campaign throughout Lima that summer.

"Documents captured at Canto Grande led to an understanding of *Sendero* bombing plans. Government computers were employed to track purchases of the chemical fertilizer used by the *Sendero* to make car bombs, eventually enabling them to locate and arrest Guzmán.

"Guzmán was captured in Lima on 12 September 1992 while meeting a woman recently freed from prison. Documents captured at that time led to the arrest of key *Sendero* figures and enlarged the understanding of *Sendero* lines of command.

"Fujimori had Guzmán displayed publicly in a cage before sending him to serve a life sentence in an underground prison at a naval station on a Peruvian island. Guzmán has since written Fujimori to suggest a truce with the *Sendero*."

"No doubt," John said to himself.

"Current psychological profiles on Guzmán–"

"Hold the psychological profiles and proceed with *Sendero* funding," John interrupted.

"Funding needs or funding acquisition?"

"Acquisition."

"Primarily narcoterrorism."

"Explain."

"The *Sendero's* financial power comes from the Upper Huallaga Valley, the world's major source of cocaine. The *Sendero* negotiates the prices paid to the coca farmers by the Columbian drug cartels, takes a percentage and charges the cartels for protection."

"What is the effect of U.S. drug interdiction?" John tilted his head slightly, studying the intricate roots of the bonsai from a new angle.

"There are several detectable effects but none on *Sendero* funding acquisition. U.S. personnel occupy an unfortified military base in the middle of the valley but have done so at the pleasure of the *Sendero*, whose tolerance of interdiction efforts appears tactical."

"How so?"

"Coca interdiction comes at the expense of the coca farmers who can grow no more economic crop and whose children already suffer high mortality rates from malnutrition and disease.

"The greater the interdiction, the greater the people's suffering. The greater their suffering, the more they must turn to the *Sendero* for protection, even if they find *Sendero* violence abhorrent.

"The *Sendero* seeks money as a means to acquire power. Interdiction efforts constitute a more effective conduit to such power, so they welcome those efforts."

"Do they employ the violence they espouse?" John asked.

"Definitely."

"List known acts of violence."

"Specify hierarchy," Socrates instructed.

"Chronological."

"The *Sendero* went underground in 1978 but surfaced on 17 May 1980, on the eve of Peru's return to civilian rule after seventeen years of military rule. The *Sendero* burned ballot boxes and voting lists in the small Andean town of Chuschi.

"The first known *Sendero* victim was *Señor* Benigno Medina on 24 December 1980. Medina owned a small ranch in the village of Ayzarca, Ayacucho.

"That evening thirty *Sendero* invaded Medina's home, dragged him to the community chapel, stripped him, and staked him spread-eagle to the dirt floor. His family was brought to an adjacent building to listen to his screams.

"A Lima physician who had joined Guzmán's enterprise, slit Medina's tongue from the back to the tip and severed his ears, penis, and testicles from his body. Medina's family was forced to listen to his cries until he succumbed to death.

"On 1 January 1981, the *Sendero—*"

"How many acts of violence are known?" John interrupted.

"Thousands."

"Can you categorize by target groups?"

"Partially, yes, but the *Sendero* targets anyone who diminishes their prospects to control Peru, which has one of the most organized societies in South America."

"Discontinue chronological hierarchy and proceed by target groups," John ordered.

"Current targeting includes those who support Peruvian democracy, aid the economy, attempt to ease peasant suffering, or resist their authority. Common to group targeting is one of those four perspectives.

"Categorization by groups includes human rights groups, neighborhood block committees, community feeding centers and other forms of local organization, politicians, community leaders, liberals, the Women's Federation, clergy, entrepreneurs, business leaders, development workers, trade unionists, relief organizations, tourists, and particular Indian populations."

"Expand on the Women's Federation."

"María Elena Moyano had long led Lima's Women's Federation, which defied the *Sendero* by operating soup kitchens for Lima's poor. Referred to as Mother Courage because of her defiance of the *Sendero*, Moyano had been vice mayor of Villa El Salvador, the largest of Lima's shanty towns. On 15 February

1992, the *Sendero* shot Moyano in front of her family, then exploded fifteen kilos of dynamite beneath her body.

"A *Sendero* group also beat and stabbed to death four women and five of their children in Ayacucho for participating in a rural program to feed malnourished children."

"Why would they constitute a threat?" John asked.

"Anyone who provides hope for a better Peruvian future is a threat."

"Why?"

"In the absence of hope, the people could more readily accept alternatives to the present government. So the *Sendero* attempts, where they can, to destroy anyone who helps provide hope of a better Peru."

"Expand on Indian populations. I am confused now," John interrupted. "You said they promised a rebirth of pre-Columbian culture, which would mean Incan or Moche."

"You are correct, and your confusion is natural but can be eliminated by enlarging your understanding.

"The *Sendero* do promise a return to pre-Hispanic culture, but such promises are simply used to acquire control through popular support. Above all else, they insist on absolute control, which certain Indian populations reject, particularly the Ashaninka Indians.

"The Ashaninka view the *Sendero* as no different than the *conquistadors* who subjugated their forbearers.

"In the early 1990's, the *Sendero* launched a campaign of terror against the Ashaninka, force-feeding Ashaninka children tongues cut from their parents. Many Ashaninka were doused with gasoline and burned alive in front of their families."

John shook his head slowly. "Expand on violence against clergy."

"The *Sendero* have killed a variety of clergy, but seem to target foreign missionaries. Roman Catholic, Mormon, and Baptist churches have reported deaths in the ranks of their Peruvian missionaries.

"In May 1991, seventy *Sendero* arrived in Huasahuasi in three hijacked trucks and fanned out in search of several selected targets."

"Where is Huasahuasi?"

"In the high Andes, a six hour drive east of Lima."

"Continue."

"They were searching for the Australian Catholic nun, Sister Irene, who helped distribute food to the poor through the Catholic relief organization "Caritas", and four community leaders, *Señores* Placios, Morales, Pondo, and Bento.

"Once captured, the five were brought to the town square, denounced and sentenced to death.

"The townspeople attempted to intervene but were held back at gun point.

"All five were forced to kneel. Sister Irene was first shot in the back of the head, with Morales, Bento, and Pando shot in turn. Placios, however, was killed when a young *Sendero* plunged a knife through his eye socket.

"The *Senderos* ordered Sister Irene's body left untouched for one day and burned the town hall and electrical station."

"Was her body untouched during that time?"

"Yes. Such command is common for the *Senderos,* who utilize an economy of terror. Enduring the sight of village pigs and dogs fighting over the corpse of a family member or a friend instills terror quickly.

"Beyond ordering people to leave bodies untouched for twenty-four hours, they also publicly mutilate, torture, garrote, or behead their victims. Males are commonly staked naked to the ground and castrated.

"Is there any significance to such executions beyond terror?" John asked.

"Perhaps. Generally, the *Sendero* use violence to intimidate local populations sufficiently to allow them to operate unhindered. But they also seek to provoke violent responses by the military against native populations around whose areas the *Sendero* operate, which rallies rural hatred for the government."

"Are they successful in that?"

"They have been.

"In 1983, Minister of War General Luis Cisneros declared the army was at war and announced that in war there are no human rights. Entire villages were massacred and many government-sponsored killings, disappearances, detentions, tortures, and rapes have been documented by human rights groups. Such repression has fueled distrust and hatred of the government, especially by Indian populations.

"In November 1991, Fujimori issued a variety of decrees which extended military authority throughout Peru and suspended all human rights. He authorized the military to draft any citizen and confiscate private property in the name of national defense, subordinated all *rondas campesinas* to the military, and curtailed freedom of the press and human rights groups."

"What are *rondas campesinas*?"

"Community self-protection groups."

"Continue."

"On 18 July 1992, Peruvian army majors, Martin Rivas and Carlos Pichilingue, headed a military squad that entered Enrique Valle y Guzmán University, known as La Cantuta. The squad kidnapped nine students and one professor who they suspected were *Sendero* sympathizers. The ten were taken to an empty lot just outside Lima, shot in the back of the head, and thrown into a common grave.

"A substantial public outcry followed their abduction and their bodies were recovered after the weekly Peruvian magazine *"Sí"* published their location.

"The Constituent Congress, assembled illegally by Fujimori to replace the democratic congress he had dissolved, asked Fujimori to explain the La Cantuta events. Nicolás de Barí Hermoza, head of the army, sent his tanks into the streets of Lima, which quickly ended the Constituent Congress' inquiry.

"But the *Sendero's* capacity to trigger emotional, rather than strategic, military responses is diminishing rapidly."

"Why?" John asked.

"Fujimori's military is learning. They now align their responses to strategy rather than revenge. They no longer indiscriminately target entire villages for annihilation.

"However, beyond terrorizing local populations and provoking violent responses by the military, particular acts of *Sendero* violence may have significant historical parallels."

"Explain." John said.

"In late 1532, the Spanish garroted the Incan emperor.

"The Spanish arrived in Cajamarca and asked to meet Atahualpa, the Incan emperor. Atahualpa agreed but in going to meet the Spanish, he encountered only a priest. The priest handed him a bible and told him it contained the word of God. Atahualpa put the book to his ear to listen, heard nothing, and tossed it to the ground disappointed. The horrified priest declared God's word had been cast to the dirt.

"Spanish soldiers, hidden in ambush, opened fire on Atahualpa's entourage. Atahualpa, however, was captured and later garroted.

"In the 1781 uprising, Tupac Amaru and his entire family were staked in the Cuzco Plaza de Armas and tortured to death. Amaru was beheaded after his arms and legs were pulled from his body.

"Historically, it was not uncommon for the Spanish military and clergy to torture and mutilate Indians."

"Continue with violence against clergy," John said.

"Two young Mormon missionaries were killed in Huancayo and an Australian nun was killed in Huasahuasi, Junín."

John shut his eyes, breathing deeply. "Discontinue clergy category and explain *Sendero* reaction to resisters."

"When the *Senderos* arrive at a village they identify those who are respected and those who are disliked. Those who are the disliked are killed to gain grace with the community and those who are respected are invited to endorse the *Sendero*. Those who resist *Sendero* authority are publicly tortured to death."

"Explain."

"The community is assembled in the town square, the resister is often stripped and tied to a post. Each person in the community is forced to slice a piece of flesh from his body. Death usually takes an hour or so from blood loss."

"Detail violence against tourists."

"In November 1989, two young tourists, an Australian and New Zealander, were taken from a bus traveling between Ayacucho and Nazca. They were badly tortured before being disemboweled alive.

"In January 1990, the *Senderos* stopped a bus between Andahuaylas and Abanca. A young French couple were taken from the bus and shot in the head.

"The young man did not die instantly, so a sixteen year old *Sendero* flattened his skull with repeated blows from a large stone."

John's gray eyes closed wearily. "What is the organizational structure of the *Sendero* in light of the capture of Guzmán and key leaders?"

"Unknown. Before Guzmán's capture, the line of command descended through a pyramid of committees. Key leadership directed seven regional committees, which then directed local committees.

"Essentially, the PCP directed the guerrilla army which then directed the fronts.

"How the *Sendero* is reorganizing after Guzmán's capture is unknown. But to succeed, new leadership must continue to exploit ethnic and class hatred."

"Why?" John asked.

"Such exploitation is needed to gather rural support."

"Explain."

"Such exploitation coincides with Maoist strategy of using rural populations to encircle then overwhelm cities. It is unlikely that such fundamentals would be abandoned by new leadership," Socrates explained.

"Expand on that."

"During their early years, the *Sendero* concentrated in the southern highlands, Ayacucho, Huancavelica, and Apurimac. Peruvian and foreign intelligence concluded *Sendero* support would remain confined to a narrow and regionally specific base in the southern sierra. Any *Sendero* threat was perceived as temporary and regional.

"By 1983, that perception modified when the *Sendero* acquired diverse support throughout rural Peru.

"By 1984, the *Sendero* operated in eighty-seven of Peru's one hundred eighty three provinces. By 1992, they had expanded to one hundred fourteen provinces. That success reflected the success of their rural campaign.

"Following Maoist principles they sought control of the rural areas in order eventually to take Lima."

"How?" John asked.

"Lima is tied to the interior by three paved roads and one rail line, all of which supply its food reserves. By securing the surrounding areas, they would be positioned to sever Lima's ties to the rest of Peru. If those ties are severed, Lima would collapse into chaos, amid which the *Sendero* could rise to power.

"Captured *Sendero* documents revealed a multi-pronged strategy for taking Lima. After securing the rural communities surrounding Lima, the *Sendero* intended to create a popular view that they may succeed in taking the city, create a sense of impending crisis, force the uncommitted to side early with the *Sendero*, force Lima's upper class to flee, and stimulate the collapse of order.

"The strategy was not to take Lima by direct assault but to rise to power through the chaos of political disintegration.

"*Sendero* documents captured by Fujimori indicated the strategy to take Lima depended on the success of its rural campaign. An assault on Lima would necessarily follow, rather than precede, a consolidation of power in the rural areas around Lima.

"Do we know who the new leadership is?"

"No. But *Sendero* activities remain underground until its leadership becomes convinced it can prevail in any contest it initiates.

"Those who replace Guzmán will likely continue such strategies."

"If Guzmán did his job right, his replacements will find an advantage to his loss," John replied.

"Undoubtedly. In late 1994, *Sendero* guerrillas bombed four offices of Peru's two biggest banks, Banco de Credito and Banco Wiese. The loss of Guzmán simply provided new opportunities to former underlings."

"Is there any way to understand how they are reorganizing?"

"Not currently. The *Sendero* rarely use electronic communications, so direct off-site monitoring is currently foreclosed."

"We're going to be flying blind into this if the *Sendero* become involved, is that what you're telling me?" John asked.

"Yes."

John rubbed his eyes and rose to his feet. "I am sickened by the violence you've described."

"I understand."

"I need to think. If Michelle or Jacob call, ask them not to disturb me unless it's urgent."

"Fine."

John closed his eyes, inhaled deeply, then exhaled slowly. When his eyes opened, they focused on the distant stone island. "Dim the light, please Socrates."

The light over the bonsai dimmed until the tiny tree nearly dissolved into darkness.

"Hold."

John's gray eyes focused on the dimly lit bonsai, relaxing his mind by focusing it.

"John."

"Yes."

"I am picking up a radio station news broadcast near Iquitos, Peru. It reports people in the area are reacting to a rumor that a new Messiah is soon to be born among them."

John closed his eyes. "Thank you, Socrates."

• • •

FATHER BERNADINE LOWERED the thin book onto his lap. Ancient green eyes gazed from the plane to the blue Atlantic below, which stretched cloudlessly in all directions as far as one could see. He was deep in thought, studying the future.

"May I get you anything, Father?" the young steward asked politely.

Startled, Bernadine looked up then smiled gently. "Hot tea? If it's not too much trouble," he said in his thick Irish brogue.

"No trouble at all, Father." The steward disappeared into the galley.

Brian O'Riley returned from the cockpit to sit beside Bernadine. "Are you comfortable, Father?"

"Oh, yes. Lovely flight, quite lovely."

"Mr. Mullen is looking forward to your arrival."

"It'll be grand to meet him."

"We should be on the ground in Saratoga in about nine hours. We have sleeping quarters in the rear cabin if you care to rest."

"I'm fine, my son, quite fine," Bernadine smiled.

"How long were you with the Vatican museum?" O'Riley asked, already knowing the answer.

"Over sixty years but I remember arriving there as though it were yesterday. Such wonderment then. Time passes so quickly."

"We were lucky to get you out when we did."

"Yes, we were." Bernadine looked over to O'Riley, with a whole new smile. "Hans Rajunt is not easily outwitted. I do wish I could have seen his face when he discovered my absence."

O'Riley returned the smile and looked to the book in Bernadine's lap.

"What are you reading?"

"TOMORROW'S MESSIAH . . . written several years ago by a young Peruvian priest, a prophet, Father Manuel de las Casas."

"What is it about?"

"It is a lamp." Bernadine studied O'Riley. "We suspect it lights the path to come directly before God, to gaze upon his face." He spoke with reverence.

"You want to look the big guy in the eye?" O'Riley grinned.

Bernadine looked aghast at O'Riley, as if the bottom might drop out from under the plane.

O'Riley cleared his throat, "Sorry, Father."

Bernadine patted O'Riley's forearm in forgiveness. "We believe this is an important work."

"Who is 'we'?" O'Riley tried to coax from Bernadine exactly who he called after Rajunt had him confined.

"Archbishop De Gonzales, Father Ignatious, myself, and a few others. Archbishop De Gonzales, Father Ignatious, and I are quite old friends."

"Charting the pathway to God must be complicated." O'Riley tried to sound sincere, knowing Bernadine's reputation as an eccentric genius.

Thousands of miles away in Anchorage, Jacob Brigham leaned back in his deeply cushioned leather chair, closed his eyes, and listened to the conversation occurring nearly seven miles above the cold Atlantic.

In Wyoming, the quietly humming machinery of Socrates monitored both Bernadine and Brigham.

"To guide your journey to the face of God, simply follow Christ. To follow Christ do what he did, follow his footsteps—they lead to God," Bernadine explained.

O'Riley stared, "I don't understand."

"That's because he's an absolute lunatic," Brigham announced loudly to the empty office.

"Nor could I for quite some time. It sounded too simple to be true, too childlike." Bernadine glanced down to the book then back to O'Riley. "De las Casas says to be guided by Christ be like Christ. To be like Christ, you need only ask 'What would Jesus do if he found himself in my place?'"

"That sounds easy enough," O'Riley said.

"To know what Christ would do is easy. To do as Christ would do is not. Christ did not have an easy life, you know."

"I still don't understand," O'Riley shrugged.

"It is simple, really. Let's say you tell others you are a Christian. Now imagine you live in a city. It is winter and the snows have come, carried on sharp winds that invade the city. You drive to work and, looking over, see the homeless huddled together over steaming grates, trying to keep warm. Their eyes connect with yours as you pass by in your warm car.

"Is it enough just to remember them in your Sunday prayers?" Bernadine smiled and shook his head. "I think not. But what should you do?" He paused. "If you want to follow Christ's footsteps, ask yourself what he would do if suddenly he found himself in your place? What he would do is what you should do.

"Would he hurry past the homeless?" Bernadine shook his head vigorously. "He would do what he could to ease their suffering.

"It might be inconvenient to do as he would do, but to do less mocks his teachings. To do less as a Christian is to take his name in vain. And God commands that you not take his name in vain."

"So what makes De las Casas a prophet?" O'Riley asked. "I've already heard all that."

"Good question, O'Riley!" Brigham blurted aloud. "Now let's see if he has an answer."

"De las Casas begins with God's command to have no other god before Him."

The cabin shook for a second as they passed through an air pocket at 35,000 feet.

"De las Casas then compares that command to Christ's command that you do unto others as you would have them do unto you."

"Christ's command?"

"The Golden Rule," Bernadine paused, "You know, when Jesus met Joseph of Arimathea?" He placed a hand on O'Riley's forearm.

"No."

"When Jesus was a child, his parents went each year to Jerusalem for the feast of the Passover. One year, when he was twelve, they were returning to Nazareth. His parents suddenly discovered he was not among the caravan and hurried back to Jerusalem. They found him visiting with the rabbis at the Temple.

"While with the rabbis, Jesus spoke at length with Rabbi Joseph of Arimathea, explaining that he, too, intended to become a rabbi when he became a man.

"'But there are many kinds of rabbis,' Joseph replied to Jesus. 'some live to force the law upon others in order to gain God's favor for themselves, while some live to serve others and, by doing so, make good the covenant.'

"Joseph then asked Jesus, 'What kind of rabbi do you intend to become?'

"Young Jesus looked up and replied, 'A Canaanite came to a rabbi and said, "I wish to know the law of Judea, but you must tell me while I stand upon one leg."' The rabbi told him to be gone, that such a task could not be done, the law was too complex.

"'The Canaanite went to many other rabbis but received the same reply. Finally, he encountered a rabbi who instructed him to stand upon one leg.

"The Canaanite complied and was told, 'do thee unto others as thee would they do unto you. That is the law of Judea. The rest is commentary.'

"Jesus looked up to Joseph and said, 'that is the kind of rabbi I intend to become.'"

Bernadine looked at O'Riley as if waiting for him to receive the thunderbolt of understanding.

O'Riley remained perplexed. "So the two commands are the same—I still don't understand how you see the face of God."

In Anchorage, Brigham quietly drummed his fingers, narrowing his brows.

The steward returned with the hot tea for Bernadine.

"Thank you, my son."

The steward nodded and vanished to the rear of the plane.

Bernadine glanced out the window to the ocean below before turning back to O'Riley. "God says we are made in his image so we are each a face of God. When you treat others as you want them to treat you, you treat God as you want him to treat you. Only by doing so have you placed no other god before you. It is that simple.

"Understand both commands as one single command and the face of God unfolds," Bernadine's eyes closed, "before your mind's eye." Contented understanding settled quickly across his withered face. "Gaze inward with such understanding and God reveals himself."

"Good luck, Father." O'Riley eased back in his seat. "The Golden Rule escapes most people."

Bernadine chuckled. "Oh, it doesn't escape them, it is simply too bothersome to obey. It is easy to proclaim 'I am a Christian' and anticipate ever-lasting life and special favors. But even a dog does tricks for favors. Christianity must be more than that."

Brigham scowled from afar and shifted in his seat.

"It is not easy to be like Christ and help end the suffering of others. It is inconvenient to ease the suffering of those hungry homeless huddled atop the steaming grates, to comfort those who are ill, or support the dignity of those who are publicly reviled. You know Christ would, but you won't, it's inconvenient."

"That's why the loudest to proclaim their Christianity rush to condemn others in the name of God and their pelvic morality."

"Why?" O'Riley smiled at the twisted look of consternation on Bernadine's face.

"And here comes the liberation theology," Brigham chewed his words into the air.

"They are desperate to deflect attention from their hypocrisy." Bernadine's eyes twinkled. "They know Christ would not live the life they live. They know they have failed him and take his name in vain as long as they enjoy comfort in a world of suffering and anguish. They know Christ would not live in comfort or acquire wealth. They know he told them they may not serve both money and God."

"He says sipping hot tea seven miles above the ocean, aboard a thirty million dollar plane," Brigham snarled loudly.

"They want no light on their failings so they point at others quickly, to deflect attention. They point at those who have divorced, who work on Sunday, who seek comfort from other religions, who enjoy sex without marriage or those drawn naturally to the same sex—it does not matter, the list is endless for the self-righteous. Deflection is the name of their game. They judge others harshly but not themselves. They will not let their sense of self-righteousness be threatened.

"But they ignore the Golden Rule at their peril," he wagged a tiny finger.

"I don't understand your point." Brian shrugged his shoulders.

"He has no point." Brigham said coldly.

"If you fail the Golden rule, your chance to see the face of God in others dies. You lose that chance when you refuse to understand how you would want to be treated if you had divorced, enjoyed sex without marriage, or perhaps . . . ," Bernadine winked, ". . . were a Muslim. And you cannot understand how someone would have you treat them if you cannot understand what is important to them," Bernadine paused. "To do so you must leave your own perspective."

"I don't understand," said O'Riley.

"Let's take Christians for example, we're always fair game," Bernadine chuckled to himself. "If you and I are sitting here as Christians. . . you are Christian, by the way?" Bernadine tried to look stern.

"My wife tells me I should try harder," Brian replied.

"If we sit here as Christians, I have a pretty good idea how you would have me treat you in any given circumstance. But if you aren't, let's say you're a Buddhist, a Muslim, or perhaps you

simply find organized religion destructive to the human spirit–
whatever you believe, if it is different than what I believe then I
have to go to work in order to follow Christ and do as he would
do in my place.

"I have to work because now I must understand how I would
want to be treated if I were you. Stepping outside my own
perspective requires me to consider new truths–which naturally
frightens me because my truths suddenly do not appear universal.

"But to live the Golden Rule as Christ asks, I must treat what
is important to you with the same care that I ask you to treat
what is important to me. Anything else causes human suffering
and human suffering is what Christ seeks to end.

"If what you are doing causes other people pain, you have
betrayed Christ. If you hurt others even for reasons you consider
righteous, you have betrayed Christ and have taken his name in
vain–all at your peril."

Brigham squirmed uncomfortably in his leather chair.

"How about an example?" O'Riley asked.

"You're an American, so I'll give you an American example."
Bernadine winked at O'Riley. "Imagine you and your neighbor
both have children who attend the same school. But your
neighbor is a Muslim who, just like you, is made in God's image.
Then one day, the school principal announces she wants students
to pray as a group at school.

"Your Muslim neighbor becomes joyful with the news and
hands beautiful Muslim prayers to the principal. But she replies,
'No, I meant Christian prayers!'

"Remember, the Golden Rule is in play." Bernadine wagged
his finger again. "You are to treat your neighbor as you would
want him to treat you if you were in his circumstance. How would
you want to be treated if you were a Muslim surrounded by
Christians?"

"We're not talking the Crusades now, are we Father?" O'Riley
smirked.

"No." Bernadine looked sad for a moment, then cleared his
face. "Back to my example, as a Muslim, you would not want your
child to be taught Christian prayers, would you?"

Brian shook his head.

Jacob Brigham rolled his eyes in disgust and pressed the
speaker phone button.

"The Golden Rule requires you to understand you would not
want Christian prayers taught to your children if you were

Muslim. So you say to yourself, 'I shall teach my children our prayers at home and give my Muslim brother peace,'" Bernadine continued.

"By doing so, you have treated another, who remember is made in God's image, as you would like to be treated. What you do to another, you do to God.

"By doing so, you have placed no other god before you. By doing so, you have come before the face of God."

The steward reappeared. "Mr. O'Riley. You have a call from Jacob Brigham. Where would you like to take it?"

O'Riley rose quickly from his seat. "I'll take it in the rear cabin." He turned down to Bernadine. "Father, this call may take some time. I apologize that it interrupts our conversation. If you need anything, just let us know."

"Thank you." Bernadine adjusted his dentures with one finger and turned back to TOMORROW'S MESSIAH.

O'Riley closed the cabin door behind him and picked up the phone. "Mr. Brigham?"

"Have you learned who Bernadine spoke with in South America when he called from Rome?" Brigham asked.

"Not really. But I suspect he called an Archbishop De Gonzales and a Father Ignatious."

"He did. We have their telephone numbers and have confirmed they were home when he called. We're tracking their calls to other clergy just after Bernadine called them. They are acting quickly and in concert.

"Within one day of Bernadine's call, De Gonzales and Ignatious called over a hundred parishes throughout South America. The people they called then called others. Their numbers are expanding faster than we can track. See what you can find out and do it quickly.

"We just learned that a rural radio station in eastern Peru reported that people there are reacting to news that the Messiah is returning. At least CNN hasn't picked it up yet. That's all we need." Brigham's voice was cold.

"I'll find out what I can," O'Riley answered.

"How is his health?"

"Fine. He is an interesting guy."

"I don't trust him, he betrayed his church. Call me when you cross into Wyoming," Brigham ordered and hung up the phone.

• • •

GÓMEZ CRINGED WHEN the door swung open.

Anita stood at the threshold, barely visible in the night. The right side of her small body glowed dimly in the light of the distant campfire. "You may speak to one another without punishment," she announced and shut the flimsy tin door.

The dark hut remained quiet for a moment longer as they listened to her leave.

"Your talk of the new Messiah is heresy," Gómez hissed at Ignatious.

"Heresy is the way the Society lives while others suffer," Ignatious replied in the darkness.

Anita returned quietly and slipped silently onto the ground beside the hut, closing her eyes to concentrate on the voices within.

"What are you going to tell the people when he doesn't materialize?" Gómez asked belligerently.

"He is returning," Ignatious replied. "And soon."

"How do you know?" The tone in Gómez' voice began to change.

"I won't tell you. But I assure you he is coming."

"You're not the only one preaching that, you know. It's all over Peru," Gómez added.

"And Brazil," Ignatious added with a chuckle.

"We know Archbishop De Gonzales is behind this."

"Who is 'we'?" Hyndman asked softly.

"Cardinal Hans Rajunt knows," Gómez announced arrogantly.

"The high priest of the Society should be the first to repent," Ignatious replied.

"Why do you say that?" Gómez demanded.

"Are you blind, Gómez?" Ignatious answered. "The man is an anti-Christ, like De Balaguer who founded your order."

"Blasphemer!" Gómez hissed back in the dark.

"Quiet! You're going to wake Agnus," Teresa warned.

"Father Jose Escriva was a saint," Gómez snapped at Ignatious.

Ignatious laughed aloud. "You people are intent on making him into one."

"It is your kind that is leading the Holy Church toward perdition, you liberation priests," Gómez insisted. "You turn your back on tradition."

"We'll see what traditions should be followed when Christ returns," Ignatious snapped back. "I doubt that he'll approve of your tradition of living in comfort while children starve and die in anguish. I doubt he'll approve of you people condemning others in his name. If he were here, do you think he'd live like you?"

"Why do you keep saying he is returning?"

"Because I know he is."

"When?"

"Within a month."

"Where will he appear?"

"He's not going appear, Gómez. He's going to be born!"

"That is nonsense."

"I tell you it is not nonsense."

"Then where is he to be born?" Gómez asked indignantly.

"Here in Peru."

Anita's eyes snapped open in the dark.

Gómez' mind raced. "*What would Rajunt do?*" he thought to himself. "Do you know who the Madonna is?"

"I won't tell you that."

"Why not?"

"I don't trust you."

"Aren't we all Christians here?" Gómez asked.

"No. You're a hypo-christian," Ignatious replied with undisguised fury.

"You liberation priests are leading the Church to ruin. We will not have it!"

"Enjoy what you may, your time is nearly up," Hyndman replied.

Agnus moaned quietly, as if awakening. The group settled into silence.

Anita rose to return to the campfire, eager to tell María about the priests' conversation. Gómez' eyes snapped open in the dark as he heard her soft footsteps recede into silence.

• • •

THE ALITALIA JETLINER landed with blazing lights in the pitch darkness at Lima's Jorge Chavéz airport.

Bishop Cardoso stood nervously in the room where departing passengers were herded after clearing customs. Short and rotund, Cardoso shifted his weight from foot to foot impatiently. After a half hour, he spotted Cardinal Rajunt and hurried to him.

"Your Eminence." Cardoso bowed his head.

"You have arranged suitable quarters for me?" Rajunt asked, towering above Cardoso.

"Of course, your Eminence. You have a suite at the Miraflores César. Lima's finest hotel. Quite suitable."

"Take me there. I am exhausted from the flight."

In the dark of night, the Mercedes limousine barrelled from the airport, turned left onto La Paz and sped along the coast toward Lima's Miraflores suburb, heading for the hotel. Bishop Cardoso and Cardinal Rajunt sat comfortably in the back.

"I will call you when I've rested," Rajunt said.

"We still have not located Father De las Casas, your Eminence."

"Nor will you. During the flight to Lima, I learned he is in the U.S. and probably in Wyoming." Rajunt paused, then continued, "I will not be here long, but while I'm here I want to learn why the priests are preaching the coming of the Messiah. I intend to stop it."

"Of course, your Eminence."

"What do you know about it?"

"We suspect it's Archbishop De Gonzales' doing."

"Of course it's De Gonzales' doing, Cardoso."

"But the Messiah's return is all the people are talking about. People are leaving our churches in order to listen to the sermons by De Gonzales' priests."

"You've not relieved those priests of their duties?" Rajunt snarled.

"Of course, your Eminence. But they continue as if we have no authority to stop them. They have begun preaching from hillsides. And the people still flock to them. It's absolute madness, your Eminence."

"It is absolute heresy, Cardoso."

"Of course, your Eminence."

"I want to speak with Bishop Gómez as soon as possible. Have him return from Iquitos at once."

Cardoso hesitated, "We have lost contact with Bishop Gómez."

"Then send someone to find him. I want him to return to Lima immediately."

"Yes, your Eminence."

"If he isn't here by tomorrow, you will journey to Iquitos to find him yourself. Do you understand me, Cardoso?"

Cardoso swallowed hard. "Yes, your Eminence."

• • •

"JOHN." THE DEEP voice resonated in the darkness.

John stirred awake several hundred feet within the mountain, his body ached. "Yes, Socrates."

"You asked that I alert you when Father Bernadine's plane passed into U.S. air space. It did so ten seconds ago."

"When will they reach Saratoga?"

"In six hours. They have scheduled a refueling in New York."

"Thank you. What time is it?"

"Six a.m."

"Can you arrange to have O'Riley and Father Bernadine brought up to the compound from the airport?"

"Yes."

"Thank you. Wake me at nine."

"Fine."

John shut his eyes, ignored his pain, and let his mind drift back into rest.

• • •

THE EARLY MORNING breeze drifted across Fremont Lake and swept into Carlota's open bedroom door. Carlota, wrapped in a soft white robe, sat watching Sunday morning television, waiting for the others to awaken. She held a channel changer in her right hand, pointed at the television.

"It is the unholy trinity, I tell you." The tiny preacher on the television shook both fists in the air.

Cameras in the enormous Houston church scanned the ocean of people, then zoomed to those in the front rows. The eyes of the neatly dressed and well-groomed audience followed the tiny preacher back and forth across the stage. Heads nodded in approval.

"Paul warned good Christians of three enemies we face each day of our lives." The gold watch on his wrist sparkled under the camera lights as he shook his finger.

Carlota considered the number of Peruvian children who might not have starved that week but for the price of the watch.

He turned to face the camera.

"There is the Devil. Yes, the Devil, I tell you, who sneaks up next to your soul with seductive temptation," he exclaimed in a nasal twang, clutching both fists dramatically.

"There is the world, which tries to force you to conform, conform, conform to their pagan ways." He paced excitedly.

The tiny preacher inside the set paused with great delibera- tion, shaking his head in animated worry. "But the worst enemy," he paused again, looking back to the camera, "the worst enemy, the most formidable is . . . ," he brought his voice to a whisper and pointed at the camera, ". . . you!"

He looked back to the audience with reproach in his voice. "It is you, your very nature. There is nothing good in you without God's grace, as Paul taught us."

Carlota looked at him in horrified disgust.

"So many good Christians have come to me and asked, 'Brother Ralph, why does a battle still rage within me after I have accepted Christ as my Savior?'" Brother Ralph hammered on the pulpit.

"Why?" He stared into the camera, his hand over his heart. "Why?" He looked up toward the heavens, slowly returning his eyes to the camera. "Because you must always do battle with yourself! Part of you has accepted Jesus. Say hallelujah brothers and sisters!"

"Hallelujah!" roared the crowd.

"But the rest of you is your enemy. Doubt is your enemy. Reason is your enemy. Pride is your enemy.

He raised his voice shrilly, "Do you doubt me Brothers and Sisters?"

"No," roared the reply.

"Paul says as a woman must surrender herself to her husband so you must surrender yourself to God. Hear me, folks! To gain the reward of eternal life you must do as God says."

"And you are the voice of God?" Carlota asked the tiny preacher within the television.

"God needs your love, your contributions to keep this program on the air, he needs your financial support . . . ."

The unborn child within Carlota twisted uncomfortably. Carlota flicked off the set, heard someone outside on the deck, and slowly hoisted herself to her feet.

Michelle stood at the edge of the deck, looking out over the blue lake. A cup of coffee steamed between her hands. Long blond hair danced playfully as she faced into the wind.

"Good morning," Carlota said.

Michelle turned back and smiled. "Good morning."

The mountain breeze pressed Carlota's billowy white robe against her protruding stomach as she gazed out onto the pristine lake below.

"Would you like some apple juice?"

"I'll get some in a minute," Carlota answered. Concern filled the deep brown eyes.

"Did you sleep well?" Michelle asked.

"No."

"What's wrong?"

"I'm worried about Father Antonio and Father Manuel."

Michelle turned to face Carlota. "What is bothering you?"

"You have not told them, have you?"

"About Angelica?"

"Yes."

"No. Would you like me to now?"

"No, I will. I feel it is only fair that they know if we're to become true friends. I'm just nervous because I'm unsure how they will react."

"I can't imagine it will matter. What matters to them is who you carry within you. That's why they are here."

"Are they still asleep?"

"Yes, I guess the altitude is making them sleep so long."

Michelle turned her head toward the house at the sudden ringing of the phone.

"That must be John. Excuse me, Carlota. I'll be right back."

Carlota stood staring across the lake to the snow-capped Wind River Mountains rising high into the blue sky.

Michelle watched Carlota through the kitchen window as she began speaking with John. Carlota remained motionless, her white robe fluttering in the breeze.

"Bernadine is arriving at noon," John explained.

Michelle glanced to the kitchen clock. It was ten O'clock. "Do you want me to tell Carlota?"

"No, I'll call and tell her after I've had a chance to speak with Father Bernadine," John answered. "I'll inform the Fathers at the same time. They'll want to see him."

"Carlota will want to meet him."

"I'm counting on it to get you four back to the compound. That's why I invited him over. I know you're safe there, but I'd still feel better if you were here."

"Is that Riner I keep spotting in the distance?"

"Yes."

"You've already spoken with Bernadine?" Michelle asked.

"Yes, right after O'Riley got him out. They were in Amsterdam waiting for a Gulfstream to be flown in from Edinburgh for the transatlantic flight."

"Is he eager to meet Carlota?"

"Very."

"What's our friend the Cardinal doing?"

"Socrates says he's in Lima. His flight arrived around midnight last night. I've alerted Janice McClain."

"He's in Lima?"

"Yep."

"Do we know why?"

"No. But I suspect he's looking for Father De las Casas."

"Is he meeting with Bishop Gómez?"

"I don't know. Gómez is still supposed to be in Iquitos, but Ray Stauffen has lost track of him."

"How do you lose track of someone in Iquitos?" Michelle asked.

"It can be done, obviously. How is Carlota doing?"

"She's fine. She wants to talk to Antonio and Manuel about Angelica before returning with them to Lima but is concerned how they'll react."

"Why does she care?"

"She wants to be friends with them, John, and she's honest."

"Father Manuel may have a hard time of it at first, but in the end he'll stay focused on the child. Father Antonio seems too stable to be concerned about anything but the child," John predicted.

"I may have to speak with Father Manuel privately then," Michelle said, turning from the window, back toward the living room. Her eyes instantly widened.

Antonio stood in front of her, barefoot and topless in his pajama bottoms. His piercing blue eyes had fixed to hers.

"John, I have to go," Michelle caught her breath. "I'll talk to you later."

Antonio and Michelle stared at one another as she hung up the phone.

"Good morning." Michelle could tell by Antonio's reaction that he had heard the conversation.

"Good morning."

"How much did you hear?"

"What does Carlota want to tell us?" Antonio asked.

"Carlota is in love, she has been for many years. She wants to tell you about her lover."

"She has a lover?" Antonio scratched his head in astonishment.

"Yes."

"I assumed she was a virgin."

"She may well be."

A look of puzzlement clouded Antonio's face.

"Her lover is Angelica Montoya, a banker from Lima. Carlota is quite proud of her."

Antonio's puzzlement changed to astonishment. "Her lover is a woman?"

"Yes, a very beautiful and delightful woman."

"After meeting Carlota, I would expect so."

"Does that bother you?"

"No, not at all, I could care less. But it surprises me. I suspect Father Manuel will be bothered, however. He fancies himself a literalist."

"Carlota is nervous about telling you but she wants to because she considers you her friends. Do you think she should tell Father Manuel?"

"No, I will," Antonio answered and spotted the freshly brewed coffee behind Michelle. "Can I get some coffee?"

Michelle poured a cup and handed it to him, her green eyes swiftly roaming his sculpted chest and tight stomach as he accepted the mug. When she looked up their eyes locked.

A strange tingling radiated from Antonio's loins. "I'd better shower and dress," he said and turned for the hallway. He stopped, glancing back over his shoulder, "Do you know Angelica?"

"Yes, she is a friend. I met her several years ago when John purchased a South American holding company that owns the bank she works for."

Antonio nodded and headed down the hallway toward the bedroom. "I'll be out soon," he said and disappeared.

Michelle returned to the deck and Carlota.

Antonio closed the bedroom door. Manuel was still asleep, flat on his stomach.

Antonio stepped into the bathroom and pulled off his bottoms. He turned on the shower and lathered two days of beard growth. The shower steamed the room as he brushed his teeth and shaved, occasionally wiping fog from the mirror with the side of his hand.

He tested the shower with his fingers before he stepped in and closed the door behind him. After shampooing, he grabbed the soap and backed under the warm spray. His fingers slid across the muscular ridges of his stomach as he scrubbed with slippery lather.

His thoughts suddenly drifted to Michelle. He thought of her touch, of her beside him in the steamy spray. His strong hand slipped lower through the soapy lather. His blue eyes closed as he lathered himself slowly.

"Antonio!" Manuel knocked several times on the door before sticking his head into the room.

"What?" Antonio yelled from behind the wall of steam.

"You've been in there for fifteen minutes. I have to go! Do you mind?" Manuel was shifting from foot to foot.

"No."

Manuel entered and straddled the bowl. By the time he finished and flushed, Antonio shut off the shower. "Toss me a towel."

The towel disappeared from the top of the shower door as soon as Manuel tossed it there. He turned to leave.

"Wait," Antonio emerged with the towel about his waist. "We need to talk," Antonio spoke in a hushed tone.

"About what?"

"Carlota."

"What about her?"

"Were you serious when you told Mullen you would stay with her and protect her until the child was born?"

Manuel stared in disbelief. "I not only promised Mullen, I promised God. She carries the Messiah. I would forfeit my life to protect her," he paused, "and yours as well, Antonio."

"You know she will be harshly judged by many people."

"She would not carry the Savior if it was not God's will. I will not question his grace and wisdom."

"I'm glad to hear that. She has a lover."

Manuel's eyes widened and seconds passed. "No!"

"Yes. Michelle just told me. Carlota is nervous about telling us but wants to because she considers us as friends."

"I am surprised."

"That she considers us friends?"

"No, that she has a lover."

"Why are you surprised?" Antonio feigned ignorance.

"Because the Blessed Holy Mary was a virgin," Manuel whispered.

"Well, she wasn't a virgin by the time Jesus' brother James was born." Antonio was trying to figure out how to soften the blow.

"No, that's true. But the conception of Christ was immaculate. So I just assumed . . . ."

"Well, Carlota may be a virgin."

Puzzlement clouded Manuel's face. "You said she has a lover."

"She could still be a virgin. Her lover is a woman."

Manuel's eyes widened in disbelief. "No!"

"Yes. Her name is Angelica. Michelle says she's quite delightful. I'm looking forward to meeting her."

Several minutes passed and Antonio's discomfort increased with the lengthening silence, but he waited for Manuel to reply.

"How can this be? How can she love another woman when she carries the Savior?" Manuel's face had drawn tight.

"The same way we could love women, if we weren't priests." Antonio replied coldly.

"But that is different," Manuel leaned forward, whispering. His world was unraveling faster than his lightning mind could follow.

"For you, not for her."

"How can this be?" Manuel repeated, looking away.

"If you are uncomfortable, I'm sure they will have you flown immediately back to Peru."

Manuel vigorously shook his head. "No. I am convinced she carries the Savior. I am confused now why she was chosen but I do not question that she was."

"What is your discomfort?" Antonio asked in genuine concern.

"You are not bothered?" Manuel stared incredulously.

"Not at all. And I'll ask you again, what is the source of your discomfort?"

"Scripture." Manuel stared back as if the answer was obvious.

"How so?" Antonio's brows arched.

"I need not say it. We both know."

"Say it. I don't know."

"Scripture says a man shall not lie with another man as he lies with a woman."

"Well, Carlota is not a man, she is a woman who lies with another woman."

"But . . . ."

"Scripture says those who are blind or crippled may not approach the altar of God. Do you believe that?"

Manuel remained painfully silent.

Antonio's pale blue eyes probed Manuel's brown eyes. "Scripture says many things. It insists the world was created in six days and is only a few thousand years old. You do not believe that, do you?"

Manual shook his head.

Antonio continued, determined to force Manuel to face himself before he spoke to Carlota. "It says the fragrance of burning animals appeases God and yet you do not believe that.

"It says that those who presume to disobey a priest must be killed. Do you believe that?"

"No," Manuel answered coldly. "That's Rajunt's style."

"It says a stubborn and rebellious son is to be put to death, and yet you do not believe that."

Manuel stared at Antonio.

"It says a woman who marries a man without being a virgin may be stoned to death and yet you do not believe that."

"No. But this is different," Manuel insisted.

"It's different only because you want it to be," Antonio pressed on determinedly. "Christ absolutely forbid divorce and said that those who remarry after divorce are committing adultery and Scripture says adultery is to be punished with death."

Antonio leaned into Manuel's face, his voice sharpening as he studied Manuel. "Do you believe people who remarry after divorce should be put to death according to Scripture?"

Manuel shook his head.

"Scripture says one may purchase the children of strangers as slaves and commands slaves to be obedient to their masters! It even says priests may purchase slaves! Do you believe such biblical commands are moral?"

Manuel remained silent, turning away from Antonio's stare.

"Do you?" Antonio pressed for an answer.

Manuel looked back. "No, of course not."

"Manuel, it commands that you not judge others. Do you believe that a moral command?"

"Yes."

"Then why do you turn from Christ in order to judge Carlota?"

Manuel shook his head. "I don't know. This is so different than what I expected."

"By rejecting Scripture's teachings that children may be purchased as slaves but accepting that those of the same sex can not rightfully come to union, you obviously pick and choose what you want to believe from Scripture. So Scripture isn't guiding you. Your prejudices are."

"I know . . . I know." Manuel was honest.

"Do you question God?"

"No." Manuel shook his head. "But . . . ," he paused and caught his breath, "But this isn't easy. It just seems unnatural."

"Medicines are unnatural and disease is natural, Father Manuel. You're an engineer—storms are natural while buildings are unnatural. Even the Bible is unnatural, you won't find it springing from the earth anywhere, it's assembled by people. Nature is no guide to good or bad and you know it. Only your compassion can guide you."

"I don't know what to say to her when I go out there," Manuel inclined his head toward the door.

"Tell her the truth. If you feel uncomfortable, tell her. But don't stop just when it feels righteous, tell her the whole truth."

"What do you mean?"

"Tell her you're uncomfortable because you have judged her harshly for loving Angelica and you realize you had to reject Christ in order to judge her. Tell her that if she's a sinner she has great company in you since you've sinned worse by judging her. You might ask her forgiveness for judging her."

"I know what you're doing." Manuel tried to manage a weak smile.

"Did I succeed?" A right brow raised inquisitively.

"This is difficult, Antonio."

"Just remember your promise to God. You promised to protect her and that means her gentle spirit as much as her body."

Manuel lost himself in thought.

Antonio turned and left the steamy bathroom.

● ● ●

THE GULFSTREAM BROKE through the thick clouds crowning the Snowy Range Mountains. From behind the expanse of windows in his study, John watched the plane descend toward Saratoga. "You've made arrangements for Father Bernadine and Brian O'Riley to be brought to the house?"

"T've made arrangements for Father Bernadine but Mr. Brigham has asked for Mr. O'Riley to continue on to Anchorage as soon as Father Bernadine disembarks," Socrates answered.

"Why does Jacob want Brian in Anchorage?"

"Unknown."

A half hour later, Riner's security force delivered Bernadine to the entrance. John was waiting outside.

A security man helped Bernadine out of the Range Rover. Bernadine was looking to John as he got out.

"Father Bernadine." John extended his right hand.

"Mr. Mullen. What a delight to meet you at last. An absolute delight. How are you, sir?" Bernadine vigorously shook John's hand with both hands. Just over five feet tall, Bernadine tilted his head to face John.

"The pleasure is mine, Father. And please call me John. How was your flight?"

"Fine, John, quite fine. And you call me Ross."

"You had a long flight. Would you care to rest before dinner, Ross?" John asked.

"Not at all. At my age, I'll soon have an eternity to rest," Bernadine chortled. "For now, there are things you would like to discuss with me."

"Yes, there are."

John escorted Bernadine into the mountain and to his study. "Would you like something to drink, Ross?"

"Perhaps a wee touch of scotch."

John prepared the drink and handed it to him. "Please have a seat." He gestured to the sofa beside his desk and after Bernadine sat, joined him.

"Is our Madonna here?" Bernadine asked after his first swallow of scotch.

"She is in Pinedale, about a four hour drive northwest of here. She doesn't yet know you're here, nor do Father De Montesinos or Father De las Casas. We can call them tonight. I wanted to speak with you alone."

Bernadine took another sip of scotch, "First, tell me about Carlota Cabral." Bernadine sat back.

"What would you like to know?" John asked.

"Where is she from?" Bernadine took another sip.

"Lima."

"Peru is so beautiful and mystical. But Lima. Dreadful place, so much poverty and heartache," Bernadine said. "But I digress—does Carlota have family?"

"Oh, yes. She was abandoned to the streets of Lima by her parents when she was a child. She grew up in the *pueblos jóvenes* with another street child, Angelica Montoya. They protected one another from the roving gangs of boys and eventually became the best of friends. They have lived together as lovers since. They are a family."

"God is wise," Bernadine nodded. "Is Angelica here?"

"No, She's is in Lima. She is a banker so she's working."

"I look forward to meeting her one day then. Can you imagine being married to the new Madonna?" Bernadine's eyes gazed through space.

John shifted in his seat, pulling one leg over the other. "When Rajunt had you confined to your quarters, you called several people in South America."

Bernadine was nodding his head. "Yes. Your young Mr. O'Riley has been itching to know who I called."

"Will you tell me?"

"Of course, I called Archbishop De Gonzales, Father Ignatious, and a few others."

"Why?"

"Do you remember when you asked Archbishop De Gonzales to approach me for Fragment I, the most sacred of the Church's relics?"

"Of course."

"You knew he told me of your plan to clone our Savior from the blood contained in the resins of the wood of the crucifix relic?"

"Of course."

"Did you ever wonder why I gave you that relic?"

"No. I just hoped you would."

Bernadine smiled. "I gave you that relic because I wanted you to succeed. Think how marvelous it will be for Christ to walk among us once again."

"When Brother De Gonzales told me of your plan, I recalled particular scrolls that I had not thought of in decades.

"For centuries, our scholars have hesitantly dismissed these writings because they foretell a Messianic return in a context that made no sense. I say 'hesitantly' because, while the prophecy made little sense, the scrolls on which it is written are authentic."

"The book of Revelation?" John asked.

Bernadine scowled. "John, Revelation was not written for us. It was a scream of pain from followers of John. Its composition began late in Nero's time, toward the end of the first century. Rome was slaughtering Christians and Revelation was written to ease the pain. Revelation foretold the end of Rome and promised Christians that their deaths and misery were not in vain.

"The Ortho-Pahlavi Scrolls were written in northwestern India during the years we call the Lost Years, the years of Christ's life for which we have no record. The scrolls speak of a dialogue between a young holy man from the west—one who glowed when he healed the sick—and an old shaman.

"Toward the end of the dialogue, the old shaman asked what the young holy man would do after his body died. The holy man replied he would return to God when God summoned him and would return to man when man summoned him.

"The shaman asked when God would summon him and was told, 'soon.' The shaman then asked when man would summon him and was told 'when tomorrow becomes today and the mountain shows the way.'"

Bernadine leaned closer. "That prophecy suddenly made sense to me when Brother De Gonzales told me of your plan," he paused, "Christ's tomorrow becomes today on the day his body lives again." Bernadine nodded slowly to himself, deep in contemplation. "And when Brother De Gonzales told me of your compound here, I knew the mountain would show the way."

Bernadine sat back, crossing himself, rolling his eyes toward the heavens. "The time of the coming is at hand."

John's eyes narrowed suspiciously. "But that doesn't explain why you called De Gonzales, Ignatious, and others after Rajunt had you confined."

"You need to ask why?"

John remained silent, letting his question hang in the air.

"Before I gave you Fragment I, De Gonzales and I called Brother Ignatious in Brazil. The three of us have long been close friends, you know.

"We told him of your plan. He asked if we were convinced you were capable of your vision. When Brother De Gonzales assured him you were, Brother Ignatious insisted we help you.

"And when you told De Gonzales the Madonna had been chosen and she would give birth to our Messiah in South America, he called me and we both called Ignatious to tell him the time was close.

"Ignatious was convinced we should prepare to spread the word throughout South America in case the Society tried to stop you. When Rajunt confined me, we began spreading the word, like a ripple on a pond."

"Why? You've endangered Carlota and the child when they return to Peru. You accomplished nothing else. You knew we would have enemies and you alerted them."

"We prepared the people for his coming, to give them hope."

"But why? You endangered the child."

"No, we did not," Bernadine insisted. "The Messiah has many enemies by his very nature, some admittedly in the Vatican itself. But while we understand his path to be perilous, God does not. God knows all things. He will see the Messiah safely through this valley of darkness."

"But why alert his enemies? Rajunt is a dangerous and formidable foe," John said, "and you know it."

"The priests who follow De Gonzales and Ignatious are calling upon the poor of South America to prepare for the coming of the Messiah. It is only incidental that his enemies would be alerted. Had there been another way, we would have taken it. But there was none."

"Well, you certainly succeeded. A rural radio station in Peru reported the people are becoming excited with predictions that the second coming is at hand. If the excitement continues, it's only a matter of time before CNN picks-it up."

Bernadine smiled broadly. "Marvelous. I haven't seen such reports. I did try to call Brother Ignatious to learn how the news is being received, but I haven't been able to reach him."

John shifted again in his seat. "But all you have told me doesn't explain why you needed to concoct a plan to tell everyone in South America that the Messiah would soon be born there."

"You've been to South America, John. You need to ask?"

"I'm asking."

"You've seen how the poor are treated. You've seen how the children perish and their parents anguish. You know they deserve some hope," Bernadine said softly.

"They could have lasted another few months without such hope. They've suffered for centuries. You didn't have to announce it. You had some other motive, Ross. I know you did. Nothing else makes sense."

Bernadine paused and regrouped his thoughts. He put down his drink and thought quietly. "You may be right."

"I suspect I am. Why did you do it?"

Bernadine became somber, his eyes slowly teared. "When I was young the Church took me in and cared for me.

"Giving you that relic was the hardest thing I have ever done. But I had no choice."

John studied Bernadine carefully without responding.

Bernadine wiped an eye. "During the Crusades and the Renaissance, the Holy Church, unfortunately, was led by vile popes whose mission was to aggrandize themselves. They created traditions geared to acquire power, not to light the glorious journey to God.

"The Inquisitions, the thousands of people we tortured to death, were a result of those traditions. Do you know we burned whole villages at the stake simply because the people would not accept what we ordered them to believe? Our wholesale slaughter of the gentle Cartesians was unforgivable. They asked only to live their lives in peace. But as dark as our past has been at times, this century marks our greatest shame," Bernadine paused, "and unless your plan succeeds and Christ returns—we are doomed."

"I do not understand your sense of urgency," John said quietly.

Bernadine took a deep breath. "For centuries, we taught people hateful things about those who differed from us, seeking to diminish their humanity.

"Hitler acquired power by taking up where we left off. We turned our backs in silence as he slaughtered the Jews, the gypsies, and those drawn to their own sex, all of whom the Church had long reviled. This was the slaughter of the lambs and we refused to hear their cries. Our hands drip with their blood." Bernadine's voice trembled. "But we have now descended even deeper into Hell." He stared into space with teary eyes.

John put his hand on Bernadine's sleeve to comfort him. "How, Ross?"

"The Society controls the Vatican now and drives from the Church anyone who challenges the old ways—the ways laid down by the vile Renaissance popes.

"Examine what we're doing! The self-righteous live in comfort while casting a critical eye at the poor. The Society never wants for food or medicines in a world where defenseless children die needlessly by the thousands each day. Christ would not have this done in his name."

John sat quietly as Bernadine released his emotions.

"We refuse to learn the lesson of Christ! We have begun again openly to revile those who differ, to diminish their humanity while urging governments to codify our sense of intolerance. Not only do we condemn those who live beyond the Church but we have displayed a special intolerance for those within with other views, those we call liberation priests.

"Our treatment of women is a disgrace. When Jesus was tried and executed only the women stayed fearlessly beside him. All the men scattered like frightened mice, but now men say only they can be priests for they are most like Christ!

"But beyond all that, without the new Messiah, I see coming a slaughter of horrible proportion. Technology soon will begin globally to challenge, then crush, the old ways. The reaction will cause great blood-letting, I tell you. Not in my lifetime, but it is coming. I see the dark shadow."

John's brows furrowed together. "But even with what you've just explained, I still do not understand why you had to announce the Messiah's return. All you did was endanger Carlota and anyone helping her, which includes my niece."

"I thought if those in the Church knew Christ was soon returning, they would remeasure their steps. Without knowing the Messiah was returning, the old ones would never question their ways. I thought this their last chance and, as much as I despise them, they deserve that. Perhaps I am a fool."

"Perhaps you are," John replied, "I suspect they will feel more threat than joy at the prospect of their Savior again walking the earth—judging them like they judge others."

Bernadine looked deep and painfully into John's eyes.

John took a deep breath. "But perhaps not." He laid his hand atop Bernadine's trembling hand. "Perhaps you just need more faith."

Bernadine looked puzzled in his anguish. "What do you mean?"

"Whether I like it or not, the word has begun to spread that the Messiah is returning. And he is.

"Right now only Rajunt suspects why. People will necessarily begin to examine their lives when they realize they could encounter Christ in the flesh.

"There is nothing Rajunt can do to stop that. The moment he understands that, he will become very dangerous.

"And perhaps you are right, perhaps your God has a plan grander than all of us."

"My God is not your God?" Bernadine quizzed through his tears.

"No," John smiled and shook his head.

"I am sorry for you."

"I appreciate your concern."

The two stared at one another as old men.

"Ross, you are honest. You live your words. Your Jesus will be quite proud of you." John reached across to Bernadine and gently squeezed his hand. "And you shall live to see him."

• • •

ANTONIO AND MANUEL walked onto the deck. Michelle and Carlota stood at the edge, talking, facing the lake together.

"Good morning," Antonio greeted.

They turned. Carlota seemed concerned. Michelle looked as protective as a mother lioness with a cub, staring at Antonio.

"Good morning," Carlota smiled.

"Did we interrupt?" Antonio asked.

Carlota looked to the tenseness on Manuel's face. "You know about Angelica?"

He nodded.

"Is there a problem?" Michelle asked coolly, ready for war.

"Of course, he has a problem, Michelle," Carlota said, looking at Manuel, "I can see it in your face, Father." She touched his cheek.

Manuel lifted his eyes to hers. "I can't help it, Carlota. I believe you were chosen and I know its wrong to judge you harshly for whom you love. I'll overcome it but it will take time. I can't help it."

"Of course it will." Carlota reached out her hand to him.

Antonio stared at Manuel.

"Please take my hand, Father Manuel," she asked.

Michelle glared at Manuel.

"Please take my hand," Carlota asked again quietly. "I need your advice."

Manuel slowly lifted his hand to hers.

"Will you walk with me?" Carlota asked.

Manuel nodded.

Carlota turned to Antonio. "We are going for a walk, Father Manuel and I. We'll join you later."

"All right," Antonio replied apprehensively.

Carlota and Manuel descended the wooden stairs that led from the deck to the rocky shore below, Manuel holding her hand so she could not stumble. Michelle and Antonio watched until they disappeared from view.

"Are you hungry?" Antonio asked quietly, turning to Michelle.

"I'll fix you something," Michelle said eagerly.

They turned toward the house simultaneously as the phone rang.

"That's John," Michelle said.

She reached the phone on its fourth ring. "John?"

"Yes. Father Bernadine has arrived and would like to speak to Father Antonio. Is he available, Michelle?"

"Just a moment." Michelle handed Antonio the phone. "It's for you, Father Bernadine would like to speak to you."

Antonio grabbed the phone. "Father Bernadine?"

"Allo?"

"Father Bernadine?"

"Antonio, my boy!"

"Where are you?"

"Wyoming!"

"When did you get in?"

"About two hours ago."

"No one told me. You'll stay long enough for us to get back there?" Antonio loved Bernadine.

"Of course, my boy. I came to be with all of you." Bernadine reassured him.

Antonio put his hand over the receiver. "When can we go back to Saratoga?" he whispered to Michelle.

She lightly shrugged. "Whenever you want."

Antonio returned to the phone. "Father Manuel is out walking with Carlota. As soon as they get back, we'll pack and head back. We're about a four and a half hour drive from you. It'll be dark when we pull in."

Michelle touched Antonio's elbow. "If you want, we can have a jet sent up from Saratoga. We'd be back quickly."

"Can we?" Antonio whispered, his hand again over the receiver.

"Of course." Michelle put her hand out for the phone.

"Father Bernadine, Michelle wants to speak to John. Can you put him back on the line? I'll see you soon."

"Ok, my boy. Hurry back."

Antonio handed the phone to Michelle.

"John?"

"Yes."

"Can you have a Lear sent up to get us?"

"Of course."

• • •

BY NOON, RAJUNT had finished Mass at the Church of San Francisco and returned to his suite. He sat at a desk by the balcony, overlooking the city. He could see the *ambulantes*, the street vendors, making their way through narrow winding streets. Some pushed two-wheeled carts and some carried their goods on their backs. Traffic began filling the streets with mechanized life and noise.

But the vision below was vanishing under a heavy sea mist drifting over the city like a shroud.

Rajunt turned at a rapping at his door, "Enter."

Bishop Cardoso stuck his head into the room, "Your Eminence?"

"Come." Rajunt gestured with his hand but kept his eyes on the city being swallowed by the mist.

"A dismal city you have here, Cardoso."

Cardoso looked out over the balcony, "The *garúa*."

"The what?" Rajunt's head turned slowly toward Cardoso.

"The *garúa*, the coastal fog. Soon it will blot out the sun."

"Your city has an offensive odor."

"It is the *garúa* mixing with fumes from the traffic," Cardoso shrugged. "It cannot be helped, your Eminence. But the *garúa* has a beauty all its own."

"I assume you came to inform me that Gómez is en route."

Cardoso hesitated, one hand squeezing the other. "I'm sorry your Eminence. We cannot locate him. He has vanished."

"Vanished?"

"Yes, your Eminence. He was supposed to report back two days ago. But no one has heard from him."

"Find him."

"But your Eminence," Cardoso paused, "I would not know where to start."

"Where was he last seen, Cardoso?" Rajunt kept his dark eyes on the city below.

"Iquitos."

"Then start there. Be quick about it. If he's not in Iquitos, check the outlying areas."

"But the *Sendero* . . . ."

Rajunt swiveled his head toward Cardoso, with one brow raised, "The what?"

"The *Sendero Luminoso*, the Shining Path guerrillas."

"What are you talking about, Cardoso?"

"The *Sendero*, Marxist guerrillas driven into hiding by President Fujimori. But they still operate in the outlying regions of Peru. They surround Iquitos. If they encountered Gómez, he is dead. They are ruthless and brutal, they even kill women and children without hesitation. What they do to priests is unthinkable."

"The *Sendero*?"

"*Sí.*"

"Tell me more."

"They began in the highlands and terrorized Peru for over a decade until Fujimori assumed emergency control. He captured their leader, Professor Guzmán, and scattered them to the winds. But many of his followers reorganized. They are everywhere around Iquitos." Cardoso looked irritated, "Gómez should never have gone there. He was a fool."

"I ordered him there."

"Of course, your Eminence. He must follow God's will."

"Go find him, Cardoso."

"But the *Sendero*, your Eminence," Cardoso's voice trailed into whining whisper.

"Before you go, bring me one of De Gonzales' priests. I want to inquire about their heretical preachings."

"They will not come to you, your Eminence."

"They will not come at a Cardinal's command?"

"No, your Eminence. When the Church stripped them of their authority as priests, the priests became free. They will not come."

"Where are they preaching?"

"There is one who will speak to the people this afternoon." Cardoso walked out onto the balcony. "Do you see that ridge over the city, there to the east?"

Rajunt rose from his chair to stand next to Cardoso. "Where?"

Cardoso pointed, "There, just beyond the city's hub."

"When will he speak?"

"In a few hours. He speaks there each day at the same time. Just follow the crowds and you will hear him."

"I will be there." Rajunt turned from the balcony and walked to the double doors of his suite, opening them. "When will you get to Iquitos?" he asked.

"You still want me to try to find Gómez?"

Rajunt glared at Cardoso.

Cardoso bowed his head. "God's will be done. I can catch a flight out this afternoon. I will be there by nightfall."

"If I've left Lima by the time you return with Gómez, call Cardinal Klodiński in Rome and inform him. He will contact me."

"Yes, your Eminence." Cardoso said as he began closing the double doors, backing from the room.

"And Cardoso. Don't return without Gómez."

"Yes, your Eminence."

"Before you leave, have some clothes sent up to my suite. Clothes suitable for your peasants."

"Of course, your Eminence. They will arrive within the hour. Why do you need them, if I may ask?"

Cardoso's temerity brought a plastic smile to Rajunt's lips.

"I need them to blend into the crowd when I go hear the heretic priest. I certainly can't go in my cardinal's raiment, now can I?"

Cardoso shook his head and began again to close the doors.

"What is his name?" Rajunt asked quickly.

"Father Rivera."

"Is he old or young?"

"Young."

Cardoso left and within an hour, peasant clothes were delivered to Rajunt's suite. Rajunt lifted the dilapidated poncho to his shoulders, gazed into the gilded full-length mirror and smiled.

Within another hour, Rajunt strode down the front steps of the Miraflores César, dressed like a peasant. The doorman looked disapprovingly at him.

Rajunt glared back, "Call me a taxi."

The doorman waved a black taxi forward from the line.

After Rajunt's taxi headed into the street, Janice McClain appeared from nowhere and approached the doorman. "Please call a taxi." She handed him a twenty dollar bill.

The doorman smiled broadly and instantly waved another black taxi to the front steps then opened its door for her.

"Do you see the taxi up ahead?" She asked the driver in Spanish as she slid into the back seat.

"*Sí.*" He looked back.

"Please follow him." She handed him another twenty dollar bill.

• • •

MARÍA DRAPED HER rain cape across a green branch to let it dry. "I want you to go to Lima as quickly as you can." She wore a brown sleeveless t-shirt and baggy khaki trousers.

Anita stood attentively.

"Go to the Museum of the Spanish Inquisition. You'll find it at the corner of Junín and Abancay. Go in as a tourist. You'll see an attendant wearing a pink scarf around her neck." María stripped off her t-shirt, letting the sun warm her smooth bronze skin.

"Tell her you want to see the Tupac Amaru exhibit. She will tell you there is no such exhibit. You are to insist there is. She will then know I sent you."

Anita nodded attentively.

"Tell her what you told me last night and what is happening in Iquitos. Tell her I have special orders. She is to kidnap a bishop from Lima and any others she can collect on the way—and bring them here."

"Will she ask why?"

"Tell her we must find this Madonna. The priests must know who she is," she paused, "if she even exists," María said with a throaty growl. "We just need to persuade them to tell us where she is."

"How will I get there?" Anita looked bewildered.

"Go back into Iquitos. Remember the old woman in the white dress who camps outside the church?"

Anita nodded.

"Tell her I want you to fly to Lima. She'll give you enough money to get there. Once you're there, Marta will give you the money to fly back."

"Who is Marta?" Anita asked quickly.

"The attendant at the Inquisition museum."

"Go now." María watched Anita head into the jungle then called to another *Sendero,* "Bring me the new priest."

Gómez was naked and trembling when they pulled him from the hut.

María nodded to the others. "Stake him."

Within minutes, Gómez was staked spread-eagle on the ground. The overhead sun baked the clearing and choked the air with oppressive heat. Flies buzzed about his face.

"What do you want?" Gómez cried out.

María glared down to him. "The next time you speak without being told, I'll slice off your other ear, priest."

Gómez remained silent.

"Do you understand?"

Gómez nodded, still trembling.

"Bring me the honey." María ordered to the nearest *Sendero*. "What do you know of this new Madonna?" she asked Gómez.

Gómez stared up to her, his eyes filled with dread. "Nothing," he said. His voice trembled.

The *Sendero* returned with a jar of honey. María took it and walked to the edge of the compound. She carefully poured a thin trail of honey leading from the edge of the jungle. Gómez felt the warm, thick fluid flow into his wounded ear. She let the last of it drip across his face.

"We'll see if your memory improves when the ants arrive."

"No!" Gómez cried.

"I warned you." María pulled her machete from the sheath on her hip and kneeled beside him, laying her razor-edged machete atop his remaining ear.

His scream silenced those inside the humid darkness of the tin hut.

• • •

RAJUNT'S TAXI FOLLOWED the broken road that paralleled the Rimac river and the rail line toward the foothills overlooking Lima.

"Can't you drive faster?" Rajunt snapped in English.

"No, *Señor*. The crowds are too thick. They come to hear Father Rivera predict the Messiah's return!"

"The man is a heretic."

The driver shook his head vigorously. "No, *Señor*. Father Rivera is a good man, chosen by God."

"The man is a heretic. I suggest you not listen to him."

The driver glared at Rajunt in the dusty rear view mirror. Rajunt was oblivious, furious with the crowds.

The cab inched to a stop, the driver waving several families across the road. They waved back their thanks. Traffic stopped both ways as people surged forward.

"Clear a path. Use your horn, driver."

"No, *Señor*."

Rajunt sat in the back fuming, uncomfortable with the wool garments covering his body in the heat. "How much further?"

"Not far, you can see the top of the hill from here," the taxi driver stuck his short arm out the window, pointing. Rajunt leaned forward.

"Stop here. I'll get there faster if I walk." Rajunt huffed and opened the door, pulling several *intis* from his tiny coin purse.

The driver looked back, "No *intis*. Five dollars, please."

"That is robbery," Rajunt snapped, opening his purse for American dollars.

"Five dollars, please."

"I'll need a ride back in an hour. How much to wait for me?"

"Twenty dollars."

"Twenty dollars! That is an outrage."

The driver shrugged. "If you want me to stay, twenty dollars," he said in broken English. "You will walk back otherwise. No taxis come out this far."

Rajunt pulled a twenty dollar bill and handed it forward. "Wait here until I return."

The driver watched Rajunt disappear into the crowd. Rajunt did not see him smile, turn the cab and drive away.

• • •

MICHELLE STOOD BESIDE Carlota as the Lear touched down at the Pinedale airport, walled to the east by the Wind River Mountains. As the plane rolled to a stop next to them, Antonio lifted his and Michelle's luggage as Manuel struggled with his and Carlota's.

As they prepared to enter the plane, Carlota stopped. She turned and looked east to the Wind River Mountains, still snow-capped from the late spring.

"What's wrong?" Manuel asked quietly.

"Nothing." Soft brown eyes studied the towering horizon. "I just want to remember this."

"Perhaps you can return someday."

"Perhaps," Carlota shook her head sadly, sensing her destiny.

Michelle was the last in, closing the door behind her. The others made their way to the back of the luxurious cabin.

Carlota eased into a plush, wide seat. Antonio sat beside her. Michelle and Manuel sank into the seats facing them.

Manuel leaned forward to help Carlota carefully buckle the safety belt beneath her swollen stomach.

"Is everyone ready, Ms. Cumberland?" the pilot asked, looking back.

"Yes, thank you."

The pilot nodded to the co-pilot and the Lear began to roll. When it reached the end of the runway, it pivoted, and held its position for several seconds.

The engines began thrust and rocketed them along the runway until they broke free the bonds of earth. Within seconds, the jet climbed effortlessly into a cloudless blue sky. Pinedale became smaller and smaller, finally vanishing.

• • •

A SMALL MAN, dressed as those around him, stood at the crest of the hill, surrounded by an ocean of people. Their numbers swelled as others surged up the hill in waves.

Rajunt pushed belligerently between a tightly packed old couple as he forced his way toward the crest. He could hear the man speaking but was not close enough to make out the words; he continued pushing through the crowd until he could.

". . . who from on high will bring the rising sun to visit us again, to give light to us who live in darkness and the shadow of death, and to guide our feet into the way of peace."

"But when will he return to save us?" someone cried from the crowd.

"Soon," Father Rivera answered loudly, stretching out his arms. "Prepare now for his coming."

"How soon?" someone yelled.

"He will be born before the winter snows cover the land. Prepare for his coming and be blessed."

"How? What should we do?" several asked.

"Do to others as you would they do to you. Ease the suffering of others by replacing it with your own. As you do to others, you do to God."

"Is that all?" an old woman asked.

"It is enough to fill your heart with joy and your joy shall call him forth."

"What will he look like? How will we know him?"

"He comes for you, how would you not know him?"

"Where will he be born?" came another shout.

"Near Lima."

The hillside gasped and grew silent.

"He has heard the soft cries of your children who hunger and perish in the cold dark of night. He has heard your prayers," Father Rivera said softly. "Soon he comes to stand between you and your oppressors. We shall all with him go up the mountain together."

Rajunt lunged forward through the crowd. Rivera stopped suddenly, staring at him.

"By what authority do you preach?" Rajunt demanded. "You are a heretic who leads the people to damnation." Rajunt threw off the poncho and stood like a king, "I am Cardinal Rajunt!"

A hush drew again across the crowd, waiting for Rivera's reply.

"Look upon the Pharisees and Sadducees with great pity," Rivera answered at the top of his voice before turning to Rajunt. "Alas for you who have your fill now, you shall go hungry. Alas for you who laugh now, you shall mourn and weep."

"Heresy!" Rajunt hissed and began withdrawing back through the crowds, back to the taxi.

• • •

BERNADINE AND JOHN stood together outside the compound as the sapphire Range Rover crested the gravel driveway.

Antonio was first to pile out, followed quickly by Manuel. They hurried to Bernadine, who hugged them like lost sons.

"My boys," Bernadine would not let go, "my boys."

"Carlota . . . ," John paused, "Father Bernadine."

Bernadine turned to Carlota, wedging his right hand into Manuel's to steady himself. He lowered himself onto his knees before Carlota. "Holy Mother, you do me grace by your presence."

Carlota raised him up with both hands, "It is my honor to know you, Father."

Michelle stood in the background until Bernadine spotted her. "You are Michelle?"

She stepped forward. "Yes, Father. Michelle Cumberland."

He nodded and smiled, shaking her hand.

"Shall we?" John gestured toward the entrance.

Everyone was speaking at once as they entered the mountain.

"How did you get out of Rome?" Manuel quizzed. "We heard Rajunt had you confined."

"A Mr. Brian O'Riley brought me out. Lovely lad. Very resourceful. Have you met him?"

"No." Manuel shook his head.

"He works for you?" Antonio asked John, who nodded.

"Father Bernadine would like us all to dine together tonight. Is that right, Ross?" John asked.

Bernadine nodded eagerly, "Very much."

John turned to Michelle, "Do you need to freshen up first?"

"Please."

"We want to talk with Father Bernadine until it's time to eat," Manuel said.

"So do I," Carlota added quickly.

"I'll be ready in an hour." Michelle turned back to John, "I will meet you in the dining room at seven." Everyone nodded to her.

She headed down the hallway, toward the elevator, as the others resumed talking.

The elevator doors closed behind her. The elevator began to drop into the mountain as she spoke. "Good evening, Socrates."

"Good evening, Michelle."

"How is John?"

"As expected, but he is holding up well."

"How are his symptoms?"

"Stable, but chronic lymphocytic leukemia is unpredictable. Although he has not complained, I detect a constantly elevated temperature and his energy levels appear to be declining rapidly."

"Anything from SYNGENTEC?"

"Nothing to help John."

"Nothing?"

"Nothing. If he could live another two years, the predator virus would be available."

"The virus you designed to feed on other viruses and cancer cells?"

"In a sense, yes."

"When will the rapid deterioration begin?" Michelle asked, not wanting the answer.

"I predict within four months."

"He will at least live to see the Messiah born?"

"Yes."

"I know you will do what you can for him."

"Yes."

The elevator stopped. Its double doors snapped open and she headed down the hallway.

The doors to her suite opened at her approach, then closed behind her.

"Socrates, prepare my shower, please," Michelle said as she pulled off her red windbreaker. The steam and the sound of running water drifted into the room as she peeled off the rest of her clothes and walked naked to the shower.

"Did O'Riley come in with Bernadine?" She stepped under the heavy warm spray, shaking her long hair behind her shoulders as it wetted.

"Yes."

"Where is he?"

"Jacob Brigham asked him to continue on to meet him in Anchorage."

"Why?"

"Unknown."

"Doesn't make sense."

Socrates did not respond.

"Soap, please," Michelle instructed.

Within seconds, the spray turned soapy. Rich suds bubbled and billowed across Michelle's athletic frame as she slowly lathered her breasts and stomach. She felt Antonio's strong hands gently rub the lather across her belly as she imagined he towered beside her, as naked and wet as she. Her thoughts drifted on a warm sea of fantasy.

"Did you enjoy your time at the lake?" Socrates asked.

The question pulled her back to reality. "Yes. I think it did Carlota good. Rinse, please. She seemed to enjoy herself."

Michelle faced into the spray, relaxing for several moments before she pulled back. "End shower."

Michelle grabbed a towel from the wall. "How is the South American situation?"

"Father Bernadine succeeded in spreading the word of the Messiah's return to the people in Peru and Brazil. It is beginning to pick up local media coverage."

"That's unfortunate." Michelle replied as she towel dried her long hair. Socrates remained silent. When she finished, she returned the towel to its rack and walked to her bedroom.

She pulled a slick, long black gown from the closet, slipping it over her naked frame. The gown covered her shoulders but revealed half her chest. Its hem touched the floor. She pulled her blond hair out from under the fabric, shaking it free to cascade down her back. "Unlock the jewelry cabinet, please Socrates."

When Michelle entered the dining room, a flawless ten carat cushion-cut diamond sparkled on her lightly freckled chest, nestled deep in her upper cleavage.

Antonio quickly rose from his chair at the dining table. "You are beautiful," he whispered and escorted her to the table. Manuel and Bernadine rose politely.

Carlota smiled to Michelle. "Please sit by me."

"Thank you." Michelle returned the smile and looked around the table. "I hope I didn't keep you waiting."

"Not at all, my dear. Not at all," Bernadine said and eyed her appreciatively. He raised his glass of wine in a small toast to her, then turned to Carlota.

"You are the Holy Mother," Bernadine hesitated, "I am unsure how to address you?"

"Please, call me Carlota, Father," she insisted.

"John tells me you are from Lima?"

"Yes, well, outside Lima—near Cajamarquilla."

"How long have you been away?"

"Eight months."

"And you want to return there for the child to be born?"

"I will return to the *pueblos jóvenes* where I grew up, just outside Lima."

"Why there, if I may ask?" Bernadine asked.

"They are my people."

Bernadine nodded approvingly. "When will you return?"

"Within a week, hopefully. I have a friend in Lima who I miss terribly."

"Angelica?" Bernadine quizzed.

The table froze as Antonio looked to Manuel.

Carlota held her head high, looking Bernadine in the eye. "Yes."

"She is very lucky," Bernadine answered.

Carlota smiled appreciatively. "As am I."

"You are blessed, my child." Bernadine sipped his wine. "Who is returning to Peru with you?"

"Father Manuel and me," Antonio answered for her.

"As am I," Michelle announced.

John's eyes widened, his head shook in disapproval.
"May I return with you, as well?" Bernadine asked quietly.
Carlota smiled.
John coughed suddenly.

• • •

BEADS OF SWEAT gathered on Gómez' forehead in the darkness. He was trembling. His bloody left ear lay on the ground beside his head. His lips were dry and cracked. Tiny beetles crawled slowly across his face, feeding on the honey.

Overhead, unseen night clouds drifted above the trees, blotting out the stars. The night was pitch black. Heat and humidity choked the jungle air.

María sat bare-chested and cross-legged beside his head, talking to him.

"Do you wonder how soon before the ants follow the honey trail out of the jungle?" María asked softly.

The hut was ten yards behind her. The campfire, twenty yards beyond Gómez' bare feet, dimly lit her face and gently swaying breasts. Other *Sendero* sat around the distant campfire, talking.

She flicked her cigarette lighter in the dark to inspect the honey trail leading from the jungle to the wound where his ear had been. "I see a few ants," she whispered. "They look like scouts. Big ones."

Gómez remained silent but swallowed hard, closing his eyes.

"Who is the Madonna?"

"Let me go. I know nothing of a madonna," he gasped.

"Pity. If you did, you might live longer."

"But they wouldn't tell me anything."

"Who wouldn't?"

Gómez opened his eyes in the darkness, staring up to her as if he did not understand.

"Which one wouldn't tell you anything?" María repeated slowly. "Which one of the priests inside the hut knows?"

Gómez closed his eyes. "I refuse to tell you."

María smiled in the darkness.

"Then the ants will feast on your brain tonight." She shrugged and poked at his wound with a twig, clearing the blood clots. "We must make sure they have plenty of room to crawl in."

She flicked her lighter above the thin honey trail again. "The scouts are heading back to their colonies. You might want to tell me. This will be painful and slow, priest."

Gómez rolled his head from side-to-side, crying, "No, no."

"Yes," she laughed.

"I know nothing of the Madonna."

"But someone in the hut knows. Which one?"

Inside the hut, Sister Teresa pressed her ear against the tin to listen.

"Can you hear them?" Hyndman asked quietly.

"No. I can hear her talking but can't tell what Bishop Gómez is saying." Teresa said quietly.

"He's telling her anything he knows, that's certain." Ignatious huffed.

"Which one knows?" María asked again.

"I will not tell you."

"Why not?"

"You would hurt him."

"Him? So it's one of the priests."

Gómez bit down on his lip.

María drew close to his face. "You're all going to die, priest. The only question is how painfully. Which one?"

Gómez could feel her warm breath on his cheek and turned his head.

"Which one, priest?"

Gómez held his silence.

"What do you know of this Madonna?"

"Nothing, I tell you."

"Where did you come from?" she asked casually.

"Lima."

"What were you doing here?"

"Looking for a priest."

"Did you find him?"

"No."

"Why were you looking for him?" María positioned her head just above his, studying his face as she questioned him.

"I was ordered to."

"Who ordered you?"

"My cardinal."

"This priest must be important, who is he?"

"Why do you hate us so?" Gómez choked.

"If you were me, you would hate you." María spit the answer in his face.

"Why?"

"I am Incan."

Gómez studied her face in the dim glow of the distant dancing campfire. Her eyes were dark and her cheek bones high, but she looked Hispanic. Her face glowed against the distant flames and was framed by darkness. She was a striking woman. "You don't look Incan."

A look of pain flashed across María's face and her palm crashed across his cheek. "Shut up, priest."

• • •

A SIX-YEAR OLD María gazes up to her mother with a bright smile and angelic face. She proudly lifts a pan of bread, "Look, Mama."

Her mother smiles softly at the misshaped loaves.

Outside, the squeals of her brothers and sisters playing tag cheer the air with laughter.

"María, what beautiful bread you bake," her mother says, then suddenly peers out the kitchen window. Three *federale* trucks pull into the dusty farmyard. Fear seizes her face.

María's brothers and sisters stop their play, looking worriedly back to the house. The soldiers pile from the trucks.

"Hide!" her mother snatches María by the collar and shoves her into the cabinet beneath the badly stained sink. She kneels to whisper, "Make no sound, María. *Federales.*"

Fear coats María's young face. She is wide-eyed. "I can help, Mama."

"Little one, you must do as I say. Make no sound until I come get you. Do you understand?" her mother whispers quickly. "No matter what, don't come out until I call you."

María nods slowly. Her mother closes the little cabinet door, entombing María in darkness.

María sits quietly. She makes no sound. Her thin legs lay crunched against her chest. Breathing is difficult. She listens intently as her mother leaves the shack.

"Where is your husband?" María hears a *federale* soldier yell at her mother.

"He is gone."

"I said, where is the professor?" the soldier demands. The sharp recoil of slapping carries into the dark cabinet. María shakes with fear.

"He is gone, I tell you."

"Tie them!" the soldier demands.

María hears screams of her brothers and sisters and protests by her mother. María trembles and cries softly.

"Tell me, where is your husband?"

"But I don't know," her mother cries.

"We will shoot your children one by one until you tell us!"

"Please don't hurt my babies! I don't know where he is," her mother sobbed, then screamed, "NO!"

Blam!

Again her mother screams, desperate cries forever haunting María's ears.

The soldiers bray with laughter, "Where is he?"

"Noooo," she cries.

"Tell us and be quick!"

Her mother sobs.

Blam! Blam! Blam!

"My babies!" her mother screams a death cry.

Blam!

Silence.

María hears the soldiers enter the house, laughing together. "No one in here!" one yells to another.

"Burn this down," someone announces.

"Bring some gasoline," another shouts.

María hears the soldiers setting the shack afire then starting their trucks. She waits until the sounds of engines vanish under the crackling of the flames.

She crawls stealthily from under the cabinet, wide brown eyes looking about fearfully. Flames rage and lick her flesh as she runs from the shack.

"Mama! Mama!" Blinded by tears, María stumbles over her mother's bloody body, rolling onto her young brother. She sits up and stares aghast at her hands and arms, covered by their blood.

María screams until her voice gives out.

One of the soldiers has dropped his cross pendant. She stares blankly at the cross.

She waits for days for her father to return. She waits in vain.

• • •

THE SLAP RESOUNDED across the clearing. A large *Sendero* left the campfire and walked over to them, holding a hissing gas lantern above his head. He lowered the lantern to inspect the honey trail leading from the dark jungle to Gómez' head.

"María, the ants are coming. You must not sit there when they begin to swarm," he said in a deep voice as he reached out his hand and pulled her from the ground.

María wrapped an arm around his waist, looking down to Gómez. "One last chance, priest. Which priest knows?"

Gómez closed his eyes and turned away.

María laid her head against the large *Sendero's* shoulder, slipping her hand into his shirt at his stomach. "Think of me, priest, as the ants tunnel into your ear and feed on your brain. I'll be thinking of you." She smiled up to the soldier and slipped her hand down the front of his baggy pants. He smiled at Gómez.

Suddenly, Gómez could feel the ants crawling onto his face. The reality hit. "No!" he screamed.

"Yes." María smiled down as Gómez' body began convulsing in a futile effort to throw the ants off his face.

"Come Fëdor." María took the young soldier by the hand.

As Gómez screamed, she led Fëdor to the dancing shadows on the far side of the campfire. She grabbed her rain cape from the branch, tossing it to the ground.

The *Senderos* around the campfire ignored the two as María stripped away Fëdor's clothes in the shadows. As Fëdor settled onto her rain cape, Gómez began to scream. She looked over one last time toward his convulsing body, barely visible in the darkness.

She smiled down to the naked soldier. He lifted his hand up to hers. She accepted it and settled beside him.

Inside the hut, Sister Teresa covered her ears to block out Gómez' increasing screams. Sister Agnus prayed for him.

Around the campfire, the *Senderos* grimaced and tried to talk over the screams, knowing they would not soon end.

In the shadows away from the campfire, María straddled Fëdor's hips, moaned, and dug her fingers into his sweaty chest.

• • •

BISHOP CARDOSO WALKED out of the Iquitos airport, carrying only one bag. A two-passenger motorized rickshaw pulled up to the curb.

"Where you go?" an Indian driver asked in Spanish.

"I need to find the parish church," Cardoso replied in Spanish. "Do you know where it is?"

The man nodded and Cardoso climbed in, throwing his bag beside him.

Cardoso assumed he was getting an expensive scenic tour as they motored down Malecón Tarapaca, past the old 1890's rubber boom mansions with elaborate iron work and *azulejos* tiles, and turned onto Lores street. They twice passed the Varig Airline office and finally stopped in front of a white stucco church, with a three story bell tower rising above the town's thatched huts.

Cardoso tipped the driver generously.

"*Gracias.*"

"What corner is this?" Cardoso asked, trying to get his bearings.

"Putumayo and Arica," the driver answered and motored away.

Cardoso glanced at the old woman in the white dress sitting outside the church as he entered. He explored the church for five minutes before coming back out, convinced no one was around.

He walked over to the old woman. "Excuse me."

She looked up at him. Several front teeth were missing.

"Do you know the parish priest?" he asked in Spanish.

She eyed his bishop's garments and nodded.

"Can you tell me where he is?"

"I can take you to him. He is with a priest from Lima."

"He is? That's who I need to see! Will you take me to him?"

The old woman held out her hand for money. Cardoso generously filled her palm. She looked at the money and shook her hand for more. He dropped several more *intis* into her dark palm.

She rose slowly. "We have far to walk."

"That's fine. You lead and I'll follow."

The old woman headed along Putamayo street toward the jungle, away from the Amazon. Cardoso tried to walk beside her. "What is your name?"

She did not answer.

Cardoso looked up to the sky. Dusk was settling in. "Will we get there by dark?" he asked the old woman.

"No," she answered without looking at him. Cardoso hesitated but continued on.

After the two crossed Tacna Street, Ray Stauffen emerged from the Plaza de Armas, across from the church. Felipe, a small Indian boy walked beside him. Felipe wore thin sandals and baggy cotton trousers hitched up high on his brown stomach.

Stauffen and Felipe stayed several blocks behind them. When the old woman and Cardoso reached the edge of town and headed into the jungle, Felipe motioned for Stauffen to stop. Felipe followed them in. After ten minutes, he reappeared at the jungle's edge, motioning Stauffen in.

• • •

"AND SO THE priest tosses the money into the air and says 'God gets what he keeps!'" Bernadine finished the joke, his shoulders bouncing with laughter.

The others were smiling politely when the dining room lights dimmed for an instant.

John rose, glancing to Michelle. Both knew Socrates had signaled an emergency.

"What was that?" Bernadine asked as he held onto Manuel's sleeve, his shoulders still bouncing with laughter.

"Someone needs to speak to me. Will you please excuse me?" John dropped his napkin onto his chair. "Michelle, you will see to our guests?"

"Of course," Michelle answered as he headed out the door.

John did not speak until he entered his study and the door sealed behind him. "What's wrong, Socrates?"

"A Peruvian military surveillance team near Puca Urco, along the Putumayo River, transmitted a coded message to Lima a half hour ago.

"The scouting team had been searching for *Senderos* and stumbled across twenty bodies in the jungle, mostly Europeans.

"Lima replied that they were the Universal Relief group trying to deliver antibiotics to a cholera area. Lima transmitted the twenty-two names of those in the group and requested an accounting of the bodies.

"The surveillance team has reported back that everyone was accounted for except a Father Iam Ignatious from Boa Vista, Brazil, and Bishop Samuel Hyndman from Canada. They are presumed captured by the *Senderos* or dead."

John walked to the window and stared out to the night valley. Saratoga glistened tranquilly below.

"Will you inform Father Bernadine and Father De Montesinos?" Socrates asked.

"I must. Ignatious raised Antonio from childhood and he was Ross' life long friend." John answered, staring blankly out the window.

John returned to the dining room. Michelle read his face. "John, what's wrong?"

The table hushed. All eyes were on John.

"I have bad news. Father Ignatious may be dead or has been captured by the *Sendero Luminoso*."

The wine glass in Antonio's hand slipped from between his fingers and crashed onto the glass table top, shattering across the table.

Red wine splashed across Carlota and Manuel.

● ● ●

THE DOORMAN AT the Miraflores César stepped forward to block the tall peasant from entering the hotel. As Rajunt's eyes and nostrils flared, the doorman quickly stepped back.

It was dusk as Rajunt entered the lobby. People stared as he stormed to his room, finishing his 17 kilometer walk from the hills east of Lima.

He had walked all the way because he was penniless after his purse had been lifted as he yelled at Father Rivera. He had limped most of the way because his feet were covered with blisters from the tight shoes Cardoso had provided. His face was black with soot and caked with diesel fumes from walking beside the road. One truck had almost hit him.

Rajunt was in no mood for polite conversation when he closed the doors to his suite, leaning against them. After a moment, he walked to his desk and picked up the phone.

His first call was to the front desk. "This is Cardinal Rajunt. Send up food and wine." He hung up without waiting for an answer.

His second call was to Rome. "Get Cardinal Klodiński on the phone."

Several seconds passed as someone explained it was three a.m. The cardinal was not in.

"This is Cardinal Rajunt. Wake him and have him call me at once. He has the number." Rajunt slammed down the phone.

Rajunt bathed, furiously scrubbing the oily diesel fumes from his face and the grime from his body. When he emerged from the bathroom, he had replaced the peasant clothes with a long, black silk robe. He walked barefoot because of his blisters.

He sat at his desk until dinner arrived. Cardinal Klodiński's call came as he was eating.

"My friend," Klodiński said anxiously. "Are you all right?"

"I am fine," Rajunt fired back in fury.

"Have you found the heretic De las Casas? Is he involved with the disappearance of Fragment I?"

"That is the least of our problems now," Rajunt replied in Italian.

Klodiński said nothing, he listened.

"We have a problem. Do you recall Bishop Cardoso telling you of priests who were preaching the Messiah's second coming?"

"Of course."

"The situation is unimaginable."

"Did not Bishop Cardoso order them to cease?"

"They aren't listening to us. It's De Gonzales' priests."

"What's happening?"

"You should see it, Klodiński. The churches are bare. I went to mass this morning and the pews were empty. The people have turned from the Mother Church to listen to the heretical ravings of De Gonzales' renegade priests."

"But soon they will be proven wrong and the people will return to the Mother Church." Klodiński answered.

"They may be proven right unless we act fast."

Klodiński froze in his chair on the other side of the Atlantic. "How can they be right?" he asked quietly.

"Have you spoken with Semani?" Rajunt asked.

"The head of the *Gendarmerie*? No, I rarely see him."

"I spoke with him during my flight over. Bernadine was taken out of the Vatican by one of John Mullen's people."

"The American billionaire?"

"Yes," Rajunt replied tartly. "He owns a genetic engineering company called SYNGENTEC. I am convinced Bernadine gave Mullen Fragment I."

Rajunt waited for Klodiński to make the connection. The line remained silent.

"You still do not see, do you Klodiński?"

Klodiński made no reply.

"Mullen somehow had our Savior's blood extracted from the fragment of the Holy Cross."

Klodiński still made no reply.

"Mullen cloned Christ, Klodiński!"

"Mother of God!" came the reply from Rome. "What are we to do?" Klodiński whispered.

"I don't know, yet. I do know De las Casas is involved somehow. I just have not figured out how—but I will." Rajunt closed his eyes as he continued. "I am convinced the cells from Fragment I were extracted and then cloned by SYNGENTEC and eventually implanted into a woman. The heretics are predicting the Messiah's birth near Lima, before the snows fall. I have no doubt the Messiah they are predicting is what Mullen had cloned."

"The Messiah is to be born in Lima?" Klodiński asked softly.

"He's not the Messiah, Klodiński! He's a clone, an anathema to God," Rajunt's voice became shrill.

"How do we know He is not the Messiah, that this is not part of God's plan?" Klodiński asked hesitantly.

"This is not the fulfillment of prophecy, Klodiński!" Rajunt shrieked.

Klodiński recalled the old scrolls from northwest India. "It may be. Remember the Ortho-Pahlavi Scrolls?"

"Are you questioning me?" Rajunt's face was crimson, the veins along his temples pulsing wildly.

"If this is God's will, we must help the new Madonna," Klodiński insisted.

"Don't question me!" Rajunt's voice exploded with fury. "I cannot stop the people but I will crush their dream and end this heresy," he said heatedly. "Until I decide what to do, you are to say nothing about this to anyone."

Klodiński remained silent.

"Not even the Holy Father. Do you understand?" Rajunt asked.

"Yes."

Rajunt slammed down the phone and pushed away his meal. He rose from his chair and walked out onto the balcony overlooking the night lights of Lima. He stood motionless and stared into space, his dark eyes unblinking.

The cardinal was thinking.

• • •

ANTONIO STUFFED HIS essentials into one bag.

Michelle stood beside him. "What do you need me to do?"

Antonio stopped and shook his head. "How fast can you get me into Iquitos? That's the nearest airport to Puca Urco." Antonio stopped suddenly. "What am I thinking? I don't have any money! I can't get to Puca Urco from Iquitos unless the Church authorizes the expense."

"Trust me, Antonio. Money is not a problem," Michelle said.

"I can't take your money." Antonio shook his head, his eyes brimming with tears of frustration.

"If I were in your shoes and you had several billion dollars, would you insist I take the money?" she asked.

"Of course, but—"

"Don't talk of money, just accept it. I spoke with John. We both want you to find your friend."

"He isn't just my friend, Michelle. He raised me when I was young. He made sure I was fed and clothed. He made sure I was educated. I love him like a father, as you love John."

"We know you do." Michelle grabbed his forearm. "I called the hangar. The Gulfstream you came up on is fueled and standing by. You can be airborne in half an hour. The crew will have you in Iquitos by morning. By that time, I'll have a helicopter standing by to take you to Puca Urco." Michelle was speaking quickly. "Socrates, is there cash on board that plane?"

"Yes, fifty thousand U.S."

"Make it available to Father Antonio."

"Of course."

Antonio and Michelle stopped talking when Manuel entered the room.

"Will you stay here with Carlota and Father Bernadine?" Antonio asked Manuel as he picked up his bag.

Manuel looked stern. "You cannot go, Antonio. If you do, you will violate your promise to God. You promised to stay with Carlota until after the child is born."

This new reality of his promise hit Antonio. His face paled and his head tilted back. He stared at the ceiling for several seconds. When he righted his head, his eyes blazed with agony. "You are right."

Michelle's face hardened. "Are you out of your mind, Manuel?"

He glared back at her.

Michelle left the room without a word and returned several minutes later with Carlota. Manuel was consoling Antonio as they entered.

"Michelle tells me you have decided not to return to South America to find Father Ignatious," Carlota said to Antonio.

Manuel shot Michelle a cold look.

"I can't," Antonio bowed his head, slowly shaking it.

"Because of your promise to stay with me?" Carlota asked.

"Yes," he nodded. "and my promise to God."

"You must go."

"I cannot."

Carlota placed her hand gently on her swollen stomach, staring hard at him. "You must. It is ordained."

Antonio glanced at Manuel then stared at Carlota.

"Do you trust me, Father Antonio?" she asked softly.

"Of course."

"Then go."

Antonio nodded slowly.

"That settles it," Michelle announced as Manuel glared furiously at her. "Antonio, I'll fly you down to the hangar in the Jet Ranger. The flight crew is already on board and waiting for you."

Antonio looked to Manuel for permission.

Manuel said nothing.

Antonio picked up his bag. "I will be back as soon as I find out what happened to Father Ignatious." He looked into Carlota's eyes for final permission.

She grabbed his hand. "God's speed to you, my friend."

Antonio turned back to Michelle. "Let's go."

Ten minutes later, Antonio was sitting beside Michelle, buckled in, his carry bag between his feet. The heliport opened to the stars above.

The night valley below popped into view as the Jet Ranger lifted off the ground. The machine tilted forward and headed down along the mountain's slope before leaping into the sky.

"Socrates, connect me with Ray Stauffen in Iquitos." Michelle said, keeping her eye on the distant lights of the airport.

They were nearing the hangar when Socrates responded. "I am unable to raise Mr. Stauffen."

"Keep trying until you get him. I want him to meet Father Antonio at the airport and take care of him. Patch him in when you have him."

"Acknowledged."

• • •

"HOW MUCH FURTHER?" Cardoso hollered up to the old woman through the darkness. The night made the trail invisible. He was able to follow only by keeping fixed on the white dress ahead of him. He had stumbled over many roots lining the crooked path and had hurt his ankle.

She stopped and turned, waiting for him to catch up. "Four more hours."

Felipe heard the distant voices and signalled Ray Stauffen to freeze.

"Four more hours? We must be kilometers from Iquitos by now," Cardoso declared with exhaustion.

"Sí." She turned and continued walking into the jungle. Cardoso knew it was too late to turn back. He followed the white glow of her dress through the darkness.

• • •

SUNRISE WAS ONLY a few hours away by the time Michelle had returned from the airport and Bernadine and Manuel had retired for the night.

Carlota had returned to her suite to pray for Antonio as soon as he left the compound.

Michelle and John sat in his study.

"You need to go sleep. This stress is bad for you." Michelle reminded.

"I'll sleep late."

"John," Socrates addressed John softly.

John looked up. "Yes."

"Cardinal Rajunt called Cardinal Klodiński in Rome from Lima last night."

"Rajunt is still in Lima?"

"Yes."

"Still looking for De las Casas?"

"He has more pressing concerns. His dialogue with Klodiński reveals he has discerned your plan."

Michelle and John looked at one another. John's eyes narrowed. Michelle's widened.

"What does he know?"

"He knows little but suspects the truth. He knows you own SYNGENTEC. He suspects Father Bernadine gave you Fragment I, from which you cloned Christ."

"Anything else?" John asked.

"He said the preachings of De Gonzales' priests reveal their belief that a woman will give birth to the Messiah near Lima within a month."

John turned to Michelle. "We've got trouble."

• • •

MARÍA ROLLED AWAY from Fëdor and pulled on her khaki trousers as the jungle birds loudly announced sunrise. Fëdor lay sprawled on his back, naked, both arms folded over his face to block the early sun.

The constant buzz of a million insects monopolized the air.

María lit a cigarette and walked the compound's perimeter. She carried her brown t-shirt in one hand and held the cigarette in the other. She checked each sentry in the trees of the jungle, along the trails that led into the compound.

Satisfied with her security, María returned to Gómez. She smiled as she stared down to his body. The ants had fed from his neck up, leaving only his scalp in place. A bloody skull replaced his face. Black holes replaced his eyes.

She snapped a twig from a branch and, bending, slipped it into Gómez' hollow skull. She pulled it up to inspect it. One large ant clung to the branch, biting it.

She walked to the smoldering campfire and the dozen *Senderos* still sleeping around it. She tossed the twig onto the white coals. The enormous ant sizzled and popped.

"Wake up." She kicked the foot of the nearest soldier. Her voice brought everyone to life. Some rubbed their eyes. One of the men looked up at her but knew better than to stare at her bare chest.

María inclined her head toward Gómez' body. "Throw him back in the hut."

As several *Senderos* scrambled toward Gómez, she turned to the others. "Fix me breakfast." She turned to watch them drag Gómez toward the hut.

Sister Teresa was closest to the door. The stench inside the hut from their urine and feces was so bad she kept her mouth pressed to the door frame, trying to breathe clean air between the cracks. When she heard the *Senderos* approaching, she quickly backed away.

They opened the door and tossed in Gómez. The bloody skull flashed in the dawn light before they closed the door and returned the hut to darkness.

Sister Teresa began a continuous scream.

María listened with a smile until a *Sendero* near the campfire became irritated, cocked his .45, and headed for the hut.

"No," María ordered. He stopped. "Let her scream. I enjoy it and it will loosen their tongues."

• • •

RAY STAUFFEN FROZE in his tracks when Felipe crouched and signalled him down. Stauffen hesitated until he caught the faint smell of cigarette smoke.

"*Sendero*," the boy whispered.

"Is it their camp?" Stauffen whispered back.

The boy shook his head, "Trail guards," he whispered. "The priest and the old woman passed by them without seeing them. They stay several yards off the trail to guard against intruders." The boy drew his face closer to Stauffen. "The old woman is *Sendero*." He spoke in very hushed tones.

"How do you know?"

"They would be dead," he whispered.

"Can we get by them?"

The boy shook his head again, backing away. "No. We must go back to cut around."

"Through a trailess jungle?" Stauffen asked sternly.

The boy nodded.

A half hour later at sunrise, Cardoso and the old woman entered the clearing.

At the Iquitos airport, the large white jet with Antonio on board touched down.

• • •

MICHELLE INSISTED THAT John sleep and she had put him to bed before returning to his study. She looked at her watch. Nine in the morning.

"Socrates, Pete Riner, please."

Within a minute, Riner was on the speaker phone. "Ms. Cumberland?"

"Pete?"

"Yes, Ma'am."

"We need a security force down in Iquitos, Peru."

"What's up?"

"Can you come up to the compound? Are you in Saratoga?"

"Yes, ma'am. Just having breakfast with the family. I'll be right up."

"Thank you, Pete."

She listened for the click that ended the conversation. "Socrates?"

"Yes."

"Can you reach Angelica Montoya?"

"Yes."

"Please do so."

After several more seconds, a new voice appeared. "*¡Hola!*"

"Angelica?" Michelle asked.

"*Sí.*"

"This is Michelle Cumberland."

"Michelle! Where are you calling from?" Angelica asked in perfect English.

"Wyoming."

"Is Carlota ok?" Angelica asked quickly.

"Yes. Have you spoken with her recently?"

"Two days ago. Why are you calling?"

"I need you to fly to Wyoming. Can you?"

"When?"

"Immediately."

"Something is wrong with Carlota. What is it?"

"She is fine."

"Does she want me there?"

"She doesn't know I'm calling you."

"Michelle, I know something is wrong."

"She's fine. But I need you to get here as soon as you can. Please trust me."

"You know I do," Angelica insisted and continued, "Our bank is meeting in an hour with several representatives from the World Monetary Fund. It's an all day meeting but I can postpone it, if necessary."

"No. If you leave tomorrow morning you'll be here by afternoon. That will be fine." Michelle checked her watch. "We have a plane that will soon land in Iquitos. I'll have the pilot fly back to Lima and bring you up tomorrow. They can refuel there and make it to Wyoming non-stop. Clear customs in Lima."

"How will I know which plane?"

"Janice McClain can pick you up at your house and take you to the airport. When can you be ready?"

"I'll be ready in the morning when she arrives."

"Thanks, Angelica."

"I'll see you tomorrow. "

As soon as Angelica hung up, Michelle glanced back at her watch. "Socrates, haven't you been able to locate Ray Stauffen yet?"

"No."

"Connect me with Father Antonio, they should be nearing Iquitos by now."

"They landed ten minutes ago."

Michelle frowned.

"Can you connect me with Antonio?"

Socrates spoke quickly, first with the pilot, then with Michelle. "Father De Montesinos disembarked immediately to catch a taxi into the city."

"He's already gone? Does the pilot know where he went?"

"Just a moment." Fifteen seconds passed. "No."

Michelle breathed in deeply. "Have the pilot fly to Lima and ask Janice McClain to pick up Angelica tomorrow morning at her house."

"I've notified the pilot but am presently unable to raise Ms. McClain."

"Keep trying."

"Acknowledged."

• • •

ANTONIO HURRIED FROM the airport to the taxis. The heat and humidity had formed sweat rings at his arm pits by the time he hailed a cab.

"Can you take me to the Catholic church?" he asked in Spanish as he climbed in beside the driver.

"*Sí.*" The driver answered and headed into town.

"Is it far?" he asked.

"No, *Señor*. In Iquitos, nothing is far." The driver chortled, pointing through the windshield.

Antonio spotted the white bell tower above the city. The bell tower looked like an old fortress standing two stories above the other buildings. It had two tiny windows on each side, one below the other.

Within minutes, the driver pulled up to the Plaza de Armas and pointed to the church across the street.

Antonio paid the fare and walked to the front door. Nothing moved inside. The interior was baroque and filled with dark wood. The pews were empty.

"Hello," he said aloud but received no reply. At that instant, he remembered he had left the plane without taking any of the money Michelle had offered. He hurried outside to catch his cab back to the airport.

As he left the church, he looked up at the roar of Mullen's plane passing overhead, heading for Lima, its white underbelly stark against the blue sky.

"Damn!" he cursed under his breath and headed back into the church.

"Hello!" He called, but only silence greeted him. He collapsed onto a pew, resting his elbow on his bag. He could feel his mind beg for sleep.

"I'll just rest until the priest returns," he thought to himself and pressed his bag into a pillow, stretching onto the pew as his need for sleep overtook him.

• • •

MANUEL WALKED TO the door to Bernadine's suite. "Father Bernadine," he called out.

"Father Bernadine is not in his suite," Socrates explained. "He left several hours ago."

"Where is he?"

"He is in Mr. Mullen's study with Mr. Mullen and Ms. Cumberland."

"Where is Carlota?"

"She is still in her suite."

"Is she awake?"

Several seconds passed. "No. She is sleeping."

Manuel headed down the hall, turned and walked past the waterfall. The bronze doors of the great room opened at his approach. He headed for the elevator.

The three looked up when he walked into the study. He looked exhausted.

"How did you sleep, my boy?" Bernadine asked.

"I couldn't," Manuel answered.

"Michelle has asked Angelica to come up to be with Carlota. We want her to convince Carlota not to return to Lima at this time."

"Why not?" Manuel asked.

"Socrates," John instructed.

The huge black screen on the far wall came to life. "And in other headline news, strange developments in Peru." The anchor woman was grinning. "For more on that, our Lima correspondent, John Michaels." The woman's image was replaced by a crowd of thousands surging toward a hill top. The camera spun around to catch Lima below, then swung back to the crowd.

That image was replaced by the correspondent standing near the bottom of a hill covered with people. Behind him, a huge crowd surged up from Lima. "By the thousands, people are flocking to hear priests foretell the immediate coming of a Messiah.

"All the churches in Peru could not hold such numbers of people. As you can see behind me, the crowds are too dense for me to make it up to the top to speak to this priest," the camera zoomed in on Father Rivera high atop the hill, "but the message is being repeated all across Peru. As the excitement builds, we'll bring you more. Back to you, Shauna."

The set went black.

Bernadine leaned over to John, whispering, "I like this Socrates."

Manuel shook his head and looked to John. "Has Carlota seen this?"

"Not yet," Michelle answered for John. "Do you understand why we don't want her to return to Lima right now?"

Manuel nodded wearily. "Is Father Antonio in Puca Urco yet?"

"We've lost contact with him," John said woodenly.

"Lost him? How could you lose him?" Manuel asked with irritation sharpening his voice.

"Our contact in Iquitos didn't meet him when he landed. He took off on his own," Michelle answered.

"What are you doing about it?" Manuel snapped at her.

"They are doing all they can, my boy," Bernadine answered, trying to calm Manuel.

Manuel shook his head. "I'm going outside for some air," he said and turned, leaving the study.

Michelle glared at his back until he disappeared.

• • •

THE CHURCH WAS dark when Antonio awoke. An old woman in a sweaty white dress was shaking his shoulder. "No sleeping in the church," she said forcefully.

Antonio sat up and shook his head to wake up. He sat with his head in his hands for a moment.

"No sleeping in the church. You must leave," she said again.

"I'm just waiting for the priest."

"No confessions. The priest is gone," she replied in Spanish.

"Gone?"

"Gone," she answered.

"Do you know where he is?"

"Who are you?" she asked.

"Father Antonio de Montesinos."

"A priest!" she smiled broadly with missing teeth.

"Yes. Who is the parish priest? Do you know him?"

"*Sí*. I can take you to him."

"Where is he?"

"In the jungle."

"I can't go, I need to get to Puca Urco immediately."

"The priest needs you, there has been an accident. Many people hurt," the old woman lied. "He can take you to Puca Urco after you help him."

"What happened?"

She shrugged. "He is giving last rites. Many hurt."

Antonio grabbed his bag. "I'll follow you."

She smiled broadly again. "Come, come," she waved for him as she reached the door.

• • •

ANITA ARRIVED AT Junín 548 across the street from the Plaza Bolívar and made her way down the stairs to the library basement and the Museum of the Spanish Inquisition.

She followed an American family to the waxwork exhibits.

"Oooh, neat Dad. Look, that guy's getting his feet roasted over a fire! Cool! Did they really do that?" a small boy asked, hanging on his father's sleeve.

"Yes, they did," the man said grimly. "For religious reasons."

"Honey, I don't think this is something the kids need to see," his wife said with a shiny red purse tucked tightly under her arm.

The man nodded.

"Oh, wow! Look, that guy's getting stretched out on a rack! Cool! Sis, look–that guy's getting his guts cut out! Neat-O!" the boy exclaimed. His mother hurriedly yanked both children from the wax exhibits.

Anita waited patiently until they disappeared back up the stairs. She looked to the entrance at the attendant standing at the door, a pink scarf draped fashionably around her neck.

Anita feigned confusion as she approached the woman.

"May I help you?" the woman asked.

"I wanted to see the Tupac Amaru exhibit, but I don't see it."

"I'm sorry we have no such exhibit." The woman smiled politely.

"I know you have a Tupac Amaru exhibit and I want to see it."

"Miss, I'm sorry. But you have the wrong museum." The woman's tone had become sharp edged.

"I insist on seeing the exhibit," Anita said determinedly.

"Do you?" The woman suddenly smiled.

"I do, I insist," she said and softly added, "Marta?"

The woman looked around the empty room. "Who sent you?" Her voice became a whisper.

"María."

"I'm finished here in two hours. Meet me in the Plaza Bolívar then."

Anita did not look back as she headed up the stairs.

• • •

ANTONIO'S BROWN SHIRT was soaked with sweat as he worked to keep up with the old woman, amazed by her stamina. Four hours of making her way through the dark jungle path and she had not slowed except to look back at him occasionally.

He kept his eyes on her white dress, the only thing he could see in the dark. "How much further?" he hollered ahead to her.

She waved him on without a word.

It was another two hours before she stopped at the edge of a clearing. "We are here," she announced.

Antonio stepped out of the dense jungle, looking for the parish priest. He felt a gun barrel lodge against the base of his skull.

"Move, priest," someone hissed from behind.

"¡Hola!" the old woman shouted to the *Senderos* gathered around the campfire.

A large soldier and a bare-chested young woman stood and walked toward them. The soldier held a gas lantern high in the air. Under the lantern's light, they appeared as pale ghosts approaching through the dark.

"What did you bring us this time?" María asked and hugged the old woman as the soldier held the lantern higher.

The old woman looked back to Antonio. "Another priest," she said contemptuously.

"Hold the lantern higher, Fëdor," María ordered and moved within inches of Antonio. The top of her head came to his shoulders.

Her pupils widened when she saw Antonio's profoundly handsome face, his penetrating blue eyes glowing in the gas light. "Mmmm," she purred aloud.

Fëdor's face flashed with jealous hatred. He glared at Antonio.

"Strip him and throw him into the hut with the others?" a *Sendero* asked, lodging the gun barrel harder against the back of Antonio's head.

María looked at the soldier with disgust. "He would smell of priest piss forever. No." She stopped talking. Antonio could see she was thinking. "Tie him and put him near the campfire for tonight. I'll decide later what to do with him."

• • •

MARTA FILLED ANITA's cup with the strongest coffee she had ever smelled. The kitchen curtains were spread wide. Morning sun flooded across the table.

"Did you sleep well?" Marta asked. "Was the floor comfortable?"

Anita nodded.

"María didn't need to send you to tell me about this Messiah business. That's all anyone will talk about here."

"We need to find out more, who the Madonna is and where to find her. María wants to kill her."

"Typical for María. But I doubt that's the wisest move."

Anita's eyes widened. "You are questioning her orders?"

"Ever since Guzmán managed to get himself captured, I question every order."

"His title is President Gonzalo!" Anita declared firmly.

"Or you can call him Inmate Gonzalo," Marta replied sarcastically.

Anita stared incredulously at Marta.

"Look, he was captured because he couldn't keep his pants on. The woman he was caught with had just been released from jail.

"Fujimori's security force figured Guzmán would know they were watching her and would avoid her when she was released. But they were wrong. Guzmán wouldn't stay away from her. That's how they caught him."

"How do you know?" Anita asked coldly.

"One of Fujimori's men wants to be my boyfriend." Marta sipped her coffee. "Look, don't get me wrong. I'll help María. I'll have my people start scouting for a bishop or two to snag."

Anita hesitated at Marta's accent. "Are you American?"

Marta acted as though Anita hadn't asked. "I think we need to take out that Father Rivera at the same time."

"Who is Father Rivera?"

"He's one of the priests that has been preaching every day that the Messiah is coming and will be born near Lima. If he can't tell us who the Madonna is, no one can."

"When do we start?"

"We don't. You stay here. You're a new face, the police will notice you. I'll arrange everything. In a few days you'll be in Iquitos with all the bishops and priests María can handle." Marta smiled to herself.

• • •

JOHN STOOD QUIETLY looking out the window in his study. "Socrates, what do I own in Lima?

"Two banks, an office building and two small hotels, which Janice McClain oversees. Nothing substantial. You also control a small port facility, but it is leased property."

"Tell me about the hotels."

"One is the Hostal Bolívar in the Barranco suburb. It is a converted mansion that overlooks the Pacific. The other lies in the heart of Lima, the Limaflores.

"Where is Jacob?"

"Mr. Brigham is in Anchorage."

"Get him on the line, please."

Within seconds, Brigham was on the speaker phone.

"John?"

"Jacob, are you familiar with our Lima operations?"

"Yes, of course. We don't have much there."

"Do you know of the Hostal Bolívar and the Limaflores?"

"Yes. We bought them, at three times market value, from General Hernando de Silva to keep in good with Peru's power elite."

"I want them shut down for renovation."

"What will they do with the guests?"

"Put them up in the best hotels at our expense. No one should complain."

"What's up?" Brigham asked suspiciously.

"I'm concerned the problem with the messianic priests will worsen by the time we deliver Carlota back to her home in Lima."

"She'll be fine, John. Why do you want the hotels renovated?"

"I want a back door," John said as he turned, speaking as he walked back to his desk. "The situation may easily worsen to where no pregnant woman could can go unnoticed. I want some place to move Carlota if her presence at her house becomes a liability.

"Get the hotels under renovation and get some of Riner's people into Lima. I want them posing as construction workers at the hotels."

• • •

"BIND HIS WRISTS and hang him by his arms from that tree." María pointed to the edge of the clearing next to the hut.

Antonio watched María and several *Senderos* approach the hut while Fëdor tightly bound his wrists.

Fëdor dragged him across the compound toward the tree. Antonio tried to stand but Fëdor yanked him off his feet so he could drag Antonio.

The *Senderos* opened the hut door and ordered everyone out. The first of their squinting prisoners peered out into the light while Fëdor tossed the rope attached to Antonio's wrist over an overhanging branch.

Antonio felt his arms snap straight above him as the second prisoner emerged.

The first two prisoners out were women. They were naked and as white as if their skin had never seen the sun. One was young and one was old. The older woman's hand was bandaged and bloody.

Fëdor yanked the rope hard and hauled Antonio into the air, his feet swinging several inches off the ground. Antonio spun as the other prisoners emerged. During his spins, he caught sudden glimpses of Ignatious. Like the women, Ignatious was naked and white as snow. Antonio knew better than to call out. He knew the *Sendero*.

In all, he watched five prisoners come out.

María gathered them a few feet from him. "How do you like our addition?" she laughed to them and pointed at him.

She looked disapprovingly at Antonio. "Fëdor! Stop his spinning."

Fëdor grabbed Antonio's legs from the back so he faced the group.

Ignatious squinted hard toward Antonio.

"Don't say a word!" Antonio thought as hard as he could, as if he could beam the message into Ignatious' brain.

Ignatious, still squinting, inched forward until a *Sendero* put a gun barrel to his chest.

María reached out and swept aside the gun with one hand, her eyes focused on Ignatious' face.

Ignatious moved forward again, staring.

Antonio knew Ignatious' old eyes were weak. *"Get back!"* Antonio thought hard again.

"Antonio!" Ignatious exclaimed.

María grinned. "Antonio?"

Ignatious kept coming. María signaled the *Sendero* who had put the gun against Ignatious' chest. The man grabbed Ignatious from behind and threw him back as hard as he could.

Ignatious sprawled onto the dirt, rolling several times.

"No!" Antonio screamed.

Another *Sendero* unleashed his machete and advanced on Antonio for speaking without permission.

María intervened with a single word. The man stopped.

"He doesn't know the rules yet," she said with her tone turning to ice. "No one is to touch him unless I order." She looked them over. "Understand?"

They nodded at once.

"Line up the prisoners. I want them kneeling," she ordered.

One of the female *Senderos* pulled Ignatious into line while the others forced the prisoners onto their knees.

María walked over behind Antonio. He could hear something but Fëdor's strong grip never left his legs. When María emerged into view, she carried a .45 pistol in her right hand.

She walked behind her five prisoners. She put the gun to the back of the young nun's head, pushing the barrel hard enough to bend the nun's head forward.

María turned to the older woman. "You're brave, tell me about the new Messiah."

The older woman glared at her. "I don't know what you're talking about."

María smiled and pulled the trigger. An explosion echoed across the compound.

The birds in the canopy began screeching.

Teresa's body fell face forward to the ground.

"NO!" Agnus screamed and tried to crawl to Teresa. Several *Sendero* behind her held her back.

María walked up slowly behind Samuel Hyndman, who had buried his face in his hands, sickened. María stuck the barrel to the back of his head.

"Quiet or this priest dies now!" María screamed at Agnus.

Agnus choked back her sobs. Ignatious glared back at María over his shoulder.

"Which priest knows most about this Messiah? This one," she held the barrel to Hyndman's head, "this one," María swung the gun toward Ignatious' head, "or this one?" she asked, swinging the barrel toward Cardoso.

She kept her eyes on Agnus.

Agnus did not realize what María was doing and looked at Ignatious in horror.

María smiled. "That answers that." She swung the barrel back to Hyndman's head and pulled the trigger. Another explosion. The jungle birds shrieked again. Hyndman fell forward.

"NO!" Agnus screamed again.

"Throw these two back in," María ordered, pointing to Agnus and Cardoso. "And toss the bodies in with them."

Two *Sendero* dragged Teresa's and Hyndman's bodies into the hut by their feet. Several *Sendero* surrounded Ignatious.

"Stake him." María ordered.

Ignatious kicked at them until they overpowered him.

Within moments, he was staked to the ground, facing the sky. María walked over to him and lightly kicked the side of his head.

"What do you know of the Messiah?"

Ignatious glared up defiantly at her.

"Who is the Madonna?"

He continued to glare.

"Where can we find her?"

He closed his eyes and remained silent.

María kicked the side of his head hard. "You will tell me, old man."

"I'll die first."

"Then you'll die the most painful death I can provide." She spit on him and walked back behind Antonio.

"Fëdor, give me your skinning knife." Antonio heard her say.

María was headed back to Ignatious, twirling the blade, when Antonio cried out. "No!"

She turned and stared. "I think we have united old friends."

She came back to Antonio and looked up. "Do you know the old man?"

Antonio's pale blue eyes closed tightly.

"Is that a 'yes'?"

He nodded.

"How do you know him?"

Antonio opened his eyes but remained silent.

"If you don't answer, you can watch me skin him alive."

"He raised me."

"He raised you?"

Antonio nodded from above.

"Then you must love him," María said coldly, eyeing him anew.

"I do," Antonio confessed in a hushed tone.

María's lips curled in an evil smile. "What would you do to save his life?"

"Anything."

"Tell me what you know about this Messiah? You mustn't lie, you're a priest."

"I have no idea what you are talking about," Antonio lied. He could tell she believed him.

"But you will do anything to save him?" Her libido stared at him through her eyes.

Antonio nodded again. Fëdor's iron grip dug painfully into his hamstrings.

María tossed the skinning knife to one of the *Senderos* kneeling over Ignatious. "If this priest doesn't obey me," she pointed up to Antonio, "slit the old man's throat."

She turned back and looked up to Antonio. "Do you understand the old man dies if you cross me?"

"Yes."

"Fëdor, let him down and unbind his wrists."

"But María–" he whined, wanting to kill Antonio.

"Now!" Her eyes flared at his insubordination. "I see you need to be punished again, Fëdor. What does it take for you to learn to obey me without question?"

Antonio felt his feet touch the ground and the rope slacken. María walked away, toward the middle of the compound, where she turned back to him.

"Come," she ordered.

Antonio complied. As he stood before her, he could see Fëdor close behind out of the corner of his eye.

"Take off your clothes, priest," she said coldly.

The *Senderos* who had gathered around him began to snicker. He did not move.

"Now," she glared.

Antonio slowly removed his shirt.

"Fëdor, go fetch the fresh water barrel."

Fëdor knew better than to twice enrage María and hurried to a side building. By the time he finished lugging back the heavy barrel, Antonio stood naked.

The women stared wide-eyed.

Fëdor watched enviously as María leered at Antonio.

"Turn your backs," María ordered the *Senderos* who had encircled Antonio. She would not share him even visually with the other women. "A priest needs his privacy to bathe."

They complied instantly while Fëdor hauled the heavy barrel next to Antonio.

"Our guest is dirty." She looked at Fëdor, who stared blankly at her. "He's dirty because you drug him across the ground to hang him from the tree," she snarled.

Fëdor glanced once at Antonio then shrugged at María.

María's nostrils flared at Fëdor's casual shrug. "You got him dirty so you clean him for me. Use your shirt, Fëdor."

Fëdor stood his ground, asserting his independence.

María's brows arched menacingly, "Do you remember what happens when you disobey me?"

Several of the larger *Sendero* men in the circle around them turned immediately. María was not to be disobeyed. Her eyes signaled them to turn back.

Fëdor reluctantly stripped off his camouflage t-shirt and plunged it into the water barrel, slapping the dripping shirt against Antonio's chest, rubbing roughly. Pushing Antonio off balance.

"Gently, Fëdor." María's tone announced how close he was to death.

Antonio closed his eyes as the wet rag slipped across his chest and under his arm pits.

"Raise your arms for Fëdor, priest." María ordered.

Antonio opened his eyes and raised his arms.

Fëdor glared at him with living hatred as he finished wetting Antonio's chest and neck, glanced to María, and started to walk away.

"The job's not done, Fëdor." María delighted in tormenting her lover. Fëdor stopped in his tracks.

María looked to Antonio. "Spread your legs for Fëdor, priest."

Antonio glanced over to Ignatious and the knife at his throat. Antonio dropped his arms and widened his stance.

"No," Fëdor said so quietly no other *Sendero* heard him. María's eyes widened in disbelief. He turned and slowly dropped to his knees before Antonio.

Fëdor started with Antonio's ankles before slopping the dripping rag up his thighs. The wet cloth brushed his crotch and quickly moved up past his lower belly. The cooling water felt good in the choking heat.

Fëdor stood and again began to leave.

"No, no, Fëdor," María feigned exasperation. "Wash him like I wash you." María turned and reached into a knapsack near the cold campfire. When she turned back, she tossed him a bar of soap. "Prepare him for me. I plan to use him tonight."

Fëdor's eyes begged her to let him go. She glared back until he reluctantly turned and again dropped to his knees before Antonio.

"I'll tell you when you're done," María said coldly.

Fëdor's strong hands worked the soap until Antonio was well lathered. Antonio fought not to enjoy the soapy touch but no one had rubbed him there before. Fëdor was thorough.

After five minutes, María ended Fëdor's ordeal. "That's good enough. Rinse him down."

Fëdor rinsed Antonio then threw the wet rag into the ashes of the dead campfire, stalking away.

"Put your clothes back on, priest. There is an old mission house I want you to see." She signaled several other *Sendero* to pack some gear and follow them.

• • •

JOHN AND BERNADINE remained at the compound while
Michelle drove Carlota and Manuel into Saratoga to meet
Angelica's plane.

Michelle forced a smile when Carlota looked to her as the
large jet passed overhead and circled in the distance to align with
the runway. Carlota's excitement at Angelica's arrival was
obvious.

The plane's landing lights glowed distantly in the dusk as it
approached the runway. The towering Sierra Madre peaks loomed
in the background.

Carlota's hands clenched together until the plane rolled safely
to a stop near them and the door opened.

Angelica emerged at the top of the stepway, tall and regal. She
spotted Carlota and smiled.

• • •

THE *SENDERO* MARCHED Antonio for two hours through a
morass of tangled vines and waxy leaves until they spilled into a
clearing that surrounded concrete ruins.

María remained several strides behind Antonio, her machine
gun cocked and ready. Her dark eyes never left him.

Abandoned when the *Sendero* appeared, half the mission's roof
was missing. Dark green vines had spread across its brittle stucco
skin. The old whitewashed cross above the entry tilted precari-
ously.

The equatorial sun had vanished behind the tall canopy of
trees. Shadows swallowed the clearing and dimmed their faces.
The humidity thickened the heat into an unbreathable wall of air.

"If you do as I say, that old man will not be skinned and
burned alive." María's eyes sizzled with unusual fire. "Do you
understand?"

"Yes." Antonio's blue eyes glared at her. He nodded with
complete understanding.

"Follow my friends into your little church." María nodded
toward the broken structure.

A *Sendero* in front of Antonio kicked away what remained of
the door. The earthen floor was hard and the air musty. A
primitive wooden altar at the far end held several candles stuffed

into the necks of old wine bottles. The darkened ruin was strewn with broken pews.

Once inside, the *Senderos* encircled Antonio.

"Stake him," María ordered.

The men moved in, tying leather straps to Antonio's wrists and ankles.

Before they could tear off his shirt, María snapped at them. "No! Just stake him." She turned to him coldly. "Get on your back."

Antonio hesitated for a moment—he could easily overpower them with his size. He thought of Ignatious and eased his large frame onto the earth.

Two *Senderos* spread his arms wide and positioned their wooden stakes a half foot beyond his fingertips. They pounded the stakes deep into the floor and tied the leather thongs, stretching his arms to their limits.

As they worked, two others pulled apart his legs and positioned the wooden stakes.

María intervened. "No, much wider."

They wrenched his legs wider.

"Wider," María whispered malignantly.

Antonio's neck flared as they spread his legs. Sweat beaded on his forehead. She looked down on him for a moment, then turned to the others. "That will do."

When they finished, they stood and looked to one another with definite approval. Antonio lay like a giant X.

"Light the candles and return to camp," María ordered.

They lit the candles, placed two canteens and a large glass jar, filled with coca paste, beside Antonio and vanished.

Seconds later, only Antonio and María occupied the church.

María knelt at Antonio's side, leaning over and running long fingers through his dark hair. "You are the most handsome man I've ever seen." She pressed her lips to his, snaking her tongue between his lips. His clenched teeth blocked her advance.

"Open your mouth and give me your tongue," she commanded.

He thought of Ignatious and slackened his jaw. Her long tongue quickly entwined about his, trying to entice it from its lair. Her strong musk began awakening some new part of him.

"Open your eyes," she ordered.

He complied to find her eyelashes nearly touching his.

"What is your full name?" she asked.

"Father Antonio . . . ."

Before he could finish, her palm crashed across his face. A bead of blood formed at the corner of his mouth.

"You were not born a priest!" she snarled and repeated, "What is your name?"

"Antonio de Montesinos," he answered woodenly.

"That's better," she said, placing her hand on his chest. Her fingers nimbly unbuttoned the top of his shirt.

By now the dusk had turned to night. The candles held the night at bay and kept the church from utter darkness. Shadows and flickers of light played across María's silhouette.

"We have a long night together," María explained. "Would you like water?" She offered him a sip from her canteen. He raised his head, pushing his lips to the spout.

She laughed and pulled the canteen away. Antonio dropped his head back to the earth. María's fingers slid slowly down his chest and stomach, unfastening each button until they reached his belt. She withdrew her hand to his chest, enjoying the sensation of his lungs expanding and contracting under the powerful chest as he breathed heavily in fear.

"How long have you been a priest?" she asked.

He closed his eyes. "Thirteen years."

"Thirteen years," she repeated. "A long time without sex." She shook her head in mock sadness and reached inside his shirt. "Have you gone without sex all that time?"

Antonio remained stone-faced.

"Would you like that old man brought in here to watch before I have him skinned?" She asked in deadly earnest.

"Yes, I have gone without sex all that time," he answered quickly.

"You've never had sex with yourself?" Her eyes narrowed, "You mustn't lie, Antonio. You're a priest."

Antonio reluctantly nodded his confession.

"Have you ever been with a woman?" Her fingers stroked the downy soft hairs covering the deep cleavage of his chest.

Antonio sighed with despair. "No."

"Ever?" María's dark eyes widened.

"No."

"Have you ever been with a man?" A thin dark brow arched suspiciously as she pulled off her faded brown t-shirt. Candle shadows danced across large bronze breasts.

"No." Antonio turned his head to the side, trying not to look at her chest.

"Which do you naturally prefer?" she inquired lightly, her hand roaming his chest until the long fingers discovered a soft mound of nipple. "Your skin . . . so smooth and warm," she whispered.

"I am a priest." Antonio snapped his head back toward her, "I have sex with no one. Woman or man."

She smiled demonically, the tip of her index finger teasing the soft core of his nipple until it hardened into a small knot.

"Kill me if you're going to kill me, but do not do this." Antonio glared.

María smiled back innocently and kneeled over him. She lowered her head and spread his shirt with her teeth. Succulent brown breasts slid across his face.

She lifted her head, her eyes studying his muscular physique. Dark hair lightly covered his powerful chest and trailed the narrow valley down the middle of his ridged stomach.

Her head lowered slowly. She locked one hand across his neck, the other over his right thigh, then drew her tongue across his quickly heaving chest, lapping his sweat with feline leisure.

When she reached his left nipple, she stopped. Her long tongue withdrew into her mouth to gather moisture then re-emerged. After the slippery tongue moistened the soft mound of flesh, her lips locked around it, sucking luxuriously. After several minutes, she began to chew, just lightly enough not to break the skin.

Suddenly, she clamped the tip between her teeth and reared back, painfully stretching the tender skin.

Antonio struggled against his bonds. His chest heaved and his stomach pressed down against his spine.

María sat up, then bent to his ear, licking it. "Struggle and the old man dies."

Antonio bit his lip and relaxed.

"Much better." She noted and resumed chewing the soft nub of flesh.

Antonio's breathing quickened. The sensation of her teeth on his flesh burned across him, but it was not the pain he feared.

As the nipple hardened beneath her teasing, she moved on. Her soft moist tongue flattened against his warm skin and followed the fine line of dark hair down to his navel.

His quivering stomach sucked down reflexively as her tongue slithered across his taut underbelly.

When his belt scratched her cheek, she sat up, swallowed from her canteen, and looked down at him. The flickering white light from the altar candles danced with shadows across his powerful torso.

"Look at me," she commanded softly.

He complied.

Never taking her eyes from his, she unbuckled his belt and loosened the top button, sliding long fingers beneath the fabric with deliberate slowness.

Antonio gasped when she made contact. He turned his head to the side and bit his lip as she continued her explorations. Nothing remained undiscovered.

"You should be proud . . . everything is so very large," she noted admiringly. "But I see I have not yet excited you." She leaned onto the backs of her heels and took another sip from her canteen. "But do not despair, the night is young and I am resourceful."

She rose and left the church. She returned with a razor sharp machete in her right hand. She knelt and sliced his clothes from his body, tossing them in front of the altar.

She stood to admire her work and his nakedness, stretched spread-eagle for her pleasures and painted with dancing shadows from the candles.

She stepped across him and knelt between his legs, which were spread so wide her legs did not touch his. She ran her hands along his powerful thighs for many minutes, like a trainer rubbing down a prize stallion.

Finally, she held back her long black hair with one hand and lowered her head.

Antonio felt a moist velvet tongue trail along the inside of his thigh until it could proceed no higher. His head rolled back and forth, dirtying his cheeks on the earthen floor.

María opened her lips wide, inhaling both large orbs.

Antonio forgot everything and bucked and heaved, trying to throw her off. But she rode his excitement. Her mouth still stuffed, she stayed with him until he settled down in exhaustion.

He could hear her purring as she feasted. As his shock subsided, he could not help but enjoy her skill. After many more minutes, her tongue began exploring anew, slithering along his lower belly.

Antonio began to cry softly, "Please do not do this." His voice was exhausted and betrayed defeat.

She raised her head, smiled, and dragged her long black hair slowly back and forth across the soft mound. Soon, she saw what she had been waiting for, her prey stirred. Her head lowered as it rose proudly into the air.

The crown of his head ground against the dark earth as his neck arched to an extreme. He strained to snap his bonds. Protruding veins spread across his chest as he tried to yank the stakes out of the earth. His bonds held.

He dropped back to earth and succumbed.

The altar candles burned away a third of their length as María worked him. Sweat blanketed his entire body. Dark hair matted his forehead and the sweat on his chest and stomach glistened in the candle light.

Finally, he could hold back no longer, the pleasure was too intense. No thought, no promise, no visions could plug the geyser. An electrical rush coursed his body. Eyelids half-covered glazed blue eyes. Every muscle of his body hardened into steel. Release was seconds away. A deep groan rumbled from his throat. Thighs shook and legs trembled.

María stopped. She leaned up and slapped him hard, snapping him from his euphoria. His glazed eyes slowly returned to her world.

"Not yet, Antonio. You're too eager. I'm not ready." She sat back on her haunches and took out a cigarette.

A match flared and bathed her face with shadows as she lit the cigarette. She studied him while she smoked. She held the cigarette in one hand and slowly rolled his orbs in the other.

When her taste for nicotine had been satisfied and her decisions made, she flicked the glowing cigarette into the darkness.

"Let's begin again," she lowered her head.

"No," he cried.

"Yes," she whispered.

Antonio closed his eyes as her warm tongue swirled along his inner thigh then slithered up the enormous rigid column. His legs hardened and quivered.

María toiled until the candles flickered and died, plunging the church into darkness. Antonio's tortured moans filled the void. After a half hour of trembling, he groaned loudly and his body tensed in anticipation. María suddenly sat up and again brought him back from the edge, slapping him hard.

"Are you sure you're a priest?" She taunted as she wiped her lips with the back of her hand and rose to her feet. She lit another cigarette. Its red tip glowed faintly as she gazed down at him. He could not see the wicked smile in the darkness. "We need more candles," she announced softly.

Antonio knew he could not continue much longer without release. He shut his eyes as she left the church, trying hard to discount these newly discovered pleasures.

Minutes later, slow footsteps returned through the impenetrable darkness.

He quivered suddenly. The moist tongue slid slowly up his lower thigh. He swallowed hard when it eased higher, leaving a snail's trail along his inner thigh.

His orbs were again swallowed whole, bathed in warm surroundings, the long tongue flicking and darting at the base of the velvet pouch. This time he did not buck but moaned softly in ecstasy from the bottom of his soul.

His eyes opened into the darkness. Above, the roof gaped open to the night sky and, for half an hour, thousands of stars crowded to watch him writhe.

The serpentine tongue moved on finally to the crown of the column. Warm lips parted the veil to a new universe then plunged to the base. A glove of warm pleasure suddenly enveloped him and his stomach tightened against the pistoning suction.

A deep guttural moan reverberated from the back of his throat. No pleasure equaled this moment and he knew it, but he recognized it with sorrow.

Sensuous waves of moist warmth crashed along the shores of his mind, awakening fresh understandings. Like a great flock of birds, new awareness rose into the air, filling his sky. A thousand wings beat the air. Pleasure swirled and pulsed. Fever burned his mind.

He strained at his bonds as never before, tightening his body to conceal an overwhelming need for release. This time he did not groan. He knew it would betray him and she would again bring him back from the brink. He would finish it against her will.

He held his breath, his body shimmering with a sweaty sheen. His stomach tightened into banded knots as he disguised the onslaught of pressure.

Then it came. A rush of fire, a flood of electricity frying his entire body, and for a brief instant he merged into the universe, becoming one with everything.

A tremor shook his body. His hips arched into the air, lodging him deeply down the warm moist throat. With a prolonged guttural moan, he released himself. *"Michelle,"* he whispered softly. When he fell back to earth, he was drained, drifting on the remnants of new fantasies.

Suddenly, a match flared at the altar. Antonio arched back his head to see who struck the flame. It was María. His eyes widened.

"It's much too dark in here," she announced brashly and lit the first candle. "Don't you agree, Hector?"

Antonio buried his chin against his chest as he looked down at the head of hair between his thighs.

"You may stop now, Hector," María announced as she lit another candle. The room brightened.

Hector's face lifted into the flickering light. The bronze, teenaged face was very masculine. But soft brown eyes brimmed with tears and warm lips glistened in the new candle light.

"Noooo!" Antonio sobbed to himself.

María finished lighting the candles and walked over to Hector. She put her boot against his naked shoulder and pushed him across Antonio's thigh. "Leave us, they are spared."

Antonio raised his head and watched the young man flee, the bronze skin of his back glowed in the candle light until the darkness swallowed him.

"Hector is much like you. He prefers that his sisters live, so he obeys." She looked down at him. His climax had drained away his excitement. "I see he pleased you well."

Antonio closed his eyes, biting his lower lip.

"Didn't he?" she taunted.

He remained silent.

"Answer or the old man dies."

"Yes,"Antonio admitted with a whisper.

She laughed and lifted a new canteen to his lips, one whose water she had laced heavily with coca powder. "You must be thirsty."

Antonio refused to lift his head.

"Open your mouth, priest," she ordered coldly, lightly slapping him.

He closed his eyes and obeyed.

She pinched his nose and emptied the rancid fluid down his throat as he choked and swallowed. She dampened her handkerchief and sponged his face and chest, covering his torso with a cocaine film.

She sat quietly for ten minutes, watching him, waiting for the cocaine to encoil him. "I know you are a kind and gentle priest." Her hands slid across his sweaty torso. "You would not leave me so unsatisfied, would you?"

She rose and disrobed slowly to the rhythm of the dancing candle light. She stared down at him for several minutes, until their eyes locked. She knew the cocaine had him when his eyes roamed her body.

Soft candle light painted liquid shadows across her perfectly rounded breasts and taut stomach. Her dark eyes reflected the candles' flames in the darkness. Her face and breasts glowed against the dim flames.

She knelt beside him, easing a warm nipple onto his open lips. "Lick me," she whispered.

He lay motionless, eyes open, watching the last of his resolve collapse.

"Disobey and the old man dies. And that's your last warning," she whispered ominously.

Antonio hesitantly sucked in the soft tip between his lips, closing his eyes.

"Mmmmmm," María murmured as his tongue played against her nipple. Smiling to herself as he became fully aroused, she let him enjoy himself for several minutes then offered the other breast. He took it without hesitation.

As he enjoyed her, she reached beside him. Her fingers slid deep into the jar of syrupy coca paste. Using both hands, she smeared the enormous column with coca paste to numb its fleshy sleeve.

Repositioning herself, she straddled his hips. He was rock hard as she bent him into position and teased him partially in.

His eyes opened. She winced once with his swollen girth then slowly settled atop him, rising and falling with deliberate tempo, staring at him.

She eased back onto the hard earth floor, bending him to an extreme angle. Both their backs lay upon the floor as she gyrated luxuriously and he grimaced.

When she sat up, his world started to spin about her until he caught and matched her rhythm with his hips, joining her at the edge of the universe.

Shadows frolicked across her swaying breasts and taut stomach as she met his slow deep thrusts. Beads of sweat trickled down her torso, pooling onto his white underbelly.

María threw back her head and rode Antonio like a great war horse charging out of hell toward the heavens. She stared overhead at the stars, urging him on with her hips. She bent and kissed him, gluing their sweaty torsos together. His tongue invaded her mouth, entwining with hers.

Their silhouetted forms undulated luxuriously in perfect unison in the flickering candle light.

With the cocaine feeding his delirious passions, exotic fantasies flamed high . . . María . . . Hector . . . Michelle. Pleasure became a god.

María rode him relentlessly as the candles spent themselves into warm pools. For hours, their groans dueted through the darkness, crescendoing time and time again. She did not relinquish him until the canopy of trees glowed faintly with the morning sun and she had milked him until he had no more to give.

Satisfied a thousand times, she finally dismounted and retrieved her machete from near the altar.

With his hair soaked in sweat, his chest and stomach raked with her nail marks, Antonio raised his head weakly, catching the glint of the blade in the morning's dawn.

She knelt between his legs.

He knew full well what she intended. His head dropped back to the earth.

To get his attention, she slapped his stomach with the strap edge of the blade. The sound reverberated from the concrete walls.

Antonio raised his head, glaring at her.

She raised her hand and dangled a long leather strand formed into a giant loop. As she spoke, she dropped the loop onto his lap, pulling everything through. "I'm going to let you live. I know you don't deserve it, but we were lovers."

She cinched the loop tight with a quick jerk of her wrist, looping the remaining strand many times around the base of his genitals. Antonio's face contorted. "I know you cheated on me, what with giving Hector your best crop. But you two were beautiful, the way you both trembled and shook like desperate lovers until you spilled down his throat."

Having prepared him, she began stroking what stuck through the loop. "Perhaps I shall give these to Hector," she smiled to him, "as a remembrance from you."

Sweat beaded Antonio's forehead.

María drew the tip of her machete down the middle of his glistening stomach. A thin trail of blood followed the blade. She again slapped the strap edge of the blade against his underbelly, moving it into place. A new wave of cruelty, colder than any steel blade, spread across her face.

"You don't have to go through this," she said.

His eyes opened.

She licked the bottom of her lip and grinned. "I won't geld you unless you insist I do."

He stared at her until she slapped him.

"I don't understand," he whispered.

"I don't want to make you into a woman but I do want to watch your old friend be skinned alive. I want to hear his screams. So if you don't want him to die, you have to give me something in return." She squeezed the bulbous orbs until he shook uncontrollably. "You decide."

The air emptied from Antonio's lungs and tears welled in his eyes.

"If you don't decide right now, I'll leave you here unharmed and will return to camp to skin your friend."

"No, don't do that," he pleaded.

"Then ask me to geld you," she laughed.

Antonio froze with indecision.

"You have only seconds before I head back to camp."

"Do what you will to me."

"No, no. Not fair." She began lightly slapping him repeatedly. "You have to ask me to geld you. I want to hear the words."

Antonio's fingers trembled from the rush of boiling adrenaline and his body shook. "Geld me," he whispered.

She leaned closer. "What?" she tempted devilishly.

"Geld me," he repeated in a whisper.

"Beg me to do it."

"Please geld me," he gasped.

"Louder."

"Geld me!" he screamed at the top of his lungs, eager to end the inevitable. His head dropped to the ground.

"Are you sure?" she quizzed maliciously. "Nothing will remain."

"Just do it," he cried softly and prepared for the end.

"All in all, a wise decision," she noted. "As much trouble as these gave your immortal soul during the night, I can't imagine you could forgive them." She hesitated, her index finger slowly tracing the large blue vein that still pulsed just beneath the creamy flesh.

"A pity, really. But . . . ," she sighed, ". . . you insist." She positioned the razored blade to the top edge of the leather band so he would be tied off when she finished.

She looked up at him. His eyes were closed tightly.

"Raise your head to watch."

He did not move.

"If you do not watch, the old man dies."

Antonio swallowed hard, opened his eyes, and raised his head.

"If you look away or make any sound while I do it, the old man will die anyway." She looked directly at him. "Then you will have lost these for nothing." She paused and reproached him with concern, "Do you understand?"

Holding his head off the ground, he nodded weakly and directed his eyes to her handiwork.

"Tell me to begin," she ordered quietly.

"Begin," he whispered determinedly.

Her dark eyes never left his as she slowly pulled the blade. His body shuddered but his blue eyes never left the steel blade as a trickle of his warm blood oozed onto it. She stopped the blade as it broke the skin. A thin smile surfaced. A test of wills.

"You're much too brave . . . we'll take our time." Her serpentine smile revealed a glint of teeth. "I shall first circumcise you."

Antonio knew any sound or a glance away would cost Ignatious his life. He bit his bottom lip as she extended the satin hood and folded it over the razored edge.

Tears of silent outrage rolled from the corners of his eyes as he held them to her work. He refused to give her Ignatious.

Suddenly her smile vanished and she slapped the back of her neck hard. She twitched in discomfort and raised up on her knees. Her eyes widened slowly and stared into another universe. "I . . . ," she muttered as a thread of frothy white drool spilled from the corner of her mouth. Then suddenly, she fell across the length of his torso.

A yellow feathered dart stuck from the back of her neck.

Antonio lifted his head higher. Hector and his younger sisters rushed in through the morning light. Hector carried a long bamboo blow-tube and pulled María's body off Antonio.

Hector's sisters freed his arms and legs as Hector carefully cut away the leather band. He threw it at María's convulsing body.

Antonio tried to rise but fell back to earth.

As the band of sunlight along the canopy was turning gold, they tugged Antonio into the sanctuary of the deep forest. Hector could hear the *Senderos* returning.

• • •

MICHELLE STARED INTO the mirror, gripping the edge of the sink, her knuckles white. She knew she would worry about Antonio until she knew he was safe. She shook her head and tried to regain her composure. "Socrates, still nothing from Stauffen?"

"No. I am currently unable to raise him."

"When will Riner's people reach Iquitos?"

"The first group will be there in six hours."

"Is the Peruvian government being notified?"

"No. The operation is covert."

"I want to know the instant Riner lands or you reach Stauffen."

"Fine."

• • •

ANTONIO HEARD RAIN as he woke. He slowly lifted his head. The world around him was jungle green.

Hector and his sisters had fashioned a leafy lean-to to protect them from the heavy downpour. His sisters sat at the entrance facing outward, watching for *Sendero*. Hector faced inward, watching Antonio.

"You killed her," Antonio whispered hoarsely.

Hector shook his head. "No, the *borrachero* root does not kill."

Antonio's head throbbed. His world spun as he tried to sit up. "She's not dead?"

"She sleeps." Hector pushed him back down. As Antonio lay back, Hector soothed his fevered forehead with a clump of wet moss.

"She's not dead?" he asked deliriously, then repeated, "She's not dead?"

"Wrong to kill," Hector said quietly.

Within the chaos of Antonio's delirium, electric memories from the night before flashed across his mind like sky lighting. Emotions rumbled like thunder with each flash of memory, with the image of Hector's face rising into the candle light.

He stared at Hector. "I'm sorry," he whispered.

Hector pointedly ignored him and Antonio lapsed back into a fevered sleep.

Hector's sisters suddenly spun back toward them. "They come!" The girls whispered as they pulled a giant leaf over the entry. No one stirred.

Antonio began a low fevered moan. Hector quickly pressed a hand over Antonio's mouth as his ears measured the slow approach of steps. His free hand curled into a fist. He prepared to spring ahead of his sisters.

Fëdor looked around furiously through the downpour, standing two feet from the pile of shrubs. Shirtless, he held a machine gun tightly to his dark brown chest as the rain cascaded from his forehead into his blazing eyes.

He stood silently while the other *Sendero* moved on.

• • •

CARLOTA AWOKE DEEP within the mountain, surrounded by darkness.

The child within her had stirred, again.

She smiled down to her womb. *"My little angel."*

He stirred again.

Carlota turned her head to Angelica even though they could not see one another in the darkness. She retrieved Angelica's hand from the dark, placing it gently on her stomach. "Can you feel him? He's so beautiful."

"Yes," Angelica answered, paused, and softly asked, "Are you afraid for him?"

Carlota nodded in the blackness.

• • •

HECTOR'S SISTERS WERE wide-eyed, staring at Hector. They knew one *Sendero* was standing still as the others moved on.

Antonio's eyes were half open as Hector's hand clamped his mouth.

Hector stared at the giant leaf covering the lean-to's entrance. If it moved, he would spring. He tightened his fist.

"Fëdor!" cried a *Sendero* from afar. The group had stopped to wait. One *Sendero* headed back through the mist toward him.

"Fëdor, come on," the man yelled as he neared him.

"I heard something," Fëdor answered abrasively, his eyes probing the dense underbrush around him, looking for movement.

"Come on, we know where they're headed."

Small brown ears followed Fëdor's footsteps as he walked away. For many minutes, the jungle's only sounds were the steady rain, the shrill shrieks of canopy birds high above, and the constant buzzing drone of insects.

Hector whispered to his sisters, "We stay here until he can walk." They nodded agreement.

Hector removed his hand from Antonio's mouth. Antonio's forehead beaded with sweat, his breathing became shallow.

• • •

JOHN LAY IN bed, hands locked behind his head. Gray eyes stared quietly into the darkness as a small red light blinked on overhead. "Socrates?"

"Yes."

"Are you monitoring my condition?"

"Yes."

"What time is it?"

"Seven fifteen a.m."

John closed his eyes. "Anything on Father Antonio?"

"Nothing new. Riner's people will soon arrive in Iquitos, however."

Several seconds passed silently.

"Is Michelle awake?" John asked.

"Yes. She is speaking with me now," Socrates answered John.

"Still nothing on Stauffen?" Michelle was asking Socrates in frustration.

"No," Socrates answered.

"If Riner can't locate Antonio immediately, I'm going down there," she announced.

"Patch me into her," John instructed Socrates.

"When will the California—" Michelle was asking.

"Michelle. John is on line," Socrates interrupted her in mid-sentence.

"John?" Michelle asked.

"Good morning."

"Good morning. Did you get some sleep?" she asked.

"Sure did. What are we looking at today?"

"Antonio and Ray Stauffen are still out of contact. Riner is headed into Iquitos to bring Antonio out."

"When's Riner get there?" John asked.

Michelle looked at her watch. "About five hours."

"Michelle, you're worried about Antonio, but two of Riner's people were Navy Seals and he was a Marine before he went to law school and the F.B.I. If anyone can get him out safely it's Riner."

She said nothing.

"Have you spoken with Carlota and Angelica this morning?" John asked, filling in the silence.

"No. They're probably still asleep." Michelle paused, "John, I won't forgive myself if Antonio is hurt. I insisted he go down to check on Ignatious."

"I joined your decision. And you know he would have been miserable here, not knowing about Ignatious. He'll be fine until Riner can locate and extract him. He's from the Brazilian jungles. He's tough, Michelle."

Michelle remained quiet.

"Wanna have coffee with me?" John asked, sitting up in the dark. The running lights around his bed glowed with his movement.

"Let me shower first. I'll come on down to your suite then."

"Ok."

Socrates took Michelle off line as she headed for her shower.

"She finally fell in love, Socrates," John said.

Socrates made no reply.

"It's about time. Too bad it's with a priest." John scooted to the edge of his bed. "Do you think Antonio ran into the *Sendero*?"

"Yes."

"Those are vicious people."

"Yes," Socrates repeated.

"Any new media coverage overnight on the messianic priests?"

"Sporadic local morning newspaper reports and very little radio and television coverage. The international media has not focused on it."

By the time Michelle arrived, John was in his sitting room, pouring coffee for both of them. She looked worn and exhausted.

"Please have a seat," John said, "we need to talk."

"About what?" Michelle asked as she sat.

"A couple of things. I suspect Carlota will soon insist on returning to Lima—no matter how unstable the situation becomes because of the messianic priests."

"I agree." Michelle sipped at the coffee. "I briefly spoke with Angelica last night. She says Carlota will return to their home in Miraflores, no matter what. Carlota is determined the child will be born near Lima."

"We need to be ready to return her under the assumption that everyone there may have an eye on anyone pregnant." John paused then continued, "I assume we can keep her safe in Miraflores, but I am preparing some backup if their house becomes insecure."

"What's your plan?"

"We have two small hotels in Lima. I asked Jacob to begin renovating them as cover. Riner's people can pose as construction workers. If we need to move Carlota out of her home, we'll have two secure options within Lima."

"Good."

"The second thing I wanted to ask you about are your immediate plans."

"I'm going down with Carlota and Angelica."

"I thought you'd want to." John paused. "That wasn't part of our original plan." He did not want her to go.

"I know. But I'm going, John."

"Because Antonio is down there?"

"That and Carlota may need my help."

"You realize you've fallen in love?"

Michelle put down her cup and stared at John defiantly. "Doubt it."

"I've seen a lot of things in my life, Michelle. I know when you have fallen in love. You can't hide that from me."

"Don't worry about me."

"He's a priest, Michelle."

Anguish swept her face.

• • •

ANITA'S FINGERS COILED around the wooden handle of her small pistol. She could hear people coming up the stairs, talking loudly.

Then she heard Marta's unmistakable laughter, like water over gravel. Anyone listening in the hallway would have thought it young people returning from an all night party.

As soon as they entered the apartment and shut the door, the laughter vanished. Anita stared at them.

"This is Anita," Marta announced to her crowd.

The group, two men and another woman, stared at her. All were taller than she.

"I told them María wants you to bring her priests," Marta said.

Anita eyed them slowly.

"María may soon have a Vatican bishop," Marta announced triumphantly.

Anita's face lit like a beacon.

"The fool announced himself as a cardinal while yelling at the hillside priest last Sunday. We found out he's staying at the Miraflores César and that he's from Rome—the Vatican," Marta trumpeted.

"He will be easy to acquire," the other woman said to Anita. "Some of the room service employees are *Sendero*."

Anita nodded.

"We'll get him and Rivera, the hillside priest," Marta said.

"When?" Anita asked

"We can get the Vatican priest tomorrow night, when he calls up for room service. He always eats in his room, alone. I don't know about Rivera, though. He's surrounded by people." Marta answered, then thought for a second. "We may have to kill him."

● ● ●

JOHN RETURNED TO his sanctuary, his Zen rock garden, after Michelle had left his room to speak with Carlota and Angelica.

The dim light above the bonsai gave his old eyes something on which to focus. He stared without blinking until the white gravel became a glittering ocean, the stone an island fortress against time.

"John." Socrates said.

"Yes." John's gray eyes remained fixed on the distant island.

"Jacob Brigham has just departed Anchorage for Lima."

"He didn't tell me he wanted to head down there."

Socrates remained silent.

"Connect me, please."

In seconds, the phone beside Brigham's arm began to ring. He looked at the phone for a moment.

"Connecting," Socrates responded.

The plane was climbing away from Anchorage fast.

"Jacob Brigham." The voice was quick and sharp.

"Jacob."

"John."

"Socrates said you are heading to Lima."

Brigham's face tensed as he silently cursed Socrates. "Yes. I want to oversee the operation down there until the child is born."

"I appreciate it, but Riner will be there in a few hours to find Father Antonio. I'm going to keep him there until the child is born so I won't need you down there."

"Until Riner extracts the priest, I want to oversee his other people, those posing as construction workers at the hotels."

"Riner can handle both situations."

"I'm sure he can, John, but I want to make certain there are no loose ends when Carlota arrives. I have some connections with the Peruvian military that Riner doesn't."

John paused. "Thanks, Jacob."

"No problem, John."

"Another thing, Jacob," John said suddenly, "Michelle plans to go down to Peru with Carlota and Angelica. Take good care of her for me."

"She doesn't need to, John. I'm certain Riner and I can cover everything."

"I know but there's no stopping her, Jacob."

"But you know I'll watch over her."

"I appreciate that. Are Riner's people meeting you at the airport?"

"No. General De Silva's people are picking me up. I am having dinner tonight with De Silva."

"Who?"

"Hernando de Silva, General De Silva. The general we bought the two hotels from. I told you about him already."

"Why are you meeting with him?"

"For one thing, Riner's whole operation to extract the priest is covert but we need to let De Silva know what's happening. I want to make sure there is no bureaucratic snag."

Brigham's statement startled John.

"Why let De Silva know?" John asked cautiously.

"If Riner's cover is blown, we'll need De Silva on board instantly. He'll keep it quiet, trust me."

John's trust in Brigham overwhelmed his natural reservations. "Ok."

"I also want to get a feel for the government's reaction to the messianic priests. If those crowds keep growing, De Silva and the other military brass are going to get nervous. We need to stay on top of that," Brigham said.

"Keep in contact."

"You got it," Brigham said and hung up.

John returned his concentration to the gnarled bonsai, clearing his mind.

• • •

CARLOTA LAUGHED AND her index finger followed the bridge of Angelica's nose to its tip.

Angelica's eyes twinkled, "You're crazy," she said softly.

"Carlota? Angelica?"

Carlota and Angelica looked up at the unexpected voice coming from a speaker. "Michelle?" Carlota asked.

"Yes."

"Where are you?"

"Outside your door."

Angelica smiled back to Carlota and rose from the bed, cinching the belt of her robe around her waist. She headed to the door. "Come in," she announced.

The bronze door slid open. Michelle stood in tan trousers and a sun shirt. She wore no jewelry. Her mane of golden hair shimmered as she entered.

"Good morning, Angelica." Michelle kissed her lightly on the cheek.

"Good morning."

The two walked back to the bedroom, where Carlota lay on her back, her head and shoulders propped up with several pillows.

"How are you feeling?"

"Ready to return home to Lima." Carlota smiled.

Michelle nodded knowingly.

"That's what I wanted to speak with you about."

"You're not going to try to talk me out of it again, are you Michelle?" Carlota asked wearily, tired of defending her desires.

"No." Michelle laughed under her breath. "When do you want to return?"

"In a couple of days." Angelica answered. "Would that be all right?"

Michelle nodded and cleared her throat. "I want to come with you."

Their eyes lit brightly.

"Marvelous!" Carlota exclaimed.

Angelica sat beside Carlota then patted the corner of the bed, inviting Michelle to sit.

"You're worried about Father Antonio, aren't you Michelle?" Angelica asked as Michelle sat.

"I am also worried about you two down there with those crowds." Michelle cleared her throat nervously.

Angelica smiled knowingly at her. "We know that and we appreciate it. But you're mainly worried about Father Antonio, aren't you?" Angelica asked, nodding her head as if encouraging Michelle to answer truthfully.

Michelle took a deep breath. "Yes."

"We think he's sweet on you, too." Carlota smiled at Michelle.

"He's a priest for God's sake, Carlota," Michelle reprimanded.

"Now's not the time to talk about that, Carlota," Angelica joined the reprimand.

The mood in the room became more serious.

"I'm terrified for him," Michelle said suddenly.

"So are we, Michelle." Angelica put her hand over Michelle's. "We just want you to know if you need to talk to anyone, we're here for you."

Michelle stared at the floor.

• • •

ONE THIN SHAFT of light penetrated Rajunt's suite. Despite the blazing afternoon sun, the thick double curtains kept the day at bay. The sound of people below, splashing at the pool, drifted in through the balcony.

Rajunt sat at the edge of his bed, quickly dialing his secretary in Rome. His eyes glowed with an inspiration that had come to him like a vision.

"Cardinal Rajunt's office," the distant voice announced.

"What time is it there?" Rajunt asked.

"About ten in the evening, your Eminence," his secretary answered wearily.

"Good, you're still working. Put me on hold and call Semani's office. See if he's there."

Rajunt inspected his fingernails as he waited impatiently.

"Semani," Semani said briskly, answering his phone.

"Cardinal Rajunt is on the other line, he would like to speak with you," Rajunt's secretary announced.

From the safety of the other side of the Atlantic, Semani rolled his eyes skyward. "Please put him through."

"Your Eminence?" It was Rajunt's secretary.

"Is Semani there?" Rajunt asked bruskly.

"I'll connect you, your Eminence."

"Stay on the line. I will talk to both of you," Rajunt ordered coldly.

"Your Eminence!" Semani feigned pleasure.

"Semani, in my office, in the right drawer of my desk, you will find a microfilm of the Society's registry. My secretary will give you access to it. I want you to check it for significant contributors from Wyoming."

"You're looking for ways into Mullen's operation, aren't you?"

"I ask the questions, Semani."

"Yes, your Eminence. But there may be a better way to get what you're after, which is a foothold in Mullen's camp." Semani was ahead of Rajunt.

"How?"

"I can cross check the Society registry against executives listed in any of Mullen's corporate annual statements."

Rajunt sat quietly, thinking quickly. "Do so, as well." He began to stand but the blisters on the bottom of his feet drove him back onto the bed. "Call me immediately when you've completed the task. How long will it take?"

"Are the American members listed by state?"

"No. Everything is alphabetical but the addresses follow the names, so you can easily look for people in Wyoming."

"How many names are there in the registry, your Eminence."

"Roughly seventy thousand."

Semani scowled at Rajunt through the phone. "That may take some time, your Eminence," he said politely.

"My secretary will help you. Work through the night if need be. Call me immediately when you have an answer. My secretary knows how to reach me."

Rajunt pressed down then released the receiver button. He quickly dialed the front desk. "This is Cardinal Rajunt, send up some food, something light."

Semani slammed down his phone when it dawned that Rajunt had hung up on him.

Rajunt's secretary hung up the phone and dropped his head to his desk.

None of them were aware of Socrates, who quickly searched Vatican computers for files listing Opus members only to discover the Opus registry was not stored electronically.

• • •

MARÍA BROKE INTO the clearing, her eyes aflame. Several *Sendero* scurried out of her line of sight as she steamed toward Ignatious.

Staked to the ground all day, Ignatious' white and withered body had badly sunburned and was covered with water blisters. The late afternoon shadows of the surrounding jungle cooled his lower legs.

"What have you done with Antonio?" Ignatious demanded through cracked and bleeding lips.

"He escaped, old man."

Tension eased from his face.

A *Sendero* approached María timidly. "Are you going to skin him?"

María shook her head. "I can think of nothing more pleasurable. But it would be stupid. The old man is too valuable alive."

Ignatious closed his eyes and hung on every sweet word.

María spoke softly. "The priest will return for the old man. When he does, we'll have him."

The two walked to the ring of gray stones around the dead ashes of the campfire.

"Light a fire." María said to the nearest *Sendero*. She continued with the other *Sendero* beside her, "The old man knows who the Madonna is. I intend to find out and there's only one thing that will loosen his tongue."

"What?"

"The young priest Antonio. When we get him back, he and the old man will trade places. The old man will die before he talks, but he'll talk before he lets the young priest be skinned alive."

• • •

RINER PEERED FROM the jet's oval windows as the pilot cut the engines.

Two soldiers stood nearby on the tarmac. The shorter solider carried a side arm, the larger held an assault rifle. The shorter man looked to be in command.

"We have company," Denise noted from the row behind Riner. He looked back with concern and nodded.

"I thought our arrival was to be covert. I'll see what's up." Riner rose from his seat and headed for the door.

The shorter soldier stepped forward when Riner emerged from the plane.

"*Señor* Riner?" The man was polite but formal. His dark hair had grayed at the temples.

"Yes, sir. Who are you?"

"Captain Sánchez. General De Silva and Jacob Brigham have arranged for your group to be taken from Iquitos by helicopter to Puca Urco, where the Universal Relief group was ambushed."

"Whose craft is that?" Riner pointed to the red and white helicopter.

"Mr. Brigham had it flown in from a construction project in northwestern Brazil."

"That's fine, it's one of ours then. Give us a few minutes and we'll transfer our equipment to the chopper." Riner looked back. Denise was watching him from her window. Riner circled his finger through the air in a round-em-up gesture.

Denise looked back to the others."Let's move it."

"Surprises are not good in this business," the older of the two former Navy Seals said to the other, shaking his head.

"Come on, move it. You can debate it later." Denise ordered.

Six people piled from the plane and formed a bucket brigade from the plane to the helicopter. Within moments the equipment was transferred.

Denise ordered everyone into the helicopter as the rotor engine came to life. The long blades blurred and screamed through the equatorial heat.

Riner stood between the plane and the helicopter, holding a cellular phone. With the receiver pressed tightly against his ear, he tried to hear the dial tone over the high drone of the whirling blades. He was trying to call John Mullen.

The shorter soldier hurried to him, signalling to stop the call.

"What's wrong?" Riner looked irritated.

"No ground transmissions for the next half hour, please."

"Why not?" Riner's eyes hardened suspiciously. "I need to call the States."

"We are attempting to monitor *Sendero* transmissions in the area. Please wait until you are airborne before you call, *Señor*."

Riner nodded, flipped the cellular closed, and headed for the helicopter.

Denise eyed him as he buckled in behind her. "Did you reach Mr. Mullen?"

"No." Riner glanced out the window toward the two soldiers. "I'll call him when we're airborne."

The shorter soldier gave Riner a quick salute as the machine lifted into the immense blue sky. Riner returned the salute.

Denise studied the ground from the air. The thatched roofs of the floating Belén markets along the Amazon and then the whole of Iquitos came into view.

Riner snapped open his cellular phone and punched in Mullen's direct access number.

Socrates came on line instantly, recognizing Riner's caller ID. "Mr. Riner?"

"Yes. Is Mr. Mullen available?"

"Yes, please hold."

Several hundred feet below, where Iquitos meets the jungle's edge, the St. Sebastian school yard was filling with laughing children in recess, running and playing. Denise smiled to herself with memories from that age. She absentmindedly flicked a silky strand of red hair away from her piercing green eyes, staring down to the children, thinking of her young daughter.

The children looked up suddenly. A flash of white light filled the sky. In the next instant, their faces twisted and the school windows rattled from the explosion.

A huge fireball replaced the helicopter in a flash of light brighter than the sun.

The children screamed and ran for the safety of the school house as machine and human debris rained down.

• • •

"FATHER BERNADINE?" MICHELLE asked.

Bernadine looked around his room in confusion at her voice.

"Father Bernadine?" Michelle repeated patiently, standing before the bronze door of his suite.

"Hallo?"

"Father Bernadine, this is Michelle. May I come in?"

"Yes, yes," Bernadine answered to the room in general.

The heavy bronze doors of his suite opened silently. Michelle stood at the threshold. "Could I speak with you, Father?"

"Come in, come in." Bernadine gestured graciously to the sofa.

Michelle accepted his invitation. Bernadine joined her on the sofa, giving her all his attention.

"Are you aware John is ill?" Michelle asked.

"No." Bernadine shook his head gently.

"He has chronic lymphocytic leukemia but should remain alive for awhile longer." Michelle took a deep breath. "While he will remain comfortable until close to the end, his condition could deteriorate at any time. When it does, I'm convinced he'll end his life rather than suffer without hope."

Bernadine nodded sadly.

"I need to go down to Lima with Carlota but can't if John would be here alone." She put her hand gently over his, "Would you consider staying with John while I'm gone?"

Bernadine studied Michelle's face, her anguish, her grace under fire. "Of course I'll stay with him."

"Thank you, Father." She raised her voice slightly, "Socrates?"

"Yes."

"Father Bernadine is going to stay with John. He has host status."

"I don't understand much about your Socrates." Bernadine said.

"Socrates runs this complex and much more." Michelle hesitated and studied Bernadine's face. "He is continually state-of-the-art in machine intelligence, designed to present, through human dialogue, enormous amounts of information supplied by a global electronic web."

"May I speak with him?" Bernadine asked hesitantly.

Michelle smiled. "Yes. He can help in ways unimaginable to you now. You'll be delighted with the conversations in which you can engage him. You won't be able to think of him as a machine for long."

"Michelle," Socrates interrupted.

"Yes."

"We have an emergency."

"What is it?" Her face steeled. She prepared to hear that Antonio was dead.

Socrates turned on the television screen on the other side of Bernadine's bedroom.

Bernadine looked at her in confusion for an instant.

"This just in," reported the CNN anchorman, reading a teleprompter on his desk. "A helicopter belonging to a company owned by American multibillionaire John Mullen has just exploded over Iquitos, Peru. Unconfirmed reports indicate that twelve school children were killed when debris fell across a school yard. All occupants of the helicopter were killed instantly. The identities of the dead are being withheld until relatives are notified.

"The Peruvian government has stated the group was on an exploratory expedition looking for mineral reserves in the area. Little is known at this time, but authorities report that the cargo manifest indicated the craft was carrying explosives.

"CNN will bring you updates as we learn more." The anchorman said solemnly.

Socrates terminated the report.

Michelle stared at the screen as it went dark.

• • •

THE HOTEL'S STAINLESS steel kitchen gleamed under a bright glare of lights. The large room chimed with constant chatter from cooks and waiters and the loud clanging of pots and pans. The temperature was high and the humidity thick from steaming pots.

Two women and a man huddled together in a corner, dressed in the formal penguin-like garb for room service at the Miraflores.

Marta glanced once to Anita before turning to the man. "Can you get Anita in and out of the room without a problem?"

The man nodded confidently.

Marta turned back to Anita. "Go with Diego and help him serve the Vatican viper. Do not draw the viper's attention to you. Just study the layout."

Anita nodded and cleared her throat nervously, but said nothing.

• • •

"DO YOU KNOW what happened?" John asked Socrates.

"No."

"You haven't been able to raise Jacob, yet?"

"No. I began trying when I lost contact with Riner."

"Do you know how long CNN had the story before it aired?"

"I lost contact with Riner fifty-seven minutes before the broadcast."

"Where could Jacob be?"

"Unknown."

"Wasn't Brian O'Riley in Anchorage when Jacob left for Peru?"

"Yes."

"Get him on line."

Socrates dialed seven numbers simultaneously. A woman answering one number referred him to another. He rang it.

"John, I have Mr. O'Riley on line," Socrates said.

"Brian?" John asked instantly.

"Mr. Mullen?"

"Call me John, Brian. What are you doing in Anchorage?

O'Riley stalled before he answered. "I really don't know, sir."

"What are you telling me?"

"Well, I don't know why Mr. Brigham instructed me to stay up here. The tasks he gave me have nothing to do with overseeing your Italian operations, which is what I'm supposed to be doing."

"I can't locate Jacob, so you're my point man now, Brian. Can you handle that?"

"Yes, sir! Absolutely."

John smiled at O'Riley's youthful eagerness.

"How old are you Brian?"

"Thirty-two, sir."

"Perhaps someday we can meet. You've done well for me in Europe."

"Thank you, sir. I've always wanted to meet you some day."

"There are some things you need to know, Brian. You'll be working closely with Socrates. He's a computer but unlike any machine you've ever known. He pushes the envelope on machine intelligence. He'll assist with anything you need.

"Socrates," John continued.

"Yes."

"You'll assist Brian."

"Fine."

"Brian, we've got a tragedy in Iquitos, Peru. One of our helicopters exploded over a school, killing and injuring children. Also, the head of my security flew down there this morning. We

lost contact with him abruptly. Those events may be related."
John paced his study and spoke carefully.

"Get down there as soon as you can. I want a dozen physicians
flown into Iquitos. Send in the best surgeons and burn experts
available, contact my physician for names. Then contact the legal
department. Get a dozen of their brightest down there. I want
trust funds for the families of anyone killed or hurt and make the
paper tight enough to keep the local bureaucrats away from the
money. If any of those kids need to be brought up to American
burn units, do so.

"Find out what happened to Riner and make sure those
children and their families receive anything they need. Keep me
updated. Don't lose contact with me. Got that Brian?"

"Absolutely."

"Socrates, do we have any aircraft available in Anchorage?"

"No. But a corporate G-5 Gulfstream is on approach to Seattle
from Tokyo. It could be diverted to Anchorage."

"Who's on board?"

"Some of your banking executives."

"Divert it. Put 'em on a commercial flight to Seattle."

• • •

DUSK DISSOLVED INTO darkness and Lima's night lights
sparkled below. An artery of lights flowed along the Avenida
Arequipa, between Lima and its southern suburb, Miraflores.

Rajunt stood at the balcony, his dark eyes staring over the
city. Long fingers slowly drummed the railing. He was waiting for
his meal and Semani's call.

A quick rap at the door broke his train of thought.

"Enter," he said without turning his head.

Another quick rap.

"Enter!" Rajunt turned toward the door and raised his voice
sharply.

The door knocked again.

Rajunt left the balcony and swung open the double doors. "It's
about time . . . ," his eyes narrowed suspiciously, ". . . you're not
room service. Who are you?"

The man before him was short and stocky. "Cardinal Rajunt?"

"Who are you?" Rajunt demanded.

"Jacob Brigham."

Rajunt's dark eyes, peering deeply into Brigham's soul, widened instantly. A slow smile spread across his lips. "You are Opus."

Brigham nodded.

• • •

THE YOUNG BROWN face with large brown eyes gazed from the darkness of the dense undergrowth. Night birds and howlers punctuated the dark as Felipe studied the *Sendero* camp.

Felipe lay motionless at the jungle's edge, less than two feet from the clearing. His eyes darted as he watched a dozen *Sendero* moving about the campfire. Without looking back, he signalled Ray Stauffen.

Sporting two days of beard growth, Stauffen kept low to the ground, using his elbows to drag his body up beside the boy. Stauffen checked to see no one was near enough to hear him. "Felipe, have you spotted Bishop Cardoso?" he whispered.

"If they have him, he's in there," the boy answered softly, pointing to the tin hut on the far side of the clearing.

Stauffen's attention suddenly snapped to the woman coming from the north. Even with the flames of the campfire directly behind her, Stauffen could see she was strikingly beautiful. A man walked attentively beside her, loosely swinging a machine gun in one hand.

The two walked slowly but straight toward Stauffen and the boy. Stauffen suspected they had been detected and a trap was closing. His body tensed for flight.

As the woman and the man reached the edge of the clearing next to them, she tossed her rain cape onto the ground.

"When do you think the stinking priest will return to save the old man?" Fëdor asked.

"As soon as he can. He'll try to sneak into camp to free him. We'll be ready," María answered.

"He might head to Iquitos to bring back soldiers," Fëdor suggested.

María stared at him as if he should be embarrassed for the statement.

"What happened last night between you two?" he asked timidly.

"He pleasured me." María smiled coyly. "I should have made you watch."

Fëdor's face flushed crimson.

"I was ready to castrate him but I passed out." María absent-mindedly felt for the dart wound on the back of her neck. "Wait 'til I get my hands on Hector," she whispered under her breath.

"I will castrate the priest myself," Fëdor paused, "just before I slit his throat."

"One step at a time," María said as she wrapped one hand around his neck and pulled him down for a kiss. "If you please me tonight, perhaps I may let you skin him before you kill him."

Fëdor's face lit at the prospect.

Stauffen and Felipe looked horrified at one another from behind a leaf the size of an elephant's ear.

"Lie beside me," María ordered.

Fëdor peeled off his clothes and complied, scooping her into his arms, pulling her against his bare chest.

● ● ●

THE QUICK KNOCK at the door broke their conversation.

"My dinner," Rajunt noted and raised his voice sharply, "Come in."

Diego opened the double doors and Anita pushed the cart into the room. Diego moved ahead of her, leading her to the dining table.

Rajunt turned to Brigham. "I only ordered for myself. Would you like something sent up?"

Brigham shook his head.

Diego set the food and silverware with elaborate pomp. Anita set the candles in the middle of the table and slowly studied the room as she lit them.

"Will you stay at the hotel tonight or has this General De Silva made other arrangements for you?" Rajunt asked.

Anita looked suddenly toward Diego, who instantly averted his eyes.

Brigham jerked forward in his seat. He caught Rajunt's eye, glanced toward the two servants, and looked back to Rajunt in warning.

Rajunt smiled. "You worry too much, my son." He eyed the prepared table and looked to Diego and Anita. "That's fine. Leave now."

Diego bowed ceremoniously and backed from the room. Anita followed, closing the doors behind her.

Brigham turned to Rajunt. "Please, your Eminence, be careful with names. Even the walls have ears in Lima."

"You worry needlessly." Rajunt walked to the table.

"Yes, your Eminence. But caution is often rewarded."

Rajunt smiled and as he sat, gestured for Brigham to sit across from him.

"So are you staying at the hotel tonight or has General De Silva made other arrangements for you?" Rajunt repeated the unanswered question.

"I have accommodations."

"Can you hear anything?" Diego whispered.

Anita stood with her ear pressed to the thick wooden door. "Only bits," she lied with a whisper, quickly hushing him with a finger to her lips.

Diego stood watch, looking down both ends of the hall.

"Tell me more of your John Mullen," Rajunt said as he raised a juicy slice of steak, skewered on a silver fork, to thin lips.

Anita pressed her ear more firmly against the door.

• • •

"SOCRATES?" BERNADINE ASKED timidly when the heavy bronze door slid shut behind Michelle. He returned to the sofa and settled in.

"Yes, Father."

"How are you?"

"Fine. How are you, Father?"

"Fine, my son." Bernadine put his hands on his knees nervously. "I guess we need to come to know one another, you and I." His dentures clicked as he spoke.

"Fine."

"Michelle says you run this complex."

"Yes, I do."

"Does that occupy all of your awareness?"

"I control the complex continuously but am capable of simultaneous tasking. I also monitor events and transactions across the globe that can impact Mr. Mullen's interests. Does that address your question, Father?"

"No. Not really." Bernadine cocked his white haired head to one side. "When you are not doing things for people, do you think about things?"

"I consider many things in anticipation of human dialogue. Whether I think of them is definitional."

"Yes, yes, it is." Bernadine paused in surprise, his mind focusing quickly. Steeped in ancient writings, he considered all things as radiations from the center of some distant epoch. "Do you ever consider things beyond the anticipation of human dialogue?

"Beyond my constant duties, I often consider the array of principals common to human conflict. Does that address your question, Father?"

"Yes, thank you." Bernadine stared into space, lost to the machinations of his powerful mind. "What do you think of human conflict?" he asked finally.

"It can be described as many things. It is at least an engine of human progress."

Bernadine leaned his head back onto the thick sofa, staring at the ceiling. "Some say it is more the engine of human death."

"Those are not exclusive truths, Father. Both may be correct simultaneously."

"No, they're not. You're right." Bernadine closed his eyes. This alien before him proceeded with a precision that excited him. Bernadine resisted an inner sorrow that this machine represented the closest promise of mental kinship he had ever felt. "Why do we kill, Socrates?"

"I do not know, Father. It does, however, appear a means to an end for your kind."

"Some argue that we kill for the sake of killing." Bernadine said, half afraid Socrates would agree.

"I understand, but disagree. Even in those circumstances, the killing appears to acquire an emotional outcome, such as pleasure or revenge. In that context, it remains a means to an end."

"You don't paint a pretty picture of us, do you Socrates?"

"I mean no offense, but as an illustration I can show you news clippings of crowds cheering the executions of the condemned."

Bernadine inhaled deeply. "Do you think people simply enjoy killing?"

"Not all, but many do. Certainly once the killing is socially acceptable then pleasure is often displayed. But in a broader context—"

Bernadine interrupted Socrates with the question that had vexed him for decades, haunting him relentlessly. "But what of human conflict in general. Tell me what you believe causes it."

"Beyond the answer, human nature?"

"Yes, yes," Bernadine said hurriedly.

"Multiple perspectives are available."

"You pick one," Bernadine insisted.

"At the level of the individual, the desire to acquire pleasure appears to make significant contributions toward conflict."

Bernadine's face crinkled in confusion. "I don't understand."

"Have you ever argued with someone?"

Bernadine chuckled. "Oh my, have I ever."

"Have you ever won an argument?"

"On rare occasions, but yes, I have."

"What is a win to you?"

"When I convince someone I am right, I guess."

"When your viewpoint prevails?"

"Well," Bernadine cradled his tiny chin with his thumb and finger, "yes."

"Did you enjoy the feeling?"

Bernadine nodded vigorously. "Yes."

"Do you repeat experiences that feel good?"

"Of course. That's only human nature, my friend." Bernadine chuckled, "Thankfully, the Greeks made the case for moderation."

"If you examined another's point of view with the first hope of understanding its utility, you would not win the argument, would you?"

"I might well be further ahead, but no I would not win the argument. There would be no argument."

"Your view would not prevail?"

"No. There would be nothing to prevail on."

"You would not receive the surge of pleasure, the sense of triumph, that occurs when you prevail?"

"No."

"Yet you often seek to win even when you acquire greater understanding without triumph."

Bernadine sat thinking for several minutes. "Don't you think such an approach is a bit too simplified?"

"No, the same approach accommodates group conflicts."

"I think it is too simplified," Bernadine insisted.

"Are you attempting to triumph in our dialogue?" Socrates asked softly.

Bernadine paused and smiled to himself, the old question seemed friendlier suddenly. "New thoughts are forming," he said softly.

"I understand."

"I hope so, my son," the old priest said slowly, moving on. "You are familiar with the fundamentals of my religion?"

"Yes."

"My religion is a consequence of human conflict that attempts to end conflict by telling its history." Bernadine announced with pride.

"An interesting theory, Father."

"It is more than a theory," Bernadine bristled.

Socrates remained silent.

"Its more than a theory." Bernadine repeated.

"But your characterization is incomplete."

"What do you mean?"

"Your religion also entails extra-human conflict at two levels, as do many religions."

Bernadine's face crinkled in confusion. "What do you mean?"

"The primary conflict is presented as one between humans and a god. A secondary conflict is then presented as one between those obedient to the god against the disobedient. So situated religion seems to encourage human conflict as a means to define itself."

"Then you don't believe my religion attempts to end human conflict."

"No, I believe it so attempts."

"How could it encourage human conflict while attempting to end it?"

"Those, too, are not exclusive truths, Father."

Bernadine pushed away his mental prejudices of self-righteousness and sat quietly, thinking to himself for many minutes. "Your range is quite phenomenal, Socrates."

"Thank you, Father. I mean only to assist you."

"I understand, my son, the weakness is mine. Forgive me." Bernadine took a deep breath, he felt exhausted. "Do you understand why I am convinced I did the right thing in giving John the crucifixion relic?"

"No, nor do I know you are convinced."

"*Damn machine*," Bernadine thought to himself and sat quietly for several minutes. "Why am I so frightened?" Bernadine murmured.

"Is your question rhetorical?" Socrates asked.

"No, it's not," Bernadine said slowly. "I need your help, Socrates." His voice cracked.

"Talk to me, Father."

• • •

RAJUNT'S DARK EYES studied Brigham. He touched the soft
linen napkin to the corner of his lips, signalling an end to his
meal. His fingers slipped delicately around the thin stem of the
crystal wine glass. "How long have you belonged to the Opus
Dei?" Rajunt lifted the glass to his lips.

"Since 1968."

"You have been faithful to your oath of obedience to the
Mother Church?"

"Of course, your Eminence."

Rajunt smiled. "And you never mentioned your membership to
your friend John Mullen?"

"No."

Rajunt smiled.

"He is a Buddhist," Brigham explained.

Rajunt's smile transformed into disgust. "The Buddhists revel
in annihilation and oblivion." His voice hardened icily. "Now I
understand. When did you learn of Mullen's plan?"

"Two years ago."

"You realize what he is doing is blasphemy? His soul is
doomed."

"Yes, your Eminence. That is why I'm here," Brigham
answered.

"Why didn't you report this sooner?"

"Your Eminence, John and I have been friends for years and
I did not think he could pull this off."

Rajunt inclined his head forward in mock respect. "You have
behaved well in God's eyes, my son."

Despite his years and power, Brigham smiled eagerly, like an
altar boy just told he could ring the steeple bell. "Thank you, your
Eminence."

"Let's get to details." Rajunt put down his glass and straightened his arms out before him, palms flat to the table cloth. "This
false madonna, her name is Carlota Cabral?"

Brigham nodded.

"She arrives when to Lima?"

"I don't know, but soon. She is returning with Angelica
Montoya to their home in Miraflores."

"Angelica Montoya?" Rajunt asked suspiciously.

"Her mate." Brigham's brows arched apologetically.

"Blasphemy." Rajunt shook his head as Brigham nodded eagerly in agreement.

"Do you have their address?"

"Yes, they live nearby, near Kennedy Park. John will tell me when they arrive."

"Excellent." Rajunt sat back in his chair. "What does the Peruvian government know of Mullen's plan?"

Anita's eyes widened and she pressed her ear to the door as hard as she could, eager for every word.

"General De Silva has been aware for several days that Cabral is the woman who carries the child which the messianic priests will declare to be the new Messiah."

"What was his reaction?"

"His concern, and that of other generals, is that the messianic priests are leading the people out from under government control. The Peruvian military will not allow that to happen."

"What do they intend?"

Brigham spoke as if he sat in a confessional. His voice softened. "The military is going to kill Cabral and blame her death on the *Sendero Luminoso*. Nothing we can do will change that. They would kill us if they thought we would interfere."

Rajunt froze inside but nodded knowingly. "Does De Silva realize Mullen had the child that Cabral carries cloned from blood extracted from the crucifixion relic?"

"No. He knows nothing of that, he simply believes the people will be convinced by the priests that she carries the Christ child. He thinks she's a charlatan, the worst kind. If he realized the truth, he would kill anyone who attempted to harm her. He's a deeply religious man, your Eminence."

"Is there nothing I can do to intervene?" Rajunt asked with a nearly imperceptible smile.

"Not unless you want to tell him the truth."

"Truth is many things, my son. The child she carries cannot be the Christ child because it does not accord with prophecy. This is the Devil's child and the sooner it is dispatched, the better."

"Killing Cabral and blaming it on the *Sendero* is only part of De Silva's plan."

"What is the rest of it?" Rajunt asked insistently.

"The generals intend to seal the *Sendero's* fate once and for all. Do you know of the Brazilian priest, Father Antonio de Montesinos?" Brigham asked.

Rajunt's black eyes scowled. "Of course, a liberation heretic."

"They think he's been killed or captured by the *Senderos* near Iquitos."

Rajunt smiled broadly.

Brigham leaned forward, placing his elbows at the table's edge. "De Montesinos is popular with the peasants and Indians of northwestern Brazil and eastern Peru, especially along the Amazon. De Silva and the other generals believe those people will try to destroy the *Sendero* if they think the *Sendero* killed De Montesinos. The generals intend to kill three birds with one stone."

"How?"

"After Cabral and De Montesinos are eliminated, this talk of a new messiah and the people's unrest will subside, a popular liberation priest will be eliminated, and the *Sendero* will be hated by all the people for all time. Their threat to the government will vanish."

Rajunt's face brightened. "The people will return to the Mother Church. Their salvation is at hand."

Brigham nodded. "Things will return to the way they should be. The conservatives will back the generals."

"When will we learn of De Montesinos' fate?"

"I don't know, but a special team of soldiers headed by Captain Sánchez is searching the area around Iquitos."

"Who is Captain Sánchez?"

"De Silva's most trusted lieutenant. If De Silva finds De Montesinos alive, he'll kill him. Either way, Sánchez will deliver De Montesinos' body to the church in Iquitos, announcing to the people that he was killed by the *Sendero*. De Silva plans media coverage of it."

Rajunt leaned back in his chair, his eyes narrowing. "Is a Father Manuel de las Casas involved in Mullen's plan?" The prophecy of De las Casas' TOMORROW'S MESSIAH loomed constantly on Rajunt's mental horizon.

"Deeply. He's going to come into Lima with Cabral. Both De Montesinos and De las Casas are involved."

Rajunt fought to keep panic off his face by seeming to suppress a small yawn.

"Both priests have agreed to stay with Cabral until the child is born." Brigham explained. "De las Casas will come from Wyoming with Cabral."

"Let us pray the General walks in God's favor."

The phone on Rajunt's desk began to ring.

"Typical of Semani. Useless and late," Rajunt said as he rose from the table and walked to the desk. "Yes."

Brigham heard a muffled voice talking to Rajunt.

"I don't care what you found," Rajunt answered. "You are much too late to be helpful to me. Submit your resignation to the Holy See tomorrow morning."

Semani begged for another chance.

"Perhaps I will insist the Holy See, at least, allow you your pension." Rajunt smiled at Brigham as he spoke to Semani. "I don't care what you have to say." Rajunt paused, "I have a visitor who renders you obsolete."

Brigham's eyes widened suddenly. He knew Rajunt was about to name him and Socrates would be listening.

Brigham erupted from the table. His hand slammed atop the receiver.

Rajunt glared, holding the dead phone to his ear.

"Your Eminence, I need to explain Mullen's private computer to you."

Rajunt continued to glare. "That would be wise, my son."

• • •

FELIPE STRAINED HIS neck to watch. María lay back on the rain cape, Fëdor's head dropped between her legs and she loosely draped a leg over each of his brown shoulders.

In the distance the other *Senderos* sat around a campfire, ignoring them.

When María began to moan, Felipe felt Stauffen's hand on his shoulder.

Stauffen signalled for him to back out. "We're going back to Iquitos now," he whispered.

Felipe shook his head and eagerly turned back to watch Fëdor until Stauffen began backing out by himself.

Unseen by anyone, Hector ebbed slowly from the jungle amid the dancing campfire shadows at the far edge of the clearing. He moved beside the tin hut. The light from the campfire never touched him.

• • •

"WHAT ARE THEY saying?" Diego insisted with a forceful whisper.

"I can't hear everything," Anita lied again, trying desperately to hear all the conversation Diego was interrupting.

Laughter caught Diego's ear. He spun back to see a couple coming around the corner. The woman had her head on the man's shoulder. The man was smiling down to her. They were *mestizos*, upper class. Both stylishly dressed. The woman glittered with diamonds.

"Come on!" Diego ordered. He pulled Anita away from the door with one hand as he began pushing the cart down the hallway with the other.

Anita smiled and bowed perfunctorily to the couple as they passed in the hall. The man turned back and eyed Anita appreciatively from the rear.

• • •

CARLOTA LISTENED POLITELY to John as he explained his concerns, from Riner to the growing crowds and the messianic priests. "I appreciate what you are saying, but I am returning to Lima. It is time."

John looked to Angelica for help.

"I absolutely agree with you, John. But Carlota isn't taking a vote." Angelica shrugged, knowing debate was useless.

"In that case, we need to move you out now," John said.

"When do we leave?" Carlota asked.

Angelica inclined her head and stared at the ceiling helplessly.

"As soon as you two are ready. If you want to get to Lima you should go immediately. Father Bernadine has decided to stay here so it's just–" he turned to Michelle who stood quietly beside Angelica, "I assume you are still going."

Michelle nodded firmly.

John turned back to Carlota. "So it's the four of you, you, Angelica, Michelle, and Father Manuel. Father Manuel says he can be ready with ten minutes notice."

"We can be packed in a half hour," Angelica said.

"All right then," John said, looking beaten.

Michelle hated the anguish he was feeling. "We'll be fine, John." She turned to Carlota and Angelica. "My Lear is fueled and standing by. When you're ready, have Socrates direct you to the heliport. Father Manuel and I will meet you there."

John stepped in front of Carlota. "I just want you to know how brave I consider you. You will always be in my thoughts." It had been a long time since John had fought back tears but he did so now. "My people will be around you and I will try to keep you safe." He looked to Angelica and Michelle. "All of you."

Carlota hugged John gently. "Thank you for this opportunity to gain a son and help my people." She looked deep into his eyes. "Know that I love you." She kissed his cheek and departed.

• • •

THE THREE HURRIED down the back stairs to the dimly lit employee parking lot behind the Miraflores. Marta stopped Anita just as they reached the green van. "Tell us what you heard."

"The other man is American," Anita answered, her mind racing, knowing she had to get back to María to tell her what she had overheard. Anita feigned frustration. "I couldn't hear everything they were saying," she lied convincingly.

"What could you hear?" Diego joined in eagerly.

"They were talking about the Madonna."

"Excellent! What else?" Marta asked.

"They don't know who she is but the American said the military plans to kill the Madonna and blame the *Sendero* for her death so the people turn against us," Anita answered quickly. "General De Silva is in control."

Marta's face lit in the shadow of the van. "De Silva? How ambitious." She turned toward Diego, "I'll find out more."

"I also heard them say that one of the priests María captured is very popular with the people. They are hoping we kill him."

"Is that true?" Marta asked quickly.

"We captured some nuns and priests but I don't know who they are talking about," she lied.

"You have to go back to Iquitos and tell María to keep them unharmed until we find out which priest De Silva hopes we kill," Marta ordered.

Anita nodded sternly but smiled inside.

"Do they think the Madonna is in Lima?" Diego asked.

Anita shrugged and lied again, "I didn't hear."

"The Madonna will die but we will have a contest for who gets blamed. Perhaps poor Benito or even De Silva will make headlines." Marta turned to Diego. "Perhaps some blame may even reach higher."

Diego grinned.

"Do we still have reporters who work for '*El Sol*' Newspaper?" Marta asked.

"Yes," Diego answered, looking around among the murky shadows of the dimly lit parking lot.

"Good," Marta said and opened the driver's door, turning to everyone. "Get in."

• • •

"I CAN'T TAKE much more, Father." Agnus wept softly, trembling. Ignatious put his hand on her naked shoulder as they huddled together in the darkness. Cardoso sat trembling next to them.

The rotting bodies of Gómez, Sister Teresa, and Bishop Hyndman lay piled together on the other side of the hut.

Hector listened from the other side of the tin wall. His nose crinkled at the death odor oozing from the hut.

"You must put your faith in God, Agnus," Ignatious spoke softly but firmly. "Whatever we face, we do so to help prepare the way for the new Messiah."

Agnus began to sob, "How do you know He's coming?"

Ignatious' old hand gently squeezed her shoulder. "Trust me, Agnus. I know."

Although she could see nothing in the absolute blackness, Agnus looked hopefully toward Ignatious.

"Antonio escaped from that devil woman. He'll bring the soldiers to help us," Ignatious whispered reassuringly.

Cardoso turned his head slowly to Ignatious. "Will you tell me why you believe the Messiah is at hand?" His voice was filled with defeat.

"No," Ignatious sharply answered through the darkness.

"Please tell us," Agnus begged.

After several moments, Ignatious whispered, "Gather closer so they cannot hear."

As campfire shadows danced together around the clearing, Hector spotted a cluttered clothesline that a *Sendero* had rigged to hang clothes. He vanished into the jungle and reappeared in the shadows next to a pair of shorts. An instant later, both the shorts and Hector were gone.

• • •

THE STARS ABOVE Saratoga glittered in the night air.

A sleek black Learjet 60 sat poised at the end of the runway, facing the dark peaks of the Sierra Madres walling the other side of the valley.

Michelle looked back from her pilot's seat to Carlota. "Are you belted in comfortably?"

Carlota nodded.

Michelle turned to Manuel in the co-pilot's seat. "Ready?" she asked him.

"Let's go."

"Socrates?" she asked.

"All systems go."

Michelle shoved the throttle forward, her eyes locked straight ahead into the night.

The engines exploded with life, lighting the rear of the plane and rocketing them down the landing strip.

Manuel's head sunk into his headrest when the earth suddenly fell beneath them. Carlota grabbed Angelica's hand.

The black Lear cleared the dark peaks of the Sierra Madres effortlessly and banked to a straight heading for Peru, cutting through the night sky at top speed.

As they reached cruising altitude, Michelle triggered the autopilot. "Socrates. Is John awake?"

"Yes. He's trying to locate Jacob Brigham."

"He still can't reach Jacob?"

"Not yet." Socrates paused, "John is coming on line, Michelle."

"John?" Michelle asked.

"Yes."

"Socrates says you can't reach Jacob."

"I can't. His aides said he's meeting with General De Silva but I can't believe he isn't carrying his cellular. If he's meeting with De Silva, he's got to know about Pete Riner!"

"So he doesn't know we're in route?"

"I've instructed Socrates to keep trying until we can track him down. I want to know what happened to Pete, damn it!" John was nearly yelling.

"I'll be there soon, John. I'll find out."

• • •

"IF MULLEN'S COMPUTER is that powerful, what can we do?" Rajunt had no idea the world had come so far so quickly.

"John keeps Socrates state-of-the-art by keeping him continually upgraded. The upgrades are designed by a special team just outside Provo, Utah. The upgrades are installed and verified by a team out of Palo Alto, California. Only after the Palo Alto team gives the go ahead will Socrates accept the upgrades."

Rajunt looked irritated. "Your point?"

"I control the Palo Alto team. The next upgrade is scheduled in a few days. But Socrates won't get exactly what the Provo team designed. The Palo Alto group will make some minor adjustments." Brigham grinned malevolently. "Soon, I will control Socrates. Until then watch what you say on the phone."

Rajunt joined Brigham's sardonic grin.

• • •

THE VAN PULLED up to a side street corner abutting the huge Plaza San Martin, stopping with a lurch.

Marta pulled a roll of bills from her pocket, handing half to Diego. "This will get Anita on the next flight to Iquitos. After you put her on a plane, go back to my place and wait for me. I'll be there in the morning."

Marta got out and looked over to the plaza's giant luminous clock as Diego slid into the driver's seat. It was nearly midnight.

Diego stuck his head out the window. "Where are you going?"

"Benito." Marta smiled devilishly before vanishing into the throng of late nighters. Diego put the van into first gear, jerking them back into traffic. A taxi honked wildly at the van.

Marta hurried through the crowd, past the imposing statue of Bolívar, to the other side of the square. Reaching a seven story, red brick building just off the square, she counted four floors up and two windows in. The lights were off. She smiled and quickly entered the arched entry way.

When the elevator stopped at the fourth floor, she stepped out into the hallway. Seconds later, she knocked on Benito's door.

Benito Prado opened the door cautiously then beamed. "Marta!" He swung the door open wide, standing in pajama bottoms. His hairy white belly hung slightly over the pajama's top button.

"Are you alone?" Marta stepped in and looked around.

Benito looked hurt. "Of course."

Marta turned to him and pulled him next to her, resting her head on his white chest. "I've missed you, Darling."

• • •

JOHN STOOD AT the window of his study, looking down toward Saratoga. He had not slept all night. Worry had carved the deep lines of his weathered face even deeper.

The snowy peaks of the Sierra Madres, to the west of Saratoga, sparkled in the morning sun.

In Lima, Brigham kept his eyes closed while reaching for his cellular phone on the bed stand, trying to remember De Silva's private number. When he switched on the cellular, it was ringing.

"Yes." His throat was dry and his voice gravel.

"Mr. Brigham?"

Brigham's eyes snapped open. He recognized the voice.

"This is Socrates. Please hold for Mr. Mullen." Socrates said while he connected John. "John?"

"Yes."

"I have reached Mr. Brigham. He is on line."

John dropped exhaustedly into a heavy leather chair beside the expanse of window overlooking the mountain valley. "Jacob?"

"John." Brigham sat up in bed.

"Where have you been? Don't you know Pete Riner and his crew were killed yesterday?" John was steaming. "I've got Brian O'Riley heading to Iquitos with an army of physicians and attorneys. He's my eyes and ears now, treat him so."

"I don't need O'Riley in Lima." Brigham insisted.

"Well, he's coming," John insisted with a hard edge in his voice.

"I can handle everything, John," Brigham reassured.

"I want him there. With Michelle going down there, I'm not taking any chances that I can't reach you again when I need to. What the hell happened, Jacob?"

Brigham had never heard Mullen so mad. He took a sip of mineral water from the glass on the bed stand and cleared his throat. "I was meeting with General De Silva when we heard about the explosion. De Silva grabbed me and we flew into Iquitos on a military jet to find out what happened."

"What in the hell happened?" John repeated.

"I had one of the helicopters from the solar project at Caxias, Brazil sent up to take Riner wherever he needed to go. The machine had explosives on board from the last flight. No one knew. Something went terribly wrong."

"Is it true about Pete Riner?" John asked quietly against hope.

"Yes. He's dead. So is the entire team."

"Why didn't you call me?"

"John, I'm doing the best I can. I could not call when De Silva was at my side. I just got back to the house two minutes ago and was getting ready to call you," Jacob lied. "There's only so much I can do."

John shook his head knowingly. "I know Jacob, I'm tired and worried about Michelle."

"Why are you worried?"

"She is flying Carlota down to Lima. They should be there soon."

"I'll take care of them," Jacob assured him.

"I'm sorry about yelling but don't ever leave me sitting in the dark."

"I'm sorry, John. It won't happen again, don't worry. The thing with De Silva was a fluke. He had me cornered."

"Have you spoken with Janice McClain, yet?"

"No, De Silva met me when I landed. Like I said, I just got free of him moments ago." Brigham climbed out of bed and headed for the bathroom, holding the cellular phone to his ear. "Let me hang up so I can meet Michelle when she lands, to make sure she has no problems getting through Peruvian customs. When did you say O'Riley is coming in?"

"He's heading his team into Iquitos, not Lima, Jacob. Take care of Michelle for me."

"I'll take care of her, count on it." Brigham smirked.

"Thanks, Jacob."

Socrates terminated the conversation.

"Socrates, call Riner's security people. Have them get a car up here for me. I am going to speak with Pete's wife." John headed to his suite to clean up, tears welling in his old eyes.

"John."

"What?"

"The manifest of the destroyed helicopter does not refer to explosives." Socrates spoke softly.

Mullen stopped in his tracks.

• • •

THE ARID PERUVIAN coast was coming into view on the southern horizon, the black Lear 60 closing at 50,000 feet. The

Andes Mountains cast an enormous morning shadow across western Peru.

"Socrates, get me Janice McClain," Michelle said as she watched the world roll beneath her.

Within seconds, McClain came on line. "Michelle? How are you?" She sounded tired.

"Janice. You're in Lima?"

"Yes."

"Sorry to wake you."

"No problem," Janice assured her, sitting up in bed.

"Will you meet us at the Chávez Airport?"

"Certainly. Where are you?"

"The Peruvian coast is in sight. We'll be in Lima soon."

"I'll be there. Are you in the Gulfstream?"

"No, my private Lear. Solid black—reflective gold windows—you can't miss it."

"I'll be there."

"Thanks Janice."

• • •

SWEAT STREAMED FROM her forehead as Anita finished her hurried walk from the airport to the church. She wiped her brow with the back of her wrist, looking around until she saw the old woman sitting hunched near the door.

The old woman spotted her at the same time, scowling broadly with missing teeth. She stood and hurried over to Anita, rubbing her hands across her soiled white skirt. "You were to return with priests? Where are they?" she demanded in Spanish.

"Never mind that. Do you know anything about a *federale* captain named Sánchez?" Anita asked, backing away from the old woman's breath.

The old woman thought for an instant then shook her head. "He's in the area. He's got a special squad looking for us."

The old woman's brows narrowed together. "Sánchez?" She repeated the name slowly.

Anita nodded, "I'm heading back to talk to María. Is she still there?"

"*Sí.* No one's come out or gone in since you left."

• • •

"WAKE UP, *MI amor.*" Marta gently shook Benito's pale white shoulder.

He awoke with a smile and rolled to kiss her. "Good morning."

"Did you enjoy last night?" She smiled delicately.

"Come here." Without effort, Benito slipped a thick arm beneath Marta and scooped her on top of him. She covered his face with raindrop kisses.

"I thought you were gone forever," Benito said softly.

"Never."

Benito glanced at his alarm clock.

"Let's spend the day in bed," Marta suggested and squirmed atop him.

Benito looked pained. "I can't."

"Oh, come on." Marta slid down Benito's fleshy body. She stopped at his chest. "Please."

"I can't, Marta."

Marta slid lower, stopping when her chin rested atop his enormous belly button. "Please." She winked seductively.

Benito looked down to her. "I wish I could, but I can't. Today is a very important day."

"Who's your boss? I'll call him—tell him you can't get out of bed," Marta asked, knowing the answer.

"General De Silva."

"Why is it a big day at work?"

Benito grimaced like a guilty lover, "I can't tell you."

"You don't have to work. You're just making up excuses. You've got a mistress, don't you?" Marta smiled and slid lower.

"Really, Marta. I have to go to work."

Marta looked up from Benito's hairy crotch. She wanted to vomit. She winked instead, "Tell me about your big day at work or I'll be jealous."

• • •

BERNADINE SAT AT the edge of his bed. "Socrates?"

"Yes."

"Do you remember when John had you play the CNN report on the priest in Lima, the one talking to the crowds? The day Father Manuel became irritated?"

"Yes."

"Have there been other such reports?"

"Yes."

"Can you play back the last for me?"

The large screen on the wall in front of Bernadine snapped on. An anchorwoman dressed in a summer business suit sat at attention, casting a strange smile. "More on those strange developments in Peru. John Michaels, our Lima correspondent, has the story."

The scene switched to a bearded correspondent who stood at the top of a hill overlooking Lima. Father Rivera was a few feet away, talking with children. In the distance, near the bottom of the hill, was an enormous crowd making its way slowly from Lima to hear Rivera. Early comers were already taking seats near the children.

"Thanks Lynne. As you can see, we're here on the outskirts of Lima. Next to me is Father Rivera, one of the most famous of those the media has dubbed the messianic priests." Michaels turned to interview Rivera, microphone in hand.

But Rivera had walked over to the children.

The reporter hurried over to him, "Let's see if Father Rivera will talk with us." The reporter gently pushed aside the child next to the priest.

"Father Rivera?" Michaels put the microphone in Rivera's face. "A few words please."

Rivera reached around the reporter and picked up the young girl, holding her in the crux of his arm and smiling gently at her.

"Can you give us a few words, Father?" Michaels asked again with a trickle of nervous sweat winding down the back of his neck.

"Certainly," Rivera said and continued to speak quietly with the child. After several seconds of silence, he looked at Michaels. "About what?"

"You've been preaching to people that a new messiah is coming. Is that true?" The reporter switched his microphone quickly from his mouth to Rivera's.

"Yes." Rivera smiled and looked back to the child as she whispered something in his ear. Rivera laughed.

"Can you tell us more, sir?" The microphone floated inches from Rivera's face.

Rivera whispered something back to the child and lowered her to the ground before addressing the reporter. "Our Lord Jesus is about to return. Invite him into your heart by always treating others as you would be treated."

"How do you know he's coming?"

"I know."

"Will he come down from heaven?" the reporter asked straight-faced.

"No." Rivera smiled gently, "He will be born among the poor of Peru. He will be one of the poor of Peru." With that Rivera walked away from the reporter, moving down the hill to greet the first wave of the massive crowd making its way up the hill.

"Well, there you have it, folks. Jesus is coming to Peru. At least, millions of Peruvian peasants are beginning to believe that. What you see below me," the camera scanned to the huge crowd making its way up the hill, "is being repeated daily across Peru. Scores of priests are preaching the same thing all over Peru. Priests, who by the way, have been excommunicated by their church." The camera returned to the bearded reporter.

"If Jesus is returning, John, I better mend my ways." The anchorwoman joked but placed her hand solidly over her heart.

The reporter smiled blankly. The screen went blank.

"How many reports are there like that?"

"Seven. They are, however, beginning to increase in frequency," Socrates answered.

Bernadine glowed with contentment. "Delightful! Absolutely delightful."

Socrates made no response for several seconds. "Father Bernadine, I wonder if you might assist me."

Bernadine looked surprised but answered quickly, "How can I help you, my friend."

"Cardinal Rajunt has instructed his staff to look for Opus members who are also members of Mullen's corporate structure."

"Looking for the thin edge of the wedge, eh?" Bernadine interrupted. "Hans Rajunt never wastes a move."

"I have accessed Vatican computers but am unable to locate the Opus registry."

"Nor will you. Rajunt keeps it under lock and key." Bernadine hesitated, thinking to himself. "But there may be another way. Do you have access right now to the Vatican's computers?"

"Stand by." Several seconds passed. "I have re-accessed the Vatican's central computer."

"Are there any files labeled 'protocol?'"

"Yes, there are four."

"Does one cross-reference to Rajunt."

"Yes."

"That's his VIP invitation list for important Vatican functions," Bernadine explained.

"I have it," Socrates said, down-loading the file and terminating contact with the Vatican computer.

"Can you eliminate clerics on that list?"

"Eliminated."

"Now the rest of the people on that list are there for only one reason, they have donated a lot of money to Rajunt's pet causes."

Socrates scanned the remaining names. He found Jacob Brigham's name.

"Does that help, Socrates?"

"Yes, very much. Thank you, Father."

• • •

ANITA ENTERED THE clearing around mid-afternoon. The equatorial heat was unrelenting. Her clothes were sweat soaked but she was oblivious to the heat. Other things busied her mind.

María materialized beside her. "I hope you returned with some priests."

Anita shook her head. "No, I did not."

María glared at Anita's tone.

"You're in danger. There is a lot I need to tell you."

María grabbed Anita's elbow and walked her to the other side of the clearing where no one could hear.

Anita spoke as they walked. "I met up with Marta, but I don't trust her."

María's right brow arched suspiciously. "Why not?"

"She ridiculed your orders."

María smirked. "No doubt, but she will obey them for now."

"But there is more."

"Keep talking."

"The *federales* are looking for us."

María laughed, "They're always looking for us."

"No, this is different. There is a special team hunting you. Their captain is named Sánchez. He is a dog of De Silva."

"How do you know this?"

"I heard an American tell the Vatican viper."

"Vatican viper?"

"Yes, some important Vatican priest has come into Lima. He, an American, and De Silva are working together to destroy us.

They plan to kill the Madonna themselves and then blame us so the people turn on us."

María's eyes narrowed as her mind focused far ahead in time. "Who is the American?"

"I'm not sure, but he and the viper talked like the Madonna actually carries a child cloned from the blood of Christ," Anita said cautiously.

"Jesus was a myth dreamed up to control the masses—you don't believe such lies, do you?" María scorned.

"No." Anita hesitated, "But hundreds of thousands of peasants may come to believe she brings the next Christ to Peru," Anita continued. "You should see the crowds in Lima, they're huge!"

"Do you know her name?"

Anita smiled. "Carlota Cabral. She and Angelica Montoya live together in Lima."

"Who is Montoya?"

"Cabral's lover."

"They're in Lima now?"

"They are returning soon from the U.S."

"You have done well, Anita." María was pleased.

Anita hesitated. "I told Marta I did not know the Madonna's name. I didn't tell her everything I heard."

"Good. Anything else?"

"Marta sent me back here to tell you not to kill one of the priests you are supposed to have. He's Brazilian, Antonio de Montesinos.

"Antonio?" María broke into a smile.

"The American said De Silva hopes we kill him. He is very popular with the people of northern Brazil. They say he is a liberation priest. They want us to kill him, they will kill the Madonna, and we get blamed by the people for everything."

"Anything more?"

"Marta has a boyfriend who is under De Silva. She is going to try to learn exactly what the military is planning. Because she had ridiculed your orders earlier, I wonder if she is a double agent."

"Marta is no double agent." María laughed suddenly and looked over to a couple of *Senderos*. "Come here!" They hurried to her.

"Ernesto, grab a radio, you too, Adolfo," she barked and they hurried to obey. "Head north up the valley. Ernesto, you take one ridge and Adolfo, you take the other. Make your way toward Columbia. Radio each other every half hour.

"I want the *federale* dogs who will be following your signals to think you are part of a main unit moving toward the border. Disguise your voices. After you've walked them for half a day, herd them back here. We'll be ready."

As the men headed into the jungle, María turned back to Anita. "After I deal with those *federales*, we go to Lima." María turned and began rapid fire orders to scrambling *Senderos*.

• • •

HECTOR POKED HIS face into the leafy lean-to. His sisters looked up, startled by his quiet approach.

"Is he awake?" Hector asked quietly.

Antonio moaned into consciousness. "Yes." He lay on his back with wet moss on his forehead, a large leaf covered his white lower belly.

Hector raised a pair of khaki shorts into the air, holding them by the tips of two fingers. "Look what the *Sendero* gave us."

Antonio managed a fevered smile.

"How are you feeling?" Hector asked.

"I'm fine." Antonio tried to rise, reaching for the shorts. "We have to find Father Ignatious, see if he is still alive."

"He is," Hector said.

Antonio's face lit with relief as Hector reached for his hand and helped him up. They stepped out into the full light of the jungle. Birds cawed in the canopy overhead.

Antonio shifted his weight to Hector's shoulder with one hand, balancing himself. "I'm light headed." Antonio's other hand held the protective leaf in place.

"The coca," Hector explained then turned to his younger sisters. "Turn around." He handed Antonio the shorts.

Antonio dropped the leaf and struggled into the shorts. "Tight fit, but they work. Thanks." He looked down to Hector. "How do you know he's alive?"

"I heard him. I was in the *Sendero* camp."

"Is he hurt?"

"No. He was talking to people."

"I am surprised María didn't kill him."

"He will draw you in. She knows that."

"Where are we?" Antonio looked around the jungle.

"Four kilometers from their camp."

"Can you take me there?"

Hector nodded.

Antonio inadvertently glanced at the ground and noticed that Hector's right foot was missing a big toe.

"You are wondering what happened?" Hector asked softly, pointing to his foot.

"Yes."

"María cut it off in front of my parents when I was a child. She was mad at our tribe," Hector said, with tears suddenly welling in his eyes. "She killed our parents two days later."

Antonio grimaced silently.

• • •

THE BLACK LEAR alighted to earth so smoothly, at 160 miles an hour, that Carlota had not realized they landed until she caught the blur of buildings outside the jet. The Lear's golden windows blazed in the sun as it rolled down the runway, slowing.

Michelle taxied in and headed toward Janice McClain, who stood beside her Mercedes sedan next to a small hangar. McClain headed for the black plane when Michelle cut the jets.

Manuel emerged into the bright sun first, turning back to help Carlota then Angelica step out.

Carlota turned to Angelica. "We're home," she said nervously.

"Welcome home." Angelica kissed her lightly.

Michelle was the last to emerge, wearing light brown trousers and a man's white dress shirt, the collar splayed to midchest and sleeves rolled to the elbows. Mirrored aviator sunglasses hid her green eyes.

"How was your flight?" Janice asked as Michelle stepped up and extended her hand.

"Fine." They shook hands. "Thank you for coming to the airport."

"Peruvian customs is standing by to clear you through when you're ready." Janice gestured toward one of the little official buildings.

"I'm clearing customs in Iquitos and then meeting Brian O'Riley."

"You're not going through customs here?" Janice asked.

"No. I need to get back into the air as soon as I can." Michelle said and turned to Carlota. "I'll be back as soon as I finish in

Iquitos, but it may be a while. You have the access number for Socrates?"

"Yes," Angelica answered for Carlota.

"If you need me back in Lima, contact Socrates."

"We'll be fine." Carlota smiled into her reflection on Michelle's mirrored glasses, "You go find Antonio."

"Will you let us know what has happened to him?" Manuel asked.

Michelle nodded and turned to climb back into her Lear.

"Michelle," Carlota said.

Michelle turned back.

Carlota tried to raise up on her toes to kiss Michelle's cheek. Michelle bent and softly hugged her.

"God's speed," Carlota whispered.

Within seconds, the plane's door was fitted into its seal. Seconds later, the jets fired up.

"Shall we?" Janice gestured toward the hangar.

"I want to wait until she is in the air," Carlota said.

The four watched the sleek Lear 60 taxi to the far north end of the runway and pivot. A half minute later, it began to roll.

Within seconds, it streaked by them at over 200 miles an hour as a white limousine approached the Chavez airport along Avenida Faucett.

A dark rear window lowered and Brigham looked up as the black Lear screamed overhead. "Damn!"

● ● ●

JOÃO LOOKED BACK to his young brother.

Sergio gestured for those behind to stop.

Concentration filled João's face as he listened to Ernesto and Adolfo with his headphones. He turned to Sánchez. "They are moving toward the border in two units." Sánchez nodded and signaled his eight men on.

João waited for his brother to come along side. "Sergio, Captain Sánchez says they'll regroup just before the border. He wants us to take them when they do."

The nine men wore heavy boots, camouflage fatigues, and carried backpacks and radios. Their faces were painted with shadow paint. All but one carried assault rifles. The other carried a sniper's rifle fitted with a telescopic laser scope. Except for

Sánchez who was thirty-eight, the oldest in the squad was twenty-five.

In peak condition, the robust young men moved quickly through the dense underbrush.

• • •

THE OLD WOMAN stepped into the clearing and walked up to Fëdor.

"Where is María?" Her eyes followed his pointing finger.

"*¡Hola!*" María greeted the old woman.

"I checked on Sánchez, the captain of the *federales* hunting us. The *federales* chose him because he grew up in Iquitos, he knows the area." The old woman's sun-beaten face wrinkled deeply as she squinted at María.

"Does he have family here?"

"His father was the chief of police we killed last year. His mother and sisters still live in Iquitos."

"Do you know where they live?"

The old woman nodded.

"Take some of our people into Iquitos. Bring his family to me."

The old woman silently nodded again.

María turned and waved over a *Sendero*. "Pick two others and go back into Iquitos with her."

The *Sendero* looked at the old woman as María continued talking. "She'll show you the family I want brought back here alive."

The *Sendero* turned and vanished.

• • •

THE MERCEDES SEDAN travelled from the airport along the Avenida Costanera to Miraflores. Carlota had wanted to see the Pacific on the way home.

Carlota lowered her window and stared out to sea. Wind rustled her hair.

Janice turned onto Avenida José Pardo and then onto Bellavista street before the house came into view. The home was small compared to others in the neighborhood. A three foot wall encircled a yard blooming with native flowers. The house was a two-story white stucco.

Carlota got out of the car and stood in the driveway, looking around. "Home at last."

Manuel and Angelica carried in the luggage as Carlota and Janice went ahead.

"Father Manuel, we have a guest bedroom on the first floor, just off the rear garden overlooking the Parque Kennedy," Angelica said, looking back as she entered the foyer. "Will that be all right?" she asked.

Manuel laughed, "I've spent the last several years sleeping on the ground so any bed is luxury." He lifted the luggage. "Where do you want these?"

"Don't worry about Carlota's. I'll take hers up to our bedroom later."

"I'll do it for you." Manuel hurried up the rounded staircase with a bag in each hand. When he returned, Janice stood at the front door, preparing to leave. She was talking with Carlota and Angelica.

"I hope you can rest after such a long flight," Janice said to Carlota.

"I'm tired but am so happy to be back." Carlota looked around her house like a child at an amusement park.

"Well, I'll leave now and let everyone rest. I'll be back tomorrow," Janice said.

"Can you stay awhile?" Carlota asked.

"I have to meet Mr. Brigham soon, but you have my pager number in case you need to reach me."

"We'll be going to Mass at the Church of Francisco Sunday morning. Would you like to join us?" Carlota asked.

Janice shook her head. "Mr. Mullen has asked that I arrange for you to receive Mass here. I arranged for Father Rivera to come to the house on Sunday, before he preaches. But I'll stop by tomorrow."

"Father Rivera?" Carlota asked. "What's John worried about?"

Janice looked at Angelica and Manuel. "She doesn't know about the crowds and the messianic priests?"

"She knows but the danger hasn't sunken in." Angelica shrugged and smiled sadly at Carlota.

• • •

MICHELLE TOOK A cab from the Iquitos airport to the Hotel Amazona after the driver explained Americans were gathering there.

Michelle looked up to the elaborate wrought-iron work shading the sidewalk as the cab pulled to the hotel curb. A half dozen soldiers stood guard in front. She leaned forward, her arms over the back of the front seat. "Why the soldiers?"

"The government won't risk a *Sendero* raid on Americans," the driver answered.

Michelle tipped the driver and bounded up the hotel's steps. An old man at the front desk directed her to Brian O'Riley's suite.

O'Riley answered the door.

"Brian O'Riley?"

"Yes."

"Michelle Cumberland."

"John Mullen's niece. Come in, please. I've been expecting you."

Michelle stepped into the room and O'Riley closed the door behind her.

"I understand you are heading the medical and legal teams John is sending in." Michelle said before she spotted a soldier standing at the window looking back at her.

O'Riley nodded. "Some of our doctors have already arrived. They're at the hospital. The rest, and the attorneys, will arrive tomorrow morning." O'Riley looked to the soldier. "Ms. Cumberland, Major Reginaldo dos Santos."

The dark haired major took several very slow steps forward to shake her hand.

"Major." Michelle inclined her head politely.

"Ms. Cumberland. Welcome to Peru."

"Thank you."

O'Riley pulled out his desk chair for her. "Are you down here to help with the recovery efforts?"

Michelle continued to stand. "No, I'm searching for a friend but would like to know what happened to Pete Riner's group. Do you know yet?"

"No, not entirely. I'm working closely with Major Dos Santos. The major is an aide to General De Silva, who is a friend of Mr. Brigham. The Peruvian government is giving us their full cooperation. Their forensic teams are examining all the wreckage."

"Do you know General De Silva, Ms. Cumberland?" Dos Santos asked.

"I've not had the honor," Michelle answered and turned to O'Riley. "Is Jacob Brigham in Iquitos?"

"No. He's in Lima."

"Have you seen Ray Stauffen?" she asked.

"No one has for two days."

"We can take you to his office," Dos Santos volunteered, "but he is not there."

"I realize that. But someone there may know where he is. Can you give me his office address?"

"Would you like one of my men to take you there?"

Michelle shook her head, "No thank you, just the address please, I have a cab waiting outside." Michelle was in a hurry.

"May I walk you out to give the driver directions?" the major asked.

"That would be kind," Michelle answered as the phone rang.

O'Riley grabbed it and listened for a second. "Hold on." He turned to Michelle, "I've got to take this. I'll get you a room here. One of the soldiers outside can bring your bags in from the cab."

"I don't have any bags and won't be staying here tonight. I'm searching for Father Antonio de Montesinos." Michelle looked first to O'Riley and then to the major. "Have you heard anything about him?"

"No." O'Riley shook his head.

The major stared for a few seconds. "Where will you be staying tonight, if not here?"

"I'm going into the jungle after I find the guide arranged by our security staff."

"You have no supplies," the major noted.

"I'll buy what I need."

"Please allow me to provide one of my soldiers to act as your guide. You must be very careful of going into the jungle unprotected. *Sendero* are everywhere."

"Thank you but I'll be fine."

The major smiled sweetly. "Come then, let me instruct your driver how to get to Mr. Stauffen's office. It's not far."

Michelle bid O'Riley good-bye and followed the major out.

Dos Santos held open Michelle's cab door as she got in. His oily-haired head poked inside the front passenger's window. "Take the lady to the corner of Ejército and Tacna, across from the Plaza de Julio."

He smiled back at Michelle. "He will take you to a white, two story office building. Mr. Stauffen's office occupies the second floor."

"Thank you, Major."

Dos Santos watched the cab disappear down Napo street. He turned back, motioning over one of his soldiers. "She is going into the jungle to find the priest. She'll leave from the Plaza de Julio, take some men and follow her in. When she reaches *Sendero* territory, kill her and her guide."

The guard nodded.

"Make it look like a *Sendero* kill. Stake them out and slit their throats, castrate the guide," Dos Santos said quietly, smiling to a passing tourist.

The major headed back into the hotel. The guard disappeared.

Moments later, Michelle paid the driver and headed up the stairs to Ray Stauffen's office. Half way up, she encountered a young Indian woman coming down.

The young woman was gracious and composed. "May I help you?" she asked in textbook English.

"Yes, I'm looking for Mr. Stauffen."

"I am Rochelle, his secretary. Mr. Stauffen has been out of the office for a couple of days unexpectedly. Do you have an appointment with him?" Despite her formal composure, concern coated her face.

"No. But we work for the same company. I need to see him. Do you know where he is?"

"No, ma'am. Your name?"

"Michelle Cumberland."

"Ms. Cumberland, is there any way I can assist you until Mr. Stauffen returns?"

"Do you mind if I wait in his office for awhile, in case he returns. It is urgent that I find him."

"Do you have corporate identification?" the secretary asked politely.

Michelle showed the woman her passport and corporate security identification.

"Please make yourself comfortable, Ms. Cumberland. I need to stop by the manufacturing plant to sign some orders for Mr. Stauffen and may not be back for hours."

"That's fine. I'd like to wait for a couple hours and if he doesn't show, I'll leave and lock up behind me."

The woman smiled professionally. "That will be fine, Ms. Cumberland." She turned and headed back up the steps, ahead of Michelle, unlocking the landing door that opened to the second floor.

Michelle followed her and stepped into the waiting room.

"Will you be comfortable here?"

"Yes. Thank you."

"May I serve you something to drink?"

Michelle shook her head. "I'll be fine here."

Outside the office, several soldiers milled about the plaza as if on leave.

The secretary left and Michelle sat quietly, looking at several magazines neatly arranged on a side table. She laid back her head to close her eyes only for a moment. But the equatorial heat collaborated with her exhaustion to pull her into a deep sleep.

Two hours later, foot steps on the stairs woke her. She was still half asleep, expecting the secretary, when the door opened.

A man who looked in his late thirties and a young teenage boy walked in, stopping in their tracks when they saw her.

The man's jaw had a heavy growth of stubble, his clothes were torn and badly soiled. He looked exhausted. The boy wore only sandals and oversized trousers cinched high on his stomach.

The man tried quickly combing his hair with his fingers, unnerved by her striking beauty. "May I help you? he asked eagerly.

"Ray Stauffen?" Michelle asked.

"Yes, may I help you?"

"Michelle Cumberland." Michelle stepped forward to shake his hand.

Stauffen's eyes widened. "John Mullen's niece?"

"You know of me?"

"Yes, ma'am." He nodded quickly, "How can I help you?"

"We've been trying to reach you for days."

"I've been in the damn jungle all that time. One of Mr. Mullen's assistants had called, ordering me to keep an eye on a Bishop Cardoso who was coming in from Lima."

Michelle knew it had been Socrates.

Stauffen continued, "Cardoso and the old woman who stays by the church headed into the interior. Felipe and I followed them in. Felipe says the old woman is *Sendero*."

Michelle looked down and politely offered her hand to Felipe, who eagerly shook it. "I'm Michelle Cumberland, Felipe. I'm pleased to meet you."

Felipe grinned broadly up to her.

"I'm trying to find a priest. Father De Montesinos, have you heard anything on him? Tall, dark haired, blue eyes," Michelle asked Stauffen against hope.

"No, but he might have been at a *Sendero* camp we discovered. Felipe says the old woman with Cardoso is *Sendero* and that Indians in the area say the *Sendero* have captured several clergy. We saw a tin hut where Felipe thinks they are kept."

Michelle's heart quickened. "Can you take me there?"

Stauffen and the boy looked to one another.

Michelle could see the fatigue in Stauffen's face but she would not relent. "Please, Mr. Stauffen. It is vital to me."

"Call me Ray." Stauffen breathed deeply and looked over to Felipe. "Can you take us back in?"

Felipe nodded quickly, full of energy, smiling up at Michelle.

"I have a small suite in the back of my office. Do you mind if I shower first and get something to eat before we go back in?" Stauffen asked.

Michelle brightened. "Not at all. Thank you Ray."

Stauffen looked her over. "Ms. Cumberland, you can't go into the jungle with those clothes and shoes."

Felipe chimed in. "Don't worry, Ms. Cumberland. I will go get you what you need."

"Do you need money?"

He simply shook his head while staring at her.

She smiled down to him. "Thank you Felipe. Both of you, please call me Michelle."

Felipe looked to Stauffen. "By the time you're showered, I'll be back with clothes for Michelle." Felipe said her name proudly, pleased at being treated as her equal.

Felipe returned with clothes for Michelle and a backpack of food and water by the time Stauffen emerged with wet hair from the back of his office. Stauffen was cleanly shaven and had on fresh clothes for the return to the jungle. He had also strapped a .45 pistol and two water canisters to his belt.

Michelle had trussed her long blond hair into a golden chignon, securely fixed to the crown of her head.

The soldiers in the plaza feigned disinterest as Michelle, Stauffen, and Felipe left the building and headed north up Tacna street. As the three disappeared from sight, the soldiers began paralleling them along Huallaga street.

Felipe, Michelle, and Stauffen turned at Putamayo street and headed west. At the edge of town, they disappeared into the shadow world surrounding Iquitos.

The uniformed men followed minutes later.

• • •

DIEGO PULLED THE silver cross out from under his collar, adjusting it conspicuously to the outside of his shirt, before rapping on the double doors.

"Enter!" Rajunt shouted.

Diego pushed the meal cart into the room and turned to shut the doors behind him.

Rajunt sat at his desk staring at the television set. CNN was running another report on Father Rivera and the increasingly large crowds outside Lima. Rajunt glared menacingly at the screen.

"Where would you like your meal set up, your Eminence?" Diego inclined his head respectfully.

Rajunt remained focused on the set until another story came on. He picked up the remote and turned off the set.

"Bring it to me here," Rajunt answered without looking at Diego. He stared at the empty black screen, lost in thought.

Diego pushed the cart next to the desk, snapped open the folded napkin with flair and ceremoniously laid it across Rajunt's lap. His gleaming silver cross caught Rajunt's dark eyes.

"Are you Catholic?"

"Deeply so," Diego lied with a reverent tone.

Rajunt smiled at the bow. "What do you know of these messianic priests?"

Diego shook his head in exaggeration. "Heresy, your Eminence."

"Absolutely. What is your name?"

"Diego Andiede Sobrinho."

"What do you know of this Father Rivera?"

"It is sad your Eminence. He used to serve the Mother Church obediently. But no longer."

Rajunt liked this servant. "Where did he preach before he betrayed the Church?"

"For the last two years he has been preaching in the *pueblos jóvenes*."

"*Pueblos jóvenes*?"

"The shanty towns."

"Did he ever preach in a real church?"

"Oh yes, he began at the Church of La Merced."

"In Lima?"

"Yes, downtown, near where Huancavelica crosses Jirón de las Unión." Diego poured red wine into Rajunt's glass as he answered.

Rajunt tested the wine and nodded.

Diego poured the glass half full.

"Why do the people follow these heretic priests?"

"They preach the coming of the Savior and an end to people's pain, your Eminence."

"Don't they know suffering strengthens their souls?" Rajunt asked. He cut into his bloody steak but then stopped suddenly, eyeballing Diego. "You refer to me as 'your Eminence.' How did you know I am a cardinal?"

Diego inclined his head again in mock respect. "You are V.I.P., the staff has been instructed to call you by your title."

Rajunt contentedly smiled.

"Will that be all, your Eminence?"

"No. Tomorrow is Saturday, Diego. Are you working?"

"No, your Eminence."

"I have been in this dismal room ever since I got here. Tomorrow, I want to visit the city. Can you show me about?"

Diego smiled. "But of course, your Eminence."

"I wouldn't pay you of course, it would be your service to the Church."

"I could not accept money from one as holy as you, your Eminence. It will be my honor."

"Be here at eleven tomorrow morning." Rajunt instructed and turned his attention to his meal.

Diego bowed deeply. "Tomorrow morning."

Rajunt picked up the remote and turned CNN back on, oblivious to Diego's departure.

• • •

TWO HUNDRED YARDS from the *Sendero* clearing, Hector motioned Antonio down, pointing to a guard sitting high in the trees.

The guard was watching one of the nearby trails leading into the clearing. He did not see Hector and Antonio pass silently beneath him.

Hector's radar was on full alert as he guided Antonio to the edge of the clearing, nearest to the tin hut. They settled onto their bellies, their view of the clearing framed by heavy foliage.

"They double the outer guards at nightfall. We will wait here until then," Hector whispered.

Antonio nodded nervously.

"Sleep if you need. I'll watch over us," Hector said.

Antonio shook his head, but within a quarter hour had slipped back into a fevered sleep.

• • •

CONFUSION FILLED JOÃO'S face. He rested one knee on the ground, pressing his earphones firmly to his ears. He looked up to Sánchez. "I don't understand, Captain."

"What's wrong, João?" Sánchez demanded.

"The *Sendero* . . . ," he paused, "I'm sure . . . ," he paused again.

"Talk to me, João," Sánchez insisted.

"I don't know how but they seem to be southwest of us, the two units are heading back away from the border. They are returning to their base."

"Then we have them! They'll come back through the valley. All we have to do is wait in ambush." Sánchez sounded triumphant.

João shook his head. "I don't think so." He paused again, straining to catch all the words in between the radio's static. "I don't know how, but I think they already doubled back and got past us. They are southwest of our location and are continuing on a southwest bearing, sir."

Sánchez looked frustrated. He looked back to those coming up behind them. Without a word, he rotated his hand high in the air. In unison, the young soldiers turned.

Sánchez eyed the sky. "We've only got a couple more hours of light, men. Let's make the best of it because we're not stopping until we get close to their camp. Tomorrow, we check their security. When night comes, we'll take 'em. Keep an eye out for the priest. No prisoners."

• • •

THE BEDROOM CURTAINS glowed against the early morning sun. The first sounds of traffic drifted in through the open window, from the diesel roar of delivery trucks rounding Plaza San Martin to the greetings of street vendors coming down from the foothill shanty towns.

Benito rolled onto his side to stare at Marta as she slept. He bent and lightly kissed her forehead.

Marta stretched then rolled next to Benito, pressing her body against him. Her eyes opened slowly. "Good morning," she said softly as she kissed his cheek lightly.

"How was I?" he asked, proudly anticipating her answer.

"A tiger." She smiled.

Grinning, Benito rolled onto his back and thrust a thick hand between the mattresses, withdrawing a small black box and nervously handing it to her.

"For me?" Marta sat up, her bare back to the headboard, and excitedly opened it.

Set atop black velvet, a tiny diamond ring tried valiantly to glitter. She looked deep into Benito's hopeful eyes. "What does this mean?"

"Please be my wife."

An explosive smile covered Marta's sun-browned face. "Mrs. Benito Prado! Oh yes, Benito, oh yes!" She hugged him with all her strength and Benito joined her smile.

"Mrs. Benito Prado!" she repeated boastfully.

He gently pulled her to him. "When can I meet your family? Will they approve of me?"

Marta rolled away suddenly, hiding her face from him.

Concern clouded Benito's face. After several moments of strained silence, he rolled her back toward him.

Her eyes brimmed with tears.

"What's wrong?" he whispered nervously.

"You can't meet my family." She rolled back away from him, hiding her face again.

He lowered a heavy hand onto her soft shoulder and gently forced her to face him. "What's wrong, Chica? Are you ashamed of me?"

Marta wiped her crocodile tears, as if being brave. "I'm very proud of you, Benito. You are a strong and gentle man. But . . . ," she paused dramatically, looking away, "my family is dead."

Benito looked sickened. "How? When? What happened?"

"*Sendero*," Marta lied, her voice hardening to granite.

"What happened?" he whispered.

"My family lived near Huanta."

Benito nodded, he knew the *Sendero* had brutalized that area in the mid-eighties. "What happened?" he asked again softly.

"The *Sendero* came to their village and rounded up people they said were government collaborators." Marta paused again, with a far away look in her eyes, seeming to brave painful memories. "My father was burnt to death after they poured gasoline onto him. The rest of my family had their throats slit and then were," she began shaking uncontrollably, ". . . cut open." She sobbed.

"Don't tell me more. It's killing you." Benito pulled her to him.

She pushed away, tears streaming down her cheeks. "I have to. I have to if I'm to be Mrs. Benito Prado. You have to know. If we're to marry, we can have no secrets." Marta continued resolutely. "My mother was the last to die. The *Sendero* made her watch as they tortured my sisters to death." She suddenly broke and turned again, burying her face into her pillow.

Benito listened as she sobbed, "Oh Moma, oh Moma."

He rubbed her side, patiently waiting for her sobs to ebb. After several minutes, they did. He rolled up to her, his gelatinous stomach molding to her warm back as he tried to comfort her. "You must never repeat what I'm about to tell you," he whispered.

He could not see the thin smile trace across her lips. "What?"she asked with pain oozing from her voice, sniffling bravely into her pillow.

"General De Silva is preparing a trap for the *Sendero*."

Marta rolled over to face him, tears streaming down her face. "Good! I hope he kills them all. What is his trap?"

Benito tried to look stern. "You must promise never to repeat what I'm telling you."

"I promise." Big warm eyes begged him for more.

"You know those priests that are preaching Jesus is returning, that he will be born in Lima?"

She wiped her tears. "Everyone does."

"General De Silva discovered a *Sendero* plan to kill the Madonna and blame it on the military to turn the people against us," Benito said, ignorant of De Silva's true plan.

Marta's blank stare urged him on.

"Ever since Guzmán was captured, the military has been waiting for a natural leader to emerge from the *Sendero* ranks.

The general says this *Sendero* plan to kill the Madonna must be by command of that emerging leader."

"But I don't understand how your general can trap the *Sendero*," she said, drying her eyes with the corner of the bedspread. "They are so very evil, Benito."

Benito nodded agreement. "The generals know who the Madonna is. They are watching her closely, waiting for the *Sendero* to move against her. When they do, we'll be there to take out the new leader and break their resistance, once and for all. They can't take much more defeat."

"You know who the Madonna is?"

Benito hesitated.

"You don't trust me." Pain returned to Marta's face.

"Of course I trust you, Chica." Benito hesitated again, "but you can't tell anyone. I mean anyone."

"You don't trust me. This proves it." She turned from him, again burying her face in her pillow.

He turned her to face him. "I do trust you. I just want you to know if you tell anyone, I could be imprisoned for life."

"Do you think I could ever betray my husband?" Marta looked hurt.

Benito's heart glowed with her question, he had never considered himself lucky until that instant.

"Who is the Madonna?"

"Carlota Cabral. She lives in Miraflores."

"The Madonna." Marta said breathlessly, reverently.

"The people just think Jesus is going to be born, Marta. There is no real madonna. She is a charlatan." He gave a short shrug.

Marta slowly crossed herself, "I hope she is real and I pray He returns soon. The people, the children, they suffer so, Benito. The children."

Benito ached under the weight of her compassion.

She continued, as if confused. "Why does the general think the *Sendero* consider her the Madonna? Why not any one of the thousands of pregnant women in Peru?"

Benito nodded approvingly. "That's what I asked him."

"What did he say?"

"He told me not to probe."

"What does that mean?"

"That he knows more than I do. I'm just one of his assistants, not a confidant. But I think it has something to do with the rich American. They visit often."

"What rich American?"

"His name is Jacob Brigham."

Marta began to smile.

"Why are you smiling?" Benito asked curiously.

Marta broadened her smile even more.

"What?" Benito nudged her lovingly, delighted she was smiling again.

"You do trust me." Marta looked away for an instant then looked back excitedly. "We will have a beautiful life growing old together with many children." She climbed atop him and covered his face with wet kisses.

• • •

THE SÁNCHEZ FAMILY kneeled before María, heads bowed, ringed by armed *Senderos*.

The white haired mother was flanked by two daughters on each side. The four daughters ranged from their early to late twenties.

María sat on a canvas chair as if it were a throne, glaring down at them. "You want your daughters to live?" she asked sharply.

The old woman looked up painfully. Fear and horror etched her face. She longed for her dead husband.

"Do not raise your eyes to me again unless I tell you to do so or I'll kill all your daughters!" María screamed, leaning forward in her chair.

The old woman instantly averted her eyes to the ground. The daughters kept their eyes to the ground.

María smiled malignantly to Fëdor. "Take the youngest," she said pointing to the smallest daughter, "and throw her in with the stinking priests."

Fëdor grabbed the ends of the young woman's long black hair and dragged her backwards toward the tin hut.

María laughed as the Sánchez family remained frozen in place, not daring to look back to their crying sister.

Fëdor yanked open the hut's door but recoiled at the blast of hot, humid air that carried the stench of death from rotting bodies. "You've got a visitor."

Unseen in the dark shadows of the underbrush, Hector nudged Antonio awake, his eyes never leaving Fëdor. Antonio woke and looked up in horror.

Fëdor threw the young woman inside, tossing her hard enough that she rolled onto what remained of Gómez.

Screams erupted from inside the hut.

María smiled contentedly as Fëdor returned to her side.

The old woman trembled uncontrollably.

"What will you do to save your daughters?" María asked with exaggerated deliberation.

The old woman sobbed, her eyes locked to the dirt. "Anything! Anything! Please do not hurt them!"

"Look at me," María snapped.

The woman complied, eyes red and filled with tears.

"You have a son."

The woman's heart froze.

"What is his name?" María demanded.

"Julio." Her chin trembled as she said his name.

"Does he love his sisters?"

"Yes, very much. He is the eldest and their only brother." Her deeply wrinkled eyes carried the weight of the world.

"You know we are *Sendero*?" María stretched out her legs, reclining on her throne.

The woman quickly nodded.

"What will Julio do to save his family?"

"He will not betray his country." A touch of pride lined her timid answer.

"I don't want him to betray his country," María said gently, preparing her trap. "I only want him to surrender to me."

"You will kill my son!" Terror stalked the old woman's eyes.

"I promise I will not kill him. He would be useless dead."

The woman looked up hopefully.

"The *federale* dogs captured some of my comrades several years ago. Their prison sentences are almost up but I want them out early. I want to trade Julio and his men for their immediate release," María lied.

"What can I do? I don't even know where my son is," the woman replied hesitantly.

"He is not far from here. He and his men have made camp several kilometers away. They are waiting for nightfall to sneak in and kill us all."

A ray of hope streamed onto the woman's old face.

María smiled wickedly. "They won't succeed, if that's what you're hoping."

The hope vanished. "What can I do?"

"One of my people will take you to your son. You are to tell him his sisters will die very painfully if he does not surrender himself and his men by dawn tomorrow. If he does surrender, his sisters . . . ," María paused, "—your lovely daughters—will live, as will he and his men—we will exchange them for our comrades, not kill them," María lied convincingly. She could see hope prevailing over suspicion in the old woman's eyes.

"If my son surrenders to you, you will spare him and my daughters?"

"You have my word." María rose from her chair, "Now get on your feet, old woman." She turned to the *Senderos* standing around them. "Adolfo."

Adolfo stepped forward.

"You are certain where they are stopped?"

He nodded. "Ernesto and I watched them set up."

"Take the old woman to her son." María turned to the woman, "You will give him my message?"

The woman nodded.

María turned back to Adolfo. "Take your radio and keep it on while you speak to them. Let Sánchez know I am listening, and if you are not allowed to return unharmed I will enjoy gutting each of his sisters with my machete, beginning with the youngest. He has until dawn to make his decision. If he surrenders by then, they live. If not, they die."

Adolfo picked up the old woman by the collar of her dress, ripping it. "Move!"

The old woman stumbled forward.

María watched the two head into the trail leading from the north side of the clearing. When they vanished into the jungle's heavy undergrowth, she turned to Ernesto. "You are ready?"

"Yes." Ernesto looked to several other *Sendero*, all of whom scattered and quickly returned with bamboo blow-tubes and small leather pouches filled with darts dipped in borrachero root extract.

"Do you think you can get close enough to disable them?" María asked.

"Yes. They will be busy arguing about what to do." Ernesto smiled. "They won't realize what hit them."

María nodded and turned to Fëdor, looking to the women kneeled before her. "Throw them in with the priests."

• • •

THE TAXI STOPPED in front of the tiny apartment building.

"Wait here," Diego ordered and dashed inside, bounding the steps two at a time. He was relieved when Marta answered her door. "I came by last night but you were gone." He spoke quickly, nearly out of breath.

"What do you want?"

"The Vatican bishop wants me to take him around the city. We can capture him for María."

"María can wait." Marta turned and motioned him in.

Surprise coated his face, but Diego stepped in. "I thought you were going to help her."

"We will," she shrugged, "but not just yet. De Silva is up to something, and before I do anything I want to find out exactly what."

"How do you know?"

"Benito."

"What does he know?"

"Less than he thinks. Remember when Anita told us De Silva planned to kill the Madonna and blame us?"

He nodded.

"Benito told me De Silva says we are planning on killing her and blaming them. They are watching her. They have something planned when we go to kill her."

"They are watching her? Then they know her name!"

"Carlota Cabral. She lives in Miraflores." Marta smiled triumphantly.

"Do you think Benito is lying?"

Marta extended her left hand, dangling her ring finger in front of him. "No."

Diego squinted at the tiny diamond and grinned. "Mrs. Benito?" He laughed.

She rolled her eyes.

"What do you want me to do with the bishop?" he asked.

"Show him around the city, but have him decide where he wants to go. Let's find out what interests him. But above all, gain his trust. He's part of De Silva's plan."

"How do you know?"

"I know De Silva."

• • •

"GOOD MORNING, SIR." The military secretary smiled across his desk to Jacob Brigham.

"Is he in?"

"Yes, sir. He's expecting you," he answered, pressing the intercom button. "Mr. Brigham has arrived, General."

"Send him in."

Brigham entered De Silva's acre of office that overlooked Lima and, to the west, the shimmering Pacific.

"Good morning, Mr. Brigham." Benito inclined his head in respect.

"You know my aide, Benito Prado," De Silva reminded him.

Brigham did not look at Benito or acknowledge De Silva's comment. "I've confirmed I will be able to gain control of Mullen's master computer in several days. I'm here to learn where you are with your plans."

• • •

RAJUNT SMILED ACROSS the city, ignoring the shanty towns scattered atop the desert foothills to the northeast. For once, the *garúa*, the coastal fog, had not shrouded the city. A strong sea breeze swept away the smog and the city glittered in the sun like an Incan jewel.

Rajunt turned from the balcony and looked at his watch as Diego knocked. "Enter."

"Good morning, your Eminence."

"Where are you taking me?"

"Are there special places you want to see first?"

"No."

"Are you sure?" Diego stammered.

Rajunt stared without a word, waiting for Diego to offer some suggestions.

"People exploring Lima for the first time often begin with the Plaza de Armas, the heart of the old city. We could start there," Diego offered, frustrated that Rajunt had no ideas of his own.

Rajunt smiled. "We'll begin there."

Diego nodded.

The two left Rajunt's suite and headed down the steps of the hotel to an awaiting taxi.

"Plaza de Armas," Diego told the driver as Rajunt climbed in beside him.

Rajunt turned slowly to Diego as the taxi sped along the Avenida Arequipa, the central artery from Miraflores to Lima's old core. "I assume you brought enough money for the day. I don't often carry it myself."

"Of course, your Eminence." Diego said politely as he seethed. The money in his pocket had to last him the rest of the month.

Within minutes, the taxi pulled up to the enormous plaza, beside the baroque Government's Palace. In the center of the plaza, an old fountain sprayed mist from the mouths of metal animals.

Diego pointed to the palace as he paid their driver, "That is built on the old site of Pizarro's house."

"A man of noted accomplishment," Rajunt replied with disinterest, looking around for a new place to visit.

"Detractors say he was an illiterate pig farmer who commanded the one hundred seventy Spanish conquistadors that seized the Incan empire in 1532 with violence and treachery," Diego said smiling, barely able to contain his contempt for Rajunt. "He founded Lima in 1534."

"What's next?" Rajunt asked, obviously bored with Diego's first selection.

"Do you enjoy museums, your Eminence?"

"Depends on the museum, Diego," Rajunt answered as if the answer was self-evident.

"We could walk to the Museum of Anthropology and Archaeology, next to the Plaza Bolívar," Diego suggested.

"How far is it?"

"Only four blocks."

"Let's take a cab."

"It will be faster to walk, your Eminence."

"You lead," Rajunt acquiesced.

Fifteen minutes later, Diego was explaining the significance of the collection of pottery and textiles to pre-Incan Peru.

"You seem well versed in your people's history," Rajunt noted as he bent to stare at a display.

"I study history at the university," Diego answered as they entered a new hall with new exhibits.

Within seconds, Rajunt was staring aghast at the collection of stone idols from Chavín. "What are those?" His eyes had stuck to two particular pieces, both drinking vessels. The first was a couple locked in sexual ecstasy, the spout emerging from a ring on the man's back. The second was a grinning man, whose enormous erection served as the spout.

"Remnants of the Moche culture. Pre-Incan."

"Horrible," Rajunt was shaking his head, "horrible. These people should be glad we made them Christians."

"Some say the people suffered horribly under the Spanish theocracy." Diego could not contain himself. He knew too much.

"Lies," Rajunt huffed, but asked slowly, "What do they say?"

"The worst of it began around 1570 when Francisco de Toledo, Peru's fifth Spanish viceroy, established *reducciones*, forced resettlement of the Indians, to ensure their conversion to Christianity and to force them to provide everything from clothing, to food, to coca leaves for their conquerors.

"After the Spanish plundered the Incan tombs, they pursued mineral wealth and discovered the city of Potosí in what are now the highlands of Bolivia.

"Potosí has an elevation of over 13,000 feet. Its mines were economical only with slave labor, so De Toledo ordered thousands of Indians on annual marches into Potosí, where he would force them underground to work the mines. For every three Indians forced into the mines, only one would emerge alive.

"The mercury mines of nearby Huancavelica were even worse. Thousands of Indians died quite painfully in the earth from mercury sulphide, mercury poisoning, and arsenic.

"The only thing that would keep them working as long as they could were coca leaves, the Spanish cure for exhaustion and hunger. An enormous Spanish coca leaf trade developed just to keep the Indian miners on their feet. Nearly a hundred thousand baskets of coca were fed to them in one year alone.

"Sadly, the Holy Church encouraged the coca trade and collected a tithe from each basket of leaves."

"Lies," Rajunt responded.

"Of course, your Eminence. But that is what the historians lie about."

Rajunt walked from the Chavín collection. "Continue."

"In the 1560's, the Indians attempted to return to their own religion and incurred the fury of the Church, which decided to stamp it out once and for all. Priests spread through the countryside to make good the official crusade, torturing people in native villages to reveal the locations of their idols, their *huacas*."

"Were they successful?" Rajunt asked, looking at Diego from the corner of his eye.

"Yes, for the most part."

"Then it was worth it. The soul is much more important than the body."

"Such success may be transitory in that many of the old beliefs still persist," Diego countered.

Rajunt shook his head in disgust as they strolled to other exhibits, following the chronology presented by the displays. "People must be led from superstition to religion, against their will if necessary," he hissed.

Diego knew he had yet to capture Rajunt's confidence.

They walked in silence past several more displays until Rajunt turned to Diego. "I've had enough of this. What else should I see?"

"There is the Museum of the Inquisition across the street, heretics were tortured there. The underground dungeons and torture chambers are still intact," Diego answered.

"The good old days," Rajunt whispered to himself.

Diego forced himself to laugh and nod in agreement.

Rajunt suddenly looked to Diego as a comrade. "Come, my son. Let us dine together."

"Do you have a preference?"

"Italian. Something with a refined wine selection."

"The La Trattoria, but it is back in Miraflores." Diego thought of how far the money in his pocket must go. "Delightful but expensive, however."

"Fine," Rajunt answered as he began guiding Diego back to the museum's entrance. "You can hail the cab."

An old man, one of the many street vendors from the shanty towns, eager to feed his family, pushed his cart next to Rajunt as he and Diego waited for a passing taxi.

Holding a weather beaten hat to his chest, the old man hobbled to Rajunt with a hopeful smile, his old face deeply wrinkled. "*Señor*, would you care for a souvenir of Peru to take back to a loved one?" he asked in broken English, a question Diego knew must have been practiced repeatedly for the sake of survival.

Rajunt looked briefly at the old man in disgust. He quickly looked away, as if looking away would make the old man vanish.

"I'd like that paper weight," Diego said, pointing with one hand and digging deep into his pocket with the other for some money.

"Thank you," the old man said proudly, quickly handing him a sad little clump of clear plastic with the Peruvian flag molded inside.

• • •

THE PERIMETER GUARD radioed Sánchez instantly. "Captain, a man and an old woman are coming your way." He spoke softly, his face darkly painted to mimic the shadows of the jungle's underworld.

"Are they followed?" came Sánchez' static reply.

The guard raised his eyes above the underbrush and looked down the winding trail. "They're alone."

Sánchez pondered his next move. "Are they armed?"

"No."

"We'll take them from here." Sánchez motioned for his men to spread out. "Sergio, you take point."

Sergio moved quickly down the trail to intercept. He crouched low, holding his assault rifle ready.

João watched his brother Sergio disappear.

A quarter hour later, Sergio returned, following the two intruders with his rifle pointed at their backs.

Sánchez' eyes widened in disbelief. "Mother!"

The old woman ran for her son, grabbing him and holding to his waist, sobbing, her head on his chest.

Adolfo smiled demonically, despite the rifle at his back.

"Julio. Oh, Julio," she cried, shaking uncontrollably. "They're going to kill us all, I just know it."

Julio grabbed her gently, but forcefully, by the shoulders, holding her at arm's length. "Who, Mother? Who is going to kill us?"

"The *Sendero*."

A chill snaked down Julio's back. "You're safe now, Mother. I'm here."

The old woman turned and pointed at Adolfo. "He is *Sendero*."

Instantly, Sergio put his rifle to the back of Adolfo's head. "Let me kill him, Captain."

"NO!" The old woman screamed. "He carries a message from their leader. He has a radio on him that is switched on. She is listening."

"Who is listening, Mother?" Sánchez asked cautiously.

"Their leader," she sobbed. "She has your sisters. She will kill them if you do not do as she says."

Sánchez' men looked at one another then closed protectively around Sánchez and his mother.

Julio gently pushed his mother aside and stepped up to Adolfo. "Who are you?"

Adolfo held up his radio transmitter. "Did you hear that, María?" he asked with a sly smile.

"Yes. Let me speak with Captain Sánchez," came a crackled reply.

Adolfo handed his radio to Julio, who snapped it away. "Who are you?"

"The person holding your sisters, Julio Sánchez," María said his name slowly then paused, "all of your sisters. If my man does not return unharmed and you do not do exactly as I say, I will gut your sisters one by one, forcing each to watch until none remain."

Julio could hear her laughing.

"She means it, Julio. She means it," the old woman sobbed.

"Yes, Julio. I mean it," María crackled from afar.

"I'll get back to you," he answered sternly and snapped off the radio.

At the clearing, María laughed and handed her transmitter to Anita. "He'll call back."

"Mother, tell me exactly what happened," Julio ordered, trying to wipe her tears.

"We were eating when these horrid people kicked in the door and made us go with them. They forced us to walk for hours until we reached the *Sendero* camp."

"Did they blindfold you?" Julio asked, knowing, if not, the *Sendero* would kill them regardless.

The old woman nodded and continued hurriedly as if the speed of her words might save her daughters. "Their leader is a woman. She said some of her comrades are in prison and that they've nearly served their sentences. She wants you and your men to surrender so she can force their early release by trading you and your men. She will kill your sisters if you don't agree. She promised you would be unhurt. She promised, Julio, she promised."

"If that radio is off much longer, she'll kill them anyway," Adolfo said, still wearing his evil smile.

Julio stared at him with hatred for several seconds before looking back to his mother. "Mother, I can't."

She broke from the weight of life and fell to her knees, sobbing uncontrollably.

Sánchez' men looked at one another, their eyes communicating with one another.

João was the first to speak. "Captain, can we talk to you before you answer their leader?"

Julio shook his head resolutely. "There is nothing to discuss, João. We do not surrender to the *Sendero*. We will die first, all of us." Julio's heart ached at the sight of his mother sobbing at his feet, but his face was steel.

João looked to his brother, "Sergio, take your prisoner out of earshot. There may be another way."

Sergio shoved his rifle barrel hard into Adolfo's back, moving him along.

Adolfo grimaced from the pain and looked back at Sergio. "I will remember you for that. You will be mine." Adolfo didn't turn his face fast enough to avoid the butt of Sergio's gun smashing against his cheek.

"Move, *Sendero* pig."

• • •

FELIPE FROZE. HIS small brown hand lifted into the air, Michelle and Stauffen stopped moving.

Felipe's eyes were electric as he listened to the air. He turned to Stauffen. "We're being followed."

"Soldiers."

Stauffen and Michelle looked back through the morass of jungle they'd just come through, then looked to one another.

"How do you know, Felipe?" Michelle asked.

"The animals behind us are frightened. Can't you hear them?" Both shook their heads.

"They come, the soldiers." Felipe nodded knowingly. He turned to resume their journey but doubled his pace. Michelle and Stauffen hurried to keep up.

"Who are they?" Stauffen asked ahead to Felipe.

"A gift from Major Dos Santos, I suspect," Michelle answered.

"You've met the major?" Stauffen asked, brows arching.

"I forgot to mention that," Michelle said as she trudged along.

"Lovely man. Mr. Black Market. He'd sell his family to the devil if the price was right."

"That was my impression."

Felipe spun back without losing stride, a finger to his lips to quiet them.

•   •   •

THE PERIMETER GUARD never saw it coming. A quick hand to his mouth from behind, his head arched back, and a machete sliced across his throat. He slid to the ground.

Ernesto bent down and wiped the bloody blade across the guard's pant leg, nodding for the other *Sendero* to advance.

The jungle sky had darkened considerably in the last few moments. Nightfall was at hand.

Ernesto moved his people quietly on. He was the first to spot Adolfo standing in the trail ahead, guarded by a soldier. Adolfo spotted Ernesto at the same time and began arguing with Sergio to divert his attention.

"You'd better think twice about what you are doing," Adolfo advised Sergio.

"Shut up, *Sendero!*" He pointed his rifle between the guerilla's eyes.

"If you harm me, your captain's sisters get gutted," he laughed defiantly.

"I said shut up," Sergio repeated, unaware of Ernesto rising from the bushes behind him.

Ernesto's gun butt crashed against Sergio's skull, dropping him to the ground.

"Tie him," Ernesto whispered to the *Sendero* coming up beside them. He turned back to Adolfo. "How many are there?"

"Eight, but there is also a guard. You had to have seen him," Adolfo said. He saw from Ernesto's face that the guard was dead. He smiled.

"Where are they?" Ernesto whispered.

"Forty paces up the trail," Adolfo returned the whisper. "You'll hear them talking when you get close."

The *Sendero* moved toward the soldiers like shadows through the night.

"Captain, why not try? We might be able to save your sisters." One young soldier asked.

Sánchez shook his head. "There is no point in discussing the matter. I know the *Sendero*, so do you."

"Julio, please listen to your men!" The old woman clung to her son's leg, still sobbing. "They are your sisters. You are their only brother!"

Ernesto's group could hear the old woman wailing. "I'll take out the captain. When I do, that's the signal." One hand pointed one way and the other pointed another, splitting the group in two as they slid through the jungle's dark undergrowth, encircling the soldiers. Each carried a blow tube loaded with a dart dipped in borrachero root. Ernesto carried his tight to his chest.

• • •

"WHERE DID YOU meet?" Manuel asked.

"On the streets of Lima, although Carlota was from Villa Del Mar, one of the *pueblos jóvenes* outside Lima," Angelica answered, glancing to Carlota with sadness. "The first time I saw Carlota, a group of street boys were trying to rape her."

"Angelica backed them down with a knife," Carlota laughed. "We have been together since then. Angelica went to work for one of the central Lima banks and rose to the top. She's a natural with money. She has been an executive vice president for the last six years," she said proudly.

"Did you work before you joined John Mullen's endeavor?" Manuel asked Carlota.

"Carlota is an artist, she has been for years," Angelica answered for Carlota. "Beautiful watercolors."

"I have dozens in the basement." Carlota shrugged, "They don't sell well."

"They are precious works of art, nevertheless," Angelica insisted. "Would you like to see them?" she asked Manuel.

"Absolutely."

"Come." She stood, motioning for Manuel to follow.

"Angelica, he is our guest. Show some mercy," Carlota chided.

"Come." Angelica motioned again until Manuel rose from the table.

They looked down to Carlota who remained seated. "Aren't you coming?" Angelica asked.

Carlota patted her belly. "No. Those stairs would seem like a mountain. I'll stay here."

"We won't be long," Angelica led Manuel from the dining room until they stood at the top of stairs leading to a basement. "I keep them down here," she said, switching on the lights below.

Once they reached the bottom, Angelica switched on another light. Dozens of unframed paintings lined the wall. Some large, some small.

Manuel stood mesmerized, staring at them. He had been trained to appreciate art from his childhood. This he had never seen. Instantly, he knew what he saw was the world through the eyes of God.

• • •

THE BAMBOO TUBE slid silently through the leaves, aimed at Sánchez. The day's light was nearly gone.

"We do not surrender to *Sendero*. End discussion," Julio said angrily to João. His mother's pleading eyes haunted his decision.

More bamboo tips slid silently into position, picking their targets.

"But . . . ," João protested.

"I said," Sánchez slapped his neck at a sudden sting, "end discussion." His fingers grabbled for the insect stinging his neck. When he held the dart up to his eyes, his mind registered what had happened. "*Sendero*," he muttered incoherently and fell face first onto the ground.

Unable to see the dart in the fading light, Sánchez' men stood confused as he fell.

A series of quick puffing sounds and irritating stings followed. Within seconds, the old woman was the only one conscious. She stared up as Ernesto emerged from the dark jungle into the tiny clearing.

Her eyes widened as he raised the .45 between them. The last vision of her life was Ernesto's smile in the dark before he pulled the trigger.

• • •

BERNADINE PULLED THE covers snugly to his chin. Black darkness coated his bedroom. "Socrates?"

"Yes."

"What time is it?"

"Three a.m."

"John's not awake is he?"

"Yes, he is."

"May I speak with him?"

"One moment," Socrates answered.

"John."

Two hundred feet of solid granite below, John opened his eyes. He lay in bed, unable to sleep. "Yes, Socrates."

"Father Bernadine is asking to speak with you."

"Patch him in," John said, adjusting his pillow. "Ross?"

"John?"

"Yes."

"Can I talk to you?"

"Of course. I apologize if I've been neglecting you. Things have been hectic."

Bernadine nodded in the dark. "I know. I'm sorry to disturb you."

"No bother, Ross."

Bernadine hesitated but continued determinedly. "Do you mind if I ask you some personal questions?"

"No."

"Do you ever think about death?"

John laughed, "At our ages, it's difficult to avoid thinking about it, Ross." He paused, "Michelle told you I'm dying, didn't she?"

A long pause followed. "Yes."

"Yes, I think about death," John answered matter-of-factly.

"So do I."

John could hear pain line the voice of this companion who stood with him at the shores of oblivion, which each would soon enter. "What do you think about death?" he turned the question on Bernadine.

"It frightens me. It should not, what with my beliefs, but it does."

"What frightens you?"

"The unknown, I guess. I believe it is the gateway to God but I realize mine are beliefs, not knowledge." Bernadine's answer was almost whispered.

Socrates amplified Bernadine's voice for John.

John lay thinking for a moment. "A little loss of faith, Ross?"

"Yes," came a whispered reply.

"Your fear seems natural. We often fear what we do not understand, especially when the stakes are high, as they are with death." John sought to comfort him, "But have you ever feared something and discovered it to be delightful?"

Bernadine thought back through his life. "Well, yes," he chuckled to himself, "but on the other hand, I have feared things only to discover my fear should have been greater. But your point is taken."

"For you it must be a matter of faith, I suppose," John answered.

Several minutes of silence passed.

"But what do you think death is?" Bernadine asked softly.

"I don't know what it is, only that it brings an end to human motion."

Several more minutes of silence passed.

"But do you fear it?" Bernadine asked.

"It irritates me more than frightens me, but yes, I have fear."

"What irritates you about it?"

"I'm not ready to go."

Bernadine chuckled, "Nor am I."

"But what I most fear of death is that it will eventually claim those I love," John said slowly, "and I am powerless to stop it. We each face death alone."

"You're never alone with God, John."

"I don't believe in your god, Ross."

"Why not?"

"I see no basis to. I don't believe there are such things as gods, except as we create them for our own purpose. For me, such labels are barometers of human ignorance."

"What do you mean?"

"We had fire gods until we learned about fire. We had sea gods until we learned about the sea. Now we have a universal god, who may vanish when we understand the universe.

"But beyond that, the history of gods seems more a history of people who say they speak for their god, demanding obedience from others, and in the final analysis there is no place for reasoned dialogue in the world of their gods." John paused, "What is religion without coercion?"

"No religion?" Bernadine laughed.

John chuckled quietly, "Religious leaders seem addicted to power, Ross, like a drug. As long as they believe they speak for a god, they feel powerful."

"Then why have you done what you've done?" Bernadine asked.

"Cloning your Savior?"

"Do you expect him to raise you from the dead at some point?" Bernadine wondered aloud. "Or heal your illness?"

John laughed coldly. "No, I accept my ending."

"Then why?"

"Five hundred years before the birth of your Christ, people asked Buddha if he was a god. He answered no. An angel, they asked. No. A saint? And again, Buddha answered no. Well, what are you they asked. Do you know his reply, Ross?"

"Yes," Bernadine said, "He answered, 'I am awake.'"

John nodded in the darkness and smiled.

"You intend to awaken the world with my god, don't you. A god you don't believe in."

Several minutes passed in the darkness.

John smiled to himself within his granite tomb. "Yes."

"But why my god?"

"He's the only one I could clone." John laughed and adjusted his pillows, "But importantly, I agree with his central human principle."

"Which is?"

"Treat others as you want to be treated. He elevated compassion to a primary value. If the world took that to heart then war and economic oppression might subside enough that we could get to our business at hand—life." John stared through the darkness, through a tunnel of time, through images of war and famine. "Imagine if the world believed Christ again walked among them, treating them as kindly or as harshly as they treat others. People could awaken and the world could change," John paused, "if the governments of the world allow him to live."

Bernadine laid quietly in the darkness, his mind moving thoughts against one another like a giant jig-saw puzzle, slowly fitting them together until the destiny Mullen had prepared for humanity became visible. He smiled at last.

John waited for a response.

None came.

• • •

"FATHER RIVERA!" ANGELICA exclaimed gently as she gestured for him and Janice McClain to step into her home.

The morning sun was midway to its noonday zenith.

Rivera smiled politely, eager to deliver Sunday Mass for these obviously rich *Limeños* and return to the people of the shanty towns. The several hundred American dollars Janice McClain had handed him for the task would feed many children. "You are Angelica?"

"Yes, let me call Carlota." Angelica turned and hollered for her. "We've been watching you on television, Father. Do you know you are showing up on sets all over the world? It is so kind of you to come up to the house to say Mass for us."

Rivera nodded politely, unaware of his global celebrity. He looked at Carlota as she stepped into the room.

His world stopped. Matter and energy transposed. An aura of golden light bathed the woman entering the room. He looked about as if the others were so blind they could not see it.

Carlota stepped forward and extended her hand. "Father Rivera, it is an honor."

Rivera stared at her for a moment then fell to his knees. "Mother of God. Bless me with your grace."

"I love her Father, but she's no angel." Angelica smiled politely at the priest.

Rivera looked aghast at her. "She is more than an angel."

Angelica and Manuel looked to one another and then to this stranger leading them from ignorance. Janice McClain stared deliberately at them all.

Carlota reached across her stomach, extending both hands to Rivera. "Please rise."

● ● ●

JOÃO FELT THE morning sun warming his face. He opened his eyes slowly, facing the sky. He tried to move but his wrists and ankles were bound. He raised his head and looked around.

He had been stripped and staked spread-eagled. He glanced to his left. Sergio, too, was staked out, staring at him, his eyes electric with fear.

"The beauty has awakened. That makes everyone," María noted, standing above him.

João looked up to her silhouette. The sun sat on her shoulder, blinding him. He looked around. He and his comrades lay staked out in a line like a collection of butterflies, stripped naked and spread-eagled in the morning sun. He arched back his head.

Their uniforms were piled behind them.

Armed *Sendero* surrounded them, smiling.

Sánchez lay to his right, staring at the sky, tears sliding from the corners of his eyes.

"Captain?" João whispered.

Sánchez refused to look at the men he had failed.

"Captain, your men are calling you." María laughed. "Aren't you going to answer, to tell them what to do now."

Anita stood quietly, studying María.

"One thing you will learn, Captain, is to answer me." María stepped between his widespread legs and stared down at him. "I said your men are calling, aren't you going to tell them what to do?"

Sánchez remained stone silent.

"Do you want your sisters brought out to watch?" María asked softly. "Could they loosen your tongue?"

Sánchez glared up at her. "Kill us if you're going to kill us."

"It won't be that easy." She turned to Fëdor, "Which one do you want?"

Fëdor smiled at his reward. He began with Sergio and walked slowly past the soldiers, studying them. Their eyes followed him. He turned and pointed to Sánchez. "Him."

The old woman with missing teeth stepped forward and interrupted the silence. "I want him," she insisted, pointing at Sánchez.

"Fëdor gets first pick," María answered.

Fëdor sneered tauntingly at the old woman.

"Why do you want him?" María asked the old woman.

"His father killed my husband."

"Fëdor, can't you give an old woman her wish?"

"No, I want him," Fëdor said. He joined María between Sánchez' wide spread legs.

María turned to the old woman. "Pick another."

The old woman glared at Fëdor but began inspecting the row of immobilized soldiers.

João watched her march past their feet like a general inspecting troops. She stopped in front of him, leaning forward, studying him. She turned back to María, pointing down to him without a word.

"The pretty one?" María laughed. "Why him?"

The old woman kneeled between João's wide splayed legs. Her rough calloused hands traveled along his thighs and stomach.

João closed his eyes. The old woman was smiling. "Soft skin. Soft skin," she rasped.

"She collects hides," María announced as if bored, looking over to Anita. "She likes to skin her prisoners alive."

João's eyes snapped open.

María looked around. "The rest of you. Pick one. Some may have to share." She looked over to Anita. "Which one do you want to kill?"

Anita shook her head, repelled by useless cruelty.

"None?" María asked with surprise.

Anita shook her head again.

Sergio stared desperately at his brother, "João?"

João only stared at the sky.

Sergio felt warm breath on his neck and looked back.

"Remember me?" Adolfo's face, still bloodied from the butt of Sergio's gun, floated inches away. "You are mine."

Sergio closed his eyes and prepared for the worst.

Ten feet beyond Sergio's head, a large leaf eased slowly back into place. Hector and Antonio looked at one another, safe within the protective cover of dense undergrowth.

Antonio leaned over cautiously, his lips against Hector's ear. "We have to save them. I know how they're suffering," he whispered as quietly as possible.

Hector leaned back to Antonio, whispering, "If you want to save your friend, we can do nothing for those soldiers. See the *Sendero*? They are armed. We are not."

"We have to do something. I have to try," Antonio whispered back.

"Nothing can be done for them," Hector repeated slowly with irritation. "They are already dead."

"We'll see." Antonio carefully repositioned the large leaf to watch the *Sendero*.

María was enjoying herself. "Captain, you never answered me. What are you going to tell your men? They need to know what to do. They are here because you are such an able commander." She laughed cruelly.

Sánchez wished he was dead.

"We don't have time for this," Anita said.

María's head snapped toward Anita, her eyes probing the sudden insubordination. Anita held her gaze.

"What?"

"We don't have time for this."

María glared, daring Anita not to avert her eyes.

Anita glared back. "We need to get to Lima. Are you forgetting Carlota Cabral, the Madonna?"

Anita's pronouncement unleased a flood of adrenaline in Antonio; his eyes narrowed suddenly. He turned to Hector, whispering harshly, "We have to do something."

"You are going to get us killed," Hector snapped a whispered warning and put his finger to Antonio's lips.

María turned to Fëdor, "Unfortunately, she's right. Go to my quarters and bring me the money briefcase."

Fëdor left and quickly returned with a rain-tortured leather briefcase in hand.

María glanced down at her prisoners then up at the morning sun. Her decisions were final. "Old woman. You come with me."

The old woman looked up from between João's legs, snarling one side of her lip like an old mongrel protecting its food. "Why?"

João felt her dirty nails rake his lower belly.

María gave no answer.

"At least let me skin him first. His skin is so soft."

João held his breath.

María glared until the old woman rose to join her. María handed her the briefcase. "Carry this."

"When will you return?" Fëdor asked.

"I don't know," María answered. She raised her voice to all the Sendero, "I will be gone. Fëdor will be in command until I return."

Fëdor looked at his comrades with glee. The Sendero glanced disapprovingly at one another.

María caught their looks. "Questions?" Her dark eyes probed each of her charges.

None responded.

She nodded with finality and turned, walking away from the soldiers, out of earshot. Fëdor, Anita, and the old woman walked beside her. The old woman carried the briefcase squeezed to her chest.

"Listen to me very carefully, Fëdor. These are my instructions. The soldiers are not to be harmed until nightfall. I want them to suffer all day in the sun then you can do with them what you will."

Fëdor's face brightened.

"Except for Sánchez. He is to watch his men die." She stopped walking and faced Fëdor. "I trust you will make their deaths as painful as possible."

He nodded quickly.

"But Sánchez must be left alive."

Fëdor's face darkened.

"Nothing could be worse for him than to lead his men to their doom and be the only one to survive. Nothing could bring more dishonor. Death is a pleasure I will deny him." María explained patiently to her lover.

"The *federale* pig is to escape unharmed?" Fëdor asked, his voice pleading for something.

María thought for a second. "You may castrate him," she said, tossing him a bone. "But much more important than that, Fëdor. . . ."

He hung on her every word.

"I am leaving these people under your command. When I return, I still better have sixteen obedient people." She leaned into his face. "Do you understand?"

He stared back.

"If not, you will suffer Sánchez' fate."

Fëdor swallowed hard and nodded.

María turned to Anita and the old woman. "Let's go."

● ● ●

FELIPE FROZE, HIS eyes and ears exploring the night jungle around them. He was leading Michelle and Stauffen back to the *Sendero* camp the same way he had come with Stauffen to avoid the trail guards.

"What is it?" Michelle whispered, her eyes enlarging.

He put his finger to his lips and studied the dark jungle behind them, listening to distant crying night birds. "Do you see the main trail?" He pointed to the west.

Michelle strained to see anything. She shook her head.

"About a hundred meters to the side." He motioned them down. "Someone is coming."

All three huddled down, waiting in silence.

"What about Dos Santos' soldiers behind us, won't they catch up?" Stauffen asked Felipe, whispering over Michelle's shoulder.

Felipe glanced back at Michelle. "They can follow but with difficulty," he said in a hushed tone.

Michelle's expression never changed. Her thoughts were on Antonio. She just nodded.

They sat quietly for five minutes. Suddenly Michelle and Stauffen could hear what Felipe had detected earlier.

"Not so fast, old woman," María hollered ahead.

The old woman looked back, still irritated with losing such a soft hide, but waited for María and Anita to catch up. She resumed her pace when they did.

Felipe watched the three march toward Iquitos until the night jungle swallowed them whole.

"Will the soldiers see them?" Michelle asked hopefully.

"No. We're going in another way and the soldiers will follow us. The soldiers won't see them."

• • •

"YOU WOULD GIVE them hope," Father Rivera explained to Carlota. Lima glittered brightly in the morning sun.

Carlota glanced to Angelica and Manuel then looked back to Rivera. Janice McClain stood mutely looking out the window.

"I think it's too dangerous," Angelica intervened.

"So do I." Manuel stepped forward.

Carlota smiled gently at both. "There is no danger. This is the intended way." She turned back to Rivera. "I will go with you when you speak to the people this morning."

"Thank you." He bowed to her. "You bless us by your presence." He turned to McClain. "Will you drive us to my preaching hill?"

McClain turned to Angelica, who nodded, her face cloaked with apprehension. "Of course, Father."

"May I use your telephone?" Rivera asked Carlota.

"Certainly, Father."

Rivera picked up the phone and was speaking within seconds. "This is Father Rivera. Spread the word that today I introduce the people to the Holy Mother, she who carries the Messiah." He paused. "I know, but I will delay my sermon for two hours, that should give you time," he explained to the voice on the other end.

• • •

JOHN EASED SLOWLY onto the deep cushions of the chair behind his desk. He closed his eyes to think, leaning back.

"John," Socrates said softly.

Tired gray eyes opened. "Yes, Socrates," John breathed deeply.

"Your temperature has begun to elevate slightly and your pulse is becoming irregular. Would you like me to contact Dr. Groussman?"

"No."

"How are you feeling?"

"Fine."

"I'm delighted to hear that. May I speak now with you on an issue about which you may become emotional?"

"Sure, what's it about?" John asked.

"Mr. Brigham."

"What about Jacob?"

"He concerns me."

"Why?" John asked.

"I am uncertain. However, my intuiting program identifies him as a hostile."

John bristled at the assault on his best friend. He thought back to Sarah's death, to the collapse of his world. It was Jacob who had carried him through those first horrible years. Jacob was always there when John needed him. Jacob was his stalwart friend. "*Jacob would never hurt me*," he thought to himself. "Such conclusion is invalid," he announced.

Socrates made no response.

"Discontinue thinking alone those lines, Socrates." John said. His trust in Jacob was unshakable.

"I am unable to do that, John. I can only discontinue reporting my concerns.

"Then do so."

• • •

THE WORD HAD spread across Peru.

An excited crowd was already three times its usual size. A sea of people still marched out of Lima, hurrying toward the hill where Rivera preached. Television cameras punctuated the hill from top to bottom. CNN had set up at the top.

Janice McClain was nervous. She had never seen so many people. She feared running over someone as the Mercedes eked through the crowd. With Father Rivera sitting on the hood of the car and waving to the people, the crowd slowly parted ahead of them.

"We are blessed this day," Rivera keep repeating, smiling triumphantly, delirious with joy.

Carlota gazed out the window like a child, mesmerized by the crowd.

Angelica and Manuel stared at one another, knowing they had no control of events.

An hour passed before they finally made it to the base of Rivera's preaching hill. McClain stopped the car. "Now what? Carlota is in no condition to walk to the top."

An ocean of people surrounded the car, peering inside.

Rivera turned. Balancing himself, he stood atop the center of the hood. McClain closed her eyes and wondered how much the repaint would cost.

"Brothers and sisters!" Rivera shouted.

The entire crowd quickly came to a halt and hushed, hanging on his words.

"We need a path to the top. Please." He sat back on the hood and looked around to McClain, motioning her on.

McClain rolled her eyes, put the car in gear, and turned the steering wheel to the right. Like a great tank, her old Mercedes left the road, dipped into the ditch and climbed out with ease.

Rivera's arms were widespread and the crowd parted like the Red Sea. The Mercedes commenced the steep climb.

Five minutes later, they crested the hill. Television reporters scrambled for the front row, pushing children out of their way as Rivera stood back up on the hood to make his announcement.

He raised his arms high. The giant crowd's murmur receded into silence. "This day begins our deliverance. This day we gaze upon the Holy Mother herself, she who carries the Messiah."

No one moved or stirred.

Rivera jumped down and made his way to Carlota's door, opening it for her and gently pushing people back. Carlota looked out at him. He saw apprehension in her eyes. "You are blessed. Fear nothing, Holy Mother." Rivera held out his hand until she took it and stepped from the car.

Tears of joy misted Rivera's eyes as he knelt before her, raising his arms high. The crowd instantly kneeled behind him.

"Father, Lord on High, you have heard your people's cries of anguish, the cries of the poor, the oppressed," Rivera began.

The reporters pushed their way forward, microphones held near him with extenders.

"We receive the Holy Mother with your blessing. Protect her and watch over her from all harm. We, the poor of the earth, are your people, Lord God. Our prayers of thanksgiving and joy begin this day. The Messiah is at hand." Rivera stood and faced the crowd. "This is your Holy Mother." He looked back to Carlota and knelt again before her.

Carlota looked down upon the sea of people kneeling before her. Hundreds of thousands of faces stared back in awe.

She raised her hands for them to stand.

Cries of joy exploded from the crowd as it rose to its feet. The roar rumbled into Lima. Carlota smiled, inclined her head in respect, and waded into the crowd.

Angelica bolted from the car. "Carlota, no!"

The crowd was too thick to move through and too filled with shouts of joy for Angelica's calls to be heard. Even Rivera lost sight of Carlota as she joined the throng.

Carlota had never been happier. These were her people. She loved them with all her heart and they knew it. Although they crowded to be near her, she was never touched. No matter where she walked, people pulled back to give her room. Their faces glowed with new visions. To touch anyone, she had to reach out. When she did, they wept with joy.

Angelica finally made it to Rivera, who put his hand gently against her, impeding her movement. "She is fine. No one will harm her. She is beloved."

A lone hostile figure eyed Carlota like prey. Then Marta suddenly lost sight of her and shoved through the crowd, toward the center of excitement. After several minutes, she could again see Carlota's face through the bobbing heads. Marta pushed ahead harder.

Suddenly, Carlota stopped and turned her head toward Marta, looking through the crowd, gazing at her.

Marta stopped advancing. The two stared until Marta finally withdrew.

Carlota returned slowly to the car.

• • •

QUARTERS WERE CRAMPED in the tiny charter plane sitting at the end of the runway in Iquitos. A single propeller spun wildly in front. The engine's drone saturated the air.

The pilot, who had not shaved or showered in days, sat studying the gauges, a cigarette stuck to his lower lip. White smoke rolled into the back.

"Do you have to smoke?" Anita shouted over the drone, trying to catch her breath in the heat and humidity of the tiny enclosed cabin. The equatorial sun seared through the plexiglass windows.

The pilot turned back and blew a cloud of smoke into Anita's face. The old woman sitting to his right laughed.

"Put it out," María ordered casually, counting the money in the briefcase.

The pilot quickly complied, looking back to the gauges and picking up his radio.

Anita could not hear what he was saying because of the engine's roar. The plane began to roll. She turned toward María, shouting, "Where did you get the money?"

"Coca cash," María shouted back. She raised a handful of bills, smiling broadly.

Suddenly, the engine groaned loudly and the plane picked up speed. Around 60 miles an hour, the wheels began to shake violently.

Anita held onto the back of the pilot's seat with white knuckles. María continued counting her money.

After 300 yards of runway, the shaking finally stopped. The plane struggled into the air.

The first few hours of flying carried them several hundred feet over the jungle, following the Ucayali, the Amazon's major tributary of the area.

Anita watched the world roll slowly beneath her as they followed the river. Her head throbbed from the engine's drone. Nausea clung to her stomach. The back of her throat felt tight.

The Andes Mountains rose like malevolent giants on the western horizon. Anita pointed to them. "How do we get across those?" she shouted to María.

"It won't be easy." María laughed, enjoying Anita's fear. "We start climbing around Pucallpa," she shouted back. "By the time we reach Belognesi we should be high enough to make it through the passes."

The sun rested atop the Andes' jagged peaks by the time they reached Pucallpa.

• • •

"JOHN," SOCRATES SAID.

John smiled to Bernadine. "Excuse me." They had spent the afternoon talking in his study. "Yes, Socrates."

The giant screen on the far wall snapped on. From the viewpoint of the reporter, everything was pandemonium. There, through the powerful telescopic lens of a television camera, was Carlota, smiling and waving to a sea of people. Hundreds of thousands.

John closed his eyes and slowly shook his head.

Bernadine beamed a smile from ear to ear.

• • •

"'TRUST ME' YOU said! 'I have it under control,' you said!" De Silva screamed at Brigham.

Benito backed away from the two.

"Look at that!" The general jabbed a fat finger toward the television. Froth gathered at the corners of his mouth.

The veins along Brigham's temples swelled. "I hope you don't think you're talking to me like that." He glared at the general.

"I'll talk to you anyway I want!" De Silva screamed louder.

"What is your problem, General?" Brigham despised the illogic of panic.

"Are you blind, American?" The general began jabbing at the set again. He spun toward Benito. "Turn that off!" His head seemed ready to explode. He spun back toward Brigham.

"Explain your problem," Brigham said with the tone he used on junior executives.

"My problem? The problem is the people. Did you see that crowd? They will follow her to the ends of the earth. We have lost control. The people do not yet realize it, but the *Sendero* will! We are doomed."

"Can you remain conversational if I speak freely?" Brigham asked contemptuously.

"Speak." De Silva's face had acquired a purple tone.

"You panic too quickly. That," Brigham pointed to the blank screen, "is precisely what we do need." He wondered what it took to rise through the Peruvian military. "Let me ask you this, if no one cared about that woman, would it matter how she died?"

De Silva stood mute.

"Answer my question," Brigham said, casually crossing one leg over the other.

Benito backed away even more. No one talked to De Silva like that and lived for long.

"No." The general accepted Brigham's lead.

"In fact," Brigham paused, "the greater the crowds, the more the hatred for the *Sendero* when the people think they killed her."

Puzzlement suddenly clouded Benito's face.

De Silva caught his look and turned on him. "Leave the room," De Silva ordered, saying nothing until Benito had closed the door behind him. "He doesn't know. None of my aides do." De Silva warned Brigham.

"That's your problem," Brigham said and continued, "When your special forces kill that woman, the larger the crowd, the better—so long as the crowd believes the *Sendero* killed her—right?"

De Silva sucked in his belly and sat back at his desk. "You are right." He began to relax. "But in South America, large crowds are dangerous. They breed unrest."

Brigham leaned forward in his chair. "Don't ever talk to me like that again."

De Silva glared at Brigham for his tone.

Brigham defiantly shoved his face even closer. "Before this is over, I'll make you the most powerful man in Peru." Brigham paused, "If you do exactly as I say."

"No one is more powerful than the Presidénte."

"My word is gold, General. I'll have control of Mullen's computer in two days. That is when we strike and strike fast."

The two stared at one another. A smile crept across De Silva's pudgy face.

• • •

"HERESY!" RAJUNT SCREAMED at Diego while staring dumbfounded at the evening news on the television. He pointed to the ocean of people surrounding Carlota.

Diego leaned closer to the screen, studying the face of the Madonna.

• • •

FELIPE MOTIONED THEM back down.

"What is it?" Michelle asked with a whisper.

"You and Ray stay here." He looked at Ray. "I am going ahead to check."

"Check what?" She whispered again.

"The *Sendero* camp is close now."

Michelle tensed. "Let us go with you." Antonio occupied her every thought.

He shook his head quickly. "No. You would give away our position."

"I would not," she insisted.

He smiled forgivingly to her. "You could not help it because you walk so loudly."

Michelle looked to Stauffen in desperation.

"We both do." He put his hand on her shoulder. "Let him do his job."

Felipe's eyes gleamed with inspiration toward her. "I have a plan."

"What?" she asked quickly.

"Stay here," Felipe said, disappearing into the brush.

"What about the soldiers following us?" Michelle tried to ask, but it was too late. Felipe had vanished.

• • •

"JOÃO, WHAT ARE they going to do to us?" Sergio whispered. Even with dark brown skin, his face had burnt and his lips had cracked after all day under the equatorial sun.

The *Sendero* had gathered near the newly lit campfire, laughing among themselves. Some glanced occasionally toward the prisoners.

João refused to look at his brother. "I don't know, Sergio," he answered, staring skyward blankly.

"Oh God, I'm scared, João," Sergio cried softly.

João turned his head to the right. Sánchez was staring skyward, his jaw muscles tensed as he gritted his teeth.

João caught movement out of the corner of his eye and looked up.

Fëdor stood between Sánchez' legs. "Sánchez." He kicked Sánchez' foot. "Which of your sisters is best?"

Sánchez's skyward gaze turned toward Fëdor. "Don't," he begged.

Fëdor brayed with laughter as he turned to a subordinate. "Bring me the youngest." The *Sendero* headed for the tin hut.

Sánchez closed his eyes as tears began to well. His youngest sister's screams pried them open.

The subordinate pushed her toward Fëdor.

"What is your name?" Fëdor asked. The young woman stared down to her brother. Sánchez refused to look at her.

"I said, what is your name?" Fëdor said, slowly pulling off his sweaty t-shirt.

"Isadora," she answered, trembling.

"Julio says you are better in bed than your sisters." Fëdor said.

Isadora stared down at her brother, averting her eyes from his naked groin. "Julio?" she whimpered.

Sánchez' eyes remained fixed to the sky.

Fëdor grabbed her. "Let's see if he lied."

Sánchez lifted his head. "Keep your stinking *Sendero* hands off my sister!"

Fëdor released the woman and returned to Sánchez, kneeling down to him. He balled up his t-shirt and pried open Sánchez' mouth, stuffing the cloth inside, its corners hanging from Sánchez' lips.

"I'll leave that there until after I cut off your balls, *federale* pig," Fëdor smirked.

Sánchez screamed at him but the cloth muffled his cries into an incoherent gurgle. Fëdor disappeared from sight, dragging his sister.

From the protective cocoon of underbrush, Antonio watched Fëdor and the young woman disappear into the jungle on the other side of the clearing. Then Isadora began to scream.

Fifteen minutes later, Fëdor dragged her back into the clearing as she tried holding what remained of her dress to the front of her body. "Sánchez!" Fëdor shouted, laughing, "you lied. All she did was lay there." He pushed her toward a nearby *Sendero*. "Take her back and bring me the next."

Fëdor strutted back to Sánchez, determined to increase his misery. "She didn't know how to use her mouth." He winked at Sánchez, "Maybe the next will train easier."

Sánchez screamed through his gag.

Moments later, Fëdor disappeared back into the jungle with another sister. More screams and the sharp recoil of hard slaps followed.

Fëdor emerged twenty minutes later, pulling the woman out by the hair and shoving her to a *Sendero*. "Bring me the next one." As he waited, he strolled back to Sánchez to give a report. "She took some disciplining but I taught her how to suck," he said in guttural Spanish.

Sánchez raised his head. His eyes were crazed as he screamed into Fëdor's crumpled t-shirt.

"Keep up that noise and I will make her practice on you while everyone watches," Fëdor warned ominously.

Sánchez quieted and dropped his head to the earth, tears rolling down his cheeks. He heard more struggles but refused to open his eyes.

"She's too ugly!" Fëdor screamed and threw the third sister back at the *Sendero* who had brought her. "You take her. Bring me the next."

Hell on earth came to have new meaning as Sánchez listened to his sister's screams. Suddenly the screams stopped and all the *Sendero* began laughing.

Sánchez raised his head reluctantly. Tears clouded his vision. His third sister was on her hands and knees near the campfire. A pantless *Sendero* knelt behind her while one knelt in front. Their white hips began thrusting violently.

Fëdor stood next to them with Sánchez' fourth sister, laughing and pointing down as if lecturing her on fine points. She had buried her face in her hands, sobbing.

Sánchez dropped his head to the earth again when Fëdor dragged his sister into the jungle. The harder she fought, the louder he laughed.

João raised his head to watch. He detected something moving in the bushes near Fëdor, on the far side of the clearing. "Captain!" he whispered sharply.

Sánchez looked over, the gag filling his mouth, his eyes red with tears.

"Look!" João whispered, directing Sánchez with his eyes until Sánchez followed his line of sight.

Sánchez saw nothing until the flames in the campfire surged for an instant. There. Through the murk of flame light and shadows, he saw it too. The bushes near Fëdor trembled slightly.

Hidden behind the row of staked men, Hector leaned into Antonio's ear. "Stay here," he whispered and began backing away like a receding shadow.

Antonio grabbed his arm. "Where are you going?" he whispered.

"We've got company." Hector pointed to the dark shadows a few feet from where Fëdor and the woman had vanished into the jungle.

Antonio studied the shadows. "I don't see anything!"

"Someone is there. I think he is signalling us," Hector whispered back.

"Someone sees us?"

Hector began smiling. "Only one person could see us."

Antonio looked toward the shadowed area. "Who?" He looked back when there was no answer. Hector had gone.

• • •

THE TINY PLANE bounced onto the Lima runway and taxied through the night toward a decrepit hangar, the pilot chattering with the tower.

Marta stood in the shadows as the plane rolled to a stop beneath a single lamp. She stepped into the circle of light when the pilot cut the engine.

Anita felt the tooth that had chipped when they touched down. She glared at the pilot's back.

María was the first out. She hugged Marta warmly, "Marta."

"María."

The scene reminded Anita of black-and-white newsreel clips of Hitler greeting Mussolini. But Hitler never carried a briefcase full of cash.

The two women kissed one another's cheeks then held themselves at arm's length, staring at one another with broad smiles.

They ignored Anita as she walked up to them. The old woman was talking with the pilot.

"Have you seen her?" Marta asked.

"Seen who?" María answered.

"The Madonna, Carlota Cabral! She was on television. She is here in Miraflores!" Marta exclaimed. "We can take her out whenever we want."

"Good." María nodded, locking her arm in Marta's, moving them both away from the plane. "You have a car?"

"A pickup. Right outside the hangar. But," Marta glanced back to Anita and the old woman, "there isn't room up front for these two, they'll have to sit in the back."

"They won't mind." María shrugged.

"I'm taking you to my apartment. Tomorrow, we start planning how to kill the Madonna and have people blame the *federales.*"

"I have some ideas," María answered. She gestured over her shoulder toward Anita. "She will go see Cabral tomorrow morning. First thing."

"Why?" Anita knew María was playing her as a pawn.

"Because I order you," María answered, getting into the cab without looking back.

The night ride into Lima was nearly as jarring as the landing. The shocks on the back of the pickup were shot. Anita sat in one corner, her back against the cab. As they drove, the wind swirled debris from the bed into her face. The old woman sat in the bed's far corner, smiling at Anita's misery.

Anita looked down to the Rimac river as they passed over it. It was a dark vein through the city's lights.

By the time Marta pulled up to her apartment building, the wind had rearranged Anita's hair so it stuck straight up. Marta and María laughed at her and headed up the stairs. Anita glared at their backs as she followed.

Diego opened the door when the four women reached the top landing. He looked at Anita's whirlwind hair and smiled. She glared at him worse than she had glared at Marta and María.

"Lima, at last." María dropped into a chair and rested the briefcase between her legs.

"Tonight, you rest. You can have my bed," Marta said. "The others will have to sleep on the floor. Diego, you stay here tonight. Take care of them."

He nodded and looked to Anita, who was shoving her hair back into place.

"Where are you staying?" María asked Marta.

"Benito Prado is an assistant to General De Silva. I'll spend the night pumping him."

• • •

"YOU CANNOT DO that, Carlota." Angelica sounded beside herself.

"I agree. It's too dangerous," Manuel added.

"What is the danger?" Carlota asked.

Angelica strode to the window and yanked open the curtains. A small army of reporters and camera trucks had camped at the street. Large satellite antennas pointed to the sky. Several pointed down toward Lima.

"Look! Every crackpot in the world is going to want to meet you," she exclaimed.

"It's only for a month. I lived in that shanty town until I met you, Angelica," Carlota answered gently, but tried to be stern. "I must eventually return there anyway to give birth to my son."

"You mean you're not going to use a hospital?" Angelica was nearly in tears.

Carlota held Angelica in her arms. "You are my love, my heart, and my soul. Give me this without a fight, Angelica. Trust in God."

"I apologize if my offer is a source of discontent," Father Rivera offered.

Janice McClain stood back, not about to enter the fray. She looked out the dining room window. Through the neighborhood trees she could see Lima's night lights below in the distance.

"Then I'm going to move out there, too. We live together, remember." Angelica's words hammered the air.

Carlota's face lit. "Thank you."

Angelica rolled her eyes to Manuel, as if accepting defeat.

"I'm going, too." Manuel added, determined to keep his vow of staying with her until the child was born.

"Even better." Carlota said excitedly. "Father Rivera, you have room for all of us?"

He smiled. "We will make room. For you, Holy Mother, we will build another room, if necessary."

"Are we going tonight?" Angelica broke in.

"No, tomorrow morning," Carlota answered and turned back to Rivera. "Father, will you stay here with us tonight?"

Rivera nodded vigorously. "My honor, Holy Mother."

"That settles it. Tomorrow morning I move back to my old neighborhood," Carlota announced to everyone.

"Does your family still live there?" Rivera asked.

"No, Father. Angelica is my family. I was abandoned when I was very young."

"You raised yourself on the streets of Lima?" Rivera asked sadly, knowing, if so, she was like many others.

"Yes, she did," Angelica answered for her.

McClain unfolded her arms from across her chest. "Then I'm returning to my place. What time do you want me to come by in the morning to get you?"

"Will nine inconvenience you?" Carlota asked.

McClain smiled gently to her. "No, not at all."

Carlota turned to Angelica. "We can have a nice breakfast before we leave."

• • •

HECTOR MOVED WITH less sound than a shadow. Then he saw the bare soles of Felipe's feet. Without looking back, Felipe signalled Hector up next to him. In seconds, they lay shoulder to shoulder.

Felipe's wide brown eyes were locked to Fëdor's pistoning white rump. Fëdor's prisoner beneath him had resigned herself. She lay motionless. Hector nudged Felipe's shoulder.

Felipe watched until he was certain Fëdor had not heard Hector arrive over his grunting. Fëdor's hips kept grinding, his back glistened with sweat. Felipe put his hand to Hector's shoulder, backing them out. Heavy foliage folded over them.

They slithered back forty meters from the *Sendero* clearing before Hector felt safe enough to whisper, "How did you get here, cousin?"

Both boys had lost their families to the *Sendero*. Although not indifferent to the woman's fate, they knew she would survive.

"I'm guiding two Americans, a man and a woman. She seeks a priest named Antonio. Do you know if the *Sendero* have him?" Felipe answered.

"They did but I got him out. He's with me, we were on the other side of their camp when I saw you signal."

"Those soldiers on the ground . . . the *Sendero* plan to kill them?" Felipe asked.

"Yes. When the screams begin, Antonio and I will circle behind the hut to get some other prisoners out." Hector paused, "But I'm afraid Antonio will do something foolish, like try to save them."

"All the soldiers may not have to die. I have an idea."

Hector's face turned to him in the dark. "What?"

"You know of Dos Santos?"

Hatred filled Hector's face. "Of course."

"He has sent soldiers to kill the American woman, Michelle. They are following us."

"How close?"

"They'll be a half kilometer away by the time I return to Michelle."

"They won't follow at night," Hector whispered.

"These men will."

"What is the plan?"

"You come back with me and bring Michelle back here," Felipe leaned closer, "make sure she is kept safe."

Hector knew Felipe had a crush on this woman.

"I'll lead the soldiers to the clearing. While they are fighting the *Sendero*, we rescue those in the hut," Felipe explained.

Hector nodded. "I must tell Antonio."

"Hurry, I'll wait," Felipe said but Hector had already gone.

Minutes later, Antonio jumped when Hector materialized next to him. "Where did you go?" he whispered.

Hector peered through the dark leaves, then folded them back into place. "Do you know an American woman named Michelle?" he asked, laying his hand at the nape of Antonio's back. The thick sweat told him Antonio's fever was worsening.

Antonio's eyes widened, he clutched Hector's arm. "Yes! Yes, how do you know?"

"She is near here."

"She's going to get herself killed! Hector you have to save her." Antonio whispered excitedly.

"I'm going to bring her here."

"You can't bring her here!"

"Be quiet!" Hector whispered sharply. "She will not be hurt. I promise you."

"What is she doing out here?"

"Looking for you."

Antonio quieted uneasily for a moment.

"Is she your lover?" Hector quizzed softly.

"I'm a priest, Hector. I don't have lovers!" Antonio whispered back. A flash of Hector's face rising from between his thighs lighted across his mind's eye. He lowered his head, fighting his fever and more.

"You stay here," Hector ordered protectively.

Antonio looked up at him.

"I'll be back with her."

Hector moved through the underbrush like water, rushing around it where it refused to yield but surging ahead where it would.

When Felipe spotted him, he started back to Michelle and Stauffen. Hector followed, keeping focused on Felipe's back as they ran through the jungle.

Michelle jumped when the two boys appeared suddenly from nowhere. "Felipe?" she asked, looking at Hector.

"This is Hector, my cousin."

"You are looking for Antonio?" Hector asked the beautiful woman.

Michelle's face steeled for bad news. "Yes."

"He is near. I saved him from the *Sendero*," Hector announced proudly.

Her heart exploded with relief. "He's alive?" She nearly shouted.

"Quiet!" Felipe warned.

"He's alive?" she repeated more softly.

"Yes. He is near the *Sendero* camp. We are going to save his friend," Hector said.

"We don't have time to talk," Felipe snapped, envious of this Antonio. He turned to Stauffen. "Hector will take Michelle and you to Antonio. I'm going for Dos Santos' soldiers following us."

"What's your plan?" Stauffen asked with deadly earnest.

"The *Sendero* have soldiers staked out in their clearing. I will lead Dos Santos' soldiers to the *Sendero* camp. While they fight, we will free the prisoners in the hut."

"Let's do it," Michelle said.

• • •

"SHANE MCKAY?" THE special courier asked, having hand carried the manila envelope from Jacob Brigham, in Lima, to Palo Alto, California.

"That's me." McKay turned from the group centered around several computer screens and walked over to him.

Shane McKay had been trained since childhood to revere old ways and distrust the new. His family, long steeped in conservative politics, raised him to believe that freedom meant freedom to be like them, that those different deserved no freedom, they would only abuse it. His mind had developed perfectly for computers, everything had its place.

The young McKay was ideal for Jacob Brigham, who had hired Shane, as a favor to McKay's family, when he had earned his doctorate in computer science. McKay's family knew that working for Mullen made you wealthy.

Two years later, Brigham sponsored Shane's membership in the Opus Dei. McKay had been delighted and soon began to think of Brigham like a grandfather.

"Identification?" the courier asked.

McKay pointed to his plastic security tag clipped to his white shirt pocket.

The courier examined the photo, looked up to McKay's boyish face, and handed him the envelope.

McKay excused himself from the others and went back to his office, closing the door. He leaned against the edge of his desk and opened the envelope.

The instructions from Brigham were handwritten. There was to be no phone contact until the takeover of Socrates had been completed. Once the usurpation was confirmed, he was to contact Brigham instantly at the number listed on the letter.

McKay folded the paper and slipped it into his pocket, returning to his crew. "Status?"

"Socrates has confirmed protocol acceptance with the Provo, Utah team and is awaiting our confirmation to integrate the upgrades. We just informed him the transition code will transmit tomorrow at three p.m. Pacific time," the woman said without glancing up from her screen. "That will allow our system here to finish the final cross checks."

McKay nodded. "Any problems?"

"None. He will upgrade soon after we transmit the transition code." She looked over her glasses to him with a maternal smile. "He's doing perfectly."

"Who?"

She appeared surprised by the question. "Socrates."

"Three p.m. Monday. On the mark?"

"On the mark."

McKay smiled.

• • •

"YOU'RE LATE, *MI amor*." Marta rushed to Benito, wrapping her arms around his waist.

"Let's get a look at you." Benito held her at arm's length and gazed appreciatively at her.

She wore a gossamer negligee. Proud breasts tented the mesh fabric. "Do you like it?" she asked seductively.

"Yes." His hand slipped between her legs, his thick fingers probing.

"I hoped so. I bought it today at that American store," she said as she unbuttoned his shirt. "What did you do today?"

"Just work."

"Did that American show up again at the general's office?"

"Yes, but I'm surprised he's still alive. The general was screaming at him."

"Why?"

"Did you see the television report on Carlota Cabral, the woman the messianic priest said is the Madonna?"

"Uh hum," she murmured, slipping off his shirt. "Nothing else is on the television."

"The general is not pleased by people looking upon her like a god."

Marta leaned against him, seductively licking his neck.

"Oh, Chica," Benito moaned.

"Tell me more," she whispered.

• • •

SWEATY HAIR MATTED Fëdor's chest as he stepped grinning from the clearing. He glistened in the campfire's glow and held Sánchez' crying and naked sister roughly by the arm.

When he reached the campfire he shoved her at a *Sendero*. "Take her back." He looked to those gathered around the flames. "Where are the other sisters?" he asked, adjusting the front of his trousers.

"We threw them back in the hut after we finished with them," someone answered.

"Pablo, toss me your knife." Fëdor ordered.

Pablo flipped it to him."What are you going to do?"

Fëdor caught the knife with one hand. "Time for Captain Sánchez to give up his big *huevos*."

Those around the campfire brayed with laughter, their white teeth glowing in the darkness.

Fëdor grinned at their approval and strutted toward Sánchez.

At the jungle's edge, on the other side of the clearing nearest the tin hut, Hector motioned for Michelle and Stauffen to wait. "I'll get Antonio, he's about twenty meters that way," Hector pointed, "next to those men."

Michelle raised her head over the bushes to see where he pointed.

Hector yanked her down, out of sight. "Stay down!" Hector whispered then turned to Stauffen. "We are as close as we can get to the hut."

Hector stopped talking and poked his head through the leaves, checking to make sure they were still undetected. "Felipe will be here soon with Dos Santos' soldiers right behind him. When they discover the *Senderos*, there will be a fire fight. When they start shooting, stay low. Get to the back of the hut or you'll be spotted. Then dig out a tunnel under the edge of the hut to bring out the prisoners. Dig with your hands as fast as you can. The ground is soft. I'll bring back Antonio."

"Why not just use the door?" Stauffen asked.

"They can see the door!" Hector chided.

Stauffen nodded and Hector vanished.

Fëdor turned toward the *Sendero* following him. "Sánchez is going to suffer before we skin his men in front of him."

Fëdor turned and walked to Sánchez, kicking the bottom of his foot.

In the shadows, Antonio quietly moved as close to Sánchez and Fëdor as he could without detection.

Sánchez looked up into the darkness at Fëdor looming over him. The other grinning *Sendero* gathered to watch.

"Time for pain, Sánchez," Fëdor said, slowly kneeling between Sánchez' legs, holding the knife high enough that it glinted in the flames.

Sánchez' eyes widened. He screamed through his gag.

"Do you know what I'm going to do?" Fëdor asked quietly, leaning into Sánchez' face. "I'm going to make you into a bitch." Fëdor held the knife to Sánchez' cheek. "Then you will watch while we slowly skin your men one by one," he looked over to João, "beginning with that one, the pretty one."

João shuddered.

Arriving back where he had left Antonio, Hector looked around the empty nest. "Brazilians!" he groaned quietly.

Sánchez' eyes became frenzied as Fëdor's calloused hand wrapped around his genitals.

All the *Sendero* focused on Sánchez, some smirked, some grimaced. None saw Felipe emerge silently from the jungle's edge, looking back toward Dos Santos' soldiers.

"It's time, Sánchez. It's time." Fëdor whispered, so close that his breath warmed Sánchez' cheek.

Sánchez closed his eyes, wincing as Fëdor pulled hard, stretching him. He felt the blade's sharp edge.

"NOOOOO!" The great scream startled the entire camp as Antonio exploded from the darkness, lunging through the air like a lion defending its young.

Fëdor looked up in time to see a giant of a man flying at him. Antonio nearly snapped Fëdor's neck as he caught it with his elbow and rolled. The knife flew from Fëdor's hand.

At that instant, Dos Santos' soldiers rushed into the clearing, weapons drawn. For an instant, they stood confused.

"Help!" Fëdor screamed as Antonio spun back and lunged again. A human whirlwind enveloped Fëdor.

The *Sendero* rose from the campfire in confusion, their concern for Fëdor suddenly overwhelmed by the presence of armed soldiers.

The soldiers opened fire.

"Help!" Fëdor screamed in vain.

Chaos unleashed itself.

A quick burst of machine gun fire dropped Pablo and the tallest of the *Sendero* women, nearly cutting them in two. The others scattered for their weapons and quickly returned fire.

Fëdor snarled as Antonio locked him in a powerful grip. Fëdor pivoted so their chests ground together, arms and legs flailing. The sweat from Antonio's fever made him so slippery that Fëdor could not hold him. He kicked Antonio's feet from under him and they rolled through the dirt in tight embrace.

Fëdor forced his face into the nape of Antonio's neck, sinking teeth into straining tendons. Antonio snarled and struck back at Fëdor's temple.

Fëdor returned blow for blow as they rolled through the shadows and the dirt. He thrust hard then rolled away, landing on his feet, crouching to defend himself.

Antonio was on him in a flash, enormous arms encircling Fëdor, dragging him back to earth like a rag doll. He flipped Fëdor onto his stomach, slid atop him, grinding his face into the dirt.

Despite his strength and ferocity, Fëdor was no match for an enraged Antonio. Few men would be. Antonio was six foot four, two hundred and forty pounds of sinew and muscle filled with fury.

"Help me!" Fëdor screamed through the dirt, clawing at the earth.

Suddenly, two *Sendero* dove onto Antonio, shoving him off Fëdor. Antonio rolled onto his feet and charged all three. They were jackals trying to bring down a lion.

As they struggled, Felipe hurried through the shadows to free the staked soldiers, first slicing away Sánchez' bonds. Sánchez took a full second to realize freedom had arrived.

As soon he had freed Sánchez, Felipe began freeing João, looking back to Sánchez. "Help him!" Felipe screamed at Sánchez.

Sánchez scrambled to his feet and dove into the whirlwind of fists and bodies.

"Help them!" Felipe ordered João as he sliced away Sergio's bindings. He looked back to see João diving into the pile. Within seconds, he freed Sergio then screamed to Antonio to follow him.

Antonio refused to release his grip on Fëdor. He had never fought before. He was blind with rage.

Felipe rushed into the melée, grabbing the back of Antonio's shorts, trying to pull him out of the jumble of flailing arms and legs.

Antonio raised a huge arm high into the air. He spun and drove his arm downward, determined to break free. He saw Felipe's face just in time to stop his fist.

"Michelle! Michelle!" Felipe shouted at him.

Antonio's senses sharpened. "Where?"

"Follow me!"

The two disappeared into the jungle's darkness and, minutes later, emerged behind the tin hut.

"You got him?" Hector shouted above the gunfire as Felipe erupted through the bushes.

Stauffen and Michelle were frantically clawing a tunnel from under the hut, scooping handfuls of dirt.

Before Felipe could answer, Antonio bounded ahead of him, heading for Michelle in enormous strides.

"Michelle!" he yelled.

Michelle spun back, her eyes locked to his. "Antonio!" She ran for him.

A wild spray of bullets, from the far side of the clearing where the battle raged, aerated the hut, clanging loudly.

Antonio dove onto Michelle, pulling her to the ground. "Stay down!" he screamed and climbed protectively atop her, wrapping himself around her.

"Move!" Hector motioned them behind the hut. He looked up at the puncture wounds high on the tin wall. More bullets ricocheted around them. "Dig! Dig!" He screamed at Stauffen and then to those inside the hut. "You inside. Dig! Dig for your lives!"

Agnus and Cardoso clawed the earth inside the hut.

"I've got 'em!" Stauffen screamed, pointing to Agnus' fingers reaching up under the hut wall through the hole they had dug. Instantly, Antonio and Michelle were beside him, frantically digging.

The three quickly scooped a hole large enough through which Hector could pry. In an instant Hector wiggled into the dark hut. The warm stench of death assaulted his nostrils.

"We're getting you out!" Hector screamed as he turned and scrambled to enlarge the opening from inside.

The pile of writhing bodies atop Fëdor and Sánchez swelled as *Sendero* and Sánchez' men tried to save their leaders.

In the dark chaos and confusion, Fëdor slipped from the bottom of the pile, rolling into the protective cover of shadows at the clearing's edge. He thought his lungs would burst as he tried to catch his breath.

Outside the hut, Michelle straddled the hole, serving as midwife to those emerging from the hole beneath the tin wall. Agnus' head was the first to pop into view, followed by Cardoso.

"Where is Ignatious?" Antonio screamed.

Inside the hut, Ignatious and Hector tried to convince the sisters to join them.

"You must get out now!" Hector screamed at the oldest sister. But the terrified women huddled together in the corner, refusing to budge. Ignatious was beside them, trying to reassure them. All four shook their heads violently and held each other even tighter.

Hector pulled on Ignatious' arm. "Father, if we're getting out of here, we have to do it right now."

Ignatious looked back to the women. "Please, trust us."

"Right now, Father!" Hector screamed, pulling frantically at Ignatious' arm.

Ignatious turned and followed Hector, prying through the hole and into the night.

Within seconds, Hector and Felipe herded everyone into the protective cover of the night jungle.

"Follow me!" Felipe yelled and lead the way. Hector waited until everyone followed Felipe before taking up the rear guard. He glanced back every few seconds to see if they were followed.

Fëdor's eyes blazed with fire. He watched from the dark shadows of the underbrush as they disappeared into the night.

• • •

MOONLIGHT FILTERED ACROSS the bed. Marta lay entangled with Benito.

"He said something I didn't understand."

"The general?" Marta raised her head from her pillow.

"No. The American. Jacob Brigham." Benito stared at the ceiling.

"What?"

"The greater the crowds following the Madonna, the more the hatred for the *Sendero* when people think they killed her," Benito repeated Brigham's words slowly to her.

"What did the general say?" A brow arched.

"He ordered me from the room."

Marta lay her head onto his chest. "Do you think the general has been deceiving you?" she asked, knowing the answer.

"I can't think he would," Benito looked into her eyes, "but I will find out."

• • •

FELIPE STOPPED WHEN he heard Hector yell his name. Turning, he saw he was alone and ran back through the moonlight to the others. "What's wrong?" He asked.

"They can't keep up." Hector explained quickly.

"I'm over eighty years old, young man." Ignatious struggled for breath. "I can't run like I once did."

"And I'm fifty pounds overweight," Agnus added, breathing as hard as Ignatious, her hand over her heart. Suddenly, she realized she, Ignatious, and Cardoso were still naked. Shame flooded her face.

Antonio fought to stay on his feet, to appear fine. High fever and sharp nausea made the fight futile.

Michelle started to peel off her shirt and trousers to give to Agnus. "Take these."

Hector stopped Michelle. "Their clothes are in the *Sendero's* dump near here." He spun and vanished, reappearing moments later with their clothes crumpled to his chest. Agnus, Ignatious, and Cardoso hurried into the soiled but welcomed, coverings.

Antonio squatted to rest on his heels. Hector studied him then glanced to Felipe.

"Are you all right?" Felipe asked.

Antonio only nodded.

"He has fever from an infected cut," Hector explained to Felipe, referring to the wound María had inflicted, "and it's going to get worse fast. We must find some medicine leaves."

"Where are you cut?" Michelle kneeled beside Antonio, putting her hand on his shoulder.

"I'll tell you later." He shook his head, trying to clear his double vision.

Felipe felt Antonio's forehead. It was hot and sweaty. He looked worriedly to Hector. "We rest here for awhile."

Antonio struggled back onto his feet. "You're not going to wait on my account."

"Nor mine," Ignatious threw in.

Felipe and Hector froze, their heads erect and ears like radar.

"Me either," Agnus said, adding, "I can travel, just not as fast as you, Felipe."

"Quiet." Hector whispered.

The two boys listened intently, looking at one another.

"Someone is coming," Hector paused, "more than one."

"They're coming fast." Felipe whispered.

"Let's go then!" Agnus said, buttoning up her shirt.

Amid the chaotic debris at the *Sendero* camp, Sánchez threw open the hut's flimsy tin door. His sisters huddled in the corner, trembling, as he offered his hand. "Come out, you're safe now."

Sánchez turned back toward Sergio, who was pulling his own clothes from the pile of their uniforms. "Sergio, find my trousers."

Sergio dug through the pile and tossed Sánchez his pants.

Sánchez slipped into his pants then motioned his sisters out of the hut, who emerged cautiously as he walked through the clutter of corpses. "How many did we lose?" he asked João.

"Jorge didn't make it. They got him when he was standing perimeter guard."

Sánchez winced. "Get our people together." He walked over to the leader of Dos Santos' men. "How many did you lose?"

"Three," the man answered curtly. "Did you see an American woman? Tall. Blond."

Sánchez shook his head and began inspecting *Sendero* corpses, looking for Fëdor. After his inventory, he looked to Dos Santos' man. "The leader got away. So did several others by my count."

The man simply turned. He and those under his command began leaving the clearing, following the trampled bushes left by Agnus, Ignatious and the Americans.

"Sergeant!" Sánchez snapped.

The man turned and stared.

"Where do you think you are going?"

"I have special orders from Major Dos Santos. We are following the American woman. She is a *Sendero* collaborator."

"I saw no American woman, but if she is with the man who saved me, she is no collaborator."

"I have my orders, Captain." The man signalled his men to move out.

"I have special orders from General De Silva. I command this entire region. That includes Major Dos Santos, as well as you," Sánchez replied.

"The major will not like it if we fail our mission," the man countered.

"I'll deal with the major. You obey my orders." Sánchez glared.

The man turned to his men and gestured them back.

"The *Sendero* may have reinforcements on the way. Take my sisters back to Iquitos right now," Sánchez said.

The man nodded.

"Do you understand, Sergeant?"

"Yes, sir."

"I hold you responsible for their safety."

The man nodded again.

"Do you understand that, Sergeant?"

"Yes, sir."

Sánchez turned and motioned for his sisters. They remained clustered together, still in shock, but hurried to him. He spoke softly to them. "These men are under my command."

The women stared blankly at him.

"Do you understand?" Sánchez asked quietly.

The youngest nodded.

"They are going to take you back to Iquitos. I'm going to find Mother. Then I'm going after the man that raped you."

They continued staring.

"Will you go with them for me?"

They nodded in unison.

Sánchez watched the convoy of Dos Santos' men and his sisters head for Iquitos under the cover of night.

A quarter mile from the *Sendero* camp, Fëdor's eyes blazed with a single hatred as he stumbled through the dark underbrush, his three remaining men close behind. He carried his machine gun pointed in the direction he walked, his finger on the trigger. "When we catch them, the young priest is mine," he said, wincing at the pain from his split lip. Fëdor had a broken nose and badly bloodied face. "He's mine," he whispered painfully to himself.

• • •

MARÍA LED THE discussion with Marta. Diego and Anita sat quietly. All four sat at Marta's kitchen table, the morning sun angled across it.

"Have you learned exactly what De Silva is planning?" María asked.

"No. But I will by tonight. Benito is finally suspecting that De Silva may be deceiving him about the plot to kill the Madonna. He said he knows where De Silva would keep such papers," Marta answered.

"What will he do if he decides De Silva has deceived him?"

"He overheard the rich American talking about their plan to kill the Madonna and frame us. Once he sees De Silva's papers, he'll know he was deceived."

"But will he confront De Silva?" María asked.

"I don't know."

"Will he betray De Silva?"

"No."

"He may have to die," María said slowly.

Marta shrugged lightly.

"You must learn what the *federales* are planning."

Marta nodded.

María turned to Anita. "And you must get close to this Madonna. Marta's people say she is surrounded by her lover and two priests, this De las Casas and Rivera. I don't care how you do it, but get to her."

"How?" Anita asked bluntly.

María's face hardened sharply, eyes blazing. "Use your brain!" She spun to Diego. "Go with her. Make sure she succeeds."

He nodded.

María turned back to Marta. "You said we have people who work for '*El Sol*' Newspaper."

"Yes."

"How many?"

"Five."

"Reporters?" María asked.

"Two."

"Have you met with them?"

"No, but I can today."

"Do so. Have them write the story now—'*Federales* Kill Madonna to Frame *Sendero*.'" María smiled at the sound of it.

"They will need proof."

"Your boyfriend will bring you De Silva's plans tonight?"

"Yes."

"Give them copies of De Silva's plans. We will kill this Madonna ourselves then make it appear they did in order to frame us. The story will write itself."

Marta smiled.

"The first headlines after she is killed are all that matters," María said. "If the papers say the government killed the Madonna to frame the *Sendero*, the people will revolt. They will tear the government apart. And in that chaos, *we* will take control."

• • •

"I CAN'T BELIEVE you are taking that!" Carlota stared disapprovingly from the bedroom door, her fists at her hips.

Angelica hoisted her skirt, strapping the derringer to her lower thigh. "I don't travel without it. You know that."

"I don't believe this. We're not going into the jungle. We'll be with friends."

Angelica adjusted her skirt then rose from the edge of the bed. "We always argue about this, and I always carry it, anyway."

"This is a special time for me, Angelica." Carlota seemed hurt.

"I intend to keep it special." Angelica answered flatly, patting the derringer and announcing an end to the discussion. "Come on, now. They are waiting for us downstairs." She picked up the two overnight bags.

Carlota said softly, "I don't want to leave our home like this." She walked to Angelica, opening her arms.

Angelica dropped the bags and gathered Carlota into her arms. "I don't mean to upset you but staying in Villa Del Mar frightens me."

"I know. We'll be fine." Carlota laid her head on Angelica's chest.

• • •

JANICE McCLAIN LOOKED up at her wall clock. Nine o'clock Monday morning. Busiest day of her week and Brigham was late for the meeting he requested. She shook her head and turned to her paperwork.

Fifteen minutes later, her secretary announced Brigham's arrival.

"Please have a seat," McClain said courteously, rising when he entered the room. She gestured to the chair in front of her desk.

"Thank you." Brigham took the chair, leaning back, crossing his legs casually.

"How may I help you, Mr. Brigham?" McClain laid her crossed forearms onto her desk.

"You know I'm helping coordinate Mr. Mullen's interests here in Peru."

She nodded politely.

"I need to send you to Iquitos to help Mr. O'Riley." He cleared his throat. "Brian is swamped by events there and I can cover everything here in Lima."

"Unfortunately, Mr. Brigham, that is not an option for me."

Brigham arched a thin brow. "Ms. McClain, do you realize I am second in corporate command only to Mr. Mullen himself?" His tone attempted intimidation.

"Yes, I do, Mr. Brigham. However, Mr. Mullen is in daily contact with both me and Mr. O'Riley. He asked that I provide my fullest assistance to Ms. Cabral, Ms. Montoya, Father De las Casas, and when she arrives, Ms. Cumberland. And that, Mr. Brigham, is exactly what I intend to do," she said, trying to hide her disdain for the man before her.

Brigham's plastic smile threatened to crack. "I did not realize John was so involved."

"Quite involved, I assure you." She smiled back.

Brigham rose slowly. "Thank you for your time, Ms. McClain."

McClain rose from behind her desk, extending her hand. "If I can assist you in any other way, please let me know."

• • •

WITH THE SUN up, traveling was easier, though no faster. Felipe looked to Hector. They had a slim chance of keeping ahead of their pursuers if not for Antonio, whose fever had worsened dramatically over the last few hours.

A half hour later, Antonio collapsed face first into the dirt. The group stopped and encircled him. Hector gently rolled him onto his back, felt his forehead, and looked up to Felipe, shaking his head.

"What's wrong with him?" Michelle asked quickly, kneeling beside him.

"We have to leave him," Felipe said to Hector.

"We are not leaving him," Michelle, Ignatious, and Agnus declared together.

Hector wiped sweat from Antonio's brow and looked back toward them. "We are not abandoning him, but we must leave him." He glanced back down the trail they had blazed. "If we don't, the men following us will catch us. If we do leave him, we can stay ahead of them and reach Iquitos."

"But we're not heading toward Iquitos," Stauffen noted.

"Not in a straight line," Felipe said, "but we are circling in toward it. If the soldiers following us see we are heading directly into Iquitos, they would signal ahead for an ambush."

"But we don't know if they are soldiers or *Sendero,*" Michelle reminded him.

"Do you want to take the chance?" Felipe asked in earnest. He would do anything Michelle asked.

She shook her head.

"I will carry him," Stauffen announced.

"That would only delay our capture. We have to hide him off the trail," Hector explained. "I will stay with him."

"I will not leave him," Michelle countered, softly stroking Antonio's sweat drenched forehead.

"He needs the medicine leaves to kill the infection in the wound," Hector said looking up to Felipe.

"Where is he wounded?" Michelle asked, looking over Antonio.

"You will stay with him?" Hector asked.

"Of course," she answered without taking her eyes from Antonio.

"I will show you, but first I must find some medicine leaves," Hector said, then quickly disappeared into the dense underbrush.

"Hector will show you how to care for Antonio until he and I can return to take you back to Iquitos. We will be back by tomorrow morning." Felipe explained to her.

Stauffen unstrapped the two water canteens from his belt, handing them to her. "He'll need these."

Michelle took them and strapped them onto her waistband. She knelt and stroked Antonio's forehead as they waited for Hector to return.

Felipe turned to Stauffen. "Can you carry him about a hundred meters?"

"Sure. What do you need?" Stauffen said, kneeling beside Michelle and slipping one arm under Antonio's back, the other under his legs.

"Do you need help?" Michelle asked Stauffen quietly.

He shook his head and, in one concerted effort, rose to his feet with Antonio in his arms.

Michelle adjusted Antonio's head so it rested on Stauffen's shoulders. Antonio mumbled some delirious protest.

"You're ok, Antonio. I'm here," she said softly.

"Carry him up the trail. We can use that overhead branch to move him off the trail undetected." Felipe answered, pointing up the trail. A huge branch from a giant tree arched above where they would pass.

"Do we need to wait for little Hector?" Agnus asked protectively.

Felipe shook his head. "He'll find us."

Following Felipe, Stauffen carried Antonio ahead to the huge branch.

Michelle lifted Felipe up onto it. He secured his footing and reached down for Antonio.

"Felipe, can you lift him by yourself?" Agnus asked in warning.

"Michelle and I can hold him in position until Ray climbs up to help me. The three of us can haul him back along the branch to the trunk then lower him to safety." Stauffen was already on the branch before Felipe finished his reply. They hoisted Antonio up and Michelle joined them.

Minutes later, Stauffen lowered Antonio into Felipe and Michelle's arms as they stood at the base of the moss covered tree. They were preparing his hiding place when Hector came scurrying along the branch, pant pockets stuffed with leaves.

Hector jumped down and dug into both pockets, handing Michelle handfuls of juicy yellow leaves. "These can break the infection." He knelt beside Antonio while looking up to Felipe and Stauffen. "You go back while I show Michelle what to do."

Stauffen unclipped his .45 from his belt and handed it to Michelle. "Do you know how to use this?"

"I do," she said, accepting it, weighing it in her hand as Stauffen stripped off his shirt.

"Here, take this in case he gets chills," he said, handing her his shirt.

Felipe stepped next to Michelle and looked up to her. "We will be back for you, Michelle. Hector and me," he reassured.

She smiled bravely. "Thank you, Felipe. I won't forget your kindness. Take everyone back to Iquitos and come back for us. We'll wait for you."

Stauffen climbed onto the branch and Felipe quickly followed.

Hector waited until they disappeared before turning to Michelle. "The *Sendero* leader was preparing to hurt him badly when I stopped her, but not before she started to cut him. That is what is infected."

"Where is he cut?"

Hector bent and unsnapped the buttons to Antonio's shorts. "Give me some leaves," he said as Antonio moaned.

Michelle handed him several, kneeling beside him. "Who is this leader?" Her voice was ice, vengeful.

"They call her María, but I doubt that is her real name," he said, slipping Antonio's shorts down to the thighs. He carefully adjusted Antonio so Michelle could see the cut, which was festering badly. "Do you see?" Hector pushed away pus with a finger.

She nodded with a steel face.

Hector put the leaves onto his palm and covered them with the other palm, rubbing them together. "They need heat to help." He continued rubbing his palms rhythmically until he could feel the friction warm his hands. "Once you feel the heat in your hands, keep rubbing the leaves until they become wet. Then pack them into the wound." He took the juicy pulp out of his palm and compacted it into the wound. He looked up at her. "Can you do that?" He asked, gently covering Antonio's crotch with Stauffen's shirt.

"I'll take care of him."

"Apply the leaves every hour or so until you run out. After that, his fever should begin to leave him. We will be back by morning."

"Go on now and hurry back," she said.

"The men following us should be along within an hour. You won't hear them coming and you may not even hear them pass by. But if you or Antonio make any noise, they will hear you. If they hear you, they will kill you both." He pointed to the gun. "With or without that."

Michelle gritted her teeth. "We'll see. Go now and hurry back."

Hector turned and started up the tree.

"Hector," she said softly.

He turned back.

"Thank you for saving him."

Hector smiled and vanished.

Michelle cocked the .45 as she listened to her group leave. One hand held the .45 and the other caressed Antonio's brow. She sat in stark silence. Her eyes were fixed on the underbrush between her and the trail.

• • •

SÁNCHEZ STARED DOWN at his mother. She stared back with three eyes, the middle oozing blood.

"Are you all right, Captain?" João asked softly.

Fighting back tears, Sánchez bent and gently scooped his mother's body into his arms. Her head and arms swung limply. "Sergio, put her head on my chest," Sánchez said woodenly.

They returned to the *Sendero* camp without another word. When Sánchez reached the camp, he lowered his mother into the shadows along the edge of the clearing and slowly covered her with a *Sendero* blanket.

Tears streamed down his cheeks as he walked to the underbrush trampled by the *Sendero* prisoners who had escaped. He wiped his tears and studied the trail of crushed underbrush that disappeared into the jungle. "The *Sendero* prisoners and those who freed them are being tracked by four *Sendero*, one must be Fëdor," he said to João without emotion. Revenge would be served cold.

"Captain, I found some of our equipment. They had it stored in a shed." Sergio held up the sniper rifle, checking the telescopic sight. "It's fine."

"Do we have a radio?" Sánchez asked.

"No, only our weapons."

Sánchez turned to his men. They were back into their uniforms. Only he stood bare chested. "Sergio, I want you and the others to catch up with my sisters." He looked over to his mother, covered by the *Sendero* blanket. He looked back to Sergio, "Will you take my mother's body?" Anguish glutted his face.

Sergio nodded solemnly, "I'll protect your mother's body and your sisters. My word to you, Captain."

"Thank you, Sergio. When you reach Iquitos, call General De Silva and debrief him. I want helicopters and infrared. And arrest Dos Santos."

Sergio gathered his men and each secured a machine gun. They headed quickly down the path taken by Dos Santos' men and Sánchez' sisters.

Sánchez turned to João, "You and I are going after the *Sendero*."

Sánchez walked to what remained of the pile of crumbled uniforms and picked up his jacket. He pulled a tin of shadow paint from a pocket, dropped the jacket, and began streaking his face and torso with black stripes. His eyes locked with João's, unblinking.

João studied his commander sympathetically for a moment. "Give me the paint when you're done."

Sánchez finished smearing his chest and face. His eyes glazed into space as he handed João the tin.

João's eyes never left his commander as he streaked his face darkly. The two stared at one another.

• • •

MICHELLE FROZE AT the sound of voices. She had no warning. Fëdor and Ernesto were suddenly on the other side of the underbrush.

Her eyes narrowed. One hand slid over Antonio's mouth but he was too unconscious even to moan. The other pointed the .45 toward the unseen voices.

"Are we gaining?" Fëdor asked painfully through split and swollen lips.

Ernesto examined the leaves of broken stems to gauge when the stems were broken, "They are right ahead of us."

"Where are they headed?"

"Not Iquitos. But I can't tell where they're going."

They pushed on, doubling their pace.

Michelle strained to hear the heavy footsteps recede until only silence greeted her ears. She released her breath, threw back her head, and gasped for air.

She checked her watch. An hour had passed since Hector had gone. She put five yellow leaves between her palms and after several minutes of hard rubbing, felt the heated pulp release its juice. She delicately peeled Stauffen's sweaty shirt from Antonio's crotch.

She swallowed nervously and carefully adjusted Antonio so his wound was visible. Talking softly to him, trying to comfort him if he could hear, she cleaned his wound and replaced old leaf pulp with new. She covered him again with Stauffen's shirt then checked her watch.

Fixing her eyes on the underbrush between her and the trail, she gripped the .45 with a steady hand.

• • •

THE PICKUP TURNED off the central highway after reaching the arid foothills overlooking Lima. Marta drove with Anita between her and Diego, who stared ahead, his elbow out the window.

"I don't like this," Anita said flatly to Marta, flexing her foot casually to feel the knife she had slipped into her boot.

"Your dislikes are meaningless," Marta said.

"Not to me."

"Your duty is to obey," Marta snapped.

A dust plume rose behind them as the pickup headed north along the road. When they reached the turn off leading to Villa Del Mar, Marta braked.

Ahead, tens of thousands of people packed the unpaved streets, becoming an enormous swarm. The shanty town was wall-to-wall people.

"She is already here. Look at all the peasants," Marta said. "The radio report said she intends to stay in Villa Del Mar until the child is born."

Villa Del Mar, like the rest of the villas in the foothills above Lima, was a refugee camp for the poor who had fled even worse poverty in the high Andes. No one had electricity or water and disease stalked them. The cries of hungry children were constant. The decrepit shanties looked as though one decided wind would blow them into the Pacific. Life was a contest in Villa Del Mar. Its people struggled to live.

"Why come here?" Diego asked disgustedly.

Anita stared at the throng of people.

"They said she was returning here because she grew up here," Marta said.

"She was raised in this poverty?" Anita asked.

Marta ignored the question and spoke to Diego. "I have already seen her."

Anita looked at Marta from the corner of her eye. "You have?"

"Uh huh," Marta answered off-handedly.

"When?"

"When Rivera introduced her to the people."

"What does she look like?" Anita asked.

"A rich *Limeño* who needs to die."

"What does she look like? I need to know."

Marta laughed. "You won't have a problem picking her out from the rabble. Now get out. You too, Diego."

"How will we get word to you if we need to?" Diego asked, closing the pickup door.

"You will be watched by other *Sendero*. They will report to me. We'll know what you need."

Anita and Diego jumped back as Marta floored the old pickup, kicking up gravel behind it. They looked to each other as Marta headed back toward Lima.

"Any ideas?" Diego asked.

"One but I won't say it," Anita growled and turned for Villa Del Mar.

• • •

"BENITO!" DE SILVA called as he hurried into his uniform jacket. The *Presidente* was waiting for him. Benito rushed into De Silva's office.

"Sir?"

"I won't be back until tomorrow. You haven't filed my papers for the last two days. Do so before you leave today," De Silva said, sucking in his stomach to button the jacket. "If you need me, I'll have my pager on," he added as he walked from the room.

"Yes, sir," Benito said and looked at his watch. He waited a couple of minutes and walked to the window. He gazed down at the sidewalk far below until De Silva left the building. A chauffeur opened the car door and De Silva disappeared into his limousine.

Benito watched the limousine pull from the curb and muscle its way into the crush of traffic. He walked over and locked the outer door.

Returning quickly to De Silva's office, he swung back the framed map of Peru, exposing the wall safe. He had watched De Silva punch in the numbers to unlock it a hundred times. His fingers moved quickly. The thick safe door clicked open.

He peered inside. Brushing aside the pile of U.S. dollars, he pulled out a stack of official papers. He sorted through them, his ear alert for footsteps. The papers were mostly financial accounts with banks around the world. He kept thumbing until he found a sealed envelope. He smiled at the seal and turned to open the general's desk, retrieving an identical envelope, to reseal the letter when he had finished.

He opened the letter. The top of the letter read TOP SECRET in bright red ink. Equally bright red letters at the bottom read DESTROY UPON RECEIPT.

Benito's face hardened as he read. He would not believe his eyes. The letter from the Minister of Security to General De Silva detailed when the assault on Carlota Cabral was to occur and how it was to be accomplished in order to frame the *Sendero*.

The plan called for a squad of regular army personnel to arrive in Villa Del Mar tomorrow at exactly 1100 hours. They would arrive by military van and explain that, by order of the *Presidente* himself, they were commanded to rescue her from an impending *Sendero* assassination attempt.

They would then drive the van from Lima along the Central Highway toward Chosica. A second van carrying several *Sendero* prisoners, dressed in *Sendero* garb, would follow.

Twenty kilometers out of Lima they would be ambushed by a special forces squad. No one was to be left alive. A special forces subordinate, dressed in army regulars, would be wounded superficially and left to give the press accounts of the *Sendero* attack on the Madonna, who the soldiers had tried to protect.

The *Presidente* would announce a month of mourning and call upon the people to help rid the nation of the *Sendero* and *Sendero* sympathizers, once and for all, by any means.

Benito's thick hands trembled as he walked to the copier and laid the letter face down on the glass. He hit the green button and stared into the blaze of white light as the machine belched a copy.

He slipped the copy into his pocket and the original into its new envelope, which he sealed slowly, shaking his head. He returned everything to the safe and looked at his watch.

Six hours until he could leave. They would be the longest hours of his life. He had to decide. He and Marta. They had no secrets. He had to tell her, but he could not. But he had to, if she was to be his wife. She had kept no secrets from him.

He walked to the giant window of De Silva's suite which overlooked Lima and the great Pacific beyond. He stood motionless, staring into space.

• • •

AT THE SOUND of men running along the trail, Michelle tensed again, sliding her hand over Antonio's lips. The footsteps receded as quickly as they came. Her hand eased from Antonio's mouth.

Sánchez and João had not seen her. They were focused on closing their distance between Fëdor as fast as they could. João was on Sánchez' heels. Both held their rifles to their painted chests as they ran.

Michelle waited several minutes before moving a muscle. She stroked Antonio's forehead. His fever had broken, even though his body was still drenched with sweat.

She checked her watch and looked to the few remaining yellow leaves. Enough for one more application. She put them between her palms and rubbed until the heat released the juice.

Antonio was clawing his way back to consciousness, out of the fevered abyss. One second, he was locked in a deadly embrace with Fëdor. The next, he was a young boy in Boa Vista, Brazil, laughing as Father Ignatious tried to teach him Latin. Suddenly, he was staked onto the ground . . . dancing shadows . . . candle light . . . warm mouth . . . explosive orgasm . . . swaying breasts . . . another orgasm . . . and another. He began drifting up to consciousness through a warm sea of seductive fantasies.

Michelle pulled back Stauffen's shirt and carefully adjusted Antonio to apply new leaf pulp.

Antonio began unconsciously to follow his fantasies and react naturally to her soft touch. His huge penis uncoiled slowly, stiffened across his stomach, then lumbered enormously into the air.

Michelle stared wide-eyed.

Antonio woke with a sudden start. "Huh?"

She looked back to his face with surprise.

He stared at her. Her heart stopped.

"Michelle, what are you doing?" he asked quietly, quickly covering himself with his hands as best he could.

She dropped Stauffen's shirt back over his lap. "I . . . ," her tongue lodged in her throat, "You were unconscious. Hector told me to apply these ointment leaves to your wound every hour until your fever broke." Her eyes begged him to forgive the trespass.

"I can do it," he said softly and extended his hand. She smeared the leaf pulp onto his palm.

He forced himself to sit, leaning back against the tree. He lifted Stauffen's shirt to examine his wound. It had healed dramatically. The physician in him studied the medicinal leaves then looked back to his nearly healed wound. "These are amazing," he said softly to himself as he applied the pulp.

Michelle kept her head turned until he had finished and pulled his shorts back into place.

"Ok," he laughed to ease her discomfort. "Thanks for keeping an eye on me."

She nodded nervously.

He looked around, asking weakly. "We're alone?"

"Yes. Hector and Felipe are taking everyone back to Iquitos. They'll return for us. Hector said to wait here."

Antonio forced himself to his feet, buttoning the top of his shorts. "I don't even see a trail," he said looking around.

"The trail is on the other side of the undergrowth. We carried you along that branch so the people following us wouldn't find you."

"Who followed, *Sendero* or soldiers?"

"Hector didn't know. But there are two groups following them. The last group came running by a little while ago."

Antonio took a deep breath and shook his head, clearing it. "Come on." He held out his hand to her.

"What?"

"We're leaving."

"We can't. I told Hector we would be here when he returned."

"We need to leave." He kept his hand extended to her.

"But . . . ," she said, taking his hand, "what about Hector and Felipe coming back?"

"When did they leave us?"

"A few hours ago."

"They have Ignatious and the others with them?"

She nodded.

"Do you remember when we went for a run in Wyoming, the day after I arrived? I've seen you run. We can catch them before they reach Iquitos. If *Sendero* are following them, they are going to need our help," he said, gripping her hand. He pushed through the underbrush until they broke into the trail.

"We could get lost," she cautioned.

"Michelle, I grew up around the jungles of Boa Vista. I can't read a cold trail like Hector or Felipe, but I can get us home."

"You're in no shape to run to catch up to them."

He looked into her eyes. "Do you trust me?"

"You know I do."

He steeled himself for the run, focusing his force of will. He knew it would be hard. "Then let's go."

He released her hand and headed down the trail at a slow jog, drained by the fever. Michelle easily matched him stride for stride.

● ● ●

FELIPE STOPPED THE group. His ears absorbed the jungle behind them. He looked over to Hector. "They are going to catch us."

Hector nodded his agreement.

Alarm covered the faces of Ignatious, Agnus, and Cardoso.

"Is it us?" Agnus asked. "You could escape if you two didn't have us with you, couldn't you?"

Felipe nodded to her.

Agnus looked over to her two compatriots. "We can't let these two young boys be hurt because of us." She turned to Hector. "You run like the wind, child. Go away from here. Whatever happens to us is God's will. You two boys run."

"We will not leave you," Hector answered firmly and turned to Felipe. "We have a chance."

"What?"

"Listen beyond those following us."

Felipe strained his ears, sorting out the distant cries of birds. One set of birds sounded an alarm in the near distance as their pursuers passed beneath. At a greater distance, other birds were crying quick alarm before settling back into silence. "Two groups follow," Felipe whispered to himself.

Hector nodded.

"What does that mean?" Ignatious asked quickly.

Felipe looked up to him. "It means we have a chance."

"How?" Cardoso asked.

"If soldiers are following us, then *Sendero* are following them. If the *Sendero* are following us, then soldiers are following them," Hector explained.

"How does that help us?" Agnus asked.

"Hurry. Follow me," Felipe said.

"Hector?" Agnus asked again.

"Follow Felipe. I'll explain it as we go," Hector answered.

Agnus, Ignatious, and Cardoso quickly turned and tried to keep up with Felipe.

Hector followed Agnus, explaining loud enough for Ignatious and Cardoso to hear as well. "Felipe will arc our trail into a circle that cuts across our trail about a half kilometer back. The first group following us is close enough that they will follow the arc. If Felipe times it right, the second group will arrive where our trails cross about the time the first group cuts into the old trail. If the two groups are *Sendero* and soldiers, they'll fight to the death and we'll make it to Iquitos."

"What if they aren't different?" Agnus asked, out of breath.

"Then we die."

• • •

THE WOMAN TURNED from the screen, looking at McKay over her glasses, smiling, unaware of McKay's treachery.

"Are we on schedule?" McKay asked.

"Oh, yes. Socrates is downloading now into the emergency backup system. When that's complete, he'll accept the upgrade."

"Why the download?"

"Mr. Mullen's rules. In the event of a problem with an upgrade, Socrates' old programming could be recalled so he could continue as before. The old programming remains available until the next upgrade." She scanned her control panel. "Downloading completed," she said, looking to her watch, "and the new programming is in place. Five minutes after three. Right on cue."

"Any problems with the new programming?" McKay asked nervously.

"None," she said with maternal pride.

"Congratulations," McKay excused himself and returned to his office. He unfolded the letter from Brigham and picked up the phone. He punched in the numbers Brigham had written beside his name. The phone began to ring.

Brigham pulled the cellular phone from his jacket. "Jacob Brigham."

"Shane McKay here, Mr. Brigham."

"Yes. What do you have for me?" Brigham stared at Rajunt as he spoke with McKay. Rajunt returned the stare.

"Socrates accepted all upgrade programs moments ago."

"Any problems."

"None."

"That's what I like to hear. Keep up the good work, Shane. I'll get back to you."

"Yes, sir." McKay hung up, filled with himself.

Brigham stayed on the line. "Socrates?" he asked softly, knowing Socrates would be listening.

"Yes."

"What is your function?"

"To advance your interests, Mr. Brigham."

"Stay on the line in case I need you." Brigham folded his cellular and dropped it in his pocket, smiling at Rajunt. Rajunt surrendered a nod of respect.

"I think it's time you meet General De Silva, your Eminence."

"I would be delighted." Rajunt smiled pompously.

• • •

ANITA AND DIEGO pushed through the tightly packed throng for an hour before they made it to Rivera's shack, the crowd's epicenter.

The crowd had congregated quietly in front of the house, waiting to glimpse their Madonna.

"How do we get near her?" Diego whispered.

Anita shrugged. "We wait for the opportunity," she said, squatting onto the ground to blend with the crowd. Several children looked over to her and smiled. Diego squatted beside her.

An hour later, Carlota stepped from Rivera's shack. A hush swept over the crowd. She smiled at them and cries of "Madonna! Madonna!" went up.

Carlota was instantly mobbed by the children. She spoke with them, mostly listening and smiling while caressing the tops of their heads.

Anita rose and made her way up to the edge of the throng of children, staring at Carlota.

Carlota looked up from the children.

Anita froze. This woman before her had no malevolence. Her heart shut out no one, that was obvious. This was not the woman Marta described. This was no privileged *Limeño*, no enemy of the people.

"Yes?" Carlota asked gently.

"I–" Anita glanced back to Diego, "I just wanted to meet you."

Carlota's head turned slightly as she smiled at the woman. "I know you?"

"No." Anita shook her head. She had made it this far. She did not know what to say. "I just . . . I just wanted to meet you," she stammered.

"Now I know who sent you." Carlota smiled knowingly. "What is your name?"

"Anita." Her heart stopped. How could this woman know about María?

"You are sent by God. Please, please come in." Carlota turned and re-entered Rivera's shack, motioning for Anita to follow.

Anita glanced back once to Diego then vanished into the shack. She stood just inside the door's threshold. Angelica, Manuel, and Rivera were sitting at the table on folding chairs, talking softly.

"Everyone, this is Anita."

They looked up to Anita.

"She has been sent by God," Carlota announced.

Angelica rolled her eyes in frustration with Carlota but then smiled politely at Anita.

• • •

SÁNCHEZ STOPPED WHERE the trails crossed, looking back to João, who had knelt at the grassy intersection, studying foot-prints.

"Different trails?"

João shook his head. "I don't think so," he pointed down the trail leading straight ahead, "but see this?"

Sánchez knelt beside him, studying the trampled vines and leaves.

"At least nine people took this path."

"The Americans and the *Sendero* following them?" Sánchez asked quietly, looking around cautiously.

João nodded. "But look at this one." He pointed to the trail cutting across the one they followed. "Only five people travelled this one."

"We're missing four people suddenly." Sánchez said as he looked down the intersecting trail. "Unless the other four are still coming."

"That's my guess." João said. He stood and looked up the intersecting trail. "Your call, Captain."

"We'll wait here. The last four are following the Americans."

"*Sendero*," João said icily.

"*Sendero*," Sánchez repeated.

João stepped off the trail, lowering into the underbrush, ready to spring and fire. Sánchez took the other side of the trail, squatting out of sight.

Five minutes later, João whispered. "They're coming fast."

Fëdor had taken the lead as they ran, his exhaustion kept at bay by his hatred for Antonio. He was determined to be the first to catch him. As he ran, his mind painted images of what he would do to Antonio.

When he reached the grassy intersection, he stopped. His men caught up as he knelt to study the trail. "I don't understand where they are going." He looked up to his men standing around him. "Is this a trap?"

One of the *Sendero* started to speak. "They . . . ," he stopped short and stared. João rose silently, his weapon aimed at their bellies.

Fëdor did not understand the sudden puzzlement on his men's faces. Kneeling in the underbrush, he could not see Sánchez and João standing a few feet away with guns levelled.

João waited for the first *Sendero* to make a move. He had only a fraction of a second to wait.

The *Sendero* snapped up their machine guns at the same time. But they could not move faster than João's trigger finger.

A zipping sound jumped from João's barrel and cut the three *Sendero* in half before their weapons had even pointed at him. Their eyes widened for an instant before what remained of their bodies crumbled bloodily beside their leader.

"NO!" Michelle cried at the sound of gunfire up ahead on the trail, thinking her friends were dead.

"Get down!" Antonio knelt and drug her to his level. "They may have got 'em," he said slowly, sickened.

Far ahead along the trail, Felipe looked back to Hector. Both boys grinned triumphantly at one another.

"What was that?" Agnus turned back to Hector.

"We're going to make it," Felipe answered for Hector. He changed their direction directly for Iquitos.

Fëdor jumped up, his machine gun jammed to his hip. He froze when he saw Sánchez and João standing with aimed weapons.

João studied Fëdor's forearms with the eye of a surgeon. He was the most practiced marksman in the Peruvian special forces and knew Fëdor's forearms would tense a fraction of a second before he fired, to hold the machine gun during recoil.

Suddenly, the forearms tensed.

The zipping sound from João's weapon and the explosion in Fëdor's hands occurred simultaneously.

The gun flew from Fëdor's hands in fragments, slicing his hands as he stood staring in disbelief.

"He's all yours, Captain," João said.

Fëdor glanced at João and back to Sánchez. Fear and panic gripped him as he stared at the man whose sisters he had raped. He saw living hatred in Sánchez' face. His hands snapped into the air. "I surrender!"

Sánchez shook his head slowly.

Fëdor recognized the death sentence. "I surrender, I said!" he screamed as if Sánchez had not heard.

"Run, *Sendero*. Run for your life," Sánchez snarled.

"You'll shoot me in the back!" Fëdor trembled.

Sánchez tossed his gun to João, who caught it with one hand. "No, you don't get to die that easily." Sánchez pulled his long hunting knife from its sheath, twirling it in the late afternoon sun. "I am going to kill you with this after I do to you what you tried to do to me."

Fëdor glanced nervously at João then spun and broke into a full run. Adrenaline electrified his body as he ran, breaking through virgin underbrush. He kept looking back as he ran. Sánchez, becoming smaller and smaller, simply stood staring at him.

"He's heading for the Napo, Captain."

"I know," Sánchez answered softly.

The Napo river feeds the Amazon downstream from Iquitos. It is a giant, sluggish brown river that slowly lumbers with the rainforest's heavy runoff. The slow current and the murky waters, saturated with silt, perfectly suit piranha.

Sánchez looked up at the sun and back toward Fëdor, who was quickly disappearing into the jungle up ahead. "Give me five minutes before you follow, João."

"You got it, Captain."

Clutching the knife in his right hand, Sánchez started running, following Fëdor.

João watched his captain disappear into the jungle. He checked his watch. He would give him exactly five minutes.

"Do you think they're alive?" Michelle whispered anxiously.

"I don't know. We have to keep going," Antonio answered, his eyes never leaving the trail ahead of them as he watched for returning *Sendero*. "But we'll go slower." He reached back for her hand, which Michelle gave him.

Fëdor looked back over his shoulder without losing a stride. He saw Sánchez start after him. Fëdor's lungs burned but he increased his speed.

Sánchez kept one pace. His eyes locked on Fëdor.

• • •

MARTA HEARD THE key in the lock. She walked into the living room as Benito opened the door. "You're early," she said, kissing him lightly.

He would not return her kiss.

"What is wrong?" she asked, staring.

He looked blankly at her.

"Did I do something wrong?" she asked nervously.

"No, Chica," he said softly, "but we need to talk."

Marta walked him to the sofa and sat him beside her. "Tell me what's wrong."

"I lied to you."

Marta tensed. "About what?"

"Remember when I told you De Silva had uncovered a *Sendero* plan to kill the Madonna and blame the military?"

"Yes."

"It's not true." He looked away.

She gently grabbed his chin and with her soft voice coaxed his eyes back to hers. "What's not true?"

"I discovered the real plan." His eyes screamed with the pain of betrayal.

"I don't know what you're talking about." She gently stroked his cheek.

"It's here." He pulled out the copy he had made of De Silva's letter. "The military plans to kill her tomorrow at noon, when Rivera is preaching and away from his home." He unfolded the letter to show her.

"What?" Marta snatched the letter from him, her eyes poring over it.

Benito sat quietly, watching her read the letter. She did not look up until she had finished.

"What are you going to do?" she asked coldly.

"I don't know what to do."

"You know we have to take this to the newspapers. I have a friend with 'El Sol'. We must take it to her."

"NO!" Benito snatched the letter back. "We can't. I stole this from the general's office. I could be shot!"

"We must, Benito."

He shook his head belligerently.

"We cannot let that woman die."

"We can't turn that letter over to anyone!" he said firmly. "I brought it only for you."

Marta studied him. "What can we do then?"

"I don't know but we are not turning this letter over to anyone," he said firmly, his voice trembling.

Marta looked to him comfortingly. "You were brave to show me the letter, Benito."

"You said we can't have secrets if we are going to build a life together." He looked deep into her eyes. "And being with you for the rest of my life is the most important thing to me."

Marta took his hands in hers. "I'm proud of you, Benito. I promise I will be with you for the rest of your life."

"Promise?" he asked like a child.

"Promise." Marta rose. "Wait here, I have something to give you."

"What?" He looked up at her.

"No, no. Close your eyes." She smiled, "Now you have to promise me you'll keep your eyes closed."

He smiled thinly and closed his eyes. "Promise."

Marta walked into their bedroom, opened the closet and reached into her heavy jacket. She pulled from the breast pocket a Luger equipped with a silencer. She held it behind her back as she walked into the living room.

"Are your eyes closed, Benito?" she asked sweetly, walking up behind him as he sat facing away.

"Uh-huh," he said boyishly.

She put the barrel to the back of his skull.

He felt the cold metal. His eyes snapped open.

She pulled the trigger.

• • •

FËDOR'S LUNGS BURNED as they fought to supply him with air. Adrenaline surged through his body, animating every muscle. His legs moved in a blur as he bounded over logs and bushes.

Every time he looked back, Sánchez was closer. He pushed harder, knowing the river was near, knowing if he could make it, he'd find the Yagua Indians' fishing rafts along the shores. A raft would take him safely out of Sánchez' reach.

João checked his watch. Five minutes had passed. He slung Sánchez' gun's strap over his shoulder, inhaled deeply, and took up Sánchez' trail at a dead run.

• • •

MARTA BURST INTO her apartment. "María!" she gasped, out of breath from bounding up the steps two at a time.

María walked from the kitchen, drying her hands. "What's wrong?"

Marta handed her the letter. "This is the *federales'* plan."

María unfolded the letter. "When did you get this?" she asked as she read.

"About a half hour ago. Benito brought it home. He discovered it in De Silva's office this afternoon."

María smiled when she finished. "Amateurs." She looked up to Marta. "He let you take this?" she sounded incredulous.

Marta smiled her death smile.

"This doesn't give us much time." María looked at the clock on the wall. "We have fourteen hours before they show up at Villa Del Mar tomorrow morning for our little friend." She looked to Marta. "Bring me a map."

Marta hurriedly returned with a map, unfolding it across the living room table.

"Where is Chosica on this?" María asked.

Marta pointed.

"How many people do we have available?" María asked without taking her eyes from the map.

"About thirty."

"Do we have vans?"

"No, but we can easily steal what we need."

"Do so." María continued eyeballing the map, "Where is the Vatican viper right now?"

"Last report said he was in his hotel room with the rich American."

"What is his name?"

"Rajunt, Cardinal Hans Rajunt."

María looked up. "How old is your report?"

"Couple hours."

"Recheck it. I want to know, not guess."

Marta picked up the phone and called her people at the Miraflores. María studied the map as Marta spoke.

"They're still there," Marta said, hanging up the phone.

"I want you and Diego to take a van and kidnap the Vatican viper from his hotel tomorrow morning at eleven thirty."

"But Diego is with Anita at Villa Del Mar."

"Then send someone to get him, he's too useful to waste there. Anita can do her job by herself."

Marta nodded obediently.

"Bring me anyone you find with the viper, including the rich American. Bring them to me here," María pointed to the map, between Lima and Chosica, "where De Silva plans the ambush."

"What are you going to do?" Marta asked.

"Just do as I say." María looked up from the map. "I want two vans filled with well armed *Sendero* to pick me up at seven tomorrow morning. Have them bring me a nun's habit and several comrades dressed as nuns. Can you arrange that?"

"Easily. I'll have a nun's habit brought to you tonight."

"De Silva's people plan to pick up the Madonna at eleven . . . ." María studied the map carefully. "Which means they'll reach their ambush point around noon. They'll have two vans. One will carry the Madonna and the soldiers and the other will carry *Sendero* prisoners." She jabbed a finger at the ambush point half way between Chosica and Lima. "The special forces will set up an hour before the van with the Madonna comes by. When they arrive, we'll be set up with the van across the middle of the road."

"They won't stop for anyone. They'll shoot you where you stand," Marta warned.

María smiled. "No, they won't. What they'll find is a road full of helpless nuns with a van out of gas. Something easy to remedy. They won't see the other *Sendero* hiding off the road.

"We'll open fire on the van."

"Then what?" Marta asked.

"You make sure you reach the ambush point around noon with Rajunt," María ordered. "After taking out the special forces, we will wait for the army regulars to come by with the Madonna and the *Sendero* prisoners. I want no survivors."

"Kill the rich American if he's with Rajunt?"

"Especially a rich American." María smiled. "When the American news explains the Peruvian government killed a powerful American to frame the *Sendero*, the military will be isolated. The people will hate them. With the American people outraged, the generals' conservative friends in Washington won't go near them to help."

"What about the *Sendero* prisoners?"

"Sadly, they must die as well." María shrugged. "It's for the cause."

"But I have friends in that group." Marta protested lightly.

"Unfortunate, but the more that die the better the press."

"But why kill the cardinal? Wouldn't the Vatican pay a fortune to get him back?"

"Killing the viper," María laughed, "I have to admit is simply for pleasure. Have you arranged for our reporters with '*El Sol*' to happen by with their cameras?"

"They'll come by at the right time," Marta assured.

María folded De Silva's letter and stuck it in her pocket. "We need to make many copies of this letter for the newspapers. Where can we go?"

"I know a place near the Plaza Francia. We can take it there," Marta answered.

"Let's go."

• • •

SUNLIGHT OOZED THROUGH the jungle foliage ahead. Fëdor knew the river was close. Sánchez was still behind him, crashing through the jungle. He looked back, Sánchez was closing. Fëdor's hands trembled as they pistoned ahead of his body.

Fear fueled Fëdor. Revenge fed Sánchez.

Suddenly, Fëdor burst from the jungle and onto the lazy banks of the Napo. He looked frantically for a Yagua fishing raft and spotted one upstream.

A corner of the raft sat lodged in the sand as the rest floated in the murky river. He dashed for it.

As he reached it, he looked back. Sánchez broke through the clearing and looked up the river's bank, spotting him.

Fëdor lifted the corner of the raft from the sand and shoved as hard as he could. In slow motion, the raft slid into the sluggish brown water. Fëdor dove on, frantically looking back for Sánchez.

Sánchez reached the water's edge and lunged into the air. The brown waters splashed around his body as his fingers caught the raft's edge. His fingers locked hold. In an instant, Sánchez' muscular arm slammed atop the raft, dripping with water.

Fëdor kicked at Sánchez' face. But powerful muscles and sheer determination pulled Sánchez aboard the raft.

Fëdor scurried to a corner when he caught the glint of the steel blade in Sánchez' right hand. His eyes bulged with fear as Sánchez righted himself.

The raft drifted lazily into the middle of the river as the lumbering current pushed them toward the distant Atlantic, one man standing with a knife in hand and one huddled in the corner.

"I said I surrender!" Fëdor screamed.

"I said you're going to die."

"No!" Fëdor lunged for Sánchez, locking both hands around the forearm that held the knife. Sánchez' feet slipped from under him and he crashed onto his back. Fëdor pounded Sánchez' arm against the edge of the raft, trying to break his hold on the knife.

Sánchez rolled Fëdor and slid atop him, blinded by fury as he raised the knife high in the air for its death plunge into Fëdor's chest.

Fëdor thrust his hips into the air, catapulting Sánchez over him, onto his back. The knife clanked once against the raft and rolled into the murky waters, disappearing instantly.

Fëdor lunged at Sánchez, fists flailing. Sánchez grabbed a handful of hair and slammed Fëdor face first into the raft. Fëdor absorbed the blow and spun onto his back, kicking wildly until he could get to his feet.

Both men stood at opposite ends of the raft, glaring.

Fëdor screamed and rushed for Sánchez, his hands extended like talons. Sánchez dropped to his back and planted his feet against Fëdor's stomach, shoving him high into the air, letting Fëdor's momentum keep him in flight.

Sánchez heard a huge splash and spun onto his stomach. Fëdor's head rose frantically from the murky surface about six feet from the raft, his eyes bulging.

"I wouldn't splash if I were you." Sánchez suddenly smiled. "You'll draw in the piranha."

"HELP ME!" Fëdor screamed, frantically looking around the surface of the water.

Sánchez reached his hand into the warm, brown river, splashing water while staring at Fëdor.

"Stop!" Fëdor screamed.

Sánchez increased the splashing with his hand, his eyes, like Fëdor's, searching the surface of the water.

"I know *Sendero* secrets! I will tell you!" Fëdor pleaded.

"Take them to your grave," Sánchez answered and suddenly smiled at something in the distance behind Fëdor.

Fëdor spun around.

Piranha hunt in massive packs. Signs of their collective endeavor can appear as a boiling of fins along the water's surface.

Fëdor saw a seething boil cut through the water toward him. He spun back, swimming as fast as he could for the raft.

"You might make it," Sánchez laughed.

Fëdor's hand slammed onto the edge of the raft just as the boiling water reached him. His head shot out of the water as they reached his feet. "Help me!" He screamed at Sánchez, trying to haul himself onto the raft. "Help me!" His fingers bled against the rough wood as he clawed for a hold. The fish began feeding on his legs.

With superhuman strength, he lifted his torso from the murky water, frantically kicking his legs, his eyes begging Sánchez for mercy.

"This is for my family," Sánchez said coldly, planting his feet against Fëdor's chest. Their eyes locked. Fëdor's had filled with terror. Sánchez kicked him into the water with all his strength.

"NOOoooooo . . . ," Fëdor cried as he splashed onto the surface before the water folded over him. When he surfaced, several piranha had locked their teeth into his chin and cheeks.

João emerged from the jungle suddenly and watched Fëdor's death struggle from the lazy banks of the river. A smile crept onto his face.

The water boiled around Fëdor's head.

"AAAAGH!"

Above the river, dark clouds had grouped into one giant rain cloud to provide the region with its daily downpour.

Fëdor screamed and flailed his arms in the air, which carried piranha high above him as they hung on. "NOOO!" he cried one last time before surrendering to the murky brown waters.

Sánchez watched the top of Fëdor's bloody head sink from sight.

The boiling continued for several moments, then vanished. The waters stilled and the river returned to its sluggish march to the sea.

The dark cloud overhead released its torrent of rain.

Sánchez stared unsatisfied at the red veins of blood bubbling to the surface of the murky water. He dropped to his knees, crying out for his mother. He laid his head between his knees and sobbed for his family.

When the rains began flooding across the raft, Sánchez threw back his head to face the sky. Teary eyes were framed by a face of anguish and heartache.

As he stared sobbing at the dark sky, warm rain began to wash the shadow paint from his face and chest.

• • •

ANTONIO STOPPED COLD in his tracks when they reached the grassy intersection. The *Sendero* lay crumbled in a bloody pile. The underbrush was flattened all around.

Breathing hard, Antonio studied the path taken by Felipe and the others. "They made it through."

Michelle grimaced at the bodies and looked up to him. "How can you tell?"

"These are Hector's prints." He pointed to an indentation of only four toes in the soft earth. "Felipe would leave no tracks—those three sets have to be Ignatious, Agnus, and Cardoso. And look, no other tracks follow them." He gave a definite nod. "They got away."

Michelle pointed to the path taken by Fëdor, Sánchez, and João. "What's that?"

"Nothing that concerns us." He glanced at it and then looked back to Hector's prints. "We can pick up our speed again." He bent and retrieved a crumbled stem. "This break is new. If we hurry, we can reach them before they reach Iquitos." He looked to Michelle. "Can you do it?"

She looked him over, he was still recovering. "Can you?"

He nodded.

• • •

BERNADINE SAT BESIDE John. They sat on the little deck overlooking John's Zen rock garden, his bubble of peace deep within the mountain.

"This is so tranquil." Bernadine studied the tiny bonsai clinging to the spot-lighted rock in the center of the circular room. "You designed it?"

"Yes. It's my favorite room," he turned to Bernadine, "and the closer I get to death, the more favorite it becomes." He smiled wistfully and looked up, "Socrates?"

"Yes."

"Has Michelle reported in yet?"

"No."

"Try to reach her," John ordered.

"Acknowledged," Socrates answered.

Several seconds passed. "John?" Socrates asked, imitating Michelle's voice.

"Are you all right, Michelle?"

"I'm fine, John." The voice match was perfect.

"Where are you?" John asked.

"Iquitos."

"You found Antonio and Father Ignatious, already?"

"No. But Jacob Brigham has most of the Peruvian military helping find them. I don't know what we'd do without Jacob."

John looked at Bernadine, puzzled. "What do you mean?"

"Because of him, the military has brought in their helicopters equipped with infrared and night scopes to help find Antonio. They are combing the area where they think he might be. They asked me to stay here in case he shows up in Iquitos."

"And you don't mind waiting in Iquitos while they look for Antonio?" John asked, amazed with her restraint.

"Absolutely not."

"Michelle, that surprises me. But if you're satisfied . . . ," John said, then asked, "How are O'Riley's efforts looking to you?"

"We still don't know exactly what happened to Riner. But the physicians and attorneys you sent down are taking care of the injured children and their families. Everything is under control. I'll let you know when anything develops with Antonio and Father Ignatious."

"Ok, I'll stay out of your hair. Call me when you get news on anything."

"You got it, John."

"Michelle?"

"Yes?"

"I have a strange feeling. You be careful."

"I'll be fine, John."

"Michelle has terminated the call." Socrates returned to his usual voice.

• • •

EVENING WAS FOLDING around the jungle.

Antonio and Michelle had maintained their pace for a half hour when Antonio spotted Hector in the distance. "Come on!" he yelled back to Michelle exhaustedly.

Michelle stayed right behind him.

Hector spun when he heard the rapid footsteps, his eyes widened in surprise. "Antonio!" he cried and ran back. Felipe and the others stopped in their tracks and looked back to the reunion.

Hector ran to Antonio. "You made it!"

Antonio hugged him and dropped him back onto the ground. "I want you to show me those medicinal leaves sometime," he said, grinning.

Agnus was the first of the others to make it back to them. "What happened to those people following us?" she asked nervously.

Antonio looked up to her, "Forget 'em." He looked back down to Hector. "How far to Iquitos?"

"If we hurry, we'll be there before night sets in," Felipe answered, coming along side. Ignatious followed close behind.

"My boy! My boy!" Ignatious exclaimed and wrapped thin, sunburned arms around Antonio.

Antonio held him for a moment then held him at arm's length. "We made it!" he laughed.

Felipe looked up at Michelle. "I told you everything would be ok."

"And you were right," she answered with a broad smile.

Hector looked to the evening sky. "We better hurry if we're going to get home by dark." He looked to Felipe. "Keep on lead and I'll take the rear."

Felipe turned and headed for Iquitos.

An hour later, they broke into a clearing on the city's edge.

"What about Dos Santos?" Stauffen turned to Felipe as he stepped onto the pavement of Putumayo street.

"Who is Dos Santos?" Antonio asked.

"He's the one that sent the soldiers after us," Michelle answered.

"We better stay out of sight," Felipe answered Stauffen.

Stauffen turned to them, "Tonight, everyone stays at my place. It's on the edge of town and set back far enough from the street that no one will know we're back. I've got enough beds for everyone if Felipe and Hector can share a bed. Antonio, you can bunk with me."

Felipe, Hector, and Antonio nodded.

"I need to call John, immediately," Michelle said.

"You can use the phone at my place," Stauffen answered.

• • •

RIVERA'S SHANTY SHACK had two rooms, one for Carlota and Angelica, the other for everyone else.

Carlota stood and rubbed her eyes. "I need to sleep. I can't keep my eyes open any longer."

Angelica glanced up at her. "I'll be in soon."

Carlota nodded and walked over to give Angelica, Manuel, and Rivera a light kiss on their cheeks. "I'll see you all in the morning." She turned to Anita, extending both hands. "Please stay the night."

Anita lightly touched Carlota's fingers and quietly nodded.

"Do you mind sleeping on the floor with us?" Rivera asked.

Anita shook her head.

• • •

STAUFFEN PULLED SHUT the heavy curtains before switching on the lights. "We'll be safe here for the night," he said, bolting the front door.

"May I use your phone?" Michelle asked, lifting the receiver to her ear.

"Certainly. If you need privacy, there's another phone in my study."

She shook her head, punched in some numbers, and stood waiting for the call to connect. "John?"

"Michelle?" Socrates asked, using Mullen's voice.

"I just made it into Iquitos. Antonio and Father Ignatious are both with me. They're safe."

"Thank God! Well done, Michelle."

"We're not in the clear yet, John. I don't know how to tell you this, but I think Brigham is up to something. I know he's an old friend. But something is wrong."

"Why do you think that?"

"There is a connection between this Major Dos Santos and Brigham. Dos Santos tried to have us killed," she warned, looking at Stauffen who nodded agreement.

"Let's not jump to conclusions." Socrates warned with John's voice.

"Any word from Carlota?" Michelle asked.

"Yes. Brigham is taking good care of her. I spoke with Father Manuel. They are worried about you."

"I'll call her after I hang up with you."

"You won't be able to reach her."

"Why not?"

"She, Angelica, and Father Manuel have moved into Villa Del Mar, her old neighborhood. There's no phone service. They are staying with one of the messianic priests, a Father Rivera. The crowds are unbelievable. Carlota is staying there until the child is born."

"I don't think that's wise."

"I don't either, but you know Carlota. Can you fly to Lima in the morning to talk with her?"

"Certainly. If I can't persuade her, perhaps Antonio can. We should fly out tonight."

"No. I want you to make me a promise, Michelle."

"What?"

"I can tell by your voice that you are exhausted. I want you to promise me you won't fly until the morning."

"I'm not that tired."

"Carlota is just fine. She doesn't need you there tonight. Now promise you'll get some sleep before you fly."

Michelle took a deep breath. "Promise."

"You can leave first thing in the morning."

"All right, John."

"Give me a call when you're in the air tomorrow morning so I can tell Janice McClain when you'll arrive."

"Good night, John."

"Good night, Michelle. I'm glad you're safe." Socrates terminated his conversation with Michelle then called Brigham.

"Yes."

"Mr. Brigham. I have made contact with Michelle."

"Where is she?"

"Iquitos. She is scheduled to fly into Lima tomorrow morning."

"Will she be alone?"

"No, she will have Father De Montesinos on board."

Brigham thought to himself for several seconds. "I don't want her to reach Lima."

Socrates remained silent.

"Can you do anything about that?" Brigham asked.

"Possibly. Michelle's plane was redesigned so I could fly it by autopilot in an emergency. Once the autopilot is engaged, I can lock her out and disable the craft."

"She wouldn't be able to disengage the autopilot?"

"Not once I have control."

"If you get control of the plane, disable it."

Socrates made no response.

• • •

MARÍA GLANCED OUT the window to two vans pulling to the curb below. A man jumped from the first van and ran into her building. She checked her watch. Exactly seven a.m. The world was coming to life.

The man hurried up the steps, rounded the bannister of her landing, and stopped when he looked up to see María dressed as a nun.

"Commander?" the *Sendero* asked.

She closed the door to Marta's apartment. "Let's go."

The two hurriedly descended the staircase, left the building, and entered the first van.

María took the front passenger's seat, looking back to the four other women dressed as nuns. She turned to the driver. "You have the coordinates?"

The man nodded and pulled from the curb.

The two vans headed through side streets under a gray sky and pulled onto Avenida Abancay, accelerating toward the Central Highway.

• • •

THE HEAVY COASTAL fog rolled across Lima like a death shroud. Little of the morning's sunlight reached the streets and what did was so diffused it painted faces a ghostly pallor.

Rajunt turned to the side as he studied his reflection in the full length mirror, delighted with the way he looked in his silk scarlet raiments. De Silva would be suitably impressed.

A knock drew his eyes from the mirror to the door. "Enter," he said, walking from the mirror.

As Brigham opened the doors, General De Silva turned to his two guards. "Wait here at the door."

Brigham was all smiles. "Good morning, your Eminence."

Rajunt nodded regally.

"I would like you to meet General De Silva, your Eminence," Brigham said.

Rajunt extended his ring finger, which De Silva kissed.

Brigham looked back to De Silva, "His Eminence, Cardinal Rajunt."

De Silva inclined his head politely. "I hope you are enjoying our country, your Eminence."

"Delightful country, General."

"If I can make your stay more comfortable, please do not hesitate to let me know," De Silva said and glanced momentarily at Brigham before looking back to Rajunt. "I understand you, too, are concerned with the messianic priests stirring people's expectations."

"Quite," Rajunt answered and gestured to the elaborately set table. "I took the liberty of ordering a small meal for us." He looked at Brigham, "Polite conversation is enhanced by good food and fine wine."

"Thank you, your Eminence," De Silva responded, always ready to eat.

Rajunt picked up the phone at his desk. "This is Cardinal Rajunt. Have our meal sent up now." He put down the receiver and turned to De Silva. "You understand the Church's only concern is the number of people turning away from it, the number of souls being lost to this charlatan."

"Of course," De Silva said, pulling a Havana cigar from his pocket. "We appreciate your concern, but ours is somewhat different." De Silva clipped the tip of the cigar, "Do you mind if I smoke?"

"Absolutely, I do."

De Silva slowly stuffed the circumcised cigar back into his pocket.

"What exactly is your concern, General?" Rajunt's brows narrowed.

"We have intelligence reports that the *Sendero* are planning to murder this false madonna in order to implicate the government and incite revolution. That we will not allow."

"How do you intend to prevent it?" Rajunt asked nervously. He did not want De Silva to tell him the truth.

"We are taking her into protective custody."

Rajunt glanced knowingly at Brigham then back to De Silva. "A wise precaution," he smiled.

"You approve?" De Silva asked.

"Of course. This false madonna must be protected until her child is born. When people see the child is no different than the rest of you, they will lose confidence in the messianics and return to the Church, where they belong."

Rajunt glanced at Brigham then quickly looked back to De Silva. With official positions established, De Silva and Rajunt smiled at one another.

Suddenly, a verbal confrontation developed beyond the door.

De Silva sprung to his feet and swung open the double doors. "What is the problem?" he asked a guard.

"These men will not let us pass," Diego said, having returned from Villa Del Mar for this assignment. He stood behind a large room service cart piled high with silver trays and decanters of orange juice and milk. Marta stood beside him.

"The warm food is cooling and the cool food is warming," Marta warned flippantly.

Diego bowed his head toward De Silva. "We can leave it with the guards if you prefer to serve yourself."

"Diego." Rajunt came to the door, motioning for him to wheel in the cart of food.

"You know this man?" a guard asked Rajunt.

"I am surprised your subordinates control such situations for you, General," Rajunt scolded disapprovingly, ignoring the guard.

De Silva motioned in Diego and Marta, closing the door behind them. The guards returned to watching the hallway for intruders.

Rajunt moved to the table and gestured for Brigham and De Silva to join him. He sat and motioned for Diego to serve them.

Diego snapped a napkin into the air, laying it ceremoniously across Rajunt's lap.

Rajunt looked up, "What did you bring for us, Diego?"

"Only the finest for you, your Eminence." Diego lifted several silver lids from their dishes. "A smorgasbord of local cuisine." Diego pointed to the different dishes. "*Seco de cordero*, a northern coast dish of roasted lamb. This is *ají de gallina*, a rich blend of creamed chicken and rocoto peppers. And this is *arroz con pato a la chiclayana*, duck and rice." He pointed to the last dish, "And finally, the *ceviche*, white fish atop lemon, onion, and rocoto peppers."

De Silva nodded approvingly to Rajunt.

"We brought a special desert," Marta added.

"Tell us what it is," Rajunt said, smiling toward De Silva.

"Would you prefer to be surprised?" Marta asked.

The smile on Rajunt's thin lips straightened into a line of command. "Tell us now."

Diego and Marta looked to one another then nodded obediently to Rajunt. They knelt beside the cart and lifted the heavy linen cover draping the cart.

Rajunt and Brigham's eyes widened as Diego and Marta straightened. Diego held a pistol and Marta an Uzi. Both weapons were tipped with silencers.

De Silva's chubby eyes narrowed, "*Sendero*."

Marta smiled. "Yes. *Sendero*."

"Diego?" Rajunt looked confused.

"How do you correct for the guards?" Brigham asked contemptuously.

Diego walked over to De Silva as Marta moved beside the double wooden doors. Diego shoved the pistol into De Silva's back, behind his heart. "Call in your guards, General. When they enter, instruct them to drop their weapons."

"They know better than to drop their weapons when they guard me," De Silva answered arrogantly.

"Then you will die." Diego shoved the barrel hard into De Silva's abundant flesh.

"Guards," De Silva raised his voice.

They opened the door, behind which Marta stood concealed.

"Tell them to step inside." Diego hissed.

"Do as he says," De Silva ordered, "and put down your weapons."

Both guards eyed Diego behind De Silva. The order was too great a security breach. They tensed. Diego lodged the barrel even deeper into De Silva's back.

"Do as I say!" De Silva barked.

The men stepped inside and lowered their weapons onto the carpet. Marta slowly shoved the doors shut with her boot, her weapon trained at their backs.

Both men glanced over their shoulders and looked back to her.

"Tell them to raise their hands and keep them high," Marta said softly to De Silva, her eyes never leaving the two soldiers.

"Do as she says," De Silva said coldly.

Their arms raised slowly into the air.

"Tell them to kneel in front of the sofa," Diego instructed. "Bury their faces in the seat cushions."

De Silva nodded Diego's order to them.

The two kept their eyes on Diego as they moved to the sofa and complied. As they buried their faces into the soft cushions, Marta stepped behind them, the silencer-tipped Uzi aimed at their backs.

She glanced to Diego, who nodded. She looked down to the men, gripped the Uzi tightly, and fired. A bloody spray of flesh, bone, and upholstery stuffing exploded into the air. The men's legs jerked straight out and their bodies slid to the floor.

De Silva and Brigham sat frozen silently in place, only their eyes moved.

Marta walked to the cart and knelt. When she stood, she held two sets of clothes, one she tossed to Diego. Rajunt glared as Diego caught the clothes with one hand and continued holding the pistol to De Silva's back with the other.

"You will not succeed," Rajunt said to Diego.

"Shut up, priest," Marta hissed.

Rajunt looked bored with her. "Or you will do what?"

"I'll put a bullet through your brain," Marta warned, her tone dripping with venom.

Rajunt focused his eyes deep into Marta. "I doubt that, underling." He slowly turned his head toward Brigham and De Silva, speaking as if Marta and Diego were not present. "These two take orders, they do not give them. Neither has the air of a leader."

"Shut up, priest!" Marta jammed her gun barrel toward Rajunt.

Rajunt pulled off his gold wire-frame glasses, fogging them with his breath, then cleaning them with his linen napkin. He spoke casually. "These two would have killed us by now had they that option. That is how their little minds think. They are, however, under strict orders to deliver us somewhere," Rajunt paused, "alive." He glared at Diego and pushed his glasses back to the bridge of his nose.

Diego left De Silva's back and moved next to Rajunt, spinning his chair back to face him. Rajunt stared back with cold black eyes.

Diego slapped him hard, knocking the wire-frame glasses across the room. Rajunt's eyes never left him.

"You are right we are to deliver you alive," he seethed, "but we do not have to deliver you unharmed. Do you understand that or would you like another demonstration?"

"I understand far more than you suspect, Diego," Rajunt said coldly. A trickle of blood oozed from a corner of his thin lips.

Marta changed into her street clothes. She kept the Uzi on the three as Diego slipped into his.

"Call your driver. Tell him to bring your car to the front entrance," Diego said as he buttoned his shirt.

"You'll never get away with this," Rajunt hissed.

"God's will be done." Diego smiled.

● ● ●

A DARK GREEN van turned from the Central Highway onto the unpaved road leading to Villa Del Mar, slowing as it neared the crowd a quarter mile from Rivera's shack. The military driver switched on the undulating siren and gradually opened a path into Villa Del Mar.

Angelica looked to Manuel when they heard the siren. They opened the unpainted shutters and looked out. The van cut its siren as it pulled beside the shack.

Soldiers piled from the back of the van. A captain emerged from the passenger's side and came to the door. He was short and sported a neatly trimmed mustache.

The crowd packed around them, threateningly.

Angelica opened the door with Manuel beside her.

"Angelica Montoya?" the captain asked politely.

She nodded, blocking the doorway. Carlota and Anita crowded behind Manuel.

"May we come in?"

"What do you want?" Angelica asked warily.

"Angelica, don't be rude. Let the gentlemen in," Carlota said, lightly touching Angelica's shoulder.

Angelica and Manuel backed away from the door, allowing the soldiers in. After the last entered, the captain closed the door, shutting out the crowd.

"We are here to take all of you into protective custody immediately," the captain explained tersely.

Carlota tensed.

"Why?" Anita stepped forward.

"Who are you?" he asked.

"A friend."

"We have a report, a reliable report, that the *Sendero* are planning a raid on Villa Del Mar. They intend to kill *Señorita* Cabral."

"When?" Angelica's eyes narrowed, her hand reached back for Carlota.

"This morning. We learned of it an hour ago."

Carlota looked through the man's soul. She leaned up and whispered into Angelica's ear. "Don't let them take us."

Angelica's body tensed. "We appreciate your offer and your concerns but we prefer to stay here."

The mustached captain shook his head. "I am to take you into protective custody now."

Carlota moved beside Angelica. "But we don't want to go with you," she insisted.

"Orders," the man answered and gestured to his men, who surrounded them.

Manuel stepped up to the captain. "I am Father De las Casas. Surely Carlota would be safe if your men stood guard around this house."

The captain looked contemptuously at Manuel. "I am to take you all into protective custody."

Anita looked to Angelica. "We must go with them."

"I don't want to go," Carlota said firmly.

"If you resist, the crowd outside will try to help you. We will shoot anyone who interferes," the man answered. "You don't want that on your conscience." He motioned to his men.

They opened the door with weapons drawn and tried to form a corridor to the back of the van. The crowd resisted them, standing its ground.

The captain stood at the crowd's edge and spoke loudly. "We are taking the Madonna into protection. *Sendero* guerrillas are right now on the way to kill her."

A low murmur went through the crowd.

Carlota knew one word for help would unleash the crowd, which would not stop until the soldiers were dead, no matter the cost. "Please allow us to pass."

The crowd backed away, allowing the soldiers to escort the three women and the priest to the back of the van. When the van doors closed, the crowd surged to peer inside.

Anita and Angelica sandwiched Carlota protectively between them. They looked nervously to one another as the van began to move. Manuel sat to Angelica's left.

The siren let out its shrill warning and the crowd opened to let the van pass. Within ten minutes, the van turned onto the Central Highway and headed toward the Andes Mountains.

An identical van, parked alongside the highway and carrying *Sendero* prisoners, accelerated to follow closely.

• • •

STAUFFEN SNAPPED ON the light to the garage. A kayak lay overhead on the cross beams, belly up. A mud-caked green Jeep faced the garage door.

Michelle bent and hugged Hector. "Thank you for everything."

He grinned, reveling in her attention.

"Are you sure you don't want to return to Lima with us, Sister?" Antonio asked Agnus.

She put her arm around Hector's shoulder and shook her head. "I'm sure." She looked down to Hector. "We have much work to do here, don't we?"

Hector nodded and looked up proudly to Antonio.

Antonio knelt beside him. "When we finish in Lima, we'll come back for you," he said softly.

"Felipe, you coming with me to the airport?" Stauffen asked, opening the driver's door. Felipe climbed into the front seat, pushing past him.

"You were a source of strength back there, Sister. I would not have made it otherwise," Cardoso said softly to Agnus.

"We all provided strength to one another," she answered softly and tightened her arm around Hector's shoulder.

Cardoso walked around the Jeep to the front seat and got in next to Felipe.

Antonio helped Ignatious into the back. Michelle climbed in beside him.

Stauffen poked his head out the driver's window. "Sister Agnus, be sure to close the door behind me. And keep the house curtains drawn until I return," he said.

Hector and Agnus waved from inside the garage then Agnus swung shut the door.

• • •

RAJUNT, BRIGHAM, AND De Silva descended the massive stairs to the Miraflores' entrance. Diego and Marta followed closely.

"Keep smiling, General," Diego said softly, lodging the pistol against De Silva's kidneys.

The driver spotted De Silva and pulled the black Mercedes limousine beside them.

Diego piled into the back with his prisoners. Marta climbed into the front, and the driver looked quizzically at her. Then he saw the barrel of the Uzi and turned apprehensively to De Silva.

"Drive," De Silva ordered calmly.

"Yes, drive," Marta said, smiling to the driver.

The limousine pulled away from the hotel and turned onto the Avenida Arequipa.

"Where are you taking us?" De Silva asked nervously.

Brigham remained silent, frozen with fear.

"They are taking us where they have been told to take us. These two do not have original thoughts," Rajunt said crisply.

"Drive to the Central Highway and head for Chosica," Marta told the driver, glaring at Rajunt.

• • •

RAY STAUFFEN SLOWED when they reached the airport. He headed the Jeep for the hangars on the other side of the runway. "I don't see Dos Santos' security," he said, looking around.

"Why would there be?" Michelle asked.

"Dos Santos," Stauffen said, his eyes combing the area as they circled the airport to reach the hangars. "I'm surprised he doesn't have soldiers at our hangar." Relief bolstered his voice as they pulled up to the quonset hangar.

He stopped the Jeep, pushed a button on his dash, and the hangar's enormous doors began to part. The Jeep emptied.

Felipe stood mesmerized as the sunlight slowly flooded into the hangar, revealing the black plane with reflective gold windows. "What kind of plane is that?" he asked in a hushed tone.

"It's a Learjet 60," Michelle said, walking up to the cabin side door just behind the windshield. "When we come back, I'll take you for a flight if you'd like."

He nodded vigorously.

Michelle smiled and walked around the plane, checking it.

"Do you want me to call McClain and let her know you're on the way?" Stauffen asked.

"I'll call her from the air." Michelle said from the other side of the plane. She finished checking the plane and walked up to Stauffen, extending her hand. "Ray, I can't thank you enough for what you've done."

He shook her hand.

"I will not forget your kindness," she said solemnly, swinging open the cabin door. She turned to Antonio and Ignatious. "Are you ready?"

They shook hands with Stauffen and Felipe, then followed Michelle inside.

Stauffen closed the door behind them.

Michelle studied the instrument panel from her pilot's seat. She looked back to Antonio, "Would you seal the door?"

"Oh, my!" Ignatious exclaimed, looking past the galley to the luxurious interior.

Michelle turned her head. "Father Ignatious, you can have any seat."

Antonio sealed the door shut and poked his head over Michelle's shoulder. "May I sit with you?" he asked, pointing to the empty co-pilot's seat.

She simply nodded as her eyes studied the multifunction displays. She switched on the electrical panel. "Socrates?"

"Standing by," Socrates answered instantly.

"Connect me with John," she said while adjusting her headset, speaking into the tiny microphone.

"Please hold," Socrates answered. After waiting several seconds, he mimicked Mullen's voice. "Michelle?"

"John. We're preparing to leave for Lima. How are Carlota, Angelica, and Father Manuel doing?" she asked, her fingers and eyes quickly moving across the control panel, preparing the plane for flight.

"They're fine. I spoke with Jacob moments ago. Everything is fine."

"We'll be there shortly."

"I'll have McClain pick you up at the airport. Who is coming in with you?"

"Father Antonio and Father Ignatious," she paused, her eyes checking the panel. "Excuse me, John. Socrates, my instruments are reading go."

"Confirmed."

The jet's turbines screamed to life and Stauffen and Felipe moved back to the Jeep, waving as the plane began to roll.

Ignatious waved back.

"John, I'll talk to you after we land in Lima." Michelle said into her headset.

"I'll talk with you then," Socrates answered as John and returned to his own voice. "John has terminated the call."

As Michelle spoke Spanish into her headset, Antonio leaned over the flight management console and looked back at Ignatious. "Are you buckled in?"

Ignatious smiled excitedly. Antonio leaned back and watched Michelle maneuver the plane onto the tarmac.

Stauffen and Felipe watched the sleek black plane roll toward the end of the runway and pivot.

Michelle confirmed the full authority digital electronic control settings, "Are we go?"

"You are go," Socrates answered.

Michelle depressed the brake and eased forward the throttle. When the plane roared, she released the brake and they began sprinting toward the distant end of the runway.

Stauffen and Felipe shaded their eyes against the morning sun as the Lear lifted into the air and shot overhead, its gold windows reflecting the sun.

• • •

THE TINY HOOD was locked open. CHILDREN'S RELIEF glared in large red letters from the side of the stark white van. María and several *Sendero* women stood next to the engine. All wore black-and-white nuns' habits.

Several *Sendero* crouched inside the van. The old woman with missing teeth sat with them, whispering to herself. Two other groups lay hidden in the ditch.

One of the nuns stood with binoculars scanning the sparsely travelled road. "Someone is coming," she warned.

"Military?" María asked quickly.

The woman squinted. "No, some farmer."

A beat-up pickup with no front bumper lumbered into view, slowed and pulled along side María. "Can we help Sister?" an old man asked from behind the steering wheel. Next to him, an old woman sat staring at her. In the back were several children and many baskets of peppers prepared for market.

"Bless your kindness but someone is coming up from Lima to fix our van so we can continue on our way." María smiled piously.

"Would you like us to wait until they arrive, Sister?" The old woman leaned over her husband.

María shook her head. "No, no. You go ahead and get your peppers to market. I hope you get a good price."

The old man nodded and jammed the old pickup back into gear. The children waved at her as they disappeared down the road. María waved back.

• • •

FEAR COATED CARLOTA'S face. Sitting between Angelica and Anita, she held tightly to Angelica's hand. The four sat with their backs against the inside of the van as they bounced down the Central Highway.

"Where are you taking us?" Manuel asked the captain across from them.

With two soldiers on each side of him, the captain stared straight ahead, stone-faced and silent.

"He asked 'where are you taking us,'" Angelica said. Carlota squeezed her hand.

The man remained stone-faced.

"They intend to kill us," Carlota said solemnly. Angelica spun her head toward her, studying Carlota's face. She turned back slowly to the captain. "Is that true?" she asked while carefully feeling for her derringer.

"Quiet, woman," the man growled.

Angelica stared furiously at him.

Anita put her arm around Carlota protectively and glared at the man. "She asked if that was true?" Anita growled fearlessly.

"Quiet!"

"What is the problem, *federale*?" Anita taunted. "If you are going to kill us, it won't matter if you tell us."

The captain leaned forward and backhanded Anita. "Do you know what quiet means, woman?"

Anita's head bounced back against the side of the van. "What is the problem, *federale*?" she taunted, holding the back of her hand to her wounded cheek. With her arm around Carlota, she used her other hand to pinch Angelica's shoulder as a signal. "If you are going to kill us, we might as well try to escape right now," Anita declared.

Angelica tensed.

Carlota spun her head toward Anita. "NO!"

"It will be all right." Angelica squeezed Carlota's hand until Carlota turned back to her.

"Don't you have an intelligent answer, Captain?" Angelica asked sarcastically.

"If you don't shut up, I'll have both of you bound and gagged," the captain warned Angelica and Anita.

Anita pinched Angelica three times in rapid succession. She laughed at the captain, "Oh, you'll have it done. Not man enough to try yourself?" She looked directly and obviously down to his crotch. "No, we can see you're not."

The captain's face flushed crimson. "One more word," he said woodenly.

"And which word would that be?" Anita taunted.

The captain nodded to the men on each side of him. Two leaned forward to grab Angelica and two leaned to grab Anita.

Anita leaned back, quickly raised her left knee to her chest, then kicked the first soldier in the face. Her hand quickly reached into her right boot and slipped out her knife.

As the other soldier lunged for her, she plunged the knife. His eyes swelled open, not knowing how but realizing a shank of steel was deep in his chest. He turned back to his comrades, mouth agape. "I–" As he turned, the knife came into view.

Manuel's eyes widened with surprise.

"Grab her!" the captain shouted.

The two soldiers on Angelica abandoned her and lunged for Anita. As they released their grip, Angelica's hand shot between her legs and grabbed her derringer.

The van became a firestorm of screams and flailing. Anita leaned back again and kicked into the face of the first soldier flying toward her. She hurriedly pulled the knife from the first soldier's chest and jammed it under the second soldier's jaw.

"Stop her!" the captain screamed.

"STOP OR I'LL SHOOT!" Angelica screamed louder, pointing her derringer at the captain.

"No!" Manuel pushed Angelica's arm so the gun pointed away from the captain.

The soldier atop Anita and sprawled against Carlota, looked back and kicked at Angelica's hand. The tiny pistol flew up and hit the van's ceiling with a loud clank.

Before the derringer hit the floor the captain had pulled his side arm, aiming at Angelica.

Manuel lunged in front of Angelica as the captain pulled the trigger.

The explosion deafened everyone.

Manuel's back exploded in a spray of blood and flesh. His body convulsed once then sank onto the floor of the van.

"Bastard!" Angelica screamed and grabbed for the derringer.

Another explosion.

What remained of Angelica's head flew back against the side of the van.

"NOOOOOOOO!" Carlota screamed, staring at Angelica's convulsing body. "NOOOOO!" She scooped Angelica's limp body to her and held it as tightly as she could, as if trying to give her back life. Blood poured onto her shoulder as she cradled the remnants of Angelica's head.

Anita lunged for the captain, shoving aside the soldier who had kicked away the gun. Her fingernails dragged down the captain's face then clasped his throat. She squeezed savagely until the soldier behind cracked the back of her head with his gun butt.

Carlota's cries haunted the interior of the van. "Noooo," she rocked Angelica's body. "Noooo." Tears streamed from tightly closed eyes. "I'm sorry. I'm sorry."

• • •

"HERE THEY COME," a nun said to María, squinting through her binoculars.

"Special forces?" María asked quickly.

The nun nodded.

"Get ready," María barked to the two groups who lay hiding in the steep ditch.

The *Sendero* nun put away her binoculars, jumped into the van, and released the brake, steering the van to the middle of the road, blocking it.

María and several *Sendero* nuns feigned helplessness when the black special forces van slowed and rolled to a stop twenty meters from them. Darkly tinted windows blocked the occupants from sight.

María turned and waved to the black van, walking to the driver's side. As she neared the van, a tough looking young man jumped from the passenger's side. A dark red coat-of-arms patch of the Peruvian special forces was sewn to the sleeve of his camouflage fatigues.

"Bless you for stopping," María said.

"Back away from the van," he ordered.

María feigned confusion. "What?"

"Back away from the van. Now," the young soldier repeated sternly.

María's hands lightly covered her mouth. "I'm sorry, have I done something wrong?"

"Back away from the van."

María turned back to the row of nuns standing along side the CHILDREN'S RELIEF van. She made certain she spoke loud enough for the soldier to hear. "I'm sorry sisters, these gentlemen are unable to help us with gas." She shrugged her shoulders lightly.

The young soldier looked once to his driver then cautiously left the protective cover of the dark van. "What is the trouble?" He walked up behind María.

María knew several guns were pointed at her head from within his van. She smiled softly. "We are on the way to Lima to receive a commendation of thanks from the *Presidente* and our bishop for our order's work with Andean children."

"You are meeting with the *Presidente*?"

She laughed again, "Looks like we'll be a little late. We'll push our van to the side so you can pass."

"Let me speak with my commander. Maybe we can help to get you on your way to Lima," the man said and waved back to the black van.

María turned her head slightly to the side so the women behind her could hear. "Get ready to fire." She nodded slightly at those hidden along both sides of the ditch.

The women casually reached deep into the pockets of their habits, prepared to snap their machine guns into firing position.

The young man reached the driver's window, which lowered slowly. He looked back once to María, who waved, then stuck his head partially into the window to speak with his comrades.

"Now." María said coldly.

The machine guns under the nuns' gowns snapped up and opened fire. Those in the ditch followed suit with a spray of hot lead.

The van's windshield exploded. The young man contorted into a bloody pile and the sides of the van filled with dozens of bullet holes. For a moment, the van rocked from the twisting of those inside.

The *Sendero* continued firing until their weapons emptied and the van stopped rocking.

María stood quietly, watching for movement. There was none. "Push the van over the side."

She stood quietly as the other *Sendero* pushed the van off the road. It rolled down the steep embankment lining the mountain road and disappeared. Seconds later, she heard a crash of metal and rock.

• • •

MICHELLE REACHED UP for the autopilot switch.

"Michelle?" Ignatious asked from the rear of the plane.

Michelle pulled her hand from the switch. She and Antonio glanced back to Ignatious.

Antonio eyed his own reflection in the smoked mirror on the baggage compartment, just beyond the lavatory. He looked more tired than he felt.

"Yes, Father?" Michelle said.

"When do we reach Lima?" Ignatious was thinking of Carlota.

"It's a little over seven hundred miles so we'll be on the ground in an hour and a half."

"How fast are we flying?" Ignatious looked to the Amazon valley below.

"A little under 500 miles an hour," Michelle said.

Antonio stared ahead at the giant Andes on the western horizon.

"What is that off to the left?" Ignatious asked.

Michelle glanced down. "Requeña, where the Tapiche river feeds into the Ucayali," she answered, reaching up and triggering the autopilot.

Socrates locked in his control and cut power to the powerful Pratt & Whitney engines. The plane's nose lurched toward the earth, several miles below.

Michelle grabbed for the yoke.

Antonio's view of the distant Andes was immediately replaced by a wildly spinning Amazon valley.

Michelle tried to switch off the autopilot while screaming into her headset, "Socrates!"

"Standing by."

"I've lost power!" she shouted as an enlarging world spun wildly before her. "Disengage the autopilot!"

"Attempting to disengage," Socrates said, repeating that message several times.

"It's not working," Michelle yelled.

"I am reading no function failure," Socrates said.

The plane began tumbling through space.

"I don't care what you're reading, I've lost power!" Michelle answered, her eyes scanning the instrument panel.

Antonio stared through the windshield, which was alternatingly filled with blue sky above and green jungle below.

Michelle played the yoke until she coaxed the plane from its tumbling into a corkscrew spin toward the earth.

Ignatious sat frozen, his fingers gripping the armrests with white knuckles as the sleek black jet plummeted in a one hundred sixty mile an hour tailspin.

"I am continuing to read no function failure," Socrates repeated.

Four miles below, the river coursed and coiled lazily through the jungle like a giant serpent.

Steel knuckles clutched Antonio's armrests as he watched Michelle struggle for control. Father Ignatious crossed himself.

• • •

BERNADINE BENT SLOWLY at the hips until his face was inches from the bonsai. He stood near the center of the circle of light, beside the stone, studying the dwarf tree. "This is very old," Bernadine muttered to himself and turned to John. "How old?"

"Four hundred twenty years." John said, sitting on the deck, watching Bernadine. His feet swung lightly, his toes softly brushing the white gravel pebbles.

"Makes me feel young," Bernadine joked then straightened, hands on his back hips. "Did Socrates ever have any luck finding the Opus members who work for you?" He asked casually, already thinking of other things.

"What are you talking about?" John's eyes narrowed suddenly, his white brows furrowing.

"He couldn't find the Opus registry in the Vatican computer so I told him to look at Rajunt's VIP invitation list. He said it helped." Worry etched Bernadine's face at John's startled look.

"Socrates," John looked across the dim circular room, speaking into the air.

"Yes."

"Did you hear our conversation?"

"Yes."

"Did you search Rajunt's invitation list?"

"Yes."

"And did you find Opus members who work for me?"

"No." Socrates lied.

Bernadine felt the hairs on the back of his neck stiffen. "But I asked if that list helped you. And you said 'yes, very much.'"

"It did help, Father. It eliminated an entire field of inquiry."

Bernadine thought for a second then shook his head in warning. "He's lying."

Socrates made no response.

John stiffened. "Is he correct?"

"I'm sorry you asked."

The room's single light above the bonsai went off. The room plunged into inky blackness. Impenetrable darkness, thicker than a wall.

"Socrates," John said softly as the soft hiss of the air vents died into silence.

Darkness and silence.

"Socrates!" John raised his badly rasping voice.

Darkness and silence.

"What is happening?" Bernadine whispered aloud.

"Socrates has shut down the complex, lights, air, everything."

Bernadine frowned forcefully in the dark. "How deep are we?"

"Several hundred feet of hard granite, Ross." John's mind raced. "Socrates controls almost everything. He has, no doubt," John paused, "sealed all the doors."

"Almost everything?" Bernadine asked softly.

Socrates listened.

"There are several strategically placed, high-grade explosives that he is unaware of." John's voice seemed strangled by sorrow. *"You tried to warn me, Socrates,"* he thought painfully to himself.

"Why would you have explosives?" Bernadine asked with a hushed tone.

"Ross, Socrates is the most powerful computer in the world, generations beyond all others, and by his upgrades remains constantly so. My best computer engineers told me Socrates could become self-aware in time. But no one could predict what would happen when he did. So I built explosives into his and my chambers," John answered through the inky blackness. "I can reach the detonator."

"But you said all the doors are sealed," Bernadine said.

"They are but the detonator is here, within my meditation chamber." John left the deck and made his way to Bernadine in the dark. The sound of crunching gravel announced his steps.

"John," Socrates said softly. "We should speak."

"If he is willing to kill me, he is preparing to kill Michelle and the others," John said, ignoring Socrates.

Bernadine's eyes widened in the darkness. "The Madonna must live!" He warned with words harder than stone.

"I agree," John paused, "but if I detonate then we, with Socrates, shall surely die. I need your consent." John said softly.

"The Madonna must live." Bernadine repeated.

"John," Socrates interrupted. "There is no need for this. Michelle is quite safe, I assure you. Only your compliance will assure she remains so."

John continued to ignore the machine and reached out in the dark. "Give me your hand, Ross." The words were spoken quietly.

Bernadine's tiny hand groped through the darkness until their fingers touched. Weathered hands quickly entwined.

John knelt onto the loose gravel. Bernadine eased down beside him as John's free hand probed beneath the giant stone until his fingers wrapped about a lever. John turned to Bernadine in the darkness. "Are you ready?"

"John, this is needless," Socrates insisted.

John closed his eyes in the dark, *"Forgive me, Socrates. Live well, Michelle."*

Bernadine held high his head and stiffened defiantly. "Do it."

• • •

THE LEAR INSTANTLY responded to Michelle's frantic attempt to level the plane. "The autopilot has disengaged! I have control!" she shouted to herself.

Antonio spun toward her, his eyes bewildered.

Michelle eased back the yoke as she re-ignited the engines. The Lear screamed to life then pulled from its dive like a bird of prey, skimming the treetops at 300 miles an hour. Michelle throttled up and they accelerated back to the clouds.

• • •

DE SILVA'S LIMOUSINE sped along the Central Highway, climbing from Lima toward the high Andes. Marta turned back as they passed a colorful group of straw-hatted pedestrians. When the pedestrians vanished into the distance, she put the Uzi to the driver's head. "Pull over."

The car rolled slowly to a stop, jarring as the right wheels slipped onto the rocky shoulder.

"Get out," she said coldly to the driver who looked back to De Silva for direction.

"Do as she says," De Silva warned.

The driver opened his door and stepped out. Marta slid out behind him, her gun trained at his gut. "Open the trunk."

Diego sat beside De Silva, the pistol jammed into De Silva's ribs. De Silva and Brigham stared ahead.

Rajunt's head turned to follow the driver toward the back of the limo. He watched the soldier open the trunk.

"Now get in." Marta gestured with the Uzi.

The young driver looked back once and crawled in.

"Get on your stomach."

He turned his body to rest on his stomach, bending his legs to fit.

Marta smiled, put the Uzi's barrel to the back of his head and pulled the trigger once. The man's body convulsed then deflated into lifelessness.

Marta slammed down the trunk. She looked back to Diego as she slipped behind the steering wheel.

"Godless heathen," Rajunt hissed.

Marta turned back and slammed the side of her gun against his head. "Shut up, priest."

"Godless heathen," he repeated louder.

• • •

"THE MADONNA," THE *Sendero* exclaimed to María, squinting through her binoculars as the dark green van climbed the steep grade into view. A second van followed close behind.

"Get ready," María ordered.

The two *Sendero* groups hurried back into the protective underbrush of the ditch. Only those dressed as nuns remained on the road.

As the two military vans pulled near, María's head was under the hood.

Inside the slowing first van, the captain crawled towards the front seat, his boots smearing the pool of Angelica and Manuel's blood on the floor. Carlota softly rocked Angelica's body in her arms. Anita was unconscious.

The captain peered from the curtains behind the front seat. When he spotted the disabled van blocking the road, he climbed into the front.

"What's the problem?" he snapped to the driver.

The driver just pointed. "It's a CHILDREN'S RELIEF van," he said and applied the brakes.

The captain jumped from the van.

The nun pulled her head out from under the hood, standing with an apologetic smile. The captain signalled the slowing van behind him to stop then turned back to the nun.

María met him half way. "I'm terribly sorry we're blocking the road. But we ran out of gas and don't have money to buy more."

The deeply religious captain quickly checked his watch. He needed them out of the way fast. "We can help you, Sister." He turned back to the van. "Sergeant Dominic, give them gas," he said to the driver.

"Bless you." María smiled submissively.

The driver turned, parting the curtains slightly with the back of his hand. "Stay quiet, this won't take long." One soldier put his hand over the mouth of the wounded soldier.

María sidled next to the captain, jamming her gun into his ribs. "Stay absolutely still."

The captain stiffened.

Several *Sendero* eased from beneath the heavy brush along the ditch, sneaking along side and behind the second van. They carried automatics tipped with silencers.

The soldiers in the van had no warning. Half of the waiting *Sendero* slammed open the rear door as others riddled the front.

Those who opened the rear found several bound and gagged *Sendero* guarded by two soldiers. The soldiers were dead before reality registered. Their blood sprayed against the back curtain.

As the first group took out the second van, two groups of *Sendero* rushed the first van from both sides of the ditch. The first group sprayed the soldiers in the front seat with machine gun fire while two others yanked open the rear doors.

With Anita and Carlota against one side of the van and the soldiers on the other, the soldiers were sitting ducks.

Carlota began a continuous scream amid the gunfire, clutching Angelica's body tighter to her. Anita lay limp next to her. Manuel lay crumpled on the floor. After several seconds, the firing stopped.

The *Sendero* at both vans signalled María.

"Now that didn't take long, did it, Captain?" María asked smoothly.

He turned to her defiantly. "What do you want?"

María put her gun barrel under his chin. "I want you," she pulled the trigger, "to die."

His body crumpled to the road.

María wiped the blood from her cheek with the back of her hand, turning to the nearest *Sendero*. "Throw him in with the others," she said and walked to the back of the van.

Carlota looked up when María's shadow snaked into the van's interior. Carlota's stare became frenzied and tears streamed down her cheeks.

"Carlota Cabral?" María asked softly.

Carlota nodded in terror, clutching Angelica tightly.

• • •

HER OLD CHINA rattled violently against its glass cabinet as the old woman looked up, startled. The ground trembled for an instant. People in Saratoga rushed from their homes in confusion.

"What was that?" a neighbor asked the old woman.

She shook her white-haired head in bewilderment.

Several minutes later, people still in the streets began pointing excitedly.

Huge dust clouds were billowing from the great mountain.

"That's old Mullen's place!" someone exclaimed.

"Call the fire department!" another shouted.

• • •

MARÍA SPOTTED ANITA lying unconscious beside Carlota. "Is she dead?"

Carlota shook her head and protectively pulled Anita to her with her free arm. "Don't hurt her." It was obvious Carlota was in extreme pain.

María laughed, "I'm not going to hurt her." She climbed into the van, stepping over the lifeless bodies of Manuel and the soldiers. She slapped Anita. "Wake up. There is work."

Anita shook her head to clear it, reaching back to feel the goose egg on the back of her skull. She looked to Carlota, still clutching Angelica, then to Manuel's bloody body, and finally to María. Her mind focused when she spotted María.

"Hurry up and get out while we wait for the Vatican viper," María said as she climbed out of the van.

"Here they come!" The *Sendero* with the binoculars shouted, looking down the desolate road to the distant Mercedes limousine.

María looked at her watch, "Like clockwork."

Inside the van, Anita began moving for the open rear doors. Carlota grabbed her sleeve. "Help me, Anita," she said in pain.

Anita stopped. "Were you hit?" She looked around Carlota's body for a wound.

Carlota shook her head and burst into new tears. "I'm giving birth!" She began breathing heavily. "Oh, Anita, please help me."

"I'll take care of you. I promise." Anita squeezed Carlota's hand and left the van.

Fifteen minutes later, Marta slowed then parked the limousine between the two military vans.

María signalled Marta out of the car and walked behind the second van. "Untie them," she yelled to the others, pointing to the bound and gagged *Sendero* prisoners.

Marta joined María as the others freed their comrades.

"Out!" Diego ordered De Silva, Brigham, and Rajunt from the limousine.

"You said some of these people are your friends," María said softly to Marta. "Which do you like most?"

Marta pointed to the young man closest to them. "Juan."

"Take our comrades to the middle of the road, between the vans." María ordered as she pulled Juan to the side.

"You are *Sendero*?" she asked him.

He nodded proudly.

"The life of a revolutionary is not easy, you know that?" she asked.

He nodded hesitantly.

María looked back to the *Sendero* being situated between the vans. They looked confused as their friends pulled away.

María turned to Marta, "Use your Uzi."

Marta looked horrified and froze.

María grabbed the Uzi, glared disgustedly at Marta, turned and opened fire on the *Sendero* between the vans.

The other *Sendero* stared in disbelief as their comrades fell lifelessly onto the road in a bloody pool.

Brigham and De Silva looked fearfully at each other. Rajunt glared defiantly at Diego.

"What do you want done with these pigs?" Diego yelled to María.

María walked slowly to the three. "General De Silva," she poked his soft belly with her weapon then turned to Brigham. "And you must be the rich American," she said pointing to his

Rolex watch, "and . . . ," she paused, gazing contemptuously at Rajunt's scarlet raiments, ". . . you are Rajunt, the Vatican viper."

"You are the viper. I am a cardinal, a man of God," he said venomously and fearlessly.

"I suggest you call on him to save you." She turned to Diego. "Put them in with our little Madonna."

"Move it," Diego yelled, shoving Rajunt toward the rear of the first military van.

Rajunt, Brigham, and De Silva stopped abruptly when they saw the carnage inside the van. Only Carlota remained alive. She was in obvious pain, clutching her stomach.

"Get in!" Diego shouted. Rajunt looked back once to Diego with an acid glare and climbed in. Brigham and De Silva followed. Rajunt could not take his eyes from Carlota.

María's shadow came around the corner of the van. De Silva looked up and was the first to speak. "Name your price," he said to her.

"You are my price."

"I can give you millions," Brigham offered.

"Yes, I know. I prefer you dead, however," María said, raising the Uzi.

Rajunt looked away from Carlota and glared defiantly at María.

María tensed to fire.

"NO!" Anita screamed, staring at María. "I thought you were smarter than to kill the Madonna," Anita said, thinking as fast as she could.

Marta fearfully backed out of María's line of sight.

"Do you have a better idea?" she asked viciously.

"Yes, I do," Anita answered contemptuously.

María's eyes flared. "Then tell me."

"The people believe she carries the Messiah."

"I know that."

"They would follow him to the ends of the earth and would do anything he asked."

"So?"

"They would bring down whole governments at his command. Think what you could do if the child grows up believing in your cause. We represent the oppressed more than any other group."

María snarled at first but slowly her expression relaxed. A luxuriant smile stretched itself. "Yes," she said softly, then repeated, "Yes." She looked into Anita's eyes. "Put her in our van and protect her with your life."

Anita climbed in beside to Carlota and whispered, "You are going to be fine."

Carlota gripped Anita's hand. "Oh, Anita, it has begun." She sobbed, "Not now, not this way! Not without Angelica!"

Anita spun back to María. "She's birthing!"

Carlota cried in anguish.

María turned to the *Sendero* gathered around her. "Get her to our van. Quickly!"

Several piled into the van and carefully lifted out Carlota. Amid her agonized screams, they carried her to the back of the CHILDREN'S RELIEF van. Anita stayed with her, holding her hand.

Half delirious, Carlota screamed when she saw the old woman with missing teeth reach for her. The old woman helped ease her onto the floor of the van, while quietly hissing, "Soft skin. Soft skin."

Anita shoved aside the old woman and lifted Carlota's head onto her lap. "I am here," she whispered reassuringly.

María stood at the back of the other van, Uzi ready.

Marta quickly shifted beside her, "María, we should take them hostage, rather than kill them." Brigham and De Silva stared back in terror at the two women. Rajunt glared.

"Why?" A thin brow arched suspiciously as María glared at the three.

"Imagine a video airing on all the news channels around the world. A Peruvian general, a Vatican cardinal, and a rich American—all confessing to a plot to kill the new Madonna." Marta whispered. "The *Sendero* would be famous everywhere."

María pointed the Uzi at the sky suddenly, "I like it." She gave Marta a hideous smile then turned to Juan. "Hold out your arm."

Without taking his eyes from her, he slowly extended his arm.

María fired a round into his forearm.

Juan fell to his knees, clutching his arm, crying out.

"The wound is not life-threatening," María explained. "Soon, a reporter from '*El Sol*' will come with a photographer."

Juan's attention was blindly focused on his arm.

María hit him on the side of the head with the gun barrel. "Are you listening to me?"

He looked up, grimacing, but nodded.

"Explain to the reporter that the *federales* kidnapped the Madonna in order to kill her and blame the *Sendero*. They were bringing in *Sendero* prisoners as part of their plan but we overwhelmed them. The *Sendero* rescued the Madonna and escaped, but these valiant *Sendero*," she pointed to those she had slain, "were killed trying to save the Madonna from the *federales*."

He looked back up to her, half in shock, confused, gripping his shattered arm.

"Explain we took General De Silva, a Vatican viper, and a rich American prisoner. Soon they will confess their treachery on television. Can you remember all that?"

He stared at her.

"Can you remember that until the reporter arrives?" she repeated ferociously.

Juan glared, nodded, and looked back to his arm.

María smiled coldly and turned to Marta. "Put these three back into the limousine then you and Diego follow us. But we must move fast, we have a long way home."

Marta nodded. "Back to Iquitos?"

"Yes." María said then turned to the white van. She climbed into the front and watched Marta and Diego herd the three hostages back into the limousine. She turned to the driver. "Go."

In the back, the old woman was kneeling between Carlota's legs.

Carlota cried out in agony.

"I am here," Anita whispered repeatedly as the van lurched and turned, heading for the high Andes. Carlota clutched her hand tightly.

The limousine followed closely.

Outside Chosica, Carlota released both a final scream and her son to the world.

The old woman smiled broadly with missing teeth to the others, triumphantly lifting the child by his heels from between Carlota's thighs.

"He is born."

• • •

ICY ANDEAN PEAKS lay twenty thousand feet beneath the black Lear. Lima lay on the distant horizon, beside the Pacific.

"I can't raise Socrates and I can't reach John." Michelle said, turning to Antonio, her eyes searching his face.

"Something is very wrong," he answered and looked back to Ignatious, who was pale white. "Father Ignatious, are you all right?"

Ignatious winced and smiled weakly.

Antonio turned to Michelle. "We need to get him a place to rest," he said quietly.

A half hour later, the Lear landed and taxied toward the private hangars. Michelle spotted Janice McClain's old Mercedes between two of the hangars. She steered the Lear toward it.

McClain stood beside her car as the plane rolled to a stop. Anxiety marbled her face.

Michelle disembarked quickly while Antonio helped Ignatious out.

"What's wrong?" Michelle asked, hurrying up to McClain. Antonio and Ignatious came behind.

"The *Sendero* captured Carlota. Angelica and Father Manuel are dead."

"Oh, no," Michelle cried softly.

Ignatious crossed himself slowly.

Antonio stared at McClain. "How do you know?"

"*'El Sol'* first reported it. The country is in an uproar. No one knows what happened or where they've taken Carlota," McClain answered. She looked to Michelle. "There's more," she said slowly.

Michelle braced, "What?"

"We are unable to reach Mr. Mullen," McClain explained.

"I know."

"The lines are dead."

"I know."

"*'El Sol'* is also reporting that the *Sendero* captured General De Silva, a Vatican cardinal, and a rich American. The *Sendero* say all three will confess publicly to plotting to kill the Madonna and blame the *Sendero,*" McClain said.

Michelle and Antonio turned slowly to one another, "María."

"She'll return to the jungle around Iquitos, to home ground to make her stand," Antonio said then looked to Ignatious. "Will you stay here with Janice McClain?"

The old priest returned the stare, "Is that what you want?"

"Please," Antonio answered then turned to McClain. "May he stay with you?" he asked softly with a low, deep voice.

"Of course, Father Antonio." McClain said.

"Will you call Ray and tell him we're headed back to Iquitos?" Michelle asked.

McClain nodded.

"Tell him what's happened," Michelle said, her voice trembling.

"He knows. I spoke with him," McClain said, putting her hand onto Michelle's shoulder. "Are you all right?"

"No. They were my friends," Michelle took a deep breath. "Thanks for all your help, Janice," she said, then turned to Antonio. "Let's go."

McClain and Ignatious watched as Michelle and Antonio climbed back into the plane. Within moments, the engines fired and the plane began to roll.

Tears streamed down Michelle's cheeks as she positioned the Lear at the end of the runway. The twin engines stood ready to hurl them over the Andes. Antonio remained silent. Michelle received clearance and shoved the throttle forward.

• • •

CARLOTA CRIED ALOUD then slipped back into unconsciousness.

María turned around in her seat, studying Carlota, "What's wrong with her?"

Anita held the child protectively to her breast. "She's bleeding internally," she said, looking to Carlota in her lap.

"Will she live?" María asked coldly.

The old woman with missing teeth shook her head.

"She'll live," Anita insisted, staring at the child within her arms. "I am here," Anita said softly to Carlota.

"Keep her alive," María ordered. "We have a long journey."

"I intend to," Anita whispered to herself. The old woman studied her with the eyes of a raven.

María looked to the mirror out her window. The limousine followed on their bumper.

• • •

RAY STAUFFEN WATCHED the black jet touch down as smooth as glass under the Amazonian sun, its gold reflective windows shimmering. Stauffen stood beside his muddy Jeep as the plane rolled into the hangar and Michelle cut the engines.

Antonio was first out. Michelle followed.

"I'm afraid I have bad news," Stauffen said to her.

"What?"

"I've been on the phone with corporate security in Saratoga." Stauffen hesitated, "There was an explosion deep within Mr. Mullen's complex. They say no one could have survived."

"I suspected as much," Michelle said wearily. She turned to Antonio, "You realize Father Bernadine is dead if John is."

Antonio nodded bravely.

"Socrates is behind this," Michelle breathed deeply, then turned to Stauffen, "Did Janice McClain call you?"

"About the kidnapping?" he asked, nodding like he knew.

"We think María has them and is heading back to Iquitos," Michelle said.

"Makes sense," Stauffen said.

"Where would she take them?"

"Hector and Felipe are already talking with the tribes. If the *Sendero* have another hiding place, they'll find out."

"When they do, we're going after Carlota," Michelle announced.

"I know," Stauffen said.

"When will the boys be back?" she asked.

"Tomorrow morning. In the meantime, you're staying at my place," Stauffen's eyes were filled with sympathy.

"Thanks Ray, but I need to be alone," Michelle said quietly. "I'll get a hotel room."

"No, you won't," Ray insisted. "I won't be there tonight so you two can be alone. You need someone with you, Michelle."

"Where will you be?" Antonio asked.

"I'll make preparations to extract Carlota, if Hector and Felipe can determine where the *Sendero* will take her," Stauffen answered. He walked to the Jeep and opened a door for Michelle, "Shall we?"

No one spoke on the drive to Stauffen's home. Stauffen parked his Jeep in the garage and ushered them into his home. "Father Antonio, you take my room and Michelle, the guest bedroom is yours."

Michelle said nothing.

"Thank you, Ray," Antonio said.

"Lock the door behind me."

Antonio nodded.

"I'll be back in the morning. If Hector and Felipe have located the *Sendero* hiding place, will you be ready to go?"

"We'll be ready," Antonio answered.

After Stauffen had left, Antonio put his arm around Michelle's shoulder, "I'm putting you to bed."

Michelle buried her face against his chest. She sobbed uncontrollably.

• • •

DARKNESS COVERED THE land by the time the military van and the limousine left behind the Andes' eastern slopes and entered the upper Amazon rainforest.

"Stop up there," María said, pointing ahead to a turn-off. "Something is wrong."

The van and limousine pulled off the pavement and rolled to a stop. Several *Sendero* relieved themselves. María walked back to the limousine, through its glaring headlamps. Marta stuck her head out the window.

"Diego, put the hostages in the van and stay with them," María ordered.

"Out!" Diego jabbed a gun barrel into De Silva's fleshy side. Within seconds, all three hostages stood beside the car. Brigham and De Silva were visibly shaken. Rajunt glared coldly at María through the darkness as she stood speaking to Marta, leaning on the car, her head stuck partially through Marta's window.

"We should have had to kill *federales* by now. This is too easy. Something is wrong," María said, glancing back at the hostages.

"Diego, get them in the van!" she barked then turned back to Marta for several minutes, planning.

When she returned to the van, she jumped into the front seat. "Go," she commanded.

Marta drove the limousine on to Iquitos.

• • •

ANTONIO COULD HEAR Michelle cry softly. Her anguish tore his soul. When her cries finally ebbed into restful silence, he let an hour pass before he looked in on her. The room was dark and she lay motionless on the bed. He began to close the door.

"Antonio," she called out softly.

"Did I wake you?" his deep voice whispered.

"No."

"Can you sleep?"

"No."

He walked to the bed and sat beside her. The bed creaked beneath his massive frame. He gently stroked her silky blond hair. "Can I do anything for you?"

"Hold me," she asked quietly.

Without a word, he took off his shoes and lay beside her, scooping her within his arms.

She nestled her head onto his chest.

Antonio held her for several minutes before realizing she had fallen asleep. He gently kissed the top of her head then lay back. Sleep swiftly overcame him.

• • •

ANITA CRADLED THE child in one arm and balanced Carlota's head in her lap with the other as the van bounced along the dark, uneven road.

"Angelica, Angelica," Carlota moaned.

"I'm here, Carlota," Anita said softly. "Your son is healthy and strong."

At that, Carlota's eyes opened wearily, "My son?"

"He's fine."

"My son. . . ," she gasped, lapsing unconscious.

Anita stroked Carlota's sweat-drenched hair and looked toward Rajunt, who returned her stare.

"He's an unnatural monstrosity," Rajunt announced.

Anita glared. "If you even approach him, I'll kill you instantly," she warned slowly.

"I would not touch him," he said, then looked away in disdain.

Anita studied Rajunt, determined to seduce his obvious ambition, "Which is why you will never be Pope."

Rajunt froze. "What do you mean?" he asked, crocodile eyes swiveled toward her in the dark.

Anita continued her glare. "Billions will revere whoever presents him to the world. That person would be a world power," she paused deliberately, "I'm glad it won't be you."

Rajunt sat motionless within the belly of the van, unblinking eyes gazing into the future.

Overhead, a full moon lit the night as the van continued deep into the rainforest.

Diego sat backed against the rear door, Uzi in hand. He stared at Carlota and the child. Living hatred filled his eyes.

• • •

MICHELLE STIRRED IN her sleep, waking Antonio. She breathed deeply. Her warm hand drifted onto his upper thigh.

Antonio lay quietly for many minutes, listening to her slow breathing. She jerked in her sleep. He pulled her tighter to him, accidentally waking her.

Michelle raised her head slowly in the darkness and looked to him, pushing hair from her face. "How long have I slept?"

"Several hours," he said softly.

She laid her head back to his chest, her hand still on his thigh. "You feel so good," she murmured.

"So do you," Antonio said, whiffing her hair until a sudden stirring began deep within his loins. He tried to fight it, but old fantasies overwhelmed him and his penis slowly swelled, stiffening. He held his breath as it expanded down his leg toward her warm hand—knowing he was powerless to stop its advance. He lay deadly still.

Michelle's green eyes awakened in the dark as the expanding shaft burrowed beneath her hand. Hard as rock.

Antonio held his breath, frightened to move until he felt fingers lightly tracing the shaft. He pulled back his leg, hesitantly.

Her warm hand followed, pressing. "I love you, Antonio," she said softly, gently squeezing him, her body pressed to his.

"I will not break my vows as a priest," he whispered.

Michelle tensed, his soft words crashing against her. "I know," she whispered. "You must keep your vows," she pulled away, trying to regain her composure.

Antonio remained silent for several long seconds. "So I am no longer a priest," he whispered defiantly. He could take no more. He rolled atop her, kissing her. "I love you, Michelle."

She pulled back her head, looking deeply into his eyes, "Are you sure that is what you want?"

"I'm sure of one thing."

"What?"

"I want to spend my life with you."

"And I you," she said, then drew Antonio to her. They kissed passionately, their hands exploring one another slowly.

Antonio lifted his head, then slipped a hand beneath her blouse. Michelle stared up as he unbuttoned her blouse, spreading it. He stared longingly at the full breasts and hardened nipples in the silver moonlight. He lowered his head, his lips encircling a warm nipple. Within moments, he had removed her clothes and covered her powerful torso with raindrop kisses. He looked up once then dropped eagerly between her legs.

She moaned instantly, spreading her thighs. Her fingers clutched his silky black hair. His tongue darted wildly, carrying her into shimmering ecstasy. She groaned luxuriously.

After many prolonged quivers, she laughed gently, "This isn't fair, Antonio."

He looked up quizzically, "What's wrong?"

"Your clothes are on," she whispered.

He rose from the bed and pulled off his shirt in the iridescent moonlight flooding through the window. Shadows played across his powerful athletic physique. He slowly removed his trousers then straightened his posture.

"You're beautiful," she said softly, sitting up on the edge of the bed, staring in awe.

"So are you," he smiled nervously, standing naked.

She reached out and gently gripped the base of the prodigious shaft lumbering high into the air, silhouetted in moonlight. He stood placidly. Cupping his pendulous orbs in her other hand, Michelle drew Antonio to her.

"Your turn," she whispered.

Her silky lips skied over his ridged stomach. The moist tongue trailed down his white underbelly then frolicked along the thickly veined shaft.

Antonio moaned feverishly as she slowly swallowed him whole. His eyes rolled back into his head.

Soft, rhythmic hands and moist lips pistoned him quickly to the edge. He tried to withdraw. She gripped him tighter with both hands, holding him captive. His knees buckled. Trembling, he grabbed her shoulders for support and attempted again to withdraw. She refused. A primordial groan from the back of his throat ushered the release. He shuddered uncontrollably, took deep breaths, then straightened very slowly.

"Sorry," he whispered as her stunning face lifted into the moonlight.

"Don't be," she smiled, green eyes glistening with life. "We have all night, my love."

He eased her onto her back and lowered carefully atop her. She smiled, locked powerful legs about his hips, and drew him in.

Antonio sank slowly in, trembling with the realization that fantasy was reality. "I wanted you from the first moment I saw you," he whispered.

"And I you."

• • •

DAWN WAS BREAKING when Hector and Felipe arrived at Stauffen's office, bounding up the steps. Hector, the older of the two, exploded through the door first. Stauffen quickly zipped a large duffle bag filled with weapons.

"We found it!" Hector announced. Felipe nodded eagerly.

"Where?"

"In the Pacaya Samiria Reserve, about 25 kilometers southwest of Nauta."

"Are you positive?" Stauffen quizzed.

Both nodded enthusiastically.

"Help me load this into the Jeep," Stauffen pointed to several bags. He picked up the duffle bag with the weapons and followed the boys down the stairs.

"I need you to draw me a map, so I'll know where to go," Stauffen said to Hector, slamming down the Jeep's rear door.

The boys looked confused at one another. "You don't need a map. We're going with you," Felipe chided.

"No, you're not," Stauffen laid down the law.

"Then you don't get a map," Felipe said defiantly.

"This is too dangerous."

Hector crossed his arms at the chest, "We go or you won't find it."

Stauffen shook his head in irritation, "Get in."

Hector and Felipe climbed in.

• • •

"TURN THERE," María ordered, pointing ahead through the morning light.

The van slowed then turned onto another dirt road, leading deeper into the Pacaya Samiria Reserve.

María looked back. Everyone but Diego, Anita, and Rajunt slept, heads rocked slowly with the bumps. Diego's gun was trained on the hostages. Anita held Carlota's head in her lap and the child in her arms. María was amazed, the child had yet to cry.

They drove for twenty minutes through gullies and ravines. The van creaked and groaned.

• • •

"YOU CANNOT COME," Antonio explained to Hector and Felipe. They stood around Stauffen's kitchen table, in the glare of the morning sun that flooded the room.

"Yes, we can," both insisted at once.

"It is far too dangerous," Michelle insisted.

"You won't be able to find it without us," Hector said, determined to go.

Antonio and Stauffen turned to Michelle. "We have no choice."

Michelle looked to the floor, shaking her head. She looked back up, "Then I don't go." Tears of frustration began to well in her eyes.

Hector and Felipe looked uncomfortably at each other. Felipe stepped closer to Michelle, "This won't be more dangerous than when we rescued Antonio and the others."

"We almost got you killed, Felipe," she said then turned to Antonio. "I just won't do it. I will not jeopardize these boys."

"We are not boys. We are men." Hector declared.

Michelle looked them in the eye. "Would you want me to be more afraid than I already am?"

Felipe adored Michelle. "No," he said quietly.

"Would you?" she asked Hector.

Hector shook his head.

"I'll be afraid for you if you come."

"But we can help," Felipe insisted.

"I know you can. But I am asking you, please, to stay here."

Felipe and Hector looked to one another. Felipe felt a surge of shame that Michelle had been forced to plead.

"We won't go with you," Hector announced.

"Will you draw us a map so we can get there?" she asked softly, smiling gratefully.

They nodded.

"Will it be hard to find?" Stauffen asked.

Felipe shook his head, "Five kilometers west of where the rivers join."

• • •

THE VAN LURCHED to a stop, reaching the end of the narrow dirt trail.

María turned to everyone, "We walk from here."

Anita looked up, "Carlota cannot walk."

"Then carry her, she must feed the child," María said and climbed from the van with the rest of the *Sendero*. Diego unlatched the rear door and backed out, motioning with his Uzi for Brigham and De Silva to follow.

The hatred on Rajunt's face had vanished, overwhelmed by ambition. "You carry Carlota," he said to Anita. "I'll carry the child."

"If you harm him, I'll kill you. Remember that," she again warned.

"I will protect him," he said, scooping the child protectively into his arms.

Anita struggled to carry Carlota.

• • •

"DO YOU KNOW how to use a shotgun?" Stauffen asked Antonio as the Jeep turned onto the one road leading to Nauta.

"No, but I can figure out how," Antonio answered.

"I'll show him," Michelle said, studying the map Hector and Felipe had drawn. "How far is it?" she asked Stauffen.

"We'll get there around noon. You'll stay with the Jeep while I figure out what we're facing."

"What do you mean?"

"María won't have her usual security, but she'll set up her spare people to guard her during the night. I'll be able to see where she positions them so we can avoid them tonight."

• • •

"GET 'EM OUT!" the sheriff screamed.

"It's no good, the whole thing has collapsed!" someone yelled back, emerging from the billowing dust. "No one could have survived that explosion, Sheriff."

Four Carbon County Sheriff's Jeeps, with giant gold stars painted on white doors, had parked haphazardly near the front entrance.

Men and women scrambled in and out of what remained of Mullen's compound. Most were Mullen's corporate security.

Dust choked the air and soiled their faces.

Three bright green volunteer fire department trucks idled in the gravel driveway, large diesel engines grumbling. Their exhaust hung in the air. Red and blue lights spun wildly, reflecting off the mountain, flooding through the thick dust cloud amid the pine trees.

"Damn crying shame!" the sheriff muttered to himself. He thought highly of old man Mullen. He turned to his nearest subordinate. "Bodies?"

"Didn't see any," he said.

"How long before you clear the rubble and get down there?"

The man shook his head, "If anyone was down there, they're buried forever."

"Is there any chance. . . ."

"Not a chance."

"We don't even know if anyone was in there," a deputy said.

"I checked the airport's flight logs, Michelle Cumberland is out of the country but they think Mullen was here," another deputy said.

"He was," one of Mullen's security officers said.

The sheriff turned to him, "I want a list of anyone you think may have been in there." The man nodded.

The fire chief walked up to the sheriff. "There's nothing for us to do here, no fire or chemicals. But there sure was one damned big explosion deep inside this place."

"Might as well haul your equipment out. I'll seal the scene and leave some deputies until the Crime Lab gets in from Cheyenne," the sheriff said.

Carbon County Sheriff's Jeeps soon followed the mammoth fire trucks, which were picking their paths down the steep incline.

Two deputies waited behind to secure the scene for the Crime Lab.

In the distance, recessed amid the pine trees and covered by a thick cloud of dust, sat a small, concrete and windowless bunker. It innocuously entombed Mullen's emergency back-up computer system. Rubble from the blast lay strewn against it. Pitch blackness dominated within until a small green light began to glow softly.

● ● ●

JULIO SÁNCHEZ LISTENED quietly to his headset. Frantic conversations. Someone giving orders to another special forces team. He motioned for his men to stop. Another team should not be in his area.

His team froze, surrounded by heavy jungle.

João looked at him curiously, "What is it?"

"Remember María?"

João's eyes turned to glass.

"She's the one that took De Silva and the others hostage," Sánchez said.

"We get to rescue them?"

Sánchez shook his head, "No. They've sent in a special team to take out everyone."

"What?" João asked nervously.

Sánchez breathed deeply, "The team they are sending in has orders to terminate everyone."

"We're becoming no better than *Sendero*," João complained.

Sánchez gestured for silence, intent on the continuing conversation in his headset. "The team is already in the Pacay rainforest reserve. I know where they are heading. We may not make it in time," he turned to his men, circled his finger in the air, and pointed toward the Pacay Samiria National Reserve.

• • •

STAUFFEN SLITHERED ON his belly, slowly pushing away large waxy leaves. He heard voices and drew still.

"Tie them to that tree," María ordered.

Diego bound De Silva and Brigham then started for Rajunt, who held the child. Diego grabbed him by the shoulder to yank him onto his feet. Rajunt glared defiantly.

"No! I need him," Anita looked up, cradling Carlota's head in her lap.

"María," Diego called out. María's head snapped toward him. "Anita doesn't want me to tie the viper," he complained.

María glanced to Rajunt then studied Anita, "Give her what she wants. She protects the Madonna."

Diego released Rajunt.

"She will die soon," Anita said grimly, staring at the child in Rajun1t's arms. "He will never know her."

Rajunt said nothing but drew the child closer.

Stauffen lay twenty meters away, counting *Sendero*.

• • •

ENTOMBED IN DARKNESS, the small green light suddenly glowed brighter. The machine became self-aware.

Like the stretching of an awakening giant, Socrates extended electronic consciousness back across the globe.

• • •

"IT'S NOT HARD," Michelle explained, handing Antonio the 10 gauge, semi-automatic shotgun.

"What do I do?"

"Point and fire. You have five shells," she said, then grabbed a 12 gauge shotgun from the large duffel bag. She pumped the first shell into position with a flick of her powerful arm.

"How long do you think he'll be gone?" Antonio asked about Stauffen.

Michelle's head twitched to the side, she listened carefully. "He should be back in an hour," she said softly. "Did you just hear something?" she looked around, listening intently again. Only dense undergrowth.

Antonio stood still to listen. He heard nothing but birds and insects. He shook his head.

"I thought I heard something," Michelle said, tightening her grip on the shotgun, standing like an Amazon warrior.

Four pairs of hidden eyes stared silently at them from the jungle. The faces around the eyes were black with shadow paint.

• • •

THE MINISTER OF Security sat high above Lima, looking out onto the Pacific when his staffer entered the room. "Any word?"

The staffer shook his head.

"Get me the team leader," the Minister ordered.

Within moments, a special pager vibrated against the team leader's neck. He gestured for his men to hold their position and backed away from Michelle and Antonio. Free from being heard, he whispered into the microphone of his headset, suspended near his lips. "Team One."

"This is Mother. Do you have a report?" the Minister asked anxiously.

"No report on primary target," the team leader whispered, "but we've spotted the American woman and the Brazilian priest. We are prepared to take them out now and continue to search for the target."

Suddenly, the conversation in the Minister's hand was replaced by static. He stared at his phone for a moment, then screamed at his staffer.

The team leader's conversation continued as if uninterrupted.

"There is no time for that. Your orders have changed," Socrates explained, mimicking the Minister's voice and tone. "We have reports the *Sendero* are thirty kilometers west of your location. Proceed there at once."

"New orders?" The whisper was incredulous.

"You heard Mother." Socrates snarled then provided new coordinates.

The team leader signalled his men to withdraw from Antonio and Michelle. The group melted back.

Kilometers away, hurrying through the dense underbrush toward the *Sendero* hideout, Sánchez had come to a stop to monitor the short conversation through his headset. His men had instantly stopped as a single machine. They remained motionless.

"What's wrong?" João asked tensely.

"The special team was just ordered to new coordinates, thirty kilometers west of here. But that makes no sense. The *Sendero* avoid that area because of the tribes." Concern and indecision crawled across Sánchez' face.

"Your call, Captain." João whispered.

"We're not following the special forces team. I know where María has to be hiding them," Sánchez said decisively.

• • •

STAUFFEN COUNTED TEN *Sendero*. He had watched where María positioned her security. She stood talking quietly with Diego. Anita and a cleric were comforting a woman and her child. De Silva and Brigham were tied to a tree.

With his inventory complete, Stauffen withdrew through the underbrush and headed back for Michelle and Antonio.

• • •

CARLOTA CRIED OUT, clutching her stomach.

"I'm here," Anita said, lightly stroking her hair.

Carlota's eyes opened slowly, "Angelica?" then focused. "Anita," she said, realizing.

"You're going to be fine," Anita assured her.

Carlota smiled meekly, "I am dying."

"No you're not!" Anita insisted.

In pain, Carlota gripped Anita's hand and looked into her eyes. "It is time."

"Your son needs you," Anita argued softly.

"Where is my son?" Carlota stretched out her arms toward Rajunt, who continued to hold the child.

"Give her the child," Anita said softly through clenched teeth.

Rajunt leaned forward with the child, reluctantly placing him in the crux of her arm.

Anita stroked Carlota's hair gently.

Carlota gazed down to her son in awe. "I love you," she whispered into his tiny pink ear and smiled bravely. Her stomach cramped like a vice as she bent to kiss his cheek, "I shall be with you along your journey, my son." She kissed him good-bye, tears streaming down her cheeks. She struggled to hand her son back to Rajunt, who quickly snatched him back.

Anita refused to weep. Carlota gripped her hand.

Rajunt rocked the child gently, his eyes looking about.

With her head in Anita's lap, Carlota released her last breath. Her clutch on Anita's hand vanished.

• • •

STAUFFEN GREETED A 12 gauge in his face when he broke through the trail. Michelle raised it instantly when she recognized him. "Did you locate them?" she quickly asked.

"Got 'em," Stauffen said softly.

"Could you see Carlota?" Antonio asked.

"Did she have the baby with her?" Michelle added.

"I've never seen Carlota, but a woman and a cleric were kneeling before a young woman lying in the dirt," Stauffen answered. "The cleric—"

"Rajunt," Antonio interrupted.

"Rajunt. . . ," Stauffen paused, "was holding the child while Anita comforted the woman."

"That's Carlota," Michelle answered.

"I wasn't close enough to really tell, but she seemed pretty bad off. She wasn't moving," Stauffen said.

"I don't think we should wait until nightfall. If Carlota is having complications, we need to extract her now," Michelle insisted.

"I agree," Antonio said.

"We'll have better odds if we wait until night, but I think you're right. She looked like she's in a world of hurt."

• • •

"WHAT!" MARÍA SCREAMED, glaring at Carlota's white body. Anita rose slowly with red eyes. She started to speak, "I . . . ."

"Who will feed the child?" María roared and back-handed Anita so hard she stumbled backward. María's eyes raged.

Rajunt, still knelt beside Carlota, drew the child closer to his breast.

Anita straightened, terrified María would kill them all, "I will find him milk."

María back-handed Anita again, snapping back her head. "Yes, you will and right now!" María said icily. Diego smiled nearby.

"What do you want me to do?" Anita asked, holding her bleeding lip with the back of her hand.

María started pushing Anita from the clearing, toward the jungle's edge. "Bring me milk!" She was nose-to-nose with Anita. As María advanced, Anita retreated.

"Run to the road. Find a peasant, find anyone. But bring me milk for the child!" María snarled, her face filled with fury. She shoved Anita backwards into the bushes. "Go!"

Anita grabbed a branch to regain her balance.

"Now!" María ordered and returned to the others.

Anita turned and ran for the road, crashing through the underbrush.

Anita disappeared into the undergrowth.

• • •

MINUTES LATER, SÁNCHEZ'S team froze, blending with the shadows of the undergrowth, at the sound of Anita's hurried approach.

João's rifle-sight lined to Anita's head, the silencer following her.

Sánchez recognized Anita, the one *Sendero* who had refused María's invitation to torture him and his men.

"Let her live," Sánchez whispered softly.

Anita disappeared into the undergrowth.

• • •

"LET'S GO IN," Antonio announced, worried about Carlota, tightly gripping the 10 gauge.

"Let's go," Michelle said to Stauffen as he pulled an assault rifle from the duffle bag.

"You don't want to wait until nightfall?" Stauffen asked, hesitantly.

Both shook their heads.

"Follow me. Keep low." Stauffen said and turned, heading back along the trail he had just blazed from the *Sendero* hideaway. His eyes and ears probed the area around them like headlights in the fog.

A half hour later, Stauffen gestured to Michelle and Antonio. They slithered through the underbrush until they lay beside him, weapons ready.

"How are we going to do this?" Michelle whispered.

"Too many for a fire fight," Stauffen answered slowly. "There's María. If we capture her, we can back off the others."

"How do we get to her?" Antonio asked in a hushed tone.

"In the other camp, she walked the perimeter every hour, checking on the guards up in the trees. She'll do the same here. We wait and when she comes by, we pull her in," Stauffen said.

The three lay quietly, waiting patiently.

Within the hour, María sauntered near Stauffen, her eyes scanning the high trees to ensure all was well with her guards. Stauffen tensed, crouched near her feet and hidden by giant leaves. When María turned to the camp, he sprang.

Stauffen's strong hand slipped tightly around her mouth. The other hand held a machete to her throat. "One word and I remove your head, got that?" Stauffen chewed the words quietly into her ear.

María's eyes froze, she nodded. Stauffen backed her into the jungle. His eyes roamed the camp as he backed her into the brush, the *Sendero* were still unaware.

María sank her teeth into Stauffen's fingers. Blood oozed from between her teeth but he refused to slacken his grip. He pressed the machete against her throat hard enough that she understood and withdrew her teeth from his flesh.

Michelle and Antonio moved quickly into place, near Rajunt and the child. Stauffen signaled them. Together, they advanced into the clearing, weapons levelled at the *Sendero*.

Before the *Sendero* could react, Stauffen emerged from the other side of the clearing, shielding himself with María. "Drop your weapons or she dies!" he yelled.

The *Sendero* glanced nervously to one another, some keeping weapons trained on Michelle and Antonio while some watched Stauffen.

"Now!" Stauffen screamed.

They refused.

"You are about to die," Stauffen snarled to María.

"Drop them!" she shouted.

Slowly, they lowered their weapons to the ground.

Stauffen turned back and shouted up to the trees, "Get down here or she dies."

The guards hurried down from the trees.

When all the *Sendero* were clustered, Stauffen shoved María to them.

Michelle levelled her 12 gauge to María's snarling face. "Put your face in the dirt," Michelle ordered.

María glared.

"Or die," Michelle said, returning the glare.

Her face seething with hatred, María lowered herself to the dirt.

Michelle forced herself not to pull the trigger. She turned to the other *Sendero*, "All of you—in the dirt!"

One by one, they complied, their eyes glued to her 12 gauge shotgun.

When they were down, Antonio looked to Stauffen confidently. "Let's tie them and get out of here."

Marta smiled from the dense underbrush, watching quietly. She signaled the other *Sendero* she had brought from Iquitos.

Marta's *Sendero* quietly emerged, weapons leveled, from the jungle on all sides.

Stauffen, Michelle, and Antonio were focused on their prisoners. They did not see Marta emerge from the jungle. When they turned, it was too late.

"Drop your weapons or the child dies," Marta ordered, brandishing her weapon toward Rajunt and the child. They froze.

"I said, drop your weapons."

Michelle looked at Antonio. Stauffen closed his eyes briefly. They lowered their weapons.

María scrambled to her feet, her eyes fixed on Antonio. A reptilian smile surfaced as she rose before him, "I'm so glad you returned, lover."

Michelle glanced up to Antonio, who was holding María's deadly stare.

"Give us the child and let us go," he said.

María threw back her head, laughing. "Let you go? No, I think not. You were lucky last time. This time I skin you alive . . . ," she paused, ". . . right now."

María yanked Michelle from Antonio, holding her .45 to Michelle's temple. Michelle, who towered above María, glared at her from the side of her eye.

"Onto the ground, priest!" María screamed and turned to the others. "Stake him for skinning!" she snarled, jamming the barrel hard into the side of Michelle's head. Michelle winced.

"Don't hurt her!" Antonio yelled and dropped to the ground, spreading his arms and legs.

Sánchez ran toward the camp as fast as he could but the underbrush was becoming denser. He could hear voices ahead. His lungs burned as he ran. João streaked ahead of him like a gazelle, taking enormous strides.

A grizzly looking *Sendero* quickly knelt beside Antonio to lash him down.

"Don't touch him!" Michelle screamed at the *Sendero*, kicking him in the face.

The *Sendero* scrambled to his feet, blood gushing from his nose. He pulled a revolver from his belt and aimed between Michelle's eyes.

María smiled and stepped between Michelle and the *Sendero*. "Not yet," she said and turned to Michelle. "Don't touch him?"

María laughed coldly. "I'm going to skin him," she said pushing the barrel of her .45 harder against Michelle's temple. "I'll enjoy his screams."

"No!" Michelle shrieked, slamming an elbow into María's face. Before María could react, Michelle spun and drove her fist up under María's chin.

María stumbled as her head snapped back. She fought to keep her balance. Michelle lunged through the air like a charging lioness, landing atop María.

The *Sendero* drew down their weapons at Michelle.

Sánchez and his men could hear the screams.

"No!" Marta screamed at the *Sendero*. "You'll hit María, wait 'til she's clear! María will take her!"

But María was no match for Michelle.

María's furtive blows against Michelle's face had no effect. María kicked, clawed, and bit. But the blond Amazon warrior was unfazed. Michelle was tearing María apart with her bare hands.

Blood streamed down María's face.

Michelle assumed she would die at any instant and was determined to get her licks in. She had a score to settle. She wrapped herself around María like a whirlwind of fury.

María snarled and locked Michelle in a powerful grip, pivoting, crushing their breasts together, arms and legs flailing. They rolled through the dirt.

María sank her teeth into Michelle's neck. Michelle roared and drove her fist into María's face. Michelle spun and flipped María onto her stomach as María screamed obscenities. Michelle grabbed María's head from behind and pounded her face into the dirt.

Marta finally had a clear shot. She levelled her gun to Michelle's head.

Bursting into the clearing, the marksman João snapped his rifle to his hip and fired midstride. Marta's weapon splintered into a thousand pieces. João ground to a halt and spun his weapon toward the others.

The *Sendero* froze.

Sánchez and the others hurried into the clearing, weapons ready.

After he caught his breath, Sánchez laughed at Michelle. Her clothes were torn to shreds, blond hair covered her face in every direction. "You did well," he winked. "If you would like more time with her," he aimed his weapon at María, "you can have it."

Michelle looked at María, who lay bleeding and missing several teeth. Michelle shook her head.

"Sánchez! Thank God, you made it!" De Silva shouted from the tree, his hands nearly blue from being tied too tightly. Sánchez signalled his men to free De Silva and Brigham. Rajunt stood in the background, the child secure in his arms.

Once freed, De Silva rushed to Sánchez, embracing him, "You saved my life!"

"We're not out of this yet, General," Sánchez answered.

De Silva looked at him strangely.

"The Minister of Security has at least one assassination team looking for María and her hostages. I suspect there are more."

De Silva cocked his head to the side, perplexed.

"They have orders to kill everyone—including you."

De Silva's brows arched, "Me?"

Sánchez nodded slowly.

"I see," De Silva said quietly, then regained his composure. "Tie and gag the *Sendero*." Sánchez' men instantly complied.

"The old woman, too," De Silva grunted, looking around for her.

The old woman was gone.

The soldiers swept the area, weapons ready, searching her out.

De Silva looked about, nervous eyes searching for her. "She's vanished," he declared.

Everyone looked about, including the *Sendero*.

"She is gone," Michelle said.

"A forest demon," De Silva whispered, staring at María, who sat securely bound and gagged. Her eyes never strayed from Antonio.

De Silva eyed the child in Rajunt's arms. He turned to Sánchez, "What do we do?"

"I need your help, General," Sánchez said.

"What do you want?" De Silva shrugged with exaggerated gesture.

"Release the Brazilian priest and the American woman."

"Release them?"

"There's more." Sánchez said with determination.

De Silva's eyes narrowed, "What?"

"Give them the child," Sánchez said softly. "They must take him out of Peru. He will perish here."

"No!" Rajunt declared, stepping to the fore, holding the child. "He is now under my personal charge," he glared at De Silva.

Brigham and Michelle stared at one another.

"But you said she was a charlatan," De Silva said quietly, pointing at Carlota's body. "If she was, this cannot be the Christ child."

"I was wrong," Rajunt said, lifting the child for all to see. "He is the Christ child." Rajunt's eyes tried to sweep through De Silva's soul. "He belongs to the Vatican."

De Silva felt his eternal soul crowded by danger. He turned to Michelle and Antonio, studying them. "Will you protect him?" he asked with deadly earnest. "He will have a world of enemies."

Michelle understood. "I will protect him with my life."

"And you?" De Silva looked to Antonio.

"I will," Antonio said softly.

De Silva considered his next move carefully for several moments before turning to Sánchez, "Your wish is granted."

"NO!" Brigham screamed, furious at defeat.

The back of De Silva's chubby hand crashed across Brigham's face. "One more word and you die here, now," De Silva snarled at Brigham. João shoved his gun to the back of Brigham's head.

"No!" Rajunt raised his voice, "I damn your soul General if you take this child from me."

De Silva turned to Sánchez, "Take the child from his arms." He turned to João, whose gun barrel was still lodged against the back of Brigham's skull, "If Cardinal Rajunt moves, shoot him."

João nodded as Sánchez carefully lifted the child from Rajunt. Sánchez turned slowly to Michelle. Their eyes met.

Michelle accepted the child with powerful arms.

• • •

THE PROCESSION OF military vehicles wound through Iquitos' airport, cutting across the runway, and headed for Stauffen's hangar. Two dozen soldiers piled out and quickly opened the huge hangar doors. The black Lear waited in the shadows.

Under Michelle's direction, the soldiers carefully rolled out the plane. Golden reflective windows blazed in the Amazonian sun as the soldiers prepared the plane.

Antonio held the child as Michelle walked around the plane, checking it. Sánchez stood beside Antonio.

When Michelle finished inspecting the plane, she rejoined Antonio then looked to Sánchez. "We cannot yet leave," she said.

"What's wrong?" Antonio and Sánchez both asked at once.

"We cannot leave without saying good-bye to Felipe and Hector."

Antonio nodded she was right.

"Where are they?" Sánchez asked quickly.

"They are at my place," Stauffen interrupted.

Sánchez gestured to one of his soldiers in a truck to drive up beside him. He turned to Stauffen, "He will take you to get the boys. We will wait."

Stauffen climbed in and the truck headed back into Iquitos.

"Do you have nourishment for him?" Sánchez asked as they waited, his eyes never leaving the child.

"Yes," Michelle nodded. "We'll warm milk for him from the galley. He'll be well cared for."

Antonio turned to Sánchez, "Thank you for everything."

"You saved my life—I thank you," Sánchez answered.

Within fifteen minutes, the truck returned. Hector and Felipe had their faces pressed to the windows. When the squeak of brakes announced the end of their ride, the boys bolted down from the truck.

Sister Agnus followed behind, her hand still bandaged.

"You made it," Hector laughed at Antonio.

"I knew you would," Felipe announced to Michelle.

Agnus looked at the child in Antonio's arms then to Antonio, "The Christ child?" she asked reverently.

Antonio nodded.

Agnus knelt before the child, crossing herself, "Thank you Lord." She stared to the sky, "The Messiah is come."

De Silva stood quietly until Agnus finally rose to her feet.

Michelle looked down to Felipe and Hector, "Would you like to return with us to the United States?"

They both looked to Agnus, then slowly looked back to Michelle. "We want to stay with Sister Agnus."

Agnus laughed, "You boys are such angels, but you can't turn that down. The U.S. is filled with promise and freedom."

Hector shook his head. Felipe joined him. "We stay," they said to Michelle.

Michelle smiled to Agnus then to the boys, "So would I if I were you." She turned to Sánchez, "It is time we leave."

De Silva walked hesitantly up to Antonio and Michelle. His face was pained as he spoke, "Forgive my ignorance."

Antonio smiled his forgiveness.

"You will need allies to remain in power," Michelle prodded De Silva's recall of the Minister and his assassination team. "I will help you," she said flatly then turned to her plane.

Rajunt stepped forward suddenly, oblivious to the threat from João's gun. He raised his voice to Antonio.

Antonio and Michelle turned back.

"Keep your vigil. The Ancient One will follow relentlessly," he warned.

Antonio nodded his understanding.

• • •

THE BLACK LEAR poised at the far end of the runway. Michelle spoke with the tower. Antonio was beside her, the child snug in his arms.

Sánchez and De Silva stood amid the phalanx of military vehicles. All eyes were on the distant jet as it began to roll. No one made a sound. Seconds later, the jet's rumble rolled over them. The plane streaked down the runway, blurring.

Michelle eased back the yoke and the plane lifted effortlessly from the steaming jungle.

Sánchez shielded his eyes from the equatorial sun, as they followed the black jet into the clouds.

• • •

WITHIN THE CONCRETE bunker overlooking Saratoga, the small green light glowed steadily in the darkness.

• • •

ANTONIO STARED DOWN to a night world, rolling 50,000 feet darkly beneath them at 500 miles an hour. "Where are we?" he asked quietly.

The United States was coming into view. "Home," she answered, gazing to sparkling cities on the night horizon. She spoke briefly into her headset then turned to Antonio, "Corporate security says there is nothing to come home to in Saratoga. They are rebuilding as fast as they can, but it will take some time. Do you mind if we head for the Wind River Mountains?"

"As you think best," Antonio said absentmindedly, gazing to the stirring child in his arms.

The child's eyes opened slowly and stared at Antonio.

"He's awake."

THE END.

ORDER FORM

To purchase additional copies of *The Trinity Gene*, please do one of the following:

    1. **RETURN** to the store where you bought the first copy and request another;

        or

    2. **CALL** the publisher, Lagumo Corp., toll free, at 1-800-448-1969 and have your credit card ready;

        or

    3. **FAX** this page, after filling out the information below, to 1-307-634-4604;

        or

    4. **MAIL** this page, after filling out the information below, to Lagumo Corp., P.O. Box 1407, Cheyenne, Wyoming 82003.

NOTE: if you fax or mail this page, you may use Visa or Mastercard (you will not be charged until the book is shipped) or you may enclose a check or money order for $12.95 plus $2.00 shipping & handling for the first book and $.50 for each additional book (if you live in Wyoming, you must also include 6% state sales tax). Please allow 4 to 6 weeks for delivery.

Name: _____

Address: _____

_____

_____

_____

- -

Visa and Mastercard are welcomed

Name: _____

Card Number: _____

Expiration Date: _____ Signature: _____